THE
SCANDALOUS
Orsinis

Three sensational, passionate novels from
bestselling Mills & Boon® author

SANDRA MARTON

Scandalous Dynasties

June 2013
THE SCANDALOUS KOLOVSKYS
Carol Marinelli

July 2013
THE SCANDALOUS ORSINIS
Sandra Marton

August 2013
THE SCANDALOUS WAREHAMS
Penny Jordan

September 2013
THE SCANDALOUS SABBATINIS
Melanie Milburne

THE
SCANDALOUS
Orsinis
SANDRA MARTON

Published in Great Britain 2013
by Mills & Boon, an imprint of Harlequin (UK) Limited, Eton House,
18-24 Paradise Road, Richmond, Surrey TW9 1SR

THE SCANDALOUS ORSINIS
© Harlequin Enterprises II B.V./S.à.r.l. 2013

Raffaele: Taming His Tempestuous Virgin © Sandra Myles 2010
Falco: The Dark Guardian © Sandra Myles 2010
Nicolo: The Powerful Sicilian © Sandra Myles 2010

ISBN: 978 0 263 90727 8

009-0713

Harlequin (UK) policy is to use papers that are natural, renewable and recyclable products and made from wood grown in sustainable forests. The logging and manufacturing processes conform to the legal environmental regulations of the country of origin.

Printed and bound by
CPI Group (UK) Ltd, Croydon, CR0 4YY

RAFFAELE: TAMING
HIS TEMPESTUOUS VIRGIN

SANDRA MARTON

Sandra Marton wrote her first novel while she was still in primary school. Her doting parents told her she'd be a writer some day and Sandra believed them. In secondary school and college she wrote dark poetry nobody but her boyfriend understood—though, looking back, she suspects he was just being kind. As a wife and mother she wrote murky short stories in what little spare time she could manage, but not even her boyfriend-turned-husband could pretend to understand those. Sandra tried her hand at other things, among them teaching and serving on the Board of Education in her home town, but the dream of becoming a writer was always in her heart.

At last Sandra realised she wanted to write books about what all women hope to find: love with that one special man, love that's rich with fire and passion, love that lasts for ever. She wrote a novel, her very first, and sold it to Mills & Boon® Modern™ romance. Since then she's written more than sixty books, all of them featuring sexy, gorgeous, larger-than-life heroes. A four-time RITA® award finalist, she's also received five *Romantic Times* magazine awards, and has been honoured with *RT*'s Career Achievement Award for Series Romance. Sandra lives with her very own sexy, gorgeous, larger-than-life hero in a sun-filled house on a quiet country lane in the north-eastern United States.

CHAPTER ONE

RAFFAELE ORSINI prided himself on being a man who was always in control. There was no doubt that his ability to separate emotion from logic was one reason he'd come this far in life.

Rafe could look at a relatively nondescript investment bank or financial corporation and see not what it was but what it could be, given time and money and, of course, the expert guidance he and his brothers could provide. They had created Orsini Brothers only five years ago but they were already an incredible success in the high-stakes world of international finance.

They'd always been incredibly successful with beautiful women.

The brothers shared the dark good looks of their mother and the rapier-sharp intellect of their father, who'd both immigrated to the States from Sicily decades before. Unlike their old man, they'd put their talents into lawful pursuits, but there was a dangerous edge to them that worked to their advantage in bedrooms as well as boardrooms.

It had done so today, when Rafe had outbid a Saudi prince for the purchase of a venerable French bank the Orsinis had wanted for a very long time. He, Dante, Falco and Nicolo had celebrated with drinks a couple of hours ago.

A perfect day, on its way to becoming a perfect evening...

Until now.

Rafe stepped from the lobby of his mistress's apartment building—his *former* mistress's apartment building, he thought coldly—declined the doorman's offer of a taxi and dragged in a deep breath of cool autumn air. He needed to calm down. Maybe the walk from Sutton Place to his Fifth Avenue penthouse would do it.

What was it with women? How could they say something at the start of an affair even when they damned well didn't mean it?

"I am completely dedicated to my career," Ingrid had said in that sexy Germanic purr of hers after the first time they'd gone to bed. "You need to know that, Rafe. I am not at all interested in settling down, so if you are—"

Him? Settle down? He still remembered how he'd laughed and rolled her beneath him. The perfect woman, he'd thought as he began making love to her again. Gorgeous. Sexy. Independent...

Yeah. Right.

His cell phone rang. He yanked it from his pocket, glared at the number on the screen and dumped the thing back into his jacket. It was Dante. The last thing he wanted was to talk to one of his brothers. The image in his head was still too fresh. Ingrid, opening the door. Ingrid, not wearing something slinky and sophisticated for their dinner reservations at Per Se but wearing, instead... What? An apron? Not the serviceable kind his mother wore but a thing that was all ruffles and lace and ribbons.

Ingrid, smelling not of Chanel but of roast chicken.

"Surprise," she'd trilled. "I'm making dinner tonight!"

She was? But she had no domestic skills. She'd told him that. Laughed about it.

Not tonight. Tonight she'd walked her fingers up his chest and whispered, "I'll bet you didn't know I could cook, *liebling.*"

Except for the *liebling*, it was a line he'd heard before. It made his blood run cold.

The scene that played out next had been all too predictable, especially her shrill accusations that it was time to take their relationship to a new level and his blurting out, "What relationship?"

Rafe could still hear the sound of whatever it was she'd thrown at him hitting the door as he exited.

His cell phone rang again. And again, until finally he cursed, hauled the damned thing from his pocket and flipped it open.

"What?" he barked.

"And good evening to you, too, bro."

Rafe scowled. A woman walking toward him veered away.

"I am not in the mood for games, Dante. You got that?"

"Got it," his brother said cheerfully. Silence. Then Dante cleared his throat. "Problems with the Valkyrie?"

"Not a one."

"Good. Because I'd hate to lay this on you if you and she are—"

"Lay what on me?"

His brother's sigh came through the phone. "Command performance, eight o'clock tomorrow morning. The old man wants to see us."

"I hope you told him what he can do with that request."

"Hey, I'm just the messenger. Besides, Mama called, not him."

"Hell. Is he supposed to be at death's door again? Did you tell her he's too mean to die?"

"No," Dante said reasonably. "Would you?"

It was Rafe's turn to sigh. They all adored their mother and sisters even though they seemed able to forgive Cesare Orsini anything. His sons could not. They'd figured out what their father was years ago.

"Damn it," Rafe said, "he's sixty-five, not ninety-five. He's got years ahead of him."

"Look, I don't want to listen to more endless speeches about where his banks are and what the combination is to his safe and the names of his lawyers and his accountants any more than you do. But could I tell that to Mama?"

Rafe's scowl deepened. "All right. Eight o'clock. I'll meet you guys there."

"It's just you and me, man. Nick's leaving for London tonight, remember? Falco heads for Athens in the morning."

"Terrific."

There was a brief silence. Then Dante said, "So, it's over with you and the Valkyrie?"

Rafe thought of saying everything from "No" to "What makes you think that?" Instead, he shrugged.

"She said it was time to reassess our relationship."

Dante offered a succinct, one-word comment. It made Rafe laugh; he could almost feel his black mood slipping away.

"I've got a cure for Relationship Reassessment," Dante said.

"Yeah?"

"I've got a date with that redhead in half an hour. Want me to call, see if she's got a friend?"

"I'm off women for a while."

"Yeah, yeah, I've heard that before. Well, if you're certain…"

"On the other hand, what is it they say about getting right back on a horse after you fall off?"

Dante laughed. "I'll call you back in ten."

Wrong. He called back in five. The redhead had a friend. And she'd be delighted to meet Rafe Orsini.

Well, hell, Rafe thought smugly as he hailed a cab, what woman wouldn't?

He overslept the next morning, showered quickly, skipped shaving, pulled on a black cotton sweater, faded jeans and sneakers and got to his parents' place before Dante.

Cesare and Sofia lived in a town house in Greenwich Village. Half a century ago, when Cesare had bought the house, the area had actually been part of Little Italy. Times had changed. The narrow streets had turned upscale and chic.

Cesare had changed, too. He'd gone from being a low-ranking mobster to being first a *capo*—the head of the syndicate—and then the boss. A *don*, though in Sicilian vernacular, the old Italian title of respect had a meaning all its own. Cesare owned a private sanitation company and half a dozen other legitimate businesses, but his true profession was one he would never confirm to his wife, his sons, his daughters.

Rafe went up the steps of the town house and rang the bell. He had a key but never used it. This place had not been his home for many years; he had not even thought of it as home long before he'd left it.

The house was enormous, especially by Manhattan standards. Cesare had used the increasingly large amounts of money brought in by his various enterprises to buy the houses on either side and convert the three buildings into one. Sofia presided over it all with no domestic help. A proper Sicilian housewife, she had always cooked and cleaned for her family. Rafe suspected it helped her cling to the fiction that her husband was just an everyday businessman.

Sofia greeted him as she always did, with a kiss on each cheek and a hug, as if she had not seen him in months instead of a couple of weeks. The she stepped back and gave him a critical look.

"You have not shaved this morning."

To his chagrin, Rafe felt himself blush. "Sorry, Mama. I wanted to be sure I got here on time."

"Sit," she commanded, as she led him into the vast kitchen. "Have breakfast."

The oak table was covered with bowls and platters. Telling her he'd already had the half grapefruit and black coffee that was his usual morning meal would have invited a lecture on nutrition, Orsini-style, so Rafe took a little of this, a little of that and put them on a plate. Dante sauntered in a couple of minutes later. Sofia kissed him, told him he needed a haircut and pointed him at the table.

"*Mangia,*" she commanded, and Dante, who took orders from no one, sheepishly complied.

The brothers were on their second espresso when Cesare's *capo*, a man who had served him for years, appeared.

"Your father will see you now."

The brothers put down their forks, patted their lips with their napkins and stood. Felipe shook his head.

"No, not together. One at a time. Raffaele, you are first."

Rafe and Dante looked at each other. "It's the prerogative of popes and kings," Rafe said with a tight smile, his words soft enough so they wouldn't reach the ears of Sofia, who was stirring a pot of sauce at the stove.

Dante grinned. "Have fun."

"Yeah. I'm sure it'll be a blast."

Cesare was in his study, a dark room made even darker by its overabundance of heavy furnishings, walls crowded with melancholy paintings of madonnas and saints and framed photographs of unknown relatives from the old country. Wine-colored drapes hung at the French doors and windows that overlooked the garden.

Cesare himself was seated behind his mahogany desk.

"Shut the door and wait outside," he told Felipe, and motioned Rafe to a chair. "Raffaele."

"Father."

"You are well?"

"I am fine," Rafe said coolly. "And you?"

Cesare seesawed his hand from side to side. "*Cosi cosa.* I am all right."

Rafe raised his eyebrows. "Well, that's a surprise." He slapped his hands on his thighs and rose to his feet. "In that case, since you're not at death's door—"

"Sit down."

Rafe's dark blue eyes deepened in color until they were almost black.

"I am not Felipe. I am not your wife. I am not anyone

who takes orders from you, Father. I have not done so for many years."

"No. Not since the day you graduated from high school and told me you were going to a fancy university on a scholarship, and told me what I could do with your tuition money," Cesare said blandly. "Did you think I had forgotten?"

"You have your dates wrong," Rafe said, even more coldly. "I haven't taken orders from you since I discovered how you earned your money."

"So self-righteous," Cesare mocked. "You think you know everything, my son, but I promise you, any man can step into the darkness of passion."

"I don't know what in hell you're talking about and, frankly, I don't care. Goodbye, Father. I'll send Dante in."

"Raffaele. Sit down. This will not take long."

A muscle knotted in Rafe's jaw. Hell, why not? he thought. Whatever his father wanted to tell him this time might be amusing. He sat, stretched out his long legs, crossed them at the ankles and folded his arms over his chest.

"Well?"

Cesare hesitated. It was remarkable to see; Rafe couldn't recall ever seeing his father hesitant before.

"It is true," his old man finally said. "I am not dying."

Rafe snorted.

"What I wished to discuss with you that last time, I did not. I, ah, I was not prepared to do so, though I thought I was."

"A mystery," Rafe said, his tone making it clear that nothing his father could say would be of interest.

Cesare ignored the sarcasm. "As I said, I am not dying." Another beat of hesitation. "But I will, someday. No one ever knows the exact moment but it is possible, as you know, that a man in my, ah, my profession can sometimes meet an un-anticipated end."

Another first. Cesare had never made even token acknowl-edgment of his ties before.

"Is this your not-so-subtle way of telling me something's coming? That Mama, Anna and Isabella might be in danger?"

Cesare laughed. "You have seen one too many movies, Raffaele. No. Nothing is, as you put it, 'coming.' Even if it were, the code of our people forbids harming family members."

"They are *your* people," Rafe said sharply, "not 'ours.' And I am not impressed by honor among jackals."

"When my time comes, your mother, your sisters, you and your brothers will all be well taken care of. I am a wealthy man."

"I don't want any of your money. Neither do my brothers. And we are more than capable of taking good care of Mama and our sisters."

"Fine. Give the money away. It will be yours to do with as you wish."

Rafe nodded. "Great." He started to rise from his chair again. "I take it this conversation is—"

"Sit down," Cesare said, and then added the one word Rafe had never heard from him. "Please."

The head of the New York families sat forward. "I am not ashamed of the way I've lived," he said softly. "But I have done some things that perhaps I should not have done. Do you believe in God, Raffaele? Never mind answering. For myself, I am not certain. But only a foolish man would ignore the possibility that the actions of his life may one day affect the disposition of his soul."

Rafe's lips twisted in a cool smile. "Too late to worry about that."

"There are some things I did in my youth—" Cesare cleared his throat. "They were wrong. They were not done for the good of *la famiglia* but for me. They were selfish things and they have stained me."

"And this has what to do with me?"

Cesare's eyes met his son's. "I am asking you to help me put one of them right."

Rafe almost laughed. Of all the bizarre requests…

"I stole something of great value from a man who once helped me when no one else would," Cesare said gruffly. "I want to make amends."

"Send him a check," Rafe said with deliberate cruelty. What did all this have to do with him? His father's soul was his father's business.

"It is not enough."

"Make it a big check. Or, hell, make him an offer he can't refuse." Rafe's lips thinned. "That's you, isn't it? The man who can buy or intimidate his way into anything?"

"Raffaele. As a man, as your father, I am pleading for your help."

The plea was astounding. Rafe despised his father for who he was, what he was…but, unbidden, other memories rushed in. Cesare, pushing him on a swing at a playground. Cesare, soothing him when the clown hired for his fourth birthday party had scared him half to death.

His father's eyes burned with guilt. What would it take to hand-deliver a check and offer a long-overdue apology? Like it or not, this man had given life to him, his brothers and his sisters. He had, in his own manner, loved them and taken care of them. In some twisted way, he had even helped make them what they were. If he'd developed a conscience, even at this late date, wasn't that a good thing?

"Raffaele?"

Rafe took a deep breath. "Yeah. Okay." He spoke briskly because he knew how easy it would be to change his mind. "What do you want me to do?"

"I have your word that you will do it?"

"Yes."

Cesare nodded. "You will not regret this, I promise."

Ten minutes later, after a long, complex and yet oddly incomplete story, Rafe leaped to his feet.

"Are you insane?" he shouted.

"It is a simple request, Raffaele."

"Simple?" Rafe laughed. "That's a hell of a way to describe asking me to go to a godforsaken village in Sicily and marry some—some nameless, uneducated peasant girl!"

"She has a name. Chiara. Chiara Cordiano. And she is not a peasant. Her father, Freddo Cordiano, owns a vineyard. He owns olive groves. He is an important man in San Giuseppe."

Rafe leaned across his father's desk, slapped his hands on the brilliantly polished mahogany surface and glared.

"I am not marrying this girl. I am not marrying anyone. Is that clear?"

His father's gaze was steady. "What is clear is the value of the word of my firstborn son."

Rafe grabbed a handful of his father's shirt and hauled him to his feet. "Watch what you say to me," he snarled.

Cesare smiled. "Such a hot temper, my son. Much as you try to deny it, the Orsini blood beats in your veins."

Slowly Rafe let go of the shirt. He stood upright, drew a deep, steadying breath.

"I live by my word, Father. But you extracted it with a lie. You said you needed my help."

"And I do. You said you would give it to me. Now you say you will not." His father raised his eyebrows. "Which of us told the lie?"

Rafe stepped back. He counted silently to ten. Twice. Finally he nodded.

"I gave my word, so I'll go to Sicily and meet with this Freddo Cordiano. I'll tell him you regret whatever it was you did to him decades ago. But I will not marry his daughter. Are we clear about that?"

Cesare shrugged. "Whatever you say, Raffaele. I cannot force your compliance."

"No," Rafe said grimly. "You cannot."

He strode from the room, using the French doors that

opened into the garden. He had no wish to see his mother or Dante or anyone.

Marriage? No way, especially not by command, especially not to suit his father—especially not to a girl born and raised in a place forgotten by time.

He was a lot of things, but he wasn't crazy.

More than four thousand miles away, in the rocky fortress that her father called his home and she called her prison, Chiara Cordiano shot to her feet in disbelief.

"You did what?" she said in perfect Florentine Italian. "You did *what?*"

Freddo Cordiano folded his arms over his chest. "When you speak to me, do so in the language of our people."

"Answer the question, Papa," Chiara said, in the rough dialect her father preferred.

"I said, I found you a husband."

"That's insane. You cannot marry me to a man I've never even seen."

"You forget yourself," her father growled. "That is what comes of all the foolish ideas put in your head by those fancy governesses your mother demanded I employ. I am your father. I can marry you to whomever I wish."

Chiara slapped her hands on her hips. "The son of one of your cronies? An American gangster? No. I will not do it, and you cannot make me."

Freddo smiled thinly. "Would you prefer that I lock you in your room and keep you there until you grow so old and ugly that no man wants you?"

She knew his threat was empty. He would not lock her in her room. Instead he would keep her a prisoner in this horrible little town, in these narrow, ancient streets she'd spent most of her twenty-four years praying to leave. She had tried leaving before. His men, polite but relentless, brought her back. They would do so again; she would never be free of a life she hated.

And he would surely not permit her to avoid marriage forever. She was a bargaining chip, a means of expanding or securing his vile empire.

Marriage.

Chiara suppressed a shudder.

She knew what that would be like, how men like her father treated their women, how he had treated her mother. This man, though American, would be no different. He would be cold. Cruel. He would smell of garlic and cigars and sweat. She would be little more than his servant, and at night he would demand things of her in his bed...

Tears of anger glittered in Chiara's violet eyes. "Why are you doing this?"

"I know what is best for you. That is why."

That was a laugh. He never thought of her. This marriage was for his own purposes. But it wasn't going to take place. She was desperate, but she wasn't crazy.

"Well? Have you come to your senses? Are you prepared to be a dutiful daughter and do as you are told?"

"I'd sooner die," she said, and though she wanted to run, she forced herself to make a cool, stiff-backed exit. But once she'd reached the safety of her own room and locked the door behind her, she screamed in rage, picked up a vase and flung it at the wall.

Twenty minutes later, calmer, cooler, she splashed her face with water and went looking for the one man she loved. The man who loved her. The one man she could turn to.

"*Bella mia,*" Enzo said, when she found him, "what is wrong?"

Chiara told him. His dark eyes grew even darker.

"I will save you, *cara,*" he said.

Chiara threw herself into his arms and prayed that he would.

CHAPTER TWO

RAFE decided not to tell anyone where he was going.

His brothers would have laughed or groaned, and there were certainly no friends with whom he'd discuss the Machiavellian intrigues of the Orsini *don* and his interpretation of Sicilian honor.

Honor among thieves, Rafe thought grimly as his plane touched down at Palermo International Airport. He'd had to take a commercial flight; Falco had taken the Orsini plane to Athens. But even without the benefit of coming in via private jet, he moved swiftly through Passport Control.

Rafe's mood was dark. The only thing that kept him from snarling was knowing he'd have this ridiculous errand behind him in a day.

Maybe, he thought as he stepped out of the terminal into the heat of a Sicilian early autumn, just maybe he'd buy his brothers a round of drinks in a couple of weeks and when they were all laughing and relaxed he'd say, "You'll never guess where I was last month."

He'd tell them the story. All of it, starting with his meeting with Cesare. And they'd nod with approval when he described how gently he'd told Chiara Cordiano he was sorry but he wasn't about to marry her and, yes, he would be gentle because, after all, it wasn't the girl's fault.

A weight seemed to lift from his shoulders.

Okay. This might not be as bad as he'd figured. What the hell, this was a nice day for a drive. He'd have lunch at some picturesque little *trattoria* on the way to San Giuseppe, phone Freddo Cordiano and tell him he was en route. Once he arrived, he'd shake the old guy's gnarled hand, say something polite to the daughter and be back in Palermo by evening. His travel agent had booked him into a hotel that had once been a palace; she'd said it was elegant. He'd have a drink, then dinner on the balcony of his suite. Or maybe he'd stop at the bar. Italian women were among the most beautiful in the world. Well, not the one he was on his way to see, but she'd be history by evening.

By the time he reached the car rental counter, Rafe was smiling...

But not for long.

He'd reserved an SUV, or the Italian equivalent. Generally, he disliked SUVs—he preferred low, fast cars like the 'Vette he had back home, but he'd checked a map and San Giuseppe was high in the mountains. The road to it looked as if it might be more a goat track than anything else, so he'd opted for the traction of an SUV.

What waited at the curb was not an SUV. It was the one kind of car he actually despised, a big, black American thing, a model long favored by his father and his pals.

A Mobster Special.

The clerk shrugged and said there must have been a communications error but, *scusi*, this was all she had.

Perfect, Rafe thought as he got behind the wheel. A gangster's son on a gangster's errand, driving a gangster's car. All he needed was a fat cigar between his teeth.

So much for being in a better mood.

Things didn't improve after that. He'd been far too generous, calling the ribbon of potholed dirt with the steep slope of the mountain on one side and a dizzying plummet to the valley on the other a goat track.

It was more like a disaster waiting to happen.

Ten miles. Twenty. Thirty, and he'd yet to see another car. Not that he was complaining. There wasn't really enough room for two cars. There wasn't really enough room for—

Something black bolted from the trees and into the road.

Rafe cursed and stood on the brakes. The tires fought for purchase; the big car shimmied from side to side. It took all his skill to bring it to a stop. When he did, the hood was inches from the yawning space that overhung the valley.

He sat absolutely still. His hands, clutching the steering wheel, were trembling. He could hear the faint tick-tick of the cooling engine, the thud of his own heart.

Gradually the ticking of the engine faded. His heartbeat slowed. He dragged air into his lungs. Okay. The thing to do was back up, very carefully...

Something banged against his door. Rafe turned toward the half-open window. There was a guy outside the car and he was obviously dressed for an early Halloween. Black shirt. Black trousers. Black boots.

And an ancient, long-barreled black pistol, pointed straight at Rafe's head.

He'd heard stories of road bandits in Sicily and laughed them off, but only a jackass would laugh at this.

The guy made some kind of jerking motion with the pistol. What did it mean? Get out of the car? Hell, no. Rafe wasn't about to do that. The pistol waved again. Or was it shaking? Was the *guy* shaking? Yeah. He was, and that was not good. A nervous thief with a gun...

A nervous thief with white, wispy hair and rheumy eyes. And liver spots on the hand that held the pistol.

Wonderful. He was going to be robbed and killed by somebody's grandfather.

Rafe cleared his throat. "Easy, Grandpa," he said, even though the odds were good the old boy couldn't understand a word of English. He held up his hands, showed that they were empty, then slowly opened the door. The bandit stepped to the side and Rafe got out, carefully skirting the edge of the road and the void beyond it. "Do you speak English?" Nothing. He searched his memory. *"Voi,* ah, *voi parlate inglese?"* Still nothing. "Okay, look, I'm going to take my wallet from my pocket and give it to you. Then I'm gonna get back in the car and—"

The pistol arced through the air. He tried not to wince as it wobbled past his face.

"Watch yourself, Gramps, or that thing's liable to go off. Okay. Here comes my wallet—"

"No!"

The old man's voice shook. Shaking voice. Shaking hand. This was getting better and better. It would make an even better story than the one he'd already figured on telling his brothers, assuming he lived to tell it.

"Hugoahway!"

Hugoahway? What did that mean? The old guy's name, maybe, but it didn't sound Italian or Sicilian.

The old man poked the end of the pistol into Rafe's flat belly. Rafe narrowed his eyes.

Another poke. Another gruff "Hugoahway" and, damn it, enough was enough. Rafe grabbed the barrel of the pistol, yanked it from the bandit's shaking fingers and tossed it over the cliff.

"Okay," he said, reaching for the old man, "okay, that's— Oof!"

Something hit him, hard, from the rear. It was a second thief, wrapping his arms around Rafe's neck as he climbed on his back. Rafe grabbed his assailant's arms and wrenched the guy off him. The thief grunted, struggled, but he was a light-weight, and Rafe swung him around, worked his hands down to the guy's wrists…

Hell, this one was only a kid. Not just lightweight but flyweight. The kid, too, was dressed all in black, this time including a deep-brimmed, old-fashioned fedora that obscured his face.

A flyweight, but a fighter.

The kid was all over him, kicking, trying to claw him, damn it, trying to bite him! Rafe hoisted the boy to his toes.

"Stop it," he shouted.

The kid snarled something unintelligible in return, lifted a knee and took aim. Rafe twisted away.

"Are you deaf, boy? I said, stop!"

Evidently, *stop* didn't translate well because the kid didn't. He came at Rafe and the old guy joined the fracas, pummeling him with what looked like a small tree branch.

"Hey," Rafe said indignantly. This was not how things were supposed to go. He was the tough guy here; tough guys didn't get beaten up by boys and old men. He knew damned well he could stop the attack, just a couple of good punches would do it, but the thought of hitting Methuselah and a teenage delinquent was unappealing.

"Look," he said reasonably, "let's sort this out. Gramps, put down that stick. And you, boy, I'm gonna let go of you and—"

Bad move. The kid aimed his knee again. This time, he caught Rafe where he lived with devastating accuracy. Rafe grunted with pain, drew back his fist and managed a right cross to the kid's jaw.

It must have been a good one because the boy went down in a heap.

Still struggling for air, Rafe started to turn toward the old man. "Listen to me," he gasped....

The tree limb whacked him in the back of his head.

And Rafe went down beside the kid.

He came around slowly.

Ah, God, his head hurt. Methuselah had crowned him, the kid had kneed him. He had been totally and completely humiliated.

Could the day get any worse?

The old guy was sitting in the road, holding the kid in his arms, rocking him, talking to him in rapid and seemingly anguished Sicilian. He didn't even look up as Rafe rose painfully to his feet.

"Okay," he said gruffly, "okay, old man. Stand up. You hear me? Let go of the kid and get up." The old man ignored him. Rafe reached down and grabbed a spindly arm. "I said, stand up!"

"Hugoahway!" the old guy shouted, and suddenly the words made sense. What he was saying was, *You go away.* Well, hell, he'd definitely oblige, but first he had to make sure the boy was okay. Stopping this unlikely duo from robbing him was one thing; killing them was another.

Rafe shoved the bandit aside, reached for the unconscious boy, lifted him into the crook of his arm. The kid moaned, his hat fell off, and...

And the boy wasn't a boy at all.

He was—*she* was a girl. No. Not a girl. A woman with a pale oval face and a silky mass of long, dark hair. He'd KO'd a woman. So much for wondering if the day could get any worse.

Carefully he scooped her up, ignored the old guy pulling at his sleeve and carried her to the side of the road that abutted the sloping mountain. Her head lolled back. He could see the pulse beating hard in the delicate hollow of her throat. The angle of her body made her breasts thrust against the rough wool of her jacket.

He set her down against the grassy rise. She was still unconscious.

She was also incredibly beautiful.

Only an SOB would notice such a thing at a moment like this, but only a fool would not. Her hair wasn't just dark, it was the color of a cloudless night. Her brows were delicate wings above her closed eyes; her lashes were dark shadows against razor-sharp cheekbones. Her nose was straight and narrow above a rosy-pink mouth.

Rafe felt a stir of lust low in his belly. And wasn't that terrific? Lust for a woman who'd tried to turn him into a eunuch, who'd played back-up to an old man with a pistol...

Who now lay helpless before him.

Damn it, he thought, and he caught the woman by the shoulders and shook her.

"Wake up," he said sharply. "Come on. Open your eyes."

Her lashes trembled, then slowly lifted, and he saw that her eyes were more than a match for the rest of her face, the irises not blue but the color of spring violets. Her lips parted; the tip of her tongue, delicate and pink, slicked across her mouth.

This time, the hunger that rolled through his belly made him sit back on his heels. Was this all it took? Was being on Sicilian soil enough to make him revert to the barbarian instincts of his ancestors?

Clarity was returning to her eyes. She put her hand to her jaw, winced, then shot him a look filled with hatred.

Those soft-looking pink lips drew back from small, perfect white teeth. *"Stronzo,"* she snarled.

It was a word any kid who'd grown up in a household where the adults often spoke in Italian would surely understand, and it made him laugh. Big mistake. She sat up, said it again and swung a fist at his jaw. He ducked it without effort and when she swung again, he caught her hand in his.

"That's a bad idea, baby."

She hissed through her teeth and shot a look over his shoulder at the old man.

Rafe shook his head.

"Another bad idea. You tell him to come at me, he'll get hurt." Disdain shone in her eyes. "Yeah, I know. You figure he got me the first time but, see, here's the thing. I don't get taken twice. You got that?"

A string of words flew from her lips. Rafe understood a

couple of them but you didn't need a degree in Italian to get their meaning. The look in her eyes told him everything he needed to know.

"Yeah, well, I'm not a fan of yours, either. Is this how you and Gramps welcome visitors? You rob them? Hijack their cars? Maybe send them tumbling down into the valley?"

Her mouth curled, almost as if she'd understood him, but of course she hadn't. Not that it mattered. The question was, what did he do with this pair? Leave them here was his first instinct—but shouldn't he notify the authorities? Yes, but he'd heard stories about Sicily and the cops. For all he knew, this pair were the Italian equivalent of Robin Hood and Little John—except, Little John had turned out to be Maid Marian.

The woman had a faint mark on her jaw where he'd slugged her. He'd never hit a woman in his life and it bothered him. For all he knew, she needed medical care. He didn't think so, not from the way she was acting, but he felt some responsibility toward her, even if he'd only done what he had to do to protect himself.

He could just see telling that to a local judge: "Well, you see, sir, she came at me. And I hit her in self-defense."

It was the absolute truth but it would probably just give the locals a laugh. He was six foot three; he weighed a tight 240 pounds. She was, what, five-six? And probably weighed 120 pounds less than he did.

Okay. He'd drive the duo home. Maybe what had happened had taught them a lesson.

Rafe cleared his throat. "Where do you and Gramps live?"

She stared at him, chin raised in defiance.

"Ah, *dove è—dove è* your house? Your *casa*?"

The woman jerked her hand free. She glared at him. He glared back.

"I'm willing to drive you and Grandpa home. You got that? No cops. No charges. Just don't push your luck."

She laughed. It was the kind of laugh that made Rafe's eyes

narrow. Who in hell did she think she was? And what was there for her to laugh about? She'd come at him, yes, but she was the one who'd lost the fight. Now she was out here in the middle of nowhere, at the mercy of a man twice her size.

A man who was angry as hell.

It would take him less than a heartbeat to show her who was in charge, that she was at his mercy, that he had only to cup that perfect, beautiful face in his hands, put his mouth to hers and she'd stop looking at him with such disdain, such coldness, such rage.

A kiss, just one, and her mouth would soften. The rigidity of her muscles would give way to silken compliancy. Her lips would part, she'd loop her arms around his neck and whisper to him and he'd understand that whisper because a man and a woman didn't need to speak the same language to know desire, to turn anger to something hotter and wilder...

Rafe shot to his feet. "Stand up," he growled.

She didn't move. He gestured with his hand.

"I said, stand up. And you, old man, get in the back of the car."

The old man didn't move. Nobody did. Rafe leaned toward the woman.

"He's old," he said softly, "and I really have no desire to rough him up, so why don't you just tell him to do what I said."

She understood him. He could see it in her face.

Rafe shrugged. "Okay, we'll do it the hard way."

Her violet eyes flashed. She got to her feet, rattled off a string of words, and the old man nodded, walked to the car and climbed into the back.

Rafe jerked his thumb toward the car. "Now you."

One last glare. Then she turned away, marched to the car and started to climb in beside the old guy.

"The passenger seat," Rafe snapped. "Up front."

She said something. It was something women didn't say, not even on the streets of his youth.

"Anatomically impossible," he said coldly.

Color rose in her face. Good. She *did* understand English, at least a little. That would make things easier. She got into the car. He slammed the door after her, went around to the driver's side and climbed behind the wheel.

"How far up the mountain do you live?"

She folded her arms.

Rafe ground his teeth together, started the car, carefully backed away from the sheer drop and continued up the road in silence. Minutes passed, as did miles. And just when he'd pretty much given up hope he'd ever see civilization again, a town appeared. A wooden signpost that looked as if it had been here forever announced its name.

San Giuseppe.

He stopped the car and took in his first sight of the Sicily of his father.

Houses overhung a narrow, cobblestoned street that wound its steep way up the mountain. Washing hung on clotheslines strung across rickety-looking balconies. The steeple of a church pierced a cloudless sky that overlooked a line of donkeys plodding after a small boy.

Cesare had insisted on showing him a couple of grainy snapshots of the town, taken more than fifty years ago. Nothing had changed, including the castle that loomed over it all.

Castello Cordiano.

Rafe put the car in gear. The woman beside him shook her head and reached for the door.

"You want to get out here?"

An arrogant lift of her chin brought into prominence the bruise he'd inflicted. Guilt racked him and he took a deep breath.

"Listen," he said. "About your jaw…"

Another flash of those violet eyes as she swung toward him.

"Yeah, I know. Believe me, the feeling's mutual. All I'm trying to say is that you should put some ice on that bruise. It'll keep the swelling down. And take some aspirin. You know what aspirin is? As-pi-rin," he said, knowing how idiotic he must sound but not knowing any other way to get his message through.

She snapped out an order. The old man replied; his tone suggested he was protesting but she repeated the order and he sighed, opened the door and stepped from the car.

Rafe caught her elbow as she moved to follow the old guy.

"Did you understand what I said? Ice. And aspirin. And—"

"I understood every word," she said coldly. "Now see if *you* understand, *signor*. Go away. Do you hear me? Go away, just as Enzo told you to do."

Rafe stared at her. "You speak English?"

"I speak English. And Italian, and the Sicilian form of it. You, quite obviously, do not." Those stunning eyes narrowed until only a slash of color showed. "You are not welcome here. And if you do not leave of your own accord, Enzo will see to it that you do."

"Enzo? You mean Grandpa?" Rafe laughed. "That's one hell of a threat, baby."

"He is more a man than you will ever be."

"Is he," Rafe said, his voice gone low and dangerous and instead of thinking, he caught her by the shoulders and lifted her across the console, into his lap. She struggled, beat at him with her fists but he was ready. He caught both her hands in one of his, slid the other into her hair, tilted her head back and kissed her.

Kissed her as he'd fantasized kissing her, back on that road. She fought, but it was pointless. He was hot with fury and humiliation…

Hot with the feel of her against him. Her mouth, soft under his. Her breasts, tantalizing against the hardness of his chest. Her rounded backside, digging into in his lap.

His body reacted in a heartbeat, his sex swelling until he was sure it had never been this huge or throbbed with such urgency. She felt it happen; how could she not? He heard her little cry of shock, felt it whisper against his mouth. Her lips parted and she tried to bite him but he turned the attempt against her, used it as a chance to deepen the kiss, to slip his tongue into the silky warmth of her mouth. She gasped again, made a little sound of distress...

And then something happened.

Her mouth softened under his. Sweetened. Turned warm and willing, and the knowledge that he could take her, right here, right now, made his already-hard body turn to stone. He let go of her wrists, slid his hand under her jacket, cupped the delicate weight of her breast...

Her teeth sank into his lip.

Rafe jerked back and put his hand to the tiny wound. His finger came away bearing a drop of crimson.

"Pig," she said, her voice shaking. "No good, filthy pig!"

He stared at her, saw her shocked eyes, her trembling mouth, and heard his father's voice reminding him that any man could step into the darkness of overwhelming passion.

"Listen," he said, "listen, I didn't mean—"

She opened the door and bolted from the car, but not before she'd flung a string of Sicilian curses at him.

Hell, he thought, taking his handkerchief from his pocket and dabbing it against his lip, for all he knew, he deserved them.

CHAPTER THREE

WAS the American going to come after her?

Chiara ran blindly into the narrow alley that led to a long-forgotten entrance to Castello Cordiano, following its twists and turns as it climbed steeply uphill.

No one knew this passageway existed. She'd discovered it when she was a little girl, hiding in the nursery closet with her favorite doll to get away from her father's callousness and her mother's piety.

It had been her route to freedom ever since, and there was the added pleasure of fooling her father's men when she seemed to vanish from right under their noses.

The alley ended in a field of craggy stone outcroppings and brambles. A thick growth of ivy and scrub hid the centuries-old wooden door that led into the castle. Panting, hand to her heart, Chiara fell back against it and fought to catch her breath. She waited, then peered through a break in the tangled greenery. *Grazie Dio!* The American had not followed her.

Behaving like the brute he was must have satisfied him.

No surprise there. She'd always known how the world went. Men were gods. Women were their handmaids. The American had gone out of his way to remind her of those truths in the most basic way possible.

Chiara took a last steadying breath, opened the heavy door

and slipped past it. A narrow corridor led to a circular stair-case that wound into a gloomy darkness broken by what little light came through the *balistraria* set into the old stone walls. Long moments later, she emerged in the nursery closet. Carefully she stepped into the room itself, eased open the door, checked the corridor, then hurried halfway down its length to her bedroom.

Her heartbeat didn't return to normal until she was safely inside with the door shut behind her.

What a disaster this day had been!

Yes, she'd gotten farther from the castle than ever before, but so what? The plan to frighten the American and send him running had been a miserable failure. Worse than a failure because instead of frightening him, she'd infuriated him.

Angering a man like that was never a good idea.

Chiara touched the tip of her finger to her lip. Was his blood on her? It was not but she could still feel the imprint of his mouth, could still taste him. The warm, firm flesh. The quick slide of his tongue. The terrifying sense of invasion…

And then, without warning, that sensation low in her belly. As if something were slowly pulsing deep inside.

She blinked, dragged air into her lungs. Never mind going over what had happened. What mattered was what would happen next.

She had badly underestimated the American.

Where was the short, stocky, cigar-chomping pig she'd envisioned? Not that he wasn't a pig. He was, absolutely. The difference was that she could not have walked into a room and picked him out as one of the goons who did the work of men like her father.

He was too tall. Too leanly built. But it was more than looks that separated him from the men she knew. It was… What? His clothes? The gray, pinstriped suit that had surely been custom-made? The gold Rolex she'd glimpsed on his tanned, hair-dusted wrist?

Maybe it was his air of sophistication.

Or his self-assurance.

Smug self-assurance, even when Enzo had pointed a pistol at him. Even when she'd flung herself on his back. Even when she'd sunk her teeth into his lip to end that vile stamp of I'm-in-charge-here male domination.

That hot, possessive kiss.

Chiara jerked away from the door. She had to work quickly. *Dio*, if her father saw her now...

She almost laughed as she stripped off the ancient black suit and white, collarless shirt Enzo had found for her. Thinking about Enzo was enough to stop her laughter. What humiliation he had suffered today. And if her father ever learned what he had done...

He would pay a terrible price, and all because of her. She should not have run to him for help, but who else was there to turn to?

Enzo had listened to her story. Then he'd taken her hand in his.

"I can scare him off," he'd said. "Remember, he is not truly Sicilian. He is American, not one of us, and they are not the same. They are weak. You will see, child. We will catch him by surprise. And while he is still immobilized, I will show him my pistol and tell him to go away. And he will be gone."

When she protested that it was too dangerous, Enzo had suddenly looked fierce and said he had done things of this sort in the past.

It was hard to imagine.

The old man was her dearest friend. Her only friend. He'd been her father's driver when she was little and he'd been kind to her, kinder than anyone, even her mother, but her mother had not been made for this world. Chiara had only vague memories of her, a thin figure in black, always kneeling in the old chapel or sitting in a straight-backed parlor chair bent over her Bible, never speaking, not even to Chiara, except to whisper warnings about what life held in store.

About men, and what they all wanted.

"Men are animals, *mia figlia*," she'd hissed. "They want only two things. Power over others. And to perform acts of depravity upon a woman's body."

Chiara kicked the telltale clothing into the back of her closet, then hurried into the old-fashioned bathroom and turned on the taps over the bathtub.

What her mother had told her was the truth.

Her father ruled his men and his town with an iron fist. As for the rest…she'd overheard the coarse jokes of his men. She'd felt their eyes sliding over her. One in particular looked at her in a way that made her feel ill.

Giglio, her father's second in command. He was an enormous blob of flesh. He had wet-looking red lips and his face was always sweaty. But it was his eyes that made her shudder. They were small. Close set. Filled with malice, like the eyes of a wild boar that had once confronted her on the mountain.

Giglio had taken to watching her with a boldness that was terrifying.

The other day, walking past her, his hand had brushed her buttocks and seemed to linger. She had gasped and shrunk from him; her father had been in the room. Hadn't he seen what had happened? Then why hadn't he reacted?

Chiara blanked her mind to the memory as she sank deep into the tub of hot water. She had more important things to worry about right now.

She and Enzo had failed. The American would keep his appointment with her father. The question was, would he recognize her? Enzo could keep out of his way but she couldn't. She was, after all, the reason for the American's visit.

She was on display. For sale, like a prize goat.

All she could do was pray that he would not recognize her. It was possible, wasn't it? She'd be wearing a dress, her hair would be scraped back into its usual bun, she would speak softly, behave demurely and keep her eyes on the floor. She would make herself as invisible as possible.

And even if he recognized her, she could only pray that he would not want her, even though it would be an honor for him to wed the daughter of Don Freddo Cordiano.

A man like that would surely refuse such a so-called honor. Why take her when he could have his pick of women? Though she found all that overt masculinity disgusting, she knew there were those who'd be dazzled by the rugged face, the piercing blue eyes, the hard, powerful body.

Dio, so powerful!

Heat suffused her cheeks.

That moment, when he'd pulled her onto his lap, when she'd felt him beneath her. The memory made her tremble. She had never imagined…

She knew a man's sexual organ had that ability. She was not ignorant. But that part of him had felt enormous. Surely a woman's body could not accommodate something of such size…

A knock sounded at the door. Chiara shot up straight in the water.

"*Sì?*"

"*Signorina, per favore, il vostro padre chiede che lo unite nella biblioteca.*"

Chiara held herself very still. Her father wanted her in the library. Was he alone, or had the American arrived? "*Maria? È solo, il mio padre?*"

"*No, signorina. Ci è un uomo con lui. Uno Americano. Ed anche il suo capo, naturelmente.*"

Oh God. Chiara closed her eyes. Not just the American. Giglio was there, too.

Could the day get any worse?

* * *

Could the day get any worse?

Rafe felt a muscle jump in his cheek. Why bother wondering? It already had.

First the nonsense with Robin Hood and Maid Marian. Then the girl sinking her teeth into his lip. Now this. Twenty minutes of being trapped in an uncomfortable chair in a library even more depressing than his father's, with a similar clutch of saints and stiffly posed ancestors looking down from the walls. He had an unwanted glass of *grappa* in his hand, a fat cigar he'd declined on the table beside him and the finishing touch, a butt-ugly mass of muscle and fat named Giglio, overflowing in a chair across from his.

Cordiano had introduced the man as a business associate. His *capo*, was more like it. It was the accessory *du jour* for hoodlums.

The *capo* had not taken his eyes off Rafe, and nasty eyes they were. Small. Set too close together. Unblinking and altogether mean. At first Rafe had ignored it, but it was getting to him.

For some reason the pig man didn't like him. Fine. The feeling was mutual.

Added to all that, Cordiano seemed intent on spinning endless, self-aggrandizing tales set in the glory days of his youth, when men were men and there was nothing anybody could do about it.

Rafe didn't care. All he wanted was to get out of here, back to Palermo, back to the States and a world that made sense, but until they got down to basics, he was stuck.

His attempts to move things along had gotten nowhere.

After the handshakes, the how-was-your-trip question and his it-was-fine response—because no way was he going to tell this sly old fox and his *capo* that he'd been had by a doddering old highwayman and a woman—after all that plus the ceremonial handing over of the unwanted cigar and the obligatory glass of *grappa*, Rafe had handed Cordiano his father's sealed letter.

"Grazie," the *don* said and tossed it, unopened, on his

desk. Each time he paused for breath, Rafe tried to launch into the verbal form of his father's apology. No luck. Cordiano didn't give him a chance.

At least the marriage proposal had not been mentioned. Maybe Cesare had already explained that Rafe would not be availing himself of the generous offer to take his old enemy's obviously undesirable daughter off his hands.

Something must have shown in his face because the pig man's eyes narrowed. Rafe narrowed his in return. He felt foolish, like a kid doing his best to stare down the class bully, but what else did he have to keep him occupied?

"—for you, Signor Orsini."

Rafe blinked and turned toward Cordiano. "Sorry?"

"I said, this has surely been a long day for you and here I am, boring you with my stories."

"You're not boring me at all," Rafe said, and forced a smile.

"Is the *grappa* not to your liking?"

"I'm afraid I'm not a *grappa* man, Don Cordiano."

"And not a cigar man, either," Cordiano said, with a quick flash of teeth.

"Actually…" Rafe put his glass on the small table beside the chair and rose to his feet. The pig man stood up, too. Enough, Rafe thought. "I am also not a man who enjoys being watched as if I might steal the silver, so tell your watchdog to relax."

"Of course." The *don* chuckled, though the sound was remarkably cheerless. "It is only that Giglio sees you as competition."

"Trust me, Cordiano, I'm not the least bit interested in taking his job."

"No, no, certainly not. I only meant that he is aware that I have been searching for a way to thank him for his years of dedication, and—"

"And I'm sure you'll find an appropriate reward but that doesn't concern me. I'm here on behalf of my father. I'd appreciate it if you'd read his letter."

Cordiano smiled. "But I know what it says, *signor*. Cesare begs my forgiveness for what he did almost half a century ago. And you, Raffaele—may I call you that?—and you are to assure me that he means every word. Yes?"

"That's pretty much it." And still not a word about daughters and marriage, thank God. "So, I can return home and tell him his apology is accepted? Because it's getting late. And—"

"Did your father tell you what it is he did?"

"No. He didn't. But that's between you and—"

"I was his—I suppose you would call it his sponsor."

"How nice for you both."

"He repaid my generosity by stealing *la mia fidanzata*."

"I'm sorry but I don't speak—"

"Your father stole my fiancée." Cordiano's smile turned cold. "He eloped with her in the middle of the night, two days before we were to marry."

"I don't understand. My father has a wife. She…" Rafe's jaw dropped. "Are you saying my mother was engaged to you?"

"Indeed she was, until your father stole her."

All that "dark passion" stuff was starting to make sense. Now what? What could he say? It was hard enough to picture a young Cesare but to imagine his mother as a young woman running away with him…

"Did you think this was about something simple?" The *don*'s voice was as frigid as his smile. "That is why he sent you here, boy. To offer a meaningful apology, one I would accept. An eye for an eye. That is our way."

Rafe shot a quick look at the *capo*. Was that what this was all about? He'd put in his time in the Marines; he and his brothers had all served their country. He could give a good account of himself against, what, 350 pounds of fat and muscle, but in the end…

"An eye for an eye. Or, now that so many years have gone by, a deed for a misdeed." Cordiano folded his arms over his chest. "Your father took my bride. I will show him forgiveness by letting you take my daughter as yours. Do you see?"

Did he see? Rafe almost laughed. No way. Not even a genius would see any logic in that.

"What I see," he said flatly, "is that you have a daughter you want to get rid of."

Pig Man made a humming sound deep in his throat.

"And somehow, you and my old man cooked up this cockeyed scheme. Well, forget about it. It's not going to happen."

"My daughter needs a husband."

"I'm sure she does. Buy one, if that's what it takes."

The mountain of muscle grunted and took a step forward. Rafe could feel the adrenaline pumping. Hell, he thought, eyeing the *capo*, he could do more than put up a good fight. Angry as he was, he could take him.

"I have your father's word in this matter, Orsini."

"Then you have nothing, because it is not his word you need, it's mine. And I can damned well assure you that—"

"There you are," Cordiano said sharply, glaring past him. "It took you long enough to obey my orders, girl."

Rafe swung around. There was a figure in the doorway. Chiara Cordiano had come to join them. A weak finger of late-afternoon sunlight pierced a narrow gap in the heavy window draperies, lending a faint outline to her thin shape.

"Have you turned to stone?" the *don* snapped. "Step inside. There is a man here who wants to meet you."

Like hell he did, Rafe almost said, but he reminded himself that none of this was the girl's fault. If anything, he felt a stab of pity for her. He'd already figured that she was homely. Maybe it was worse than that. For all he knew, she had warts the size of watermelons.

She was also a woman defeated. Everything about her said so.

She moved slowly. Her head was bowed, showing dark hair pulled back in a tight bun. Her hands were folded before her, resting at her waistline, assuming she had one. It was impossible to tell because her dress was shapeless, as black and ugly as her shoes. Lace-ups, he thought with incredulity, the kind he'd seen little old ladies wearing back home on Mulberry Street.

He couldn't see her face but he didn't need to.

It would be as plain as the rest of her.

No wonder her father was trying to give her away. No man in his right mind would want such a pitiful woman in his bed.

Okay. He'd be polite. He could do that much, he thought, and opened his mouth to say hello.

Pig Man beat him to it.

"Buon giorno, signorina," the *capo* said.

Except, he didn't say it, he slimed it. How else to describe the oiliness in the man's voice? Maybe Chiara Cordiano thought so, too. Rafe saw a tremor go through her narrow shoulders.

"Signor Giglio has spoken to you," the *don* snapped. "Where are your manners?"

"Buon giorno," she said softly.

Rafe cocked his head. Was there something familiar about her voice?

"And you have not greeted our guest, Signor Raffaele Orsini."

The woman inclined her head. Not easy to do; her chin was damned near already on her chest.

"Buon giorno," she whispered.

"In English, girl."

Her hands twisted together. Rafe felt another tug of sympathy. The poor thing was terrified.

"That's okay," he said quickly. "I don't know much Italian but I can manage a hello. *Buon giorno, signorina. Come sta?"*

"Answer him," Cordiano barked.

"I am fine, thank you, *signor."*

There was definitely something about her voice…

"Why are you dressed like this?" her father demanded. "You are not going into a convent. You are going to be married."

"Don Cordiano," Rafe said quickly, "I've already told you—"

"And why do you stand there with your head bowed?" Cordiano grabbed his daughter's arm, his fingers pressing hard. She winced, and Rafe took a step forward.

"Don't," he said quietly.

The *capo* lunged forward but Cordiano held up his hand.

"No, Giglio. Signor Orsini is correct. He is in charge of things now. It is his right, and his alone, to discipline his fiancée."

"She is not my…" Rafe shot the woman a quick glance, then lowered his voice. "I already told you, I am not interested in marrying your daughter."

Cordiano's eyes turned hard. "Is that your final word, Orsini?"

"What kind of man are you, to put your daughter through something like this?" Rafe said angrily.

"I asked you a question. Is that your final word?"

Could a man feel any worse than Rafe felt now? He hated what Cordiano was doing to the girl. Why in hell didn't she say something? Was she meek, or was she stupid?

Not my worry, he told himself, and looked at Freddo Cordiano.

"Yes," he said gruffly, "it is my final word."

Pig Man laughed. The *don* shrugged. Then he clamped his fingers around his daughter's delicate-looking wrist.

"In that case," he said, "I give my daughter's hand to my faithful second in command, Antonio Giglio."

At last the woman's head came up. "No," she whispered. "No," she said again, and the cry grew, gained strength, until she was shrieking it. "No! No! No!"

Rafe stared at her. No wonder she'd sounded familiar. Those wide, violet eyes. The small, straight nose. The sculpted cheekbones, the lush, rosy mouth…

"Wait a minute," he said, "just wait one damned minute…"

Chiara swung toward him. The American knew. Not that it mattered. She was trapped. Trapped! She had to do something…

Desperate, she wrenched her hand out of her father's.

"I will tell you the truth, Papa. You cannot give me to Giglio. You see—you see, the American and I have already met."

"You're damned right we have," Rafe said furiously. "On the road coming here. Your daughter stepped out of the trees and—"

"I only meant to greet him. As a gesture of—of goodwill." She swallowed hard; her eyes met Rafe's and a long-forgotten memory swept through him of being caught in a firefight in some miserable hellhole of a country when a terrified cat, eyes wild with fear, had suddenly, inexplicably run into the middle of it. "But…but he…he took advantage."

Rafe strode toward her. "Try telling your old man what really happened!"

"What *really* happened," she said in a shaky whisper, "is that—is that right there, in his car—right there, Papa, Signor Orsini tried to seduce me!"

Giglio cursed. Don Cordiano roared. Rafe would have said, "You're crazy, all of you," but Chiara Cordiano's dark lashes fluttered and she fainted, straight into his arms.

CHAPTER FOUR

IT WAS like being trapped in a nightmare. One minute, Rafe was about to launch into his father's all-too-florid verbal apology. The next—

The next, Chiara Cordiano was lying as limp as laundry in his arms.

Was she faking it? The woman was a class-A actress. First a tough bandit, then a demure *Siciliana*, when the truth was, she was anything but demure.

A little while ago, she'd attacked him with the ferocity of a lioness.

And there'd been that sizzling flash of sexual heat.

Oh, yeah. The lady was one hell of an actress and this was her best performance yet. Claiming he'd tried to seduce her. He'd kissed her, was all, and one kiss did not a seduction make.

The *don* was holding his *capo* back with a hand on his arm and an assortment of barked commands. Rafe knew that Pig Man wanted to kill him. Good. Let him try. He was more than in the mood to take on the load of lard.

First, though, the woman in his arms had to open her eyes and admit she'd lied.

He looked around, strode to a brocade-covered sofa and unceremoniously dumped her on it. "Chiara," he said sharply. No response. "Chiara," he said again, and shook her.

Pig Man snarled an obscenity. Rafe looked up.

"Get him out of here, Cordiano, or so help me, I'm gonna lay him out."

The *don* snapped out an order, pointed a finger at the door. The *capo* shrugged off his boss's hand. Like any well-trained attack dog, he did as he'd been ordered but not without one last threatening look at Rafe.

"This is not over, American."

Rafe showed his teeth in a grin. "Anytime."

The door swung shut. Cordiano went to a mahogany cabinet, poured brandy into a chunky crystal glass and held it out. Give it to her yourself, Rafe felt like saying but he took the glass, slipped an arm around Chiara's shoulders, lifted her up and touched the rim of the glass to her lips.

"Drink."

She gave a soft moan. Thick, dark lashes fluttered and cast shadows against her creamy skin. Wisps of hair had escaped the ugly bun and lay against her cheeks, as delicately curled as the interior of the tiny shells that sometimes washed up on the beach at Rafe's summer place on Nantucket Island.

She looked almost unbelievably fragile.

But she wasn't, he reminded himself. She was as tough as nails and as wily as a fox.

"Come on," he said sharply. "Open your eyes and drink."

Her lashes fluttered again, then lifted. She stared up at him, her pupils deep as a moonless night and rimmed by a border of pale violet.

"What…what happened?"

Nice. Trite, but nice.

"You passed out." He smiled coldly. "And right on cue."

Did defiance flash in those extraordinary eyes? He couldn't be sure; she leaned forward, laid cool, pale fingers over his tanned ones as she put her mouth to the glass.

Her throat worked as she swallowed. A couple of sips and then she looked up at him. Her lips glistened; her eyes were wide. The tip of her tongue swept over her lips and he could imagine those lips parted, that tongue tip extended, those eyes locked, hot and deep, on his—

A shot of raw lust rolled through him. He turned away quickly, put the glass on a table and stepped back.

"Now that you're among the living again, how about telling your old man the truth?"

"The truth about…" Her puzzled gaze went from her father to Rafe. "Oh!" she whispered, and her face turned scarlet.

Rafe's eyes narrowed. Her reactions couldn't be real. Not the Victorian swoon, not her behavior at the memory of what had happened in the car. He'd kissed her, for God's sake. That was it. He'd lifted her into his lap and kissed her and, okay, she'd ended up biting him, but only after she'd responded, after he'd gotten hard as stone and she'd felt it and…

And he'd behaved like an idiot.

He was not a man who did things like that to women. A little playing around during sex was one thing; he'd had lovers who liked a hint of domination, but having a woman whisper "more" even as she pretended something else was not the same as what had happened with Chiara Cordiano.

What in hell had gotten into him? He'd been furious, but anger had nothing to do with sex…did it?

It was a subject to consider at another time. Right now he might just have a problem on his hands. This culture had its roots in times long gone. Its rules, its mores, were stringent.

Back home, a kiss, even a stolen one, was just a kiss. Here it could be construed as something else.

"Don Cordiano," he said carefully, "I kissed your daughter. I'm sorry if I offended her."

"And I am to accept your apology?"

The *don*'s tone was arrogant. It made Rafe bristle.

"I'm not asking *you* to accept it," he said sharply, and turned to Chiara. "I shouldn't have kissed you. If I frightened you, I'm sorry."

"Perhaps you would care to explain how you managed to meet with my daughter before you met with me."

Perhaps he would, Rafe thought, but he'd be damned if he'd stand here and admit he'd almost been bested by a slip of a girl and an old man. Besides, that part of the story belonged to Cordiano's daughter, he thought grimly, and looked at her again. But she locked her hands together in her lap, bent her head and studied them as if she had no part in this conversation.

The hell with that.

"Your turn, *signorina*," Rafe said coldly.

Chiara felt her heart thump. The American was right.

This was the time for her to say, "You have it wrong, Papa. This man didn't 'meet' me, not the way you make it sound. I stopped him on the road and tried to scare him away."

What a joke!

Instead of scaring him away, she'd brought him straight to San Giuseppe. And she couldn't explain that, not without telling her father everything, and that meant she'd have to tell him about Enzo.

No matter what the consequences, exposing Enzo's part in the mess would be fatal.

She knew her father well. He would banish Enzo from San Giuseppe, the place where the old man had spent his entire life. Or—her heart banged into her throat—or Enzo could suffer an unfortunate accident, a phrase she'd heard her father use in the past.

She was not supposed to know such things, but she did. When she was little, her father would say that Gio or Aldo or Emilio had left his employ but by the time she was twelve, she'd figured it out.

No one "left" the *don*. They had accidents or vanished, and their names were never mentioned again.

She could not risk having such a thing happen to Enzo. And yet if she didn't come up with something, who knew what her father might do to Rafe Orsini? Not that she cared about him, but she surely didn't want *his* "accident" on her conscience.

"Well? I am waiting."

Her father wasn't talking to her; he was glaring at Raffaele Orsini…but she would reply. She would make up the story as she went along and pray the American would not correct her version.

"Papa. Signor Orsini and I met when I—when I—"

"Silence!" her father roared. "This does not concern you. Signor Orsini? I demand an explanation."

"Demand?" Rafe said softly.

"Indeed. I am waiting for you to explain your actions."

Her father's face was like stone. Chiara had seen men cower from that face. Orsini, for all his studied toughness, surely would do the same. That patina of arrogant masculinity would crumble and he'd tell her father the entire story.

"I don't explain myself to anyone," the American said coldly.

Her father stiffened. "You came here to beg my forgiveness for an insult half a century old. Instead, you insult me all over again."

"I don't beg, either. I offered you my father's apology, and I apologized to your daughter. As far as I'm concerned, that ends our business."

Chiara held her breath. The room seemed locked in stillness, and then her father's lips curved in what was supposed to be a smile. But it was not; she knew it.

Still, what he said next surprised her.

"Very well. You are free to leave."

The American nodded. He started for the door as her father strode toward her.

"On your feet," he snarled.

Raffaele Orsini had already opened the door, but he paused and turned around at her father's words.

"Let's be clear about something, Cordiano. What happened—that I kissed your daughter—wasn't her fault."

"What you say has no meaning here. Now, get out. Chiara. Stand up."

Chiara rose slowly to her feet. Her father's face was a study in fury. She knew he would have hurt her if she were a man, but some old-world sense of morality had always kept him from striking her.

Still, he would not let what had happened pass. Raffaele Orsini could insist that the kiss had not been her fault until the end of eternity. Her father would never agree. A woman was supposed to defend her honor to her last breath.

She had not.

Someone had to pay for the supposed insult her father had suffered and who else could that someone be, if not her?

Her father's eyes fixed on hers. "Giglio!" he barked.

The *capo* must have been waiting just outside. He stepped quickly into the room.

"Si, Don Cordiano?"

"Did you hear everything?"

The fat man hesitated, then shrugged. *"Sì.* I heard."

"Then you know that my daughter has lost her honor."

Rafe raised his eyebrows. "Now, wait a damned minute…"

"All these years, I raised her with care."

"You didn't raise me at all," Chiara said, her voice trembling. "Nannies. Governesses—"

Her father ignored her. "I saw to it that she remained virtuous and saved her chastity for the marriage bed."

"Papa. What are you talking about? I have not lost my chastity! It was only a kiss!"

"Today, she chose to throw away her innocence." The *don*'s mouth twisted. "Such dishonor to bring on my home!"

Chiara laughed wildly. Rafe looked at her. Her cheeks were crimson; her eyes were enormous. Somehow the tight bun had come undone and her hair, thick and lustrous, swung against her shoulders.

"I've brought dishonor to this house?"

The *don* ignored her. His attention was on his *capo*.

"Giglio," he said, "my old friend. What shall I do?"

"Wait a minute," Rafe said, starting toward the *don*. Pig Man stepped in his path; he brushed him aside as if he were no more than a fly. "Listen to me, Cordiano. You're making this into something that never happened. I kissed your daughter. I sure as hell didn't take her virginity!"

"This is not America, Orsini. Our daughters do not flaunt their bodies. They do not let themselves be touched by strangers. And I am not talking to you. I am talking to *you*, Giglio, not to this...this *straniero*."

Pig Man said nothing, but his tiny eyes glittered.

"I cannot even blame him for what happened," Cordiano continued. "Foreigners know nothing of our ways. It was all my daughter's fault, Giglio, and now, what am I to do to restore our family's honor?"

Holy hell, Rafe thought, this was like something out of a really bad movie. The furious villain. The terrified virgin. And the pig, licking his thick lips and looking from the woman to the *don* as if the answer to the question might appear in neon in the space between them.

"Okay," Rafe said quickly, "okay, Cordiano, tell me what will stop this nonsense. You want me to direct my apology to you? Consider it done. What happened was my fault entirely. I regret it. I didn't mean to offend your daughter or you. There. Are you satisfied? I hope to hell you are because this...this farce has gone far enough."

He might as well have said nothing. Cordiano didn't even look at him. Instead, he spread his arms beseechingly at his *capo*.

Giglio was sweating. And all at once Rafe knew where this nightmare was heading.

"Wait a minute," he said, but Cordiano put his hand in the small of Chiara's back and sent her flying into the meaty arms of his *capo*.

"She is yours," he said in tones of disgust. "Just get her out of my sight."

"No!" Chiara's cry echoed in the room. "No! Papa, you cannot do this!"

She was right, Rafe thought frantically. Of course Cordiano couldn't do this. He wouldn't.

But Cordiano had taken a telephone from his desk. It, at least, was a symbol of modernity, bright and shiny and bristling with buttons. He pushed one, then spoke. Rafe's Italian was bad, his Sicilian worse, but he didn't need a translator to understand what he was saying.

He was arranging for Chiara and Pig Man to be married.

Chiara, who understood every word, went white. "Papa. Please, please, I beg you—"

Enough, Rafe thought, He tore the phone from Cordiano's hand and hurled it across the room.

"It's not going to happen," he growled.

"You are nobody here, Signor Orsini."

Rafe's lips stretched in a cold grin. "That's where you're wrong. I am always somebody. It's time you understood that. Chiara! Step away from the pig and come to me."

She didn't move. Rafe took his eyes from Cordiano long enough to steal a look at her. He cursed under his breath. That last faint had probably been a fake. This one wouldn't be. She wasn't just pale, she was the color of paper.

"Giglio. Let go of the lady."

Nothing. Rafe took a breath and dug his hand into his pocket, snagged his BlackBerry and shoved it forward so it made a telltale bulge. As he'd hoped, the *capo*'s eyes followed.

"Do it," he said through his teeth, "and you might have an unfortunate accident."

That was all it took. The pig's arms dropped to his sides. Despite everything, or maybe because of it, Rafe struggled not to laugh. He could almost hear his brothers' howls when he told them how he'd faked out a man who was surely a stone-cold killer with his trusty PDA.

"Chiara. Get over here."

She crossed the room slowly, her eyes never leaving his. When she reached him, he took her wrist, brought her close to his side. She was shaking like a young tree in a wind storm; her skin felt clammy under his fingers. He cursed, slid his arm around her waist and tucked her against him. She came willingly and his anger toward her gave way to compassion. Sure, this whole damned mess was her fault—he'd kissed her, but if she hadn't pulled that stupid trick on the road, it never would have happened—but her father's reaction, even for an old-line Sicilian, was way out of line.

"It's okay," he said softly.

She nodded. Still, he could hear her teeth chattering.

"It's okay," he said again. "Everything's going to be fine."

She looked up at him, eyes glittering with unshed tears, and shook her head. Her loosened hair drifted across one side of her face and he fought back the sudden crazy desire to tuck the strands back behind her ear.

"No," she said, so softly that he could hardly hear her. "My father will give me to Giglio."

Rafe felt his muscles tense. Give her away. As if she were Cordiano's property.

"He won't. I won't let him."

Her mouth trembled. She said something, so quietly he couldn't hear it, and he cupped her face, lifted it to his.

"What did you say?"

She shook her head again.

"Chiara. Tell me what you said."

She took a long, deep breath, so deep that he could see the lift of her breasts even within the shapeless black dress.

"I said he will do what he wishes, Signor Orsini, once you have gone."

Was she right? Was this only a temporary respite from her

father's crazed insistence that the only way to restore the honor she had not lost was by marrying her off?

The sound of slow applause made him look up. Cordiano, smiling, was clapping his hands together.

"*Bravo*, Signor Orsini. Nicely done. I see that your father raised you properly. In fact, you are very much like him."

Rafe shot a cold look at the other man. "I assure you, Cordiano, I am nothing like my father."

"It was meant as a compliment, I assure *you*. You are quick. Strong. Fearless. As for your earlier refusal to admit that you wronged my daughter…" The *don* smiled. "That is behind us."

Maybe he'd been mistaken. Maybe coming to Chiara's rescue had been enough to set things straight. Rafe forced an answering smile.

"I'm happy to hear it."

"Gossip can spread as swiftly as a sirocco in a town like this. And people do not forget things that steal one's honor."

Back to square one.

Rafe looked down at the woman who stood in the protective curve of his arm. She was calmer, though he could still feel her trembling. His arm tightened around her. What in hell was he going to do? Of course she was right; as soon as he drove away, the *don* would force her into a marriage, if not with the disgraced Pig Man then with someone else. Some hard-eyed, cold-faced butcher like the ones he'd seen lounging in the castle's entry hall.

Chiara Cordiano would become the wife of a thief and a killer. She would lie beneath him in her marriage bed as he forced her knees apart, grunted and pushed deep inside her….

"All right," Rafe said, the words loud in the stillness of the room.

Cordiano raised an eyebrow. "All right what, Signor Orsini?"

Rafe took a long, seemingly endless breath.

"All right," he said roughly. "I'll marry your daughter."

CHAPTER FIVE

THE private jet Rafe had rented flew swiftly through the dark night.

He'd arranged for the rental at the airport in Palermo. The alternative—a six-hour wait for a commercial flight home—had struck him as impossible.

He had no wish to spend a minute more than necessary on Sicilian soil.

The plane itself was very much like the luxuriously appointed one he and his brothers owned; the pilot and copilot were highly recommended, the cabin attendant pleasant and efficient. She'd made sure he was comfortable, that he had a glass of excellent Bordeaux on the table beside him, that filet mignon would be fine for dinner—not that he was in the mood for dinner—and then she'd faded from sight.

A night flight on a private jet was generally a great place to relax after a difficult day.

But not this time. A muscle in Rafe's cheek ticked.

This time, he was not alone.

A woman was seated across the aisle. Nothing terribly unusual in that. Women had traveled with him before. His PA. His attorney. Clients. His sisters. An occasional mistress, accompanying him for a weekend in Hawaii or Paris.

This woman was none of those things.

She sat wrapped in a black coat even though the cabin was

a steady 72 degrees Fahrenheit. She sat very still, her shoulders back, spine rigid. Last he'd looked, her hands were knotted in her lap.

She was an ill-dressed, tight-lipped stranger.

And she happened to be his wife.

Rafe felt the muscle in his cheek jump again.

His wife.

The words, the very concept, were impossible to grasp. He, the man who had no interest in marrying, had married Chiara Cordiano. He'd married a woman he didn't know, didn't like, didn't want, any more than she wanted him.

Rafe shut his eyes, bit back a groan of despair.

How in hell had he let himself get roped into this? Nobody had ever accused him of fancying himself a knight in shining armor. Well, no—but he couldn't have just stood by and let her be handed over to Pig Man.

Assuming, of course, that would really have happened.

Rafe frowned. But would it?

Her father had wanted his daughter to marry an Orsini. The *don* had no way of knowing he was not part of Cesare's organization; Cesare would never have admitted such a thing to an enemy. Cordiano surely would have figured the marriage would strengthen ties between the old world and the new at the same time it settled a debt.

Marrying Chiara to the *capo*, on the other hand, would have accomplished very little, only ensuring a loyalty that already existed. Why waste her on an underling?

Rafe cursed under his breath.

He'd been scammed.

His father had wanted him to marry his old enemy's daughter. Freddo Cordiano had wanted the same thing. But he'd said he wouldn't, and Cordiano had staged a scene straight from a fairy tale. Either the prince married the princess, or the ogre got her.

The only question was, had Chiara known about it?

Rafe folded his arms.

Dutiful Sicilian daughter that she was, what if she'd agreed to do her best to make him think everything that had happened today was real, starting with that ridiculous stuff on the road? A pair of burlesque bandits, stopping his car... Yes. That would have been good staging. Both father and daughter would have known it wouldn't send him running, that if anything, he'd have been even more determined to reach San Giuseppe.

Even that kiss in the car. Her initial struggle against him, followed by that one sweet sigh of surrender, the softening of her lips, the rich, hot taste of her...

He'd been had.

Aside from him, the only other person who hadn't been in on the con was Giglio. Chiara and her old man had used the *capo* as neatly as they'd used him.

Rafe narrowed his eyes.

Final proof? The 1-2-3 wedding ceremony. Cordiano had obviously pulled a bunch of high-powered strings. There'd been no posting of wedding banns, no formalities beyond signing a couple of papers in front of a mayor who'd all but knelt at the *don*'s feet. A handful of mumbled words and, wham, it was done.

Cordiano had beamed. "You may kiss the bride," he'd said.

Except, of course, Rafe hadn't.

Chiara had looked up at him. He'd looked down at her. Her eyes had held no expression; her lips had been turned in. "Do not touch me" had been her message, and he'd come within a heartbeat of saying, "Trust me, baby, you don't have a thing to worry about."

That kiss in the car, that one moment of heat... Easy to explain. The encounter on the road had left him pumping adrenaline. Danger, sex... One complemented the other. A man could fool himself into thinking anything when he was in that kind of state.

Rafe sat up straight.

Okay. He understood it all. Not that it mattered. He'd married the woman. Now he had to unmarry her. Next stop, an annulment. Divorce. Whatever it took.

Problem solved.

Not that he would just abandon his blushing bride. Yes, she'd trapped him, but he wasn't blameless. He, the man who prided himself on logical thinking, had not thought logically. The price for digging yourself out of a hole, even when someone else had handed you the shovel, was never cheap.

He would do the honorable thing. Arrange a financial settlement. Considering all the effort Chiara had gone to, hauling him in, she was entitled to it. Then she could return to Sicily and he could forget all about—

"Signor Orsini."

He looked up. Chiara stood next to him. He tried not to shake his head at the sight. When they were kids, his sister Anna had gone through a Goth period that had, thankfully, lasted only about a minute. She'd dressed in black from head to toe. She'd even dyed her long, blond hair black.

"You look like something the cat dragged in," he'd told her, with all the aplomb of an older brother.

But a cat would not have bothered dragging Chiara in. Or out. She looked too pathetic. Well, except for the hair. Even skinned back in that damned bun again, it had the gloss of a raven's wing.

Was looking like this part of the act?

"Yes?"

Yes?

Chiara forced herself not to show any reaction. Three hours of silence, and the best Raffaele Orsini could come up with was yes, said in a way that almost hung it with icicles?

Still, yes was an improvement. She would try not to show her annoyance.

"*Signor.* We must talk."

His eyes narrowed to dark blue slits. Chiara was puzzled, but then she realized he was considering what she'd said, as if she'd made a request, when what she'd made was a demand.

She wanted to stamp her foot in fury! What an *imbecile*! Did he think she was a stray cat he'd taken in? That she would be so grateful she would simply sit quietly and let him do whatever he wished with her life?

She had not signed herself over to this man.

Yes, she'd married him. Heaven knew she had not wanted to do it, but choosing between going to America with a hoodlum and remaining in San Giuseppe with a killer had made her decision easy.

The only surprise was that he'd gone through with the ceremony, such as it was. She'd spent the last few hours trying to come up with a reason; by now, she had several.

Her father had paid him to do it. *His* father had paid him to do it. Her father had threatened him with what would happen if he didn't, though she had to admit, that was a slim possibility. Whatever else he was, the American was not a coward.

Perhaps he had finally realized the benefits of marrying the *don*'s daughter. She had no illusions about her feminine appeal: she was mousy, skinny, nothing at all like the voluptuous females who caught men's eyes. What she was, was a link to her father, and thus, to power.

Not that the American's reasons for marrying her mattered.

He'd done it, was what counted, and she'd even felt a rush of gratitude that he had saved her from being given to Giglio—but gratitude only went so far. The bottom line, as they said in all those American movies she watched late at night on TV, was that she had no wish to be married, none to stay married. And from his silence, from the way he looked at her now, she was fairly certain Raffaele Orsini felt the same.

It was time to lay the cards on the table.

She told him exactly that.

"*Signor.* It is time to lay the cards on the table."

One dark eyebrow lifted. He seemed amused. "Whose cards?"

Chiara frowned. "What do you mean, whose cards? *The* cards. Is that not what one lays on the table?"

"Not precisely. They're either your cards or mine." That faint hint of amusement—a smirk, was closer to accurate—disappeared from his face. "Sit down."

"I would rather—"

"Sit," he barked, jerking his chin toward the leather seat angled toward his.

She bristled. Just as she'd suspected. He thought he owned her. Well, he didn't, and the sooner he knew that, the better, but there was no sense in getting sidetracked right now.

"Well?"

He had folded his arms across his chest and sat staring at her, his expression unreadable. He'd discarded his suit coat soon after they'd boarded the plane, stripped away his tie, opened the top two buttons of his white shirt and rolled back his sleeves.

The look on his face, the lack of formality in his clothing, his posture…had he done it deliberately to intimidate her? He looked—he looked very masculine. Aggressive. Those wide shoulders, so clearly defined by the fine cotton of his shirt. The strong, tanned column of his throat. The tanned and muscular forearms…

"Let me know when you're done with the inventory."

Chiara jerked her head up. His tone was silken, that hint of amusement back on his face. She flushed. Why was he making this so difficult? He had not wanted this marriage any more than she. The only reason she had kept silent the last hours was because she'd assumed he would make the first move.

She knew how it was with men like him. They needed to believe they were in charge, even when they weren't.

She drew a breath, then let it out. "What you did—asking me to marry you—"

He snorted. "I didn't ask you anything."

"No. Not if one wishes to be precise, but—"

"I *am* being precise."

"Well, yes. Of course. What I mean is, if you hadn't proposed—"

"You keep getting that wrong, baby. I didn't propose."

"I mean it only as a figure of speech, Signor Orsini."

"And I mean it as fact. I didn't ask. I didn't propose." His eyes narrowed again. "And yet, surprise, surprise, here we are."

She nodded, but it was not a surprise at all. Never mind all her speculation. He had been sent to marry her and he had done so. All the rest was meaningless.

"So?"

He was waiting. Fine. She just had to phrase this right.

"Here we are indeed," she said politely, as if the topic had to do with finding themselves in the same shop instead of in a plane heading for America. "And…and—"

She hesitated. This was the tricky part. Convincing him he had done all he had to do, that now he could take a step that would free them both, might be a challenge. She had a small fortune to offer him in exchange for a divorce. Her mother had left her all her jewelry. Her mother had never worn any of it. Vanity, she'd said, was a sin. But Mama had not been completely unworldly. She'd hidden her jewels, told Chiara where to find them in case, someday, she should need what they might buy.

Today that time had come.

She had the jewels hidden in the bottom of the small suitcase she'd packed. The American could have them all if he would grant her her freedom.

Still, she had to phrase her argument properly, not dent his macho ego.

Her throat, her mouth had gone dry. Unconsciously she swept the tip of her tongue lightly over her lips.

"And," she continued, "this isn't what I want. What either of us wants."

He said nothing, and she touched the tip of her tongue to her lips again. Rafe watched her do it, and a fist seemed to close slowly in his belly.

Did she know what she doing? Was the gesture innocent or deliberate? Her tongue was pink. It was a kitten's tongue. It had touched his, however briefly; he could remember the silken feel of it.

She was still talking, but he had no idea what she was saying. His eyes lifted; he studied her face. It was bright with animation. She had, as he'd noticed before, some fairly good features.

Good? The truth was she was beautiful.

Those big violet eyes were fringed by long, thick lashes. The straight little nose was perfectly balanced above a lush, dusty-rose mouth. Her cheekbones weren't just razor sharp, they were carved.

Why did she dress as she did? Why did she hold herself so stiffly? Why did she confine what he now remembered was a silky mane of thick curls in such an unbecoming style? Was it all illusion? Was it part of the scam?

"Why do you wear your hair like that?"

He hadn't meant to ask the question. Obviously, she hadn't expected it. She'd still been talking about something or other. Now she fell silent in midsentence and stared at him as if he'd asked her to explain how to solve a quadratic equation. Then she gave a nervous little laugh.

"I beg your pardon?"

"Your hair. Why do you pull it back?"

To keep her father's men from looking at her the way this man was looking at her now, but she knew better than to tell him that. It wasn't the same thing, anyway. When Giglio and the others looked at her, she felt her skin crawl. But her skin wasn't crawling now. It was…it was…it was tingling.

Chiara's hand flew to her hair. "It's…it's neater this—"

"Let it loose."

The American's voice was rough. His eyes were blue flames. She could see a muscle knotting and unknotting in his cheek.

Suddenly it seemed hard to breathe. "I don't...I don't see any reason to—"

"The reason is that I'm telling you to do it," Rafe said, and a shocked little voice inside him whispered, *What in hell are you doing?*

It was a good question.

He was not a man who believed in ordering women around. He'd explain that, explain that he'd only been joking...

"Let your hair loose, Chiara," he said, and waited.

The seconds crept by. Then, slowly, she put her hands to her hair. The neat bun came undone. Her hair—thick, lustrous, curling—fell down her back.

The fist in his belly tightened again.

"That's better."

She nodded. Cleared her throat. Knotted her hands in her lap.

"As I was saying—"

"It's warm in here."

She swallowed hard. "I don't find it—"

"You don't need that coat."

She looked down at herself, then at him. "I'm...I'm comfortable."

"Don't be silly." He reached toward her, caught the coat's lapels in his hands. "Take it off."

Chiara felt her heart leap. She was alone with this stranger. Completely alone, in a way she had never been alone with a man before. Enzo, yes. Her father. San Giuseppe's old, half-demented priest. But this was different.

This man was young. He was strong. He was her husband.

That gave him rights. Privileges. She knew about those things, oh God, she knew...

"The coat." His voice was harsh. "Take it off."

Heart pounding, she unbuttoned her coat and shrugged it from her shoulders.

"Listen to me," she said, and hated the way her voice shook. "Signor Orsini. I do not want to be your wife any more than you want to be my husband."

"And?"

"And we are trapped. You had no choice but to marry me and—"

His eyes narrowed again. She had already learned enough about him to know that was not a good sign.

"Is that what you think?"

"Your father wanted it." He said nothing and she hurried on. "And my father wanted it. So—"

"So, I did it to please them both?"

"Yes. No. Perhaps not." She was losing ground; she could sense it. The thing to do was speak more quickly, make him see that she understood why he'd done what he'd done and that he could gain by undoing it. American gangsters could be bought. She had watched enough films to know a great deal about America, and this was one of the things she knew.

"Perhaps my father made promises to you. Perhaps he said he would reward you."

He sat back. Folded his arms again. Watched her, waited, said nothing, everything about him motionless, his body, his face, nothing moving but that damnable muscle in his cheek.

"Did he offer you a reward, *signor*? I can make a better offer."

The corners of his lips curved. "Can you," he said, very softly.

"As soon as we get to America, we will end the marriage. It is an easy thing to do in your country, yes?"

He shrugged. "And you walk away. From me. From your charming father. From that miserable little town. Everybody lives happily ever after. Right?"

He understood! The relief was enormous. "Yes," she said, with a quick smile. "And you get—"

"Oh, I know what I get, baby. But I'd get that, anyway."

Chiara shook her head. "I don't under—"

"That black thing you're wearing."

Confused, she looked down at herself again, then at him. "The black thing? You mean, my dress?"

"What's under it?"

She blinked. "Under…?"

"Give me a break, okay? You're not deaf. Stop repeating what I say and answer the question. What's under that dress?"

Color heated her face. "My…my undergarments."

He grinned. She almost made the old-fashioned word sound real. "Silk? Lace? Bra? Panties?" His smile tilted. "Or is it a thong?"

Chiara shot to her feet. "You're disgusting!"

"You know, it took me a while but I finally figured it out. This get-up. The clothes, the hair, the 'Don't touch me' all but painted on your forehead—it was all for me, wasn't it?"

She swung away. His hands fell hard on her shoulders and he spun her to him. He wasn't smiling anymore; his face was hard, his eyes cold.

"The real Chiara Cordiano is the one I kissed in that car."

"You are *pazzo*! Crazy! Let go of me. Let go of—"

Rafe bent his head and kissed her. It was a stamp of masculine power and intent, and when she tried to twist away from him, he caught her face between his hands and kissed her even harder, forcing her lips apart, thrusting his tongue into her mouth, taking, demanding, furious with her for the lies, furious with himself for falling for them.

Furious, because he was stupid enough to want to reclaim that one sweet moment when he'd kissed her and she'd responded.

Except, she hadn't.

That, too, had been a lie just like everything else, including the way she was weeping now, big, perfect tears streaming down her face as he drew back.

If he hadn't known better, he'd have bought into the act.

"Come on, baby," he said with vicious cruelty, "what's the point in prolonging this? Get out of that ridiculous dress. Do what you undoubtedly do best." His mouth twisted. "Do it really well and I might just give you that divorce you're after."

"Please," she sobbed, "please…"

"Damn it," Rafe growled. He'd had enough. He reached out with one hand, grabbed the collar of her ugly black dress, tore it open from the neckline to the hem…

And saw white cotton.

Sexless, all but shapeless white cotton. Bra. Panties. The kind of stuff his sisters had worn beneath their school uniforms when they were kids, stuff he and his brothers used to cackle over when they saw those innocent, girlish garments drying on the line in the backyard.

He stood, transfixed, uncertain. Was this, too, part of the act?

"Don't," Chiara whispered, "I beg you, don't, don't, don't…"

Her knees buckled. Rafe cursed, caught his wife in his arms and knew, without question, he'd gotten everything wrong.

CHAPTER SIX

THE cabin spun. The floor tilted. And all Chiara could think was, *No, I am not going to pass out again!*

Once in a lifetime was enough. What she needed to do now was fight, not faint.

The American had scooped her into his arms.

"Stay with me," he was saying. "Come on, baby, stay with me!"

He wanted her conscious when he forced himself on her. That chilling realization was enough to chase the gray fog from her brain. Chiara summoned up all her strength and began beating her fists against his shoulders. One blow connected with his chin, and he captured her flailing hands in one of his and held them tightly against his chest.

"Hey," he said, "take it easy!"

Take it easy? *Take it easy?* Maybe the women in his world gave in, but she would fight to what might well be her last breath because this man was strong. Very strong. No matter what she did, she could not get free.

"Chiara! Listen to me. I'm trying to help you."

"Liar! Liar, liar, li—"

"Damn it, are you crazy?"

No, Rafe thought, answering the question himself. Not crazy. She was blind with panic and he couldn't much blame her. What in hell had he done, all but tearing off her clothes like that? For all she knew, what came next would be—

Hell.

He kept one hand clamped around her wrists, used the other to try and pull the edges of the dress together. It was impossible, especially with her fighting him all the way.

Not exactly the way a man hoped to start his honeymoon. A joke, of course, because this was never going to be a honeymoon but still...

Her head jerked back.

She had some dangerous moves. He had to remember that. The way she could get her knee up, for instance, aiming with precision. Getting in close, putting her off balance, would be his only protection. He swept his arms around her, lifted her off her feet and brought her hard against him.

"Chiara! Stop fighting me!"

The lady was a hellcat personified.

And she was soft. Very soft. Her breasts were flush against his chest. Her belly was against his groin. She was still struggling, moving against him, rubbing against him...

Desperate, Rafe sent a searching glance around him. He needed a place to put her down. Crews on private jets were trained to be discreet but if the attendant chose this minute to see if her passengers wanted something, explaining what was going on might be, at the least, embarrassing.

The Orsini plane had a private bedroom and bathroom in the rear of the cabin. Well, there was a door in the back of this one. He had no idea what was behind it. For all he knew, it might be locked but it was worth—

Chiara's sharp little teeth grazed his throat. Okay. Enough was enough. One bite a day was all she was going to get. Grunting, he upended her, tossed her over his shoulder and strode down the aisle while his crazy wife panted, raged, pounded the hell out of his back. *Please*, he thought grimly when he reached the door, grasped the knob...

Rafe breathed a sigh of relief.

The door opened. And beyond it was some kind of room. Not a bedroom. A lounge. Maybe an office. He rolled his eyes. Who cared what it was? There was a desk. A chair. A small lavatory visible beyond a partly opened sliding door. And, best of all, a small leather sofa just made for accommodating an out-of-control female, he thought, and shouldered the door shut.

He went straight for the sofa. Dumped Chiara on it and stood up.

Bad idea.

She was on her feet and trying to fly past him in a heartbeat. He grabbed her, wrestled her down onto the sofa again, squatted in front of her and clamped his hands around her forearms.

"Listen to me," he said. "I am not going to hurt you."

Chiara bared her teeth. An attack-trained rottweiler might have given him a friendlier response. Rafe shook his head in frustration. He had a mess on his hands and only himself to blame. He'd scared the life out of his bride. A joke to call her that, but that was what she was, at least for the time being.

His fault, sure, but how was he to know she'd go off like a roomful of high explosives if he touched her?

You didn't just touch her, that sly voice inside him whispered. True. He'd gone at her as if he were out of control, but whose fault was that, if not hers?

A woman couldn't play hot and cold. That kiss this morning. That one moment of incredible surrender. Was he supposed to forget it had happened?

Had it been real? Had it been a ploy to get him on her side? Who in hell knew? And what about the insults she'd heaped on him, her easy assumption that he was a villain, that she could buy him off? Did none of that count for anything?

Yes, but she'd been through a lot today. So had he, but it wasn't the same. He hadn't been threatened with wedded bliss as the wife of her father's *capo*.

If even that had been real. If it hadn't all been an act, meant to make him agree to a marriage a pair of aging *dons* on both sides of the Atlantic seemed to want.

For the moment he'd go with believing his wife hadn't been in on the deal—and why in hell think of her as his wife? She was nothing but a temporary impediment in his life. Maybe she'd calm down once she understood that. Hell, she had to. He couldn't spend the rest of the flight hanging on to her as she struggled to get away.

Rafe took a long breath.

"Look," he said, "I'm sorry I frightened you. I never— I mean, I had no idea… The thing is, I got angry. And…" And what? None of that excused what he'd done. Truth time, he thought, and drew another breath. "Here's the deal, okay? I thought you had been stringing me along. And—"

"Hah!"

"Hah?"

"Why would I string you along," she panted, "when I would like to string you up?"

How could he want to laugh at a time like this? He couldn't, not without enraging his wildcat even more. Instead he cleared his throat.

"I thought you were part of the plan. You know, to convince me to marry you." Her face registered incredulity, but they were getting somewhere: she had stopped struggling, at least for the moment. "Okay," he said carefully, "I'm going to let go of you. Then I'm going to stand up." His eyes drifted down; he'd all but forgotten her dress was torn in half, showing all that schoolgirl lingerie.

Showing the small but somehow lush breasts, the narrow waist, the flaring hips…

Rafe forced his gaze back to her face. When he spoke, his voice was hoarse.

"I'll stand up, and then I'll get your suitcase so you can change clothes. Okay?"

Chiara glared at him. "I was not part of any plan," she said with icy precision.

"You want something to wear or not?"

He could see her weighing the offer. At last she nodded.

"Good. Fine." Slowly he took his hands from her. She scrambled back as he rose to his feet. She looked like hell, not just the torn dress, but her face was devoid of color, her eyes huge and dark.

And he was the cause.

He, the idiot who'd said yes to marriage to save her, had done this.

"Be right back," he said briskly, striding from the lounge as if shredding a woman's clothes and scaring the life half out of her were just everyday occurrences.

He didn't see her suitcase. Just as well. It was probably overflowing with black dresses and he'd seen enough of them to last a lifetime. He grabbed his carry-on bag, headed back to the lounge...

And paused.

Chiara was exactly where he'd left her, clutching the torn dress together at her breasts. The only difference was in her posture. She sat with her head down, her hair tumbling around her face. The fight had gone out of her; she looked small and vulnerable. Mostly she looked defeated, just as she had in her father's house.

It killed him to see it.

She was shaking. With fear? No, Rafe thought, not this time. He dropped the carry-on bag and hurried to her. She was hovering on the brink of shock. Adrenaline spiked, then dropped, and this was the price you paid.

"Chiara," he said, when he reached her.

She looked up. He could hear her teeth chattering. He cursed softly, went down on his knees and gathered her into his arms.

She balked. He'd expected it and at the first jerk of her muscles, he drew her even closer against him, whispering her name, stroking one big hand gently up and down her back. Gradually he felt her body begin to still.

"That's it," he said softly, his mouth against her temple, his hand still soothing her, and at last she gave a shuddering sigh and leaned into him.

Rafe closed his eyes.

Her face was against his throat. Her lips were slightly parted. He could feel the delicate whisper of her breath, the warmth of it on his skin.

His arms tightened around her. He drew her from the sofa onto her knees. He felt her hands against his chest, one palm flat against his heart.

She was so small. So delicate. He could feel the fragility of her bones and he thought of the time a migrating songbird had flown into one of the windows that lined the terrace of his penthouse. It had been a windy day; when he heard the soft thud of something hitting the glass, he'd thought it must be a chair cushion, but when he went outside, he found the bird, smaller than seemed possible, lying on the marble floor, eyes glazed, heart beating so frantically that he could see the rise and fall of its feathered breast.

Helpless, clueless, he'd carefully scooped the tiny creature into his palm. Minutes had crept by and just when he was about to give up hope, the bird made a soft peep, scrambled upright, blinked, spread its wings and took to the sky.

Chiara stirred like that now. Her eyes swept over his face.

"Okay?" he said softly.

She swallowed. "Yes."

He felt the same rush of pleasure as the day the tiny bird had survived its brush with death. Still, he went on holding her in his arms. He didn't want to let her go. She might go into shock again, might need him to comfort her...

"Please let go of me, Signor Orsini."

So much for needing his comfort.

Rafe got to his feet and retrieved the carry-on bag. She was seated on the sofa again, a portrait of composure except for the gaping dress. He cleared his throat, dropped the bag on the floor and jerked his chin at it.

"Nothing in there will really fit you, of course," he said briskly.

"I have my own things. In my suitcase."

"Yeah, well, I grabbed the first bag I saw. Anyway, there's some stuff that might work. Jeans, sweats, a couple of T-shirts…" He was babbling. She could figure things out for herself, once he gave her some privacy. "I'll, ah, I'll wait outside. Let me know when you're done and then…and then, we'll talk. Okay?"

Chiara nodded. Her face gave nothing away, but all things considered, he figured he was doing pretty well. He nodded back, stepped from the room, shut the door, folded his arms…

And waited.

He waited for what seemed a very long time. Just when he'd finally decided she was going to pretend he didn't exist, the door swung open.

His throat constricted.

She was wearing one of his T-shirts over a pair of his workout shorts. The shirt hung to her knees; the shorts fell to midcalf. Her feet were bare. Her hair was a soft cloud of dark chocolate silk: he figured she must have found his brush and used it.

She should have looked comical. At least foolish.

She didn't.

She looked beautiful.

It made him smile. Big mistake. Her chin rose and he knew she was about to give him hell.

"Thank you for the clothes, *signor*."

"It's Rafe."

"Thank you, Signor Orsini," she repeated, and took a deep breath. It made the thin cotton T-shirt fabric lift in a way that drew his gaze to her breasts. "And for this," she said, in a voice that stopped him thinking about the shirt and what was under it. Looking up, he saw the unmistakable glint of steel in her hand. "Touch me again, and I will kill you!"

Well, hell. His brush wasn't the only thing she'd found. She'd found his nail scissors, too.

"Chiara," he said calmly, "put that down."

"Not until we reach New York and you set me free."

"You *are* free." His mouth twisted. "I married you. I didn't buy you."

"I told you. I want an annulment. A divorce. Whatever is legally necessary."

He could feel his temper rising. She was hardly in the position to make demands.

"I have money."

His eyebrows rose. "What?"

"I have my mother's jewels. I told you about them. Obviously, you were not listening." Her eyes met his. "They are very valuable. I will give them to you in exchange for my freedom."

The woman had a wonderful opinion of him. It annoyed him and he told himself to stay calm.

"Do you think this is a bazaar? That you can haggle with me to get what you want?"

Her face colored. "No. I did not mean—" She took a deep breath. "I see what you are trying to do, *signor*. You think, if you direct this conversation elsewhere, you will dissuade me."

He lifted one dark eyebrow. "Dissuade?"

"*Sì*. It means—"

"I know what it means. Someone taught you some fancy English in that hole-in-the wall town of yours."

"San Giuseppe is not 'my' town," she said coldly. "And yes, Miss Ellis taught me, as you say, some fancy English."

"One of your father's girlfriends?"

She laughed. Miss Ellis had been seventy. Tall, thin, about as approachable as a nun—but the best teacher in the world, until her father had decided she was filling Chiara's head with too much worldly nonsense. It still hurt to remember the day he'd dismissed her.

"One of my tutors," Chiara said, and lifted her chin. "Thanks to her, you will not be able to dissuade me in English or in several other languages."

"Am I supposed to be impressed?"

"You are supposed to be warned, Signor Orsini. I am not prepared to take what has been forced upon me by you and my father standing up."

Rafe grinned. He couldn't help it. For all he knew, she spoke a dozen languages but there was a difference between speaking English like a native and speaking it like a scholar, especially when the words came from the mouth of a woman who looked like an armed street urchin.

"You find this amusing, *signor*? I promise, I will defend myself if you approach me again."

He thought about going straight at her and snatching the scissors away. He wouldn't get hurt—it would be like taking candy from a baby—but what the hell, this was just getting interesting.

"So, you want out of our marriage."

"It is not a marriage, it is an alliance between my father and yours."

"Whatever," he said, as if he didn't know damned well she was probably right. He made a show of shaking his head. "I guess modern women just don't believe in keeping their vows anymore."

Chiara clucked her tongue. "Such nonsense! Neither of us wants this marriage and you know it."

For some reason her certainty irked him. "And you know this about me because…?"

Her eyes narrowed. The tip of her tongue came out and touched her top lip, then swept back inside, to be replaced by a delicate show of small—and, he knew—sharp white teeth that sank, with great delicacy, into her bottom lip.

His gut knotted. His entire body tensed. Ridiculous, but then, the entire day had been ridiculous. Why should things become normal now?

"I mean," he said, sounding like the voice of reason, "I'm Italian. What if I don't believe in divorce?"

What if the sun went nova? He wasn't Italian, except by heritage. He was American. That was how he thought of himself. And while he didn't believe people should bounce in and out of matrimony, he did believe in divorce when no other solution made sense.

Like now, when they'd both been forced into a union neither wanted...which was exactly what she'd said.

Yes, but why make this easy for her?

He'd been suckered into this. Even if she hadn't been party to the plan, she hadn't protested it, either. Now she wanted out. Fine. So did he. But first he wanted some answers. And this woman—his wife—was the only one who could provide them.

"I'm waiting, baby. Why should I agree to a divorce? After all, I flew across the ocean to marry you."

Chiara blinked. "But you told my father—"

"I know what I told him. I said I had no wish to marry you." Rafe shrugged. "Any good businessman knows better than to accept the first offer when he's negotiating a deal."

"A deal?" She stared at him in disbelief. "You mean—you mean, you intended to go through with it all the time? You only let my father think he could hand me off to that...that animal?"

"I didn't say that."

"You implied it."

First, *dissuade*. Now, *implied*. Tricky words, even for native English speakers, which Chiara was not. What she was, his scissors-wielding bride, was a font of surprises.

"I married you," he said calmly. "Never mind my reasons. As for you...I didn't see Daddy holding a shotgun on you during the ceremony."

"I do not understand what that means."

"It means you married me without a word of argument."

"I would have married a…a donkey if it meant I didn't have to marry Giglio!"

"You're no prize package either, baby."

Color rushed into her cheeks. "You know what I mean. And do not call me 'baby.' I am a grown woman."

Yes. She was. A beautiful grown woman, but there was much more to her than that.

Her face wasn't just lovely, it was animated. Her eyes weren't just a color that reminded him of violets, they were bright with intelligence. He'd seen enough of her body to know it was feminine and lush, but it was the proud way she held herself that impressed him, something in her stance that said she would fight to the end for what she believed.

She was, as she said, a grown woman.

His woman.

His wife.

Rafe felt his body stir. They were alone, still a few hours from landing. He'd scared the hell out of her by coming at her with all the subtlety of a hormone-crazed bull, but then, he'd misjudged her.

She wasn't a femme fatale; she was inexperienced. After all, how many lovers could a woman have in a town the size of San Giuseppe? Cesare had described her as a virgin, but obviously that was impossible. There were no virgins in today's world, not even tucked away in remote towns in the Sicilian hills.

No, things had not gone well a little while ago, but whether his wife wanted to admit it or not, she had responded to him when he'd kissed her before. She'd let him hold her in his arms. All he had to do was take those stupid scissors from her, gather her close, kiss her, slip his hand under that T-shirt…

Was he insane? For one thing, this woman was *not* his wife. Well, she was, but not for long. For another, sleeping with her would only complicate things.

Besides, if he touched her, she'd come apart in terror.

Her reaction to him hadn't been an act. It hadn't been because he hadn't used any finesse. She'd been out of her mind with fear. Real, honest fear. Something awful had happened to her. Something had hurt her so much that she hid inside those godawful black dresses.

Who had done this to her? A man, surely. Giglio? One of the other brutes her father employed?

Hot rage swept through him. He told himself he'd feel this about the violation of any woman, that it had nothing to do with Chiara in particular.

The hell it didn't.

She was his. Temporarily, until he could figure out what to do with her, her but for now she belonged to him. And he was a man who would always protect what was his.

"Chiara."

She looked at him.

"Who hurt you?"

She stared at him. The color drained from her face. "I do not know what you mean."

"Yeah, you do. Why did you scream when I touched you?"

"What you mean is, why didn't I melt with delight."

The words dripped venom, but she wasn't going to put him off that easily. Rafe folded his arms over his chest. "It's a simple question. What made you so frightened of men?"

"What you mean is, why am I unwilling to let men have their way with me?"

"How about not telling me what I mean and just answering the question? What are you afraid of?"

"If we play a round of Twenty Questions, do I win a divorce?"

He was in front of her in two strides. Her hand shot up, the little scissors glinting. Rafe didn't bother playing games. He caught her wrist, took the scissors from her and tossed them on the sofa.

"One question," he said brusquely, "and I want an answer. Why are you afraid of sex?"

"I am not afraid. Besides, what I am or am not is none of your business."

The woman was impossible! "It's every bit my business," he said sharply. "You're my wife."

She laughed. Hell, he couldn't blame her. Sure, a small-town official owned by her father had mumbled some words at them, but the truth was, she was no more his wife than he was her husband.

Except, he was. He had a piece of gilt-edged paper tucked inside his passport case that proved it.

"Was it because you thought I was going to—" he felt his face heat "—to force you?" He cupped her elbows. "Because I wasn't. I got rough, yeah, and I shouldn't have, but I would never have taken you against your will." Her eyes called him a liar; he couldn't much blame her for that, either. "It's the truth. I'm no saint, but I'd never force a woman to make love with me."

"Love," she said, with a little snort of disdain.

"That's what men and women do. They make love." His hands tightened on her. "I'd never sleep with a woman who didn't want me."

No, Chiara thought, no, he wouldn't have to.

A woman would go to him willingly. Raffaele Orsini was all the things women supposedly wanted in a man. He was strong, good-looking and so masculine there were moments he made her feel dizzy.

So, if a woman liked sex, she would like him. And there were women who liked sex. She was not a fool. She understood that, even though she would never want to be one of those women.

No matter what he claimed, sex was for the man. A woman had to go along with it, if she married. The nudity. The intimacy. The slap of flesh against flesh, the smell of sweat, the terrible, painful, humiliating invasion of your body...

Her mother had explained it all so that she would be prepared if—when—it came time for her to take a husband.

"I would not wish my daughter to go to her wedding night without knowing what awaits her," Mama had said.

A shudder went through her. The American saw it. Big, brave, macho creature that he was, he reacted instantly.

"Chiara."

She shook her head, stepped back, but he put his arms around her and drew her against him. She let him do it; the sooner she convinced him she was fine, the sooner he'd let her go.

She could feel the heat coming from him. Feel the hardness of his male body. Smell his male scent. Fear clogged her throat. He seemed to know it and he began whispering to her as he had a few minutes ago. She had to admit he had calmed her then, but she'd been in a state of shock. It was his warmth that had steadied her.

She told herself that a blanket would have had the same effect.

Still, she felt herself responding to his soothing touch, to his voice. She sighed, shut her eyes, felt one of his hands thread into her hair, cup her head, lift her face to his…

Chiara jerked back. "Do not touch me!"

Rafe lifted his hands from her with exaggerated care. She was looking at him as if he was a serial killer. Undoubtedly, the lady had a problem. But it wasn't his problem. *She* wasn't his problem. The minute they reached New York, he'd phone his lawyer and tell her to get started on whatever had to be done to end this sham of a marriage.

The sooner he was out of this mess, the better.

CHAPTER SEVEN

CHIARA'S first glimpse of New York City almost took her breath away.

Lights, what seemed like millions of them, lay winking beneath the plane like sparkling diamonds on black velvet. As the jet dropped lower, she could see that the lights were moving. They were lights from automobiles racing along endless intersecting highways.

Where were all these people going in the middle of the night? It *was* the middle of the night, American time. East Coast time. She would have to remember that. This was not like Italy, where the hour was the same if you were in Rome or Florence or Palermo.

Not that she'd ever been to Rome or Florence. Not that she'd ever been anywhere.

It should have been exciting, the realization that she was about to land on another continent, in a city she'd read of and dreamed about. But it wasn't.

It was terrifying.

She wasn't here by choice, she was here as the unwilling bride of a stranger. She knew nothing about her husband. No, she thought, swallowing hard as the plane descended, that was not true. She did know something about him. She knew that he was a man who bore her father's stamp of approval.

That could only mean he was a hoodlum, just like her father.

Except—except, he wasn't really like her father. He could be cold and hard, but sometimes there was a tenderness to him, too. And he was beautiful. She knew it was a strange word to use to describe a man but none other suited him. His height. His body. His face, *Dio*, his face, those hard, masculine angles and planes, that firm mouth…

Firm. Warm. And soft, so soft against hers…

The plane touched down, bumping delicately against the runway. The captain made a pleasant announcement, welcoming them to New York. Chiara, fumbling with her seat belt, rose quickly to her feet. The plane was still moving along the taxiway as she started blindly up the aisle.

A strong hand closed lightly on her elbow.

"I'm happy to see you're in such a hurry to reach your new home," her husband said.

She could hear the derision in his voice, feel the possessiveness of his grasp. Her heart thumped.

God only knew what lay ahead.

Whatever it was, she would face it with courage. If life had taught her anything, it was that you must never show weakness to your oppressor.

Finally the plane came to a stop. The door shushed open. Chiara stepped out into the North American night.

She'd heard all about security procedures, but they evidently didn't apply to powerful American gangsters. Her husband led her into a small building. He presented their passports to a man who hardly glanced at them. Minutes later they made their way out to a waiting automobile. A uniformed driver stood beside it.

Her steps faltered and her husband's hand tightened on her elbow.

"Keep moving," he said coldly.

As if she had a choice.

What had the poet said in the *Divine Comedy*? Something about abandoning hope, all those who entered here.

One last, free breath and Chiara stepped into the back of the limousine.

The big car moved swiftly through the night.

So far, so good, Rafe thought—assuming you discounted the fact that his wife was sitting beside him like a prisoner being driven to her execution.

At least there hadn't been a reception committee waiting, something he'd half expected. He'd figured Cordiano would have phoned his father. Cesare would have told the family....

What fun that would have been.

The old man gloating. His mother going from being upset that there hadn't been a big wedding to planning a party that would rival anything Manhattan had ever seen. His sisters teasing him unmercifully. And his brothers...

Lord, his brothers! Better not even to go there.

But the reception committee hadn't materialized. Clearly, Cordiano had not contacted Cesare. Rafe had no idea why, and frankly he didn't much care. What mattered was that he had some breathing room. Tomorrow morning, first thing, he'd call his lawyer, start the procedure that would return his life to normal. No matter what he'd told Chiara, he wanted a divorce every bit as much as she did.

The drama on the plane, all that stuff about not giving her a divorce? Meaningless. He'd been ticked off, that was all, and he'd made a threat he had no intention of keeping.

He wanted out.

Traffic was light, this time of night. The big car moved smoothly along the highway, sped along Fifth Avenue and drew to a stop before his building. The doorman greeted them politely; if he found the sight of a woman wrapped in a coat like the kind old ladies wore in bad foreign films unusual, he was too well trained to let it show.

"Do you need help with your bags, Mr. Orsini?"

I need help with my life, Rafe thought, but he tossed him a polite "No, thanks" and headed for his private elevator, his carry-on hanging from his shoulder, Chiara's old-fashioned leather suitcase clutched in one hand, the other wrapped around her elbow. It would have made things easier to let go, but he knew better.

The last thing he needed tonight was to end up running down Fifth Avenue after her.

They rode the elevator in silence. Nothing new there. They'd made the trip from the airport the same way. The door slid open when they reached his penthouse. Rafe stepped from the car. Chiara didn't. He rolled his eyes and quick-stepped her into the foyer. The elevator door shut; Rafe sent it to the lobby level and let go of his wife's arm.

"Okay," he said briskly, "we're home."

He winced. What a stupid remark, but what else was there to say? He dropped their bags, shrugged off his jacket, checked the little stack of mail on the table near the entryway, checked his voice mail, gave Chiara time to say something, do something, but when he turned around she was standing precisely where he'd left her, except she'd backed up so that her shoulders were pressed against the silk-covered wall.

She looked exhausted and terrified, lost in the awful black coat. Defiance, or an attempt at it, glittered in her wide eyes, but the overall effect was—there was no other word for it—pathetic.

Despite himself, he felt a surge of pity along with the gnawing realization that there was no point in being angry with her. Never mind his accusations. The truth was unavoidable. Neither of them had wanted this marriage.

She was as trapped as he. More so, maybe. He, at least, was on his own turf. She, however, was in a place she didn't know, a country she didn't know...

Hell, he thought, and cleared his throat. "Chiara?" She

looked at him. "Why don't you, ah, why don't you take off your coat?"

She didn't answer. Okay. He'd try again.

"Would you, ah, would you like something to eat?"

Nothing. His jaw tightened. She wasn't going to help him one bit.

"Look," he said, "I know this isn't what either of us wanted—"

"It is what *you* wanted," she said coldly.

"Me? Hell, no. Why would you think—"

"You won't agree to a divorce."

"Yeah. Right." Rafe ran his hand through his hair. "Look, about that—"

"The one thing I promise you, *signor*, is that I will never be a real wife to you!"

"Damn it, if you'd just listen—"

"You can force me to remain your property." Her chin rose. "You can force me to do a lot of things, but I will never let you forget that I do them unwillingly."

Rafe's eyes narrowed. "Are we back to talking about sex?"

The rush of color to her cheeks was answer enough. Why did her vow make him so angry? He had no intention of taking her to bed. Why would he when he could scroll through his BlackBerry and find the names of a dozen women who'd sleep with him and be happy about it? Beautiful women. Sexy women. Women who'd make this one look like Little Orphan Annie.

"I am talking about female compliance in general and, yes, that would include—it would include—"

"Sex." He smiled tightly. "You can say the word. It won't pollute you."

Her color went from deep pink to bright red. "I know it is difficult for you to believe, but not every woman wants to pretend she enjoys being the recipient of a man's most base desires."

Whoa. Her attitude definitely needed updating, but that would be some other man's problem, not his. Why not tell her she had nothing to worry about? Divorce was just a phone call away—

"Perhaps you think you are entitled to…to special privileges because you supposedly saved me from Giglio."

Whatever hackles were, he could damn near feel his rise. "Supposedly?"

Chiara shrugged. "You said it yourself. You had every intention of marrying me all along."

"I said that because I was angry. You know damned well I only did it because your old man threatened to hand you over to his *capo*."

"Why should I believe you now?" Her smile was like ice. "After all, *signor*, you lie with such ease."

Okay. Enough. He'd taken one insult too many. It was time to let the lady stew in her own juices for a while.

"You know," he said coldly, "I've had enough of this nonsense to last a lifetime. It's bedtime."

All the color drained from her face. She'd misunderstood him. He opened his mouth to explain, but before he could say a word, she spat out a Sicilian phrase he'd never heard anywhere but on the streets of his youth.

"Right," he said through his teeth, "that's precisely what I am."

He strode purposefully toward her, grabbed her arm and yanked her toward him. She cried out, struggled, and on a curse the equal of hers, he lifted her into his arms and carried her up the staircase to the second floor, down the hall and into one of the guest rooms where he dumped her in the center of the bed.

She scrambled back against the pillows. Her hair was a tangle of wild curls. Her ugly coat had come open, exposing her ludicrous outfit…

Her amazingly sexy outfit.

Her breasts, shadowed beneath the thin cotton of his T-shirt. Her nipples, pebbled and just waiting for the touch of his fingers, the heat of his mouth…

Rafe stepped back. Jerked his head toward a half-open door.

"Your bathroom's through there. There's a clean tooth-brush in the vanity. Toothpaste. Towels. Soap. Shampoo. Whatever else you might need."

"If you think I'm going to…to prepare myself for you—"

"If you did, you'd be wasting your time. I like my women soft, feminine and sexy. You don't even approach that description. No wonder your old man had to find you a husband."

It was a good line, and he made the most of it by walking out.

He was halfway down the hall when he heard her door slam hard enough to rattle the walls. For some crazy reason, it made him smile.

A hot shower, then bed.

That was what he needed.

The shower was fine. So was the bed until he turned the sheets into a tangled mess. After an hour of trying to sleep, he gave up, lay back and watched the digital alarm clock blink away the minutes.

Two a.m. Three. Four. Damn it, he had to be at work in the morning. He didn't have time for this.

Maybe he ought to phone his lawyer now. Yeah, it was the middle of the night, but so what? He had Marilyn Sayers on retainer. A big, fat retainer. The whole point of it was so that he could contact her anytime, anyplace, about anything.…

Rafe got out of bed, pulled on a pair of old gray sweatpants. What difference would it make if he spoke to Sayers now or later? She was a top-notch legal eagle; this was a simple divorce. An hour or two wouldn't mean a thing.

He'd wait.

He thought about going for a run in the park, but that would have meant leaving Chiara alone in the apartment. Somehow, that didn't seem wise. He had a bottle of sleeping tablets in the medicine cabinet, something the doctor had given him a couple of years ago after minor surgery on his knee—he'd torn a tendon in a motorcycle accident. But he'd never taken even one of the pills and he wasn't about to start now.

A shot of brandy. That would do it.

It did.

Twenty minutes after he drank the Courvoisier, Rafe got into bed and tumbled into sleep.

Something woke him.

He wasn't sure what it was. A sound, but what? Not his alarm. The red numbers on the clock were steady at 5:05 a.m., which meant he had fifty-five minutes until the thing went off.

There it was again. A noise. Faint but... A cry? That was it. A cry. Weeping.

Hell. It was Chiara.

He sat up in bed, rubbed his hands over his stubbled jaw and cheeks. Now what? Did he ignore it? Might as well. Let her cry. Who gave a damn? Every time he tried to treat her with kindness, she reacted like a junkyard dog.

He lay back against the pillows again, stacked his arms beneath his head. She was unhappy? He wasn't exactly ecstatic. If she was crying, it was her business.

But it didn't stop. Well, so what? He'd heard women cry before. Ingrid, for example, just a couple of days ago... Just a lifetime ago. But it hadn't been like this. Sad. Desperate. As if the sobs were being torn from Chiara's soul.

Rafe threw back the covers, got to his feet, headed for the door and then for the guest suite, where he paused. "Chiara?"

At first he thought the sobs had stopped. They hadn't. They'd just grown muffled. She was crying as if her heart might break.

"Chiara," he said again, and tapped lightly on the door. Still no answer. He took a breath. Then, carefully, he tried the knob.

It turned, and the door swung open.

The room was in darkness, but she'd left the bathroom light

on and the door partly open. He could see the huddled form visible in the center of the bed.

Rafe called her name again. Still, no answer. Slowly, certain he was going to regret this, certain she'd rear up, scream the bloody building down when she realized he was in her bedroom, he made his way forward and sat down, gingerly, on the edge of the mattress. He could see her now, part of her, at least; she was just a small, sad lump under the duvet, on her belly, her face buried against the pillows.

His heart constricted. She was small and frightened and he'd known that and added to it.

Without thinking, he reached out and laid his hand gently against her hair.

"Chiara, sweetheart, I'm sorry. Please, don't cry…"

The bedclothes seemed to explode. Rafe braced himself for a scream, a shout, a right to the jaw… But none of that happened. Chiara launched herself at him, wound her arms around his neck and buried her damp face against his naked shoulder.

Stunned, he sat absolutely still. Then, slowly, he slipped his arms around her. Filled them with soft, warm, trembling woman.

He shut his eyes.

Holding her felt wonderful. And she smelled good. His soap. His shampoo. And mingling with their scents, essence of woman. Of Chiara.

Of his wife.

His body stirred. Silently he cursed himself for it. There was nothing sexual happening here. Dawn was about to break over a sleeping city and he had a weeping woman in his arms.

Remember that, Orsini, he told himself sternly.

"Chiara," he said gently. "What is it? Did you have a nightmare?"

She nodded. Her hair, all those dark and lovely curls, slid like feather wisps against his skin. He shut his eyes again, drew her closer, held her more tightly against his heart.

"Do you want to talk about it?"

She shook her head.

"No. Okay. Fine. You don't have to—"

"I dreamed it was my wedding night."

A muscle knotted in his jaw. It *was* her wedding night. A hell of a thing to know that *he* was her nightmare.

"It's all right, baby. Nothing will happen to you. I promise."

"My wedding night with…with Giglio."

A nightmare, all right. Rafe's arms tightened around her.

"Shh, sweetheart. It was just a bad dream."

A shudder went through her. "It was so real. His hands on me. His mouth."

"Shh," Rafe said again, an unreasoning rage filling him at the picture she'd painted. "Giglio can't get to you. Not anymore."

Silence. Another shudder. Then, a whisper so low he could hardly hear it.

"What?" he said, and bent his head closer to hers.

"I said…I said I have been awful to you, Raffaele. You saved me from him. And instead of saying thank you, I have accused you of…of all kinds of terrible things."

He smiled. "Seems to me we've done a pretty good job of accusing each other of all kinds of terrible things."

"It is only that I never expected any of this to happen. My father had threatened to marry me to an American but—"

"Just what every guy hopes," Rafe said, trying to lighten things. "To be a beautiful woman's worst nightmare."

His little attempt at humor flew straight over her head. "No," she said quickly, "I did not dream of you, Raffaele, I dreamed of—"

"I know. I only meant… Chiara, you have to believe me. My father wanted me to marry you, yes, but I didn't have any intention of doing it. Not that a man wouldn't be lucky to marry you," he added quickly, "but—"

Her hand lifted; she placed her fingers lightly over his lips.

"It…it isn't that I don't want to be your wife. It's that I do not want to be any man's wife. Do you understand?"

He didn't. Not really. He'd been dating women since he'd turned sixteen and he'd never yet come across one whose ultimate goal, no matter what she claimed, wasn't marriage.

Then he thought of what he knew of the woman in his arms. Her father's domination. Her isolation. Above everything else, her fear of sex, a fear he'd done little to ease over the past several hours.

"Truly," she said, "it is not you. It would be any man." She drew back in his arms, her face turned up to his, her eyes brilliant, her dark lashes spiky with tears. "Do you see?"

God, she was so beautiful! So vulnerable, lying back in his arms...

"Yes," he said, his voice a little rough, "I do see. But you need to know—you need to know not all men are beasts, sweetheart."

A wan smile curved her lips. "Perhaps you are the exception."

The exception? If he were, his body wouldn't be responding to the tender warmth of hers. He wouldn't be looking at her and wondering if her mouth tasted as sweet as he remembered, if she was naked under the oversize cotton thing he assumed was a nightgown.

"I...I appreciate your decency," she said, and every miserable male instinct he owned shrieked, *Yeah? Then how about proving it?*

He sat up straight, all but tore Chiara's encircling arms from his neck and set her back against the pillows, grateful—hell, hopeful—that his baggy sweats would hide the effect she'd had on him.

"Well," he said brightly, "you'll be okay now." She didn't answer. "So, ah, so try to get some sleep." Still no answer. He cleared his throat. "Chiara? About that divorce?"

"Yes?"

The hopeful note in the single word would have thrilled him if this were Ingrid or any one of a hundred other women. As it was, it only made him feel a pang of remorse.

"I'll phone my attorney first thing in the morning and get it started."

She gave a deep sigh. "*Grazie bene*, Raffaele. The jewels—"

"Forget about them. They're yours."

"I can, at least, use them to pay my share of the legalities."

"I said, I don't want them." He knew he sounded harsh but, damn it, did she really think he'd let her pay for the severance of their marriage? Okay, it was a bogus marriage but still… "I'd prefer you keep them," he said, trying for a calmer tone.

"*Grazie.* I can use the money they bring to live on. New York is expensive, yes?"

"New York is expensive, yes. But it won't be so bad. Not with alimony."

"Alimony?"

Alimony? his baffled brain echoed. A settlement was bad enough but alimony? Why would he pay alimony to a woman who'd been his wife for, what, twenty-four hours?

"I do not expect alimony, Raffaele. We have not had a real marriage."

"Yeah, but this is America. Everybody pays alimony," he said with a straight face, even though he could already hear his lawyer screaming in legal horror.

Chiara smiled. "I think," she said, very softly, "I think, perhaps, you are an honorable man, Raffaele Orsini."

Guilt made his jaw tighten. She wouldn't think that if she could see the response of his body to the soft hand she laid upon his thigh. He took that hand, gave it a brisk little shake and stood up.

"Okay," he said brightly, "sleep time."

Her smile faded.

"You won't have that bad dream again," Rafe said softly. She didn't answer and he cleared his throat. "If you like—if you like, I'll sit in that chair until you doze off."

"Would you mind?"

"Mind? No. I'm happy to do it."

"It would be comfortable for you?"

Comfortable? Not in this lifetime. The chair in question was a Queen Anne, a Marie Antoinette, a Lady Godiva or something like that. It was puny looking. He'd put his own stamp on the living room, the library, the dining room and his bedroom, but he'd grown impatient after a while and turned the interior decorator loose on the guest rooms. One result was this chair. It might hold a dwarf but would it hold a man who stood six-three in his bare feet?

"Raffaele? I would not want you to be uncomfortable."

"I'll be fine," he said with conviction, and he pulled the chair forward, sank onto it and prayed it wouldn't collapse under his weight.

"Grazie bene," Chiara said softly.

Rafe nodded. "No problem," he said briskly. "You just close your eyes and—"

She was asleep.

He sat watching her for a while, the dark curve of her lashes against her pale cheeks, the tumble of her curls against her face, the steady rise and fall of her breasts. A muscle knotted in his jaw, and he reached out and tugged the duvet up, settled it around her shoulders.

He wanted to touch her. Her face. Her hair. Her breasts.

Determinedly he forced his brain from where it was heading. Concentrated on taking deep breaths. He needed to get some rest but it was impossible. The damned chair…

What if he slipped out of the room? She was deep, deep asleep. Yes, but what if she dreamed of Giglio again? He'd promised she wouldn't, but thus far, his clever predictions had hardly been infallible.

His back ached. His butt. His legs. He looked at the bed. It was king-size. Chiara was curled on one edge. He could sit at a distance from her—sit, not lie—and at least stretch his legs. He wouldn't touch her and she'd never know he was there.

Rafe made the switch carefully, waiting to make sure she

didn't awaken before he leaned back against the pillows. Yes. That was much better. He knew he wouldn't sleep even though he was exhausted. He yawned. Yawned again until his jaws creaked. Maybe he'd just shut his eyes for a couple of minutes....

The sun, streaming in through the terrace doors, jolted him awake.

Chiara lay fast asleep in his arms, her hand over his heart, her breath soft and warm against his throat.

Rafe's body clenched like a fist. He knew the perfect way to wake her. He'd kiss her hair, her eyelids, her mouth. Slowly her lashes would lift. Her beautiful eyes would meet his.

"Chiara," he'd whisper, and instead of jerking back, she'd say his name, lift her hand to his face, and he'd turn his head, press his mouth to her palm, then to the pulse beating in the hollow of her throat, then to her breasts, breasts that he was now damned sure had never known a man's caress—

Rafe swallowed a groan of frustration. Then he dropped the lightest of kisses on his sleeping wife's hair, left her bed and headed to his bathroom for the longest cold shower of his life.

CHAPTER EIGHT

SLOWLY, cautiously, Chiara opened her eyes.

Had she been dreaming, or had Raffaele been in bed with her, holding her in his arms?

It must have been a dream. A man wouldn't get into a woman's bed only to hold her close. Not even a man like Raffaele, who—she had to admit—seemed to have some decent instincts. Even he would not have slept with her curled against him without…without trying to do something sexual.

And yet the dream had seemed real.

His arms, comforting and strong around her. His body, warm and solid against hers. His heart, beating beneath her palm. And then, just before she awakened, the soft brush of his lips…

A dream, of course. And, at least, not a dream that had sent her into a panic.

Despite the things about him that were good—his gallantry in marrying her, his gentleness last night—he still represented everything she despised.

But she no longer despised him.

What if he'd actually slept with her in his arms? If she'd awakened, wrapped in his heat? If she had looked up at him, clasped the back of his head, brought his lips to hers…

Chiara shoved aside the bedcovers and rose quickly to her

feet. There was a cashmere afghan at the foot of the bed. She wrapped herself in it and padded, barefoot, over a rich Oriental carpet to the doors that opened onto a small terrace.

The morning air was crisp, the colors of the trees across the street, brilliant. Was that Central Park? It had to be. It surprised her. She knew of the park, of course, but she had not expected such an oasis of tranquillity.

Pedestrians hurried along the sidewalk: kids dressed for school, men and women in business suits, sleepy-looking people in jeans and sweats being tugged along by dogs hurrying to reach the next lamppost. Cars, taxis and buses crowded the road.

The street was busy. Still, it was surprisingly quiet up here. She hadn't expected that, either.

The truth was, she hadn't expected most of what had happened since yesterday. She certainly hadn't expected what little she'd discovered about Raffaele Orsini.

She had, almost certainly, misjudged his reasons for marrying her. She felt a little guilty about that. Not a lot. After all, they had misjudged each other. But everything pointed to the fact that he had not gone to Sicily to do his father's bidding.

That he had taken her as his wife only to save her from being given to Giglio.

But, as he had said, he was no Sir Galahad. He was a hoodlum, like her father. Like his father. It was in his blood, even though he looked more like a man who'd stepped out of one of the glossy magazines that had been Miss Ellis's one weakness....

Or like the *David.* Michelangelo's marble masterpiece. She had never actually seen the statue, of course, but one of her tutors had taught her about art, had shown her a photo of the *David* in a book...

Chiara swallowed dryly.

Did Raffaele look like that statue? Was his naked body that

perfect? Was all of him so…so flagrantly, blatantly, beauti-fully male?

Beautifully male?

Blindly she turned and hurried back into the bedroom.

What did it matter? He could look like one of God's angels and it wouldn't change the fact that he was what he was. That he did things, made his money—lots of money, from what she'd seen of his life so far—doing things she didn't want to think about.

That he had decent instincts was interesting, even surpris-ing, but it didn't change the facts.

Still, would it not be a good thing to make it clear she was grateful to him for what he had done? She remembered little of what they'd said to each other when he'd come into her room last night. She was pretty sure she'd said thank you, but showing her gratitude would be polite.

How?

She could find ways to make herself useful.

Yes. Of course. She could be useful. He had no wife. Well, he had her but she was not really his wife. The point was, there was no woman here to do things. Clean. Cook. She could do those things. She could start immediately. She could make breakfast. Make coffee.

Coffee! Men liked awakening to the scent of it. When her father came down in the morning, he always said the smell of good, fresh espresso was the perfect way to start a day.

Chiara tore a dress and underwear from her suitcase, rushed into the bathroom and turned on the shower.

Rafe always began the day with a shower.

He began this one with two, both icy enough to make his teeth chatter.

The frigid water did the job of quieting his still-jumpy hormones, but nothing could stanch the headache that had settled in just behind his eyes.

He downed two ibuprofen but the trolls inside his skull only laughed and drummed harder.

The headache matched his rapidly deteriorating mood. Was he crazy? He had to be, otherwise why was he taking this Boy Scout routine so far? Bad enough he'd married Chiara. What in hell had possessed him to sleep with her? To really *sleep* with her—no euphemism involved.

Waking up in bed with a woman you couldn't have plastered against you and a hard-on you didn't want in your sweats was not a good idea, especially if you were stuck with the woman and unable to do anything about the hard-on.

Uh-uh. Definitely not a way to begin the day.

And when, exactly, had he turned so accepting of the mess he was in?

Rafe glared as he stepped out of the shower stall and toweled off.

Not just a Boy Scout. At the rate he was going, he was pushing for the Order of the Arrow with oak leaf clusters. And for what reason? He'd done his good deed for her. Now, he'd do a good deed for himself.

Divorce court, next stop.

Absolutely, it was time to phone his lawyer. First, though, he needed to get his head working right. A couple of aspirin, to help move the ibuprofen along. Then coffee. Lots of coffee. Strong and black. That would do it.

When a man put, what, eight, nine thousand miles on his internal clock in twenty-four hours and got married to a woman he didn't want, that man definitely needed something to bring him down. Mileage and a marriage. It sounded like one of those self-help books, but what it was, was the reason he wasn't thinking straight.

Why else would he have suddenly felt such compassion, okay, such tenderness for the babe who'd screwed up his life?

Wanting to make it with her? That was understandable. He was male. She was female and under those crazy outfits she wore, she wasn't bad-looking. Yeah, but there was no way in the world he'd follow through on those most basic of male instincts.

He didn't know much about matrimonial law but what little he did know told him that, as of now, their quickie set of I do's could be erased in a heartbeat. No sex? No real marriage.

Sleep with the lady and that would change.

Besides, why would he want to sleep with her? She was afraid of sex. What man wanted a scared woman in his bed? Plus, she was a virgin. No question about it anymore.

Imagine. In this day and age, she was a virgin.

Rafe grimaced as he stepped into a pair of faded jeans.

He'd been with a lot of women but never with a virgin. Any man with half a functioning brain knew to avoid that situation, because taking a woman's virginity was a trap. It left you with the kind of responsibility he most assuredly did not need and did not want.

He zipped his fly, pulled on a gray cotton sweater. He didn't bother shaving. No point pretending he'd go to his office today. Nothing on his desk was as important as dissolving a relationship that wasn't a relationship.

He checked the time. It was barely seven. A reasonable hour at which to phone Marilyn Sayers, but first he'd have that coffee. Let the headache tablets do their thing. He wanted to sound cool and controlled when he told Sayers about his incredible situation. She would have questions, but all she really needed to know was where and when the marriage had taken place and that he wanted out, ASAP.

Marriage? He snorted. Ridiculous. He wouldn't dignify what had happened in San Giuseppe by calling it that. There'd been some kind of ceremony, that was all.

It sure as hell hadn't been a—

Crash!

Rafe spun toward the door. What was that? It sounded as if a two-car collision had just taken place in his apart—

There it was again, a metallic crash loud enough to make

the trolls inside his skull pick up the tempo. By the time the third crash echoed through the penthouse, he was halfway down the stairs, racing down the hall…

He skidded to a stop in the entrance to his kitchen. What the hell…?

It looked as if Bloomingdale's housewares department had decided to hold a sale right here, in his pristine—his once pristine—kitchen. The white granite countertops, the black stone floor…they were covered with pots and skillets. Big ones. Small ones. Stainless steel. Ironware. Ceramic. The place was ankle-deep in cookware, more than he'd imagined he owned, because the stuff had all been the decorator's idea, not his.

Why would a man need a million things to cook in when he didn't cook?

In the center of it all was Chiara, dressed like an undertaker in a calf-length black something and clunky black shoes, her hair scraped back in that damned bun. Chiara, who had decided to take over his kitchen. Chiara, who was, without question, about to utter those famous eight words…

"What are you doing?" he said sharply.

She spun toward him. "Raffaele!"

"I asked you a question. What are you doing?"

She hesitated, looking around her, then at him. "I suppose you had no idea I could cook."

Okay. It was a variation but the theme was the same. Man, had he ever misjudged her!

She gave him a hesitant smile. "I was making coffee."

Rafe folded his arms over his chest. "Come on, baby." His voice was like ice. Amazing, considering that he could feel his blood pressure soaring into the stratosphere. "Just coffee? How about breakfast? Eggs. French toast. Waffles. You can make all that stuff, right?"

She swallowed. Nodded. Offered another cautious smile. Rafe could feel his anger growing. She wanted out of this marriage? The hell she did, he thought in escalating fury, and his BP went through the roof.

"I have a housekeeper," he snarled. "The time comes I want something cooked, I'll ask her to cook it."

Chiara's smile vanished. "Yes. Of course. I told you, I only wished to make coffee. Espresso. But I could not find an espresso pot so—"

"You couldn't find it because I don't have one. Or did you assume having an Italian name means I came out of my mother's womb with an espresso maker tucked in my…hands?"

"No. I mean, yes." She caught her lip between her teeth. "I did not mean to make you angry."

"I am not angry," Rafe said. "Why would I be angry? Just because you've decided you don't want out of this nonsensical marriage—"

"What?"

"Just because you think the I-can-cook thing will change my mind—"

"You are *pazzo*! Of course I want—what did you call it— out of this marriage!" Her hands slapped on her hips. "And I have no idea what the I-can-cook thing is!"

"A likely story."

Chiara drew herself up. "I do not have to listen to this idiocy."

"No. You have to clean up my kitchen." Rafe glared. "Look at it. You tore it apart, and—"

The sound of something bubbling drew his attention. His gaze swept past her. His French press was on a front burner of the big Viking range. The burner glowed red-hot; the press was filled with water.

With boiling water.

He cursed, sprinted across the room, grabbed the French press and yelped when his fingers closed around the hot glass. The predictable thing happened. It slipped from his hands, smashed against the floor, and spewed hot water over his bare toes.

"Oh, *Dio mio!*"

Chiara threw out her hands. One connected with a cast-iron skillet. The predictable thing happened again. The skillet tumbled from the counter and landed on Rafe's still-naked, now scalded toes.

"Figlio di puttana!"

"Raffaele!" Chiara said, sounding shocked.

Rafe ignored her, hopped to the fridge and hit a button. Ice cubes tumbled into his hand. He squeezed his fingers around some, let the others dump on his toes.

Damn it all, his life had turned into a reality show. And it was all this woman's fault. No. It was his. Why had he brought her home with him? Okay, maybe he'd had to marry her. So what? He could have left her in Palermo. He could have dumped her at a Manhattan hotel. He could have done a hundred things that wouldn't have put her under his roof.

Chiara said his name again and he swung toward her.

"Are you...are you all right?"

"I'm fine," he said coldly.

She gestured at his hand, then at his foot. "I am sorry, Raffaele."

Her voice quavered. She was on the verge of tears. Who gave a damn?

"I only meant to do a good thing. To show you that I appreciate all you have done for me."

"The only way you could do that would be to erase yesterday, and that's not about to happen."

The tears appeared, filling her eyes until they glittered like diamonds. So what? Women were good at producing instant tears. It didn't change a thing.

"Stop that," he growled.

She turned her back and cried harder.

It made him feel bad but, hell, she probably wanted him to feel bad. She was clever. Somewhere between the ceremony in San Giuseppe and their arrival here, he'd managed to forget that. Well, he wouldn't forget it again. This was the woman who'd waylaid him on the road. Who'd kissed him as if she wanted to suck out his tonsils right before she went into her Petrified Virgin routine. Forget what he'd thought last night, that she was as much a victim as he was.

Still, he sure as hell didn't want her crying over a couple of stupid accidents.

"Okay," he said, "that's enough. It's only a kitchen."

"I burned your fingers."

"You didn't burn them, I did." He turned her toward him, held up his hand, flexed his fingers. "See? They're fine. That ice did the trick."

"I broke your toes."

"Toe. Just one. The big one." He looked down; so did she. He flexed his toes, forced himself not to wince. The damned thing probably was broken but he'd sooner have walked on nails that admit it. "See? It's fine. Ice can do wonders."

She gave a little hiccup and raised her face to his. Hell, he thought, his throat tightening, didn't they teach women how to sob delicately in Weeping 101 anymore? Because there was nothing delicate about Chiara's red eyes and runny nose. She was a veritable mess, as sorry a mess as the room and their marriage.

And yet she looked even more beautiful.

How could that be? Everything she had on was ugly. She wore no makeup. She'd wept her way into ruddy-faced disaster.

"Raffaele." Her voice broke. More tears overflowed and trickled down her cheeks. "I am so sorry. For everything. For ruining your life, ruining your kitchen—"

"Hush," he said, and then he did the only logical thing.

He cupped her face, brought his lips to hers and kissed her.

His head told him it was a mistake. You didn't kiss a woman you intended to get rid of. You certainly didn't kiss a woman who'd made it clear she was afraid of any kind of physical intimacy.

Except…except, she wasn't struggling. Wasn't gasping with fear or anger. No, he thought in wonder, no…

She was melting in his arms.

It happened so fast that it stunned him.

One second he was holding a weeping woman whose spine might have been fashioned of steel. The next, she was on her toes, leaning into him. Her arms were tight around his neck. Her heart was racing against his.

It was what should have happened early this morning, he thought…

And then he stopped thinking.

Her hands speared into his hair. She moaned, dragged his face down to hers. He whispered her name, slanted his mouth hungrily over hers, cupped her backside and lifted her up and into his straining erection. Her breath caught. He thought he'd frightened her but she moved against him, moved again, a tentative thrust of her lower body and it came as close as anything could to undoing him.

"Raffaele," she whispered.

The word trembled on her lips, wafted over his.

"Chiara. My beautiful Chiara."

His hands rose. Cupped her breasts. She cried out, said his name, made the sweet little sounds a woman makes when she wants a man.

He swept aside whatever remained on the granite counter, clasped her waist and lifted her onto it. *Not like this,* logic said, *not here, not for her first time!*

To hell with logic.

He wanted her, now. Needed her, now. He was dizzy with it, crazed with it, with wanting to kiss her, touch her, bury himself inside her.

Somehow he forced himself to slow down. He kissed her eyelids, her temples, her mouth. Sweet. Soft. Warm. Her lips clung to his. He felt the first delicate whisper of her tongue against his, and desire, hot and fierce, shot through him like an arrow.

"Raffaele? Raffaele. I want—I want—"

"Tell me," he said hoarsely, between deep, hot kisses. "Tell me what you want, sweetheart."

Everything, she thought. Oh *Dio*, she wanted everything.

Raffaele's mouth, drinking from hers. The silken intrusion of his tongue. His thumbs tracing the arc of her cheekbones, her throat, her breasts. And, yes, what he was doing now. Undoing the endless row of jet buttons on her dress. Baring her flesh to him. The curve of her breasts, rising above her bra.

He kissed the hollow of her throat. Nipped lightly at the skin. She gasped; her head fell back. She would have fallen back, too—she was boneless—but he caught her shoulders, his strong hands supporting her as he brought her to him and kissed her again and again.

It wasn't enough. None of it was enough. How could it be enough? She ached for him.

For his possession.

She sobbed his name. His eyes met hers. They were black with desire; the bones of his face stood out in stark relief.

She knew what it meant.

For the first time, a frisson of fear slid greasily through her belly.

"Raffaele," she said breathlessly, "Raffaele…"

He grasped the hem of her dress, bunched it in his big hands and raised it to the tops of her thighs. Stepped between them. Still watching her face, he laid one hand over that place between her legs, that temple of evil her mother had warned against.

She cried out.

"Raffaele," she said, and he slipped his fingers under the edge of her underpants, and now she felt the wetness in that place, the heat, the throbbing of her pulse…

"Omylord," a woman's voice squealed. "Oh, Mr. Orsini! I had no idea—"

Chiara froze. Rafe went still.

"I'll come back later, sir, shall I? Of course. That's what I'll do. I'm so sorry, sir…"

A low moan rose in Chiara's throat. She shot into motion, a blur of energy as she jumped from the counter, then tried to fight free of Rafe's arms as they swept around her.

"Easy," he whispered.

She struggled against him but he refused to let go. She was saying something in Sicilian, saying it again and again in a low, anguished voice.

He thought it might be that she wanted to die, and his heart turned over.

"Chiara."

She shook her head. Her eyes were screwed tightly shut, like a child's, as if what she couldn't see couldn't hurt her.

"Sweetheart. Look at me."

Another shake of her head. Rafe sighed, brought her face against his shoulder. For all her offer to leave and return later, his housekeeper was still standing in the entrance to the kitchen, her eyes as round as her face, one hand plastered over her heart.

Rafe cleared his throat. "Good morning, Mrs. O'Hara," he said pleasantly.

The woman bobbed her head. "Morning, Mr. Orsini. I am terribly sorry. I never meant—"

"No, of course you didn't."

He looked from his housekeeper to the woman in his arms. There were simple choices here. He could let Chiara go. She'd bolt and run and probably add this to her already distorted ideas of sex.

Or he could hold on to her while he played the scene through. It was, after all, only a minor embarrassment. Someone stumbling across a man and woman about to have sex? There was nothing original about it. Told in the right company, it would prove amusing.

He could feel Chiara trembling against him, her tears soaking his sweater.

Rafe paused. In his twenties, he'd gone bungee jumping. He remembered how it had felt, that gut-wrenching moment when he'd been about to jump off the bridge railing into the there's-no-turning-back void.

"Mrs. O'Hara," he said, "Mrs. O'Hara…I'd like to introduce you to my wife."

CHAPTER NINE

IF YOU were an anthropologist doing field work, you might have put The Bar on a threatened-species list.

No rope at the door to keep out those who might offend the fashionistas. No VIP lists. No hot babes in spandex, no guys with more money than brains, no drinks with names that made a man laugh.

In fact, the place was so low-key that you had to know it existed before you could find it. Wood-paneled, dimly lit, it was located in an unremarkable Soho neighborhood. At least, it had been unremarkable when the Orsini brothers had discovered it years ago.

They'd been just starting out back then, three of them with unused degrees in finance and business in their pockets and one, Falco, with enough university credits for a couple of degrees but not enough concentration in any one area to matter. They'd all turned their backs on the white-collar world. Cesare, sneering, said it was to find themselves.

The truth was, they'd gone off to lose their connection to everything he represented.

Rafe and Nick had ended up in the military, one in the Marines, one in the Army, both fighting wars neither wanted to talk about. Falco was even more tight-lipped about his time in Special Forces. Dante had headed north to Alaska and the dangers of the oil fields on the North Slope. He and Falco were the only ones who'd returned with money in their pockets, Dante from his job, Falco from the high-stakes poker games he loved.

Dante, Nick and Rafe had quickly figured out that they wanted to build a future together. Falco wasn't sure what he wanted.

They began getting together a couple of nights a week at a place called O'Hearn's Bar. It was a neighborhood place, located just downstairs from Rafe's one-room-with-what-passed-for-a-kitchen walkup. The beer was cold, the sandwiches were cheap, and nobody gave a damn who the brothers were.

Gradually the last booth on the left became known as theirs. It was where they met and discussed Life and Women and What To Do with Their Lives.

Eventually they figured out a way to combine their talents, temperaments and education. Rafe and Nick pooled their resources, played what was then a booming stock market, put the money into the new venture. Dante added his impressive oil field savings. Six months later Falco decided to throw in his luck with his brothers and put them over the top with the not-so-small fortune he'd made at poker.

Orsini Brothers was born.

Their corporate baby flourished. So did the neighborhood around O'Hearn's. Tired old tenements, including the one where Rafe had lived, were gutted and reborn as pricey town houses. A factory building became a high-priced club. Bodegas became boutiques.

The Orsinis could tell that O'Hearn's days were numbered.

"We've got to do something," Falco had grumbled, so they did. They bought the place, and it became the smallest and least noticed part of the Orsini Brothers' holdings.

They cleaned it up, but only a little. Had the planked oak floor refinished. Tore out the worn leather stools and banquettes and replaced them with new ones. Everything else—the scarred wood tables, the pressed-tin ceiling, the long zinc counter, the beers on draught, the overstuffed sandwiches and killer grilled-with-onions burgers—stayed the same.

To the brothers' shock, O'Hearn's Bar—by now, simply known as The Bar—became what people referred to as a "destination." Still, only the bartenders knew who owned it, and that was exactly how the Orsinis wanted it.

That way they could avoid the reporters from the *Times* and the *Wall Street Journal* as well as the ones from the tabloids. It wasn't easy to keep your privacy when you'd created a company worth billions—and your old man was still *numero uno* whenever some damned investigative reporter dredged up the *M* word.

So, The Bar was the logical place to get together every couple of Friday nights, or maybe after closing on Saturday night if a date had proved especially memorable. It was also where you went if you just wanted to talk.

Like today.

Falco and Nick, back from their business meetings overseas, were already there when Rafe arrived. Only Dante was missing. He was off somewhere in South America. Nobody knew where or why. Rafe figured it had something to do with that Sunday morning meeting with Cesare but decided it was Dante's business to talk about it, not his.

He sure as hell wasn't going to say anything about what had happened at *his* Sunday morning meeting with his father…and if he wasn't, what was he doing here? he thought, as he stepped from the sunlight into The Bar's artificial gloom.

He'd phoned Nick and Falco on the spur of the moment. They'd both been at work, as he should have been, when he called. "Got time for a beer?" he'd said, and they'd said sure.

Now, seeing them, his gut knotted.

Why he'd suggested getting together was beyond him. He had a problem on his hands but he wasn't about to lay it out for discussion. There was still time to turn around and walk away—but Nick looked up, spotted him and it was too late.

Nothing to do now but fake some casual conversation. Rafe fixed what he hoped was a smile on his face, sauntered over to their usual booth and slid in beside Falco.

"Hey."

"Hey."

So much for casual conversation.

The bartender, who'd spotted Rafe the second he walked in, came over with an icy mug of ale. Rafe nodded his thanks. His brothers watched as he took a long swallow.

"Well," he said brightly, "it's good to see you guys."

Nick looked at Falco. "At least he doesn't look as bad as he sounded."

And so much for getting through this unscathed. Rafe concentrated on his mug of beer.

Falco shrugged. "He looks worse."

Okay. Enough. Rafe looked up.

"I am," he said, "right here. No reason to talk as if I weren't."

"Sure." Nick nodded agreeably. "No reason not to tell you, to your face, that Falco's right. You look like *caca*."

"Thank you."

"You want compliments, you're in the wrong place," Falco said, but his usually hard expression softened. A bad sign, Rafe thought glumly. "So, you want to tell us what's going on?"

Rafe thought of making another clever response, but what was the point? His brothers knew him too well to be fooled. Besides, he was the idiot who'd called this meeting and brought this on his own head.

"Nothing. It's just been a long couple of days."

Nick raised his eyebrows. "That's it?"

Another shrug. Another swallow of beer. Then Rafe pressed the icy bottle against his temple, where a Chinese orchestra playing traditional Mandarin melodies had moved in to replace the departed trolls.

"I, ah, I have some things to sort out."

"Such as?" Nick asked.

"Just…things."

Nick looked at Falco. "Your turn."

Falco scowled. Nobody could scowl quite like Falco.

"You want to tell us what's happening? You don't show up at the office—"

"I'm entitled to a day off," Rafe said, trying not to sound defensive.

"You don't show up," Falco continued, "then you phone us and say you need to talk—"

"I never said that."

"You didn't have to. It's Monday, the market's in the toilet and here we are, taking a break at your request. You really think we're going to think it's just so we could all say 'hello, what's new, how was your weekend?'"

"Hello," Rafe said, "what's new, how was your—" A muscle knotted in his jaw. "Okay. It's true. I have a, uh, a slight problem."

"Blonde or brunette?"

"That's insulting, Nicolo. I mean, why jump to the conclusion that it's a female problem?"

"Blonde or brunette," Nick repeated, and Rafe sighed.

"Brunette."

"What happened to the Valkyrie?"

"She's history."

"How come?"

Rafe narrowed his eyes. "Are we going to discuss the past or the current situation?"

"Don't get testy," Falco said mildly. "Okay. So, what *is* the current situation?"

Rafe stared at his brothers. The thing was, he *did* know why he'd phoned them. Who else would he turn to when he was in a mess straight up to his eyeballs? And, damn it, yes, this thing was a mess.

He was married. Married, him, a man who'd never even contemplated marriage, who'd run like hell anytime a woman so much as breathed the word. He was married to a stranger from a world so unlike his it would have been funny if it hadn't been so unbelievable.

That was item one in the "current situation."

Item two was that even though he was going to end the marriage as quickly as he could pull it off, that hadn't kept him from, item three, damned near making it with Chiara on his kitchen counter, which led, inexorably, to item four, that she was almost certainly a virgin and having sex with her would, oh damn, item five, make ending the marriage more complicated, never mind item six, that he'd introduced her as his wife and she wasn't, well, she was, legally, and—

"Rafe?"

And what a disaster of a scene that had been. His house-keeper had all but burst into congratulatory song. Not Chiara. She'd turned bright pink.

"I am *not* your wife," she'd said, "and if you think that— that assaulting me makes it so, you are wrong!"

Then she'd fled.

He'd thought about trying to explain things to his house-keeper—who'd gone from looking at him through misty eyes to regarding him as if he'd turned into a serial killer right in front of her—given that up and gone after Chiara instead, but she'd locked her door and when he'd tried to talk to her—

"Raffaele!"

Rafe's head came up. "Why'd you call me that?" he said, glaring at Nick.

"Because it's your name. Because you're a thousand miles away. Because one of us is nuts and the odds are excellent I'm looking at him. What's the brunette's name?"

Mrs. Orsini, Rafe thought wildly, and choked back what began as an insane cackle.

"This is amusing?"

"No," Rafe said quickly, "believe me, it isn't."

"So, what's the lady's name?"

"Chiara."

Falco raised an eyebrow. "Very nice. Very sexy."

"She isn't."

"Nice? Or very sexy?"

"She's not like that, is what I'm saying. She's, ah, she's different."

"They're always different," Falco said, "until they get to feeling comfortable." He made interlocking damp rings on the beat-up tabletop with his beer mug. "I take it this one isn't feeling comfortable yet."

Comfortable? A muscle tightened in Rafe's jaw. She was living in his apartment. Somehow he didn't want to admit that. He didn't want to admit anything. He wished to God he'd never started this conversation. In another few minutes his brothers would go from calling him nuts to figuring he needed to be committed.

"Okay," Falco said, "I get it. You got involved on the rebound. Now you want out. You do, don't you? Want out? I mean, that's what this is all about?"

Rafe nodded. "Absolutely."

"I don't see the problem. Take the lady to dinner. You know, the it's-been-great-but-it's-over meal."

"It isn't like that. She wants out, too."

Nick stared at him. "Well, then there isn't any problem."

"There is." Rafe hesitated. "It's…it's complicated. I mean, we both want out. But—"

"But?"

"But, she's, ah, she's new to the city."

"Buy her a guidebook," Falco said coldly.

"And, ah, and I came on to her and that, ah, that kind of upset her."

Falco and Nick grinned at each other. "So much for those smooth Orsini moves," Nick said.

"Hey, I'm trying to be serious here. What I mean is… See, the lady in question is a little wary. Of men. Of sex. Of me.

And, uh, and now I'm wondering if I…if I—" He swallowed hard. "She won't talk to me."

This time nobody grinned. "She's frigid?" Falco said, his eyebrows aiming for his hairline.

"No. Yes. I mean, maybe. I mean, it doesn't matter because I have no intention of keeping her around very long."

His brothers were looking at him strangely. He couldn't blame them.

"Back to what Falco suggested," Nick said. "Dinner. She won't talk to you? No problem. Leave a message on her voice mail. Tell her to meet you somewhere for dinner. When she shows up, tell her things aren't working. Give her a little gift, you know, not the little-blue-box-from-Tiffany's kind of thing, but… What? Why are you shaking your head?"

"No phone. No voice mail." Rafe cleared his throat. "She's living in my apartment."

The look of incredulity on his brothers' faces said it all.

"She's—"

"—living with you?"

"It's temporary."

"You sent the Valkyrie packing a couple of days ago and moved this Clara—"

"Chiara."

"Clara, Chiara, whatever. You moved her in, what, five minutes later?"

Rafe gave one last thought to explaining, but how could he, when not even he could make sense out of everything he'd done? The only certainty was that he'd gotten himself into this mess and it was up to him to get himself out of it.

"Hey," he said brightly, after a glance at his watch, "look at the time!"

"Rafe. Wait a minute—"

But he was already on his feet. "Great seeing you guys," he said, and scrambled for the door.

Nick and Falco watched him go. Then they looked at each other.

"You got any idea what just happened?" Nick said.

Falco shook his head. "Not in the slightest."

Nick nodded and signaled for another round of beer.

Rafe had taxied downtown.

His condo was on Fifth Avenue, in the midsixties. Any way you looked at it, it was a long walk home, but that was a good thing. Long walks usually helped clear his head.

Involving his brothers had not been a good idea. Not that he'd really involved them. He hadn't told them much of anything, but what he had told them was not good.

Still, the confrontation, if you could call it that, had had one positive effect. It had made him face reality. He'd been dealing with this as if he were standing outside the problem, observing it. He wasn't. What he was, he thought as he passed a group of suburban women in for some shopping and dressed more for a New Jersey mall than for the eclectic streets of Soho, what he was, was a man standing in a hole six feet deep, busy digging himself in deeper.

He'd married Chiara, yes, but given the same circumstances, he'd have done it again. What kind of man would turn his back on a desperate woman? And it wasn't because of how she looked, those big violet eyes, that trembling mouth, or of how that mouth had felt under his, or of how she'd felt in his arms.

She'd needed help. He'd offered it. So, okay. The marrying part had been necessary.

What had been going on since then was not. The arguing. The accusations. What was the point? It was a done deal. And then, this morning... Proof of how crazy things had gotten. He couldn't imagine why he'd tried to jump her bones.

To say she wasn't his type was a laugh. She had a pretty face, yeah, but so did a million other women, and none of those million other women went around looking like little old ladies. None of them would ever look at him as if he were a mustachioed villain.

None of them was a wife he didn't want. And none of them had hang-ups about sex.

Not that Chiara had seemed to have many of those this morning. That kiss. The way she'd clung to him. Moaned into his mouth. Arched her body against his, lifted herself to him…

Just what he needed. Turning himself on while he walked down a crowded street. Oh, yes, that was a great idea.

He swung toward a shop window, found himself staring at a display of hammers and power tools while he fought for control. That was another thing. When had he ever had to struggle for self-control? Never. Not since he'd left the Marines. Now he fought for it all the time. Either he was furious at his wife or so turned on that he couldn't see straight for wanting her and—

"And she isn't your wife," he said sharply.

A couple coming out of the store gave him a wary look.

"Sorry," Rafe said, "sorry. I was just—"

He was just losing his mind. The couple moved quickly past him. He took some deep breaths, began walking again.

It was time to move on. She wanted a divorce. So did he. He pulled his cell phone from his pocket as he reached the corner. The light turned red. Time to separate the tourists from the natives. The tourists stayed on the curb. The New Yorkers, Rafe among them, kept going. A car horn bleeped. A voice shouted something. Rafe met the driver's eyes, flashed a look that silenced him.

Rafe stepped onto the curb, brought up his contact list, selected Marilyn Sayers's number. Her phone rang and rang. When it finally picked up, what he got was not her but her voice mail.

"Marilyn," he said impatiently, "it's Rafe Orsini. Pick up if you're there. Or call me back, fast. It's urgent."

He'd hardly closed the phone when it rang. He glanced at the face plate, saw with relief that it was her.

"Marilyn. Thanks for getting back to me so fast. No, I'm okay. I'm just in a messy situation, is all. See—" She interrupted. He blinked. "You're where?"

She was in Istanbul. Five thousand miles away. Something about the first vacation she and her husband had taken in years, blah-blah-blah, but Rafe didn't give a damn. All that registered was that she'd be gone another week.

"A week?" He shook his head as he navigated a particularly crowded stretch of Sixth Avenue. "Impossible. I have a problem. A personal problem. And— Marilyn?"

The call broke up, then died. Rafe cursed, hit redial. Marilyn picked up and said they had a bad connection.

"Yeah. I know. Listen, this problem I have—"

She interrupted again, told him to get in touch with her partner. He'd handle things. Rafe shook his head, as if she could see him. Sayers's partner was ninety if he was a day, a starchy old guy who wore a vest, carried a pocket watch and took ten years to shuffle across a room.

Explain to him how he'd come to have a wife who wasn't a wife? Ask him to expedite things so they could get divorced quickly because if they spent another day together, he was liable to strip his wife-who-wasn't-a-wife out of her ugly black clothes and bare all her soft, sweet flesh to his eyes and hands and mouth?

"No good," he growled. "I need you, not your partner."

It was useless. Sayers was sorry but— The line went dead. Rafe snarled and closed the phone with a vengeful snap.

Okay. What now? Easy. Get Chiara out from under his roof. A week's wait was nothing, once he'd done that. Out of sight, out of mind.

He'd find her a place to live. It was an excellent idea, one that would bolster the fact that the marriage wasn't a marriage at all. And how hard could it be to find someplace to stash her? The city was loaded with real estate agents. He just needed one who'd move his request to the top of the list.

Of course!

Rafe flipped the phone open, checked his contact list again, hit a button.

"Chilton Realtors."

"Elaine Chilton, please."

It was the perfect solution. Why deal with an agent he didn't know when he had one at his fingertips? He'd met the Chilton woman somewhere. A party, a dinner. It didn't matter. She'd tugged his phone from his hand after he'd taken a call, smiled prettily and programmed in her number.

"In case you ever need me," she'd purred.

He hadn't. He'd been involved with Ingrid at the time but he sure as hell needed her now.

"Hello?"

"Elaine? It's Rafe Orsini."

"Well, well, well," she said in a throaty whisper, "how are you, Mr. Orsini?"

He said he was fine and then he cut to the chase, said he was interested in seeing her.

"It's urgent," he said.

She gave a sexy little laugh. "How nice!"

Rafe felt a second's unease. Were they talking about the same thing?

"Where are you?" she asked.

He told her.

"Perfect. I have a rental a couple of blocks away."

"What's it like?"

Another little laugh. "I'm sure you'll think it's perfect." She gave him the address, told him to meet her there in twenty minutes.

Rafe disconnected, his concerns gone. Perfect? Absolutely. He checked his watch, turned down Fifty-seventh Street…

Half an hour later, he was striding towards his condo, furious at fate, at life, at his own stupidity.

Elaine Chilton had been waiting for him, all right…on a

pale pink sofa in a red silk teddy and black stilettos, and okay, maybe he hadn't handled things exactly right. Maybe you didn't look at a half-naked woman and say, "Oh sorry! See, what I meant was, I'm interested in finding an apartment for this woman who's living with me."

Definitely a poor choice of words, he thought as he marched into his own apartment building, glowered at the hapless doorman and stepped into his elevator.

He probably deserved the names the Chilton babe had called him, if not the slap. At least he'd stopped himself from saying, "Okay, now that that's out of the way, what about the rental?"

The car shot upward. Next step was to call a hotel. The Waldorf. The St. Regis. Not as homey as a furnished apartment but who cared? What counted was that Chiara would be there, he would be here. And as soon as Sayers was in her office, things would start to be okay.

The elevator door slid open. Rafe stepped out—and found Chiara, waiting for him as Elaine Chilton had been waiting.

Not quite.

No silk teddy. No stiletto heels. No pink sofa. Chiara was seated in his foyer in an Eames chair, back straight, knees all but locked, hands folded in her lap, dressed in yet another of those incredibly ugly black outfits.

Then, why did seeing her go through him like a surge of electricity?

"Raffaele." She rose to her feet, hands still tightly clasped. "I am sorry."

Her voice was small but her eyes were steady on his. She was that combination of vulnerability and defiance that got to him every time.

"I seem to say that to you a great deal but…" She licked her lips. He could no more have kept from following the quick swipe of her pink tongue than he could have kept from breathing. "But I overreacted. You were simply trying to save me from embarrassment in front of your housekeeper. I should have understood that."

Rafe forced his gaze from her mouth. Not a good plan. He looked into her eyes, instead, and saw that they glittered with unshed tears.

"No," he said, "it's my fault. I've handled this all wrong. I know what you want and I—" Why was his voice so rough? He cleared his throat. "I've been in touch with my attorney."

Chiara shook her head. Her hair was still loose. He'd set it free hours ago, when he'd kissed her. The wildness of her curls was in direct contrast to her black dress and sensible shoes.

"Please, let me finish. This is difficult for me but I must say it." She drew a deep breath. "The…the kissing, Raffaele. It was inexcusable."

"Yes." He swiped his hand through his hair. "I'm sorry about that, Chiara. I shouldn't have—"

"My response, I mean. It was wrong. I have no explanation to offer. I can only say I regret it and—"

"Don't," he said quickly, his voice even rougher. "Don't regret it, sweetheart. Please."

"But I…" Color flooded her face. "I should not have kissed you back."

"Chiara. That was a good thing. A healthy thing. Responding to a man's kisses. To *my* kisses."

"But I do not… I have never…"

Her voice faded. She looked away from him. She'd known this would be difficult, admitting that what happened whenever he touched her was as much her fault as his, but what she hadn't expected was that seeing him would make her feel light-headed. Almost dizzy. Afraid to keep meeting his gaze because looking into his beautiful blue eyes made her want to…want to…

She felt a light touch on her hair. His hand, stroking the curls back from her temples. His fingers, threading into the strands. A moan rose in her throat. What was happening? She wanted to sigh his name, lift her face to his…

"No," she said quickly, "no, it must not happen again. Those things I did—"

"You kissed me," he said in a low voice. "And I kissed you. Kissing isn't wrong, sweetheart."

Somehow, his hand was cupping her chin. Somehow, her face was lifting to his.

And then his mouth was on hers.

He was kissing her, kissing her gently, and she was kissing him back. She caught his sweater in her hands, knotted the soft cotton in her fists and rose to him.

His arms swept around her. He gathered her against him and she framed his face with her hands, her lips soft and warm against his. She was making little sounds, moans of pleasure and desire, and he knew she was his for the taking.

He had only to lift her into his arms, carry her up the stairs to his bed. What he wanted, what he had wanted from the first time he'd kissed her, would become reality.

He would make love to her.

Take her innocence.

Take it, and be no better than bastards like her father and Giglio, men who would exploit this beautiful, brave woman instead of honoring and protecting her.

He kissed her one last time. Then he rested his forehead against hers.

"Chiara." His voice sounded rusty; he cleared his throat. "Sweetheart. I have a great idea. Let's…let's start over."

"Start over?"

"Yes. You. Me. The situation we're in… We don't have to be enemies, Chiara. We can be friends."

She looked baffled. Why wouldn't she? It was probably the last thing she'd expected him to say. Hell, it was the last thing *he'd* expected to say. But it was right, and he knew it.

He would be her friend, not her lover, even if it killed him.

"I would like that," she said softly. "To start over with you, Raffaele."

Then she smiled, and he wondered how it was possible for everything good in the world to be captured in a woman's smile.

CHAPTER TEN

HE KNEW he had to get the two of them out of his apartment.

He was a man, not a martyr. All his good intentions could easily come undone if this sweet, intimate moment stretched on. So he flashed a quick smile, let go of her and stepped back.

"I," he said briskly, "am hungry enough to eat a bear."

She laughed. "I think it would be difficult to find a bear on Fifth Avenue."

"Oh, I don't know. This is a pretty amazing city."

Chiara nodded. "I have read that it is."

She had read about New York. Read about it, but not seen it. He'd been so wrapped up in his own selfish misery he hadn't given a thought to what might make things easier for her.

She'd just given him the answer.

He could show her his town. And in the process keep her at a safe distance. A win-win situation, he thought, and decided not to waste time. He took her hand, hurried her to the elevator. When she asked where they were going, he grinned and said they were in pursuit of that bear.

Of course, none of the restaurants he had in mind had bear on the menu, but he had a long list of favorite places. They'd all be jammed this time of day, but that wasn't a problem. He'd never needed a reservation to get a great table. It was one of the benefits of being Rafe Orsini.

When they reached the lobby and he asked the doorman to flag a taxi, Chiara held back.

Rafe looked at her. "What?"

"Nothing. Nothing at all."

Not true. Something was troubling her; she was biting gently on her bottom lip, the way she always did when she was upset, and if he kept watching her do it he was going to scoop her into his arms and ravish her, right here. The hot image made him sound brusque.

"Chiara, look, if you don't want to do this—"

"Oh, no, Raffaele." She put her hand lightly on his arm. "I just wondered…could we take the subway?"

"The what?"

"The subway. I have read about it. It is in the ground. Well, most of it is in the ground. It whisks people through the city, from one borough to another, from Bronx all the way to the end of the Brooklyn. *Sì?*"

She sounded like a tour guide. He wanted to haul her into his arms and kiss her.

"Sì," Rafe said, smiling. "But it's *the* Bronx, and just plain Brooklyn.

"Ah. I see. But it is probably foolish…"

Foolish? That his wife would prefer to ride the subway instead of a taxi? Rafe smiled and took her hand.

"It's a great idea," he said. "I should have thought of it."

He warned her it was a few blocks' walk to the nearest subway station. She smiled and told him she loved to walk. He had never known a woman who said that and meant it, but his Chiara did. She craned her neck at the skyscrapers, gaped at the shop windows, almost skipped along the crowded sidewalks.

"Oh," she said, eyes shining, "I have never seen anything like this!"

No, he thought, watching her. Neither had he.

Rockefeller Center, when they finally reached it, rated a huge gasp.

"The statue of Prometheus!"

Well, hell, was that the name of the big gilded guy? Rafe hadn't known that. Chiara told him all about it. The legend. The sculptor. How the statue had come to be placed here. He listened, but mostly he just heard his wife's voice. Soft. Silvery. Happy.

That was the word.

She was happy.

So was he.

He had never been so happy in his life, he thought in amazement, and while she was still bubbling about Prometheus, he swung her into his arms and kissed her, right there in Rockefeller Center surrounded by thousands of people. Nobody seemed to notice. This was, after all, New York. But when he finally took his lips from hers and she opened her eyes and he saw how they were glowing, he thought he might be more than happy, that he was—that he was—

"Hungry," he said, the word coming out quick and sharp, as if he were a man just realizing he'd stepped back from the edge of a cliff. "Why don't we, ah, why don't we get something to eat?"

His head was spinning. He couldn't think straight. What was nearby? Where could he take her that she would enjoy? Because that was what this was all about, wasn't it? Showing his wife—this temporary wife—his city? She was his guest. She'd never been to New York before; for all he knew, after their divorce, she might choose to return to Italy.

No. Damn it, no. She wouldn't do that. Go all the way across the ocean. Go so far away from him…

Somebody bumped into them. Rafe blinked, clasped Chiara's hand and set off at brisk pace.

La Grenouille.

That was the name of the restaurant he took her to.

Chiara knew it meant frog, though why anyone would name a place so elegant after so humble a creature was beyond her.

She also understood what Raffaele did not.

She was as out of place here as, well, as a frog.

Everyone was looking at her. Okay. Maybe not everyone, but they might as well have been. The diners were as upscale as the restaurant, the women all fashionably dressed, their faces and hair testament to time spent in the city's finest salons.

What must they think of her in her ugly black dress, ugly black shoes, ugly black coat? Not that it mattered. Her Raffaele was an amazing man, but he would never get a table here. It was too crowded. And then there was the way she looked…

But they did get a table. Immediately. A banquette, and she knew, instinctively, it was a coveted spot. Waiters appeared. Busboys. Menus, wine lists…

She told Raffaele to order for her.

It was enough to watch him select a wine, a meal, to watch him smile when she bit into her salmon and offered a sigh of approval.

And it was more than enough to watch the women watching him, their covetous glances turning to disbelief when they turned their attention to her.

Yes, she thought, her chin lifting, oh, yes, I am with this man. This beautiful man who is generous and kind and caring.

Was that why the waitstaff deferred to him? Or was it because of something darker? Was her Raffaele's power similar to that of her father?

Chiara's meal, until now so perfect, suddenly seemed inedible.

"Chiara?"

She looked up. Raffaele was watching her. He looked troubled.

"Sweetheart, if you don't like what I ordered for you—"

"No. No, it is fine. I am…I am tired, I think. All that walking…"

He was on his feet in a second, helping her from her chair, dropping a stack of bills on the table. The captain hurried toward them. Was everything all right?

No, Chiara thought, everything was not all right. She was married to a man who was everything she despised…except, she was not really married to him and she did not really despise him. What she felt for him was— It was—

A tremor went through her. Raffaele curved his arm around her.

"I'll get a taxi," he said softly, "and we'll go home."

She nodded. Except, it wasn't her home, it was his. This was all temporary. And that was good, was it not? Of course it was. She had no place in Raffaele Orsini's life. She didn't want a place in it. She didn't, didn't, didn't…

Oh, God.

She did.

When they reached his place, he wanted to call his doctor.

Chiara refused. She was still pale but at least she had stopped trembling.

"I am tired, Raffaele, that is all. A night's sleep and I'll be fine."

She went to her room. He went out to his. It was still early. He thought about phoning Falco. Or Nicolo. Thought about opening his BlackBerry and phoning a woman. The one he'd met the night he'd ended things with Ingrid…

Instead, he undressed, put on a pair of sweats and turned on the TV. Watched an old football game on ESPN. An even older movie on HBO. Clicked through the zillion channels that had absolutely nothing worth viewing and finally tossed the damned remote aside in disgust.

Taking Chiara out today had been a stupid idea.

She wasn't his guest any more than she was his wife. She was an encumbrance. A beautiful encumbrance, but that didn't change a thing. The sooner he called Sayers's law partner, the better. He'd get a couple of hours' sleep and do it first thing in the morning.

But he couldn't sleep. Just as well because somewhere around dawn he got an idea. A really good one.

He had that place on Nantucket. Why not put it to good use? Phone the couple who looked after it when he wasn't there, tell them to prepare for a guest, arrange for the helicopter service he occasionally used to fly Chiara to the island.

Brilliant, he thought as he showered and dressed, then went down the hall to her room and knocked on the door. She would be there. He would be here. No more nonsense, no more temptation—

The door swung open. Rafe stared at his wife. She was wearing another ugly outfit, her face was, as always, bare of makeup, her hair was loose and wild, still damp from the shower.

"Raffaele," she said shakily, "I am so sorry I spoiled our evening…"

Rafe groaned, hauled her into his arms and kissed her, and when she rose on her toes and kissed him back, he knew there wasn't a way in the world he was going to send her anywhere.

"Baby," he said gruffly, "you don't owe me an apology."

"Yes. I do. I thought—I suddenly thought that all this made no sense. You. Me. Our marriage…"

Who you are.

The words ran through her mind but she didn't speak them. For now, it was enough to know who her Raffaele seemed to be.

A man in whose arms she felt safe and wanted.

For as long as it lasted, she would not think of anything more than that.

They had breakfast.

She cooked. Bacon. Eggs. Toast. He ate it all, every bite, and never once thought about the grapefruits languishing in the refrigerator. But he made the coffee, teasing her about it until she laughed and said he had to buy an espresso pot and she would show him how to make real coffee.

Then they went out to see the city. Because, Rafe decided, what was the sense in asking Sayers's partner to start the ball rolling? Surely, waiting another few days wouldn't be a problem.

They rode the subway. Up to the Bronx, out to the end of the line in Brooklyn. It was a warm day. They strolled the boardwalk at Coney Island. The rides were closed, but Rafe told Chiara what the big amusement park was like when it was open, what it had been like years ago when he and his brothers had played hooky a couple of times and spent the day here.

"Hooky?"

"Yeah. You know. Cut school."

She didn't understand that, either, so he explained. It made her laugh.

"A couple of times, huh?"

He grinned and said, well, yeah, just a couple of times. The other times, they'd gone to other places.

He told her about Dante. And Nicolo. And Falco. She said, wistfully, that it must have been nice, growing up with brothers. He said there were times they were a pain in the— in the behind but that mostly they were great guys.

Around noon he suggested they head back to Manhattan to have lunch.

Chiara cast a longing look at Nathan's hot dog stand.

"I do not suppose," she said, "I do not imagine you would prefer to have—"

"Hot dogs?" Rafe laughed, picked her up, swung in a circle with her while she tried to keep a serious face as she demanded he put her down. "A kiss, and I will," he said, and letting her go after that one modest peck on the lips was the hardest thing he'd ever done.

They went into Nathan's. He ordered his hot dog with mustard. She ordered hers with sauerkraut. And onions. And relish.

"May I have French fries, too, please, Raffaele?"

He wanted to tell her she could have anything she wanted, that she already had—that she already had—

"Fries," he told the kid behind the counter, and told himself to stop thinking, because wherever his head was taking him made absolutely no sense at all.

He'd heard people say that seeing the city with someone who'd never seen it before was eye opening.

Seeing it with his Chiara was more than that. It was wonderful. It was amazing. It was incredible.

It was agony.

The days flew by, and he knew they were living on borrowed time. No matter how many places he showed her, how many little parks and mews they explored, no matter how many chestnut vendors his wife charmed by telling them their chestnuts were perfectly roasted, this was all going to end, and soon.

A good thing, of course. He had his life to lead. That he hadn't gone to the office in days, that he had no desire to go to it, well, that was not good.

Neither was taking so many cold showers.

What choice did he have? A man walked a beautiful woman to the door of her room every night, kissed her, told himself the kiss would be on the cheek or on the forehead and, instead, ended up capturing her lips with his, ended up with her arms wound tightly around his neck and her sweet, lush body pressed to his...

A man had that happening to him, the only way to save his ass was to stumble down the hall and step into a long, icy shower. Well, if that was the price he had to pay for hours of laughter and companionship—companionship with a woman!—he'd pay it.

The truth was, he loved everything they did. Going to the museums. Walking in the park. Even riding the upper deck of a sightseeing bus. He'd felt like a jerk at first. Then his Chiara had turned her shining, excited face to his and he'd gone from feeling stupid to feeling like a lucky man.

The one thing they hadn't done, the one thing he longed to do, was buy his wife new clothes to replace those awful things she kept pulling out of her seemingly bottomless suitcase.

But he wasn't a fool. His Chiara was proud. If he so much as suggested buying her new stuff, he knew he might hurt her. And he'd sooner have slit his throat than do that. Besides, she was beautiful to him just as she was and anytime he caught some idiot looking at her and smirking, Rafe turned the smirk to panic with one cold glance.

So, the days were perfect. But there was, inevitably, that time each evening he left Chiara at her bedroom door.

He was a healthy, heterosexual male with healthy appetites. He'd wanted a lot of women in his life…but he had never wanted one the way he wanted her. His body ached for her. Well, why wouldn't it?

The problem was, his heart ached, too.

Crazy, he knew, because sex and desire had nothing to do with the heart.

That was what he was busy telling himself at the end of yet another long day. They'd had fun but without warning, over dinner at a little place in Chinatown, somewhere between the steamed dumplings and the Szechuan beef, Rafe looked at his wife and that aching heart of his suddenly hardened.

What kind of game was she playing?

This was her fault. All of it. That they were married. That they were in this mess. That he was going crazy, torn between wanting to drag her into his bed and believing he had to treat her as if she were made of glass.

And she knew it. Women always knew these things.

What did it all mean? Was it an act? The country mouse bit. The give-me-the-simple-life thing. The hot kisses that she had to know ended for him in the kind of anguish he hadn't experienced since he was sixteen.

Was it an act?

What else could it be? he thought coldly. And while she was in the middle of saying something about something—who gave a damn what—he tossed his chopsticks on his plate and got to his feet.

Chiara looked up. "Raffaele?"

"It's late," he said gruffly. "And I'm going back to work tomorrow." He hadn't known that until he said it, but, by God, it was one damned fine idea. He yanked out his wallet, tossed some bills on the table. "Let's go."

She was staring at him. He didn't blink, not even when her eyes began to glitter. Not tears, he told himself. A trick of the light. Or maybe a trick of hers.

"Let's go," he repeated, and she put down her chopsticks and stood up.

By the time they got a taxi, she was crying. Silently, but she was crying. Was she upset because he'd pulled aside the curtain and taken a good look at what was behind it?

Frankly, he didn't care. This was it. No more. Sayers would be back tomorrow. Perfect timing. He'd phone her, set the divorce in motion, and that would be that.

They rode the taxi in silence, took the elevator to his place the same way. Was she still crying? He couldn't tell. Her head was turned away; her dark hair hid her face. Good. He'd looked at that face once too often.

When they stepped into the foyer of his penthouse, she swung toward him.

"Raffaele." Her voice trembled. Resolutely he folded his arms over his chest. "Raffaele. What did I do?"

"Nothing," he said calmly. "I'm the one. I should have dealt with reality sooner. We're nothing to each other, Chiara, just two people forced into something neither of them wanted by two old men. Well, it's time to stop the charade."

She winced. He felt his throat constrict but, damn it, somebody had to say it.

She looked away. A long moment passed. Then she turned her face to his. Her expression startled him. She was calm. Composed. She looked…she looked relieved.

"Thank you for speaking the truth." There was no tremor in her voice now. No tears in those violet eyes. "And you are right. There is no sense in continuing this…this charade. I would be grateful if you phoned your attorney tomorrow."

He nodded. She went up the stairs. He watched until she vanished from sight, heard her door open, heard it close…

And knew he had just lost the only thing in the world that mattered.

"Chiara," he said, and then he shouted her name and ran for the stairs, taking them two at a time, racing down the hall, throwing open the door to her bedroom. "Sweetheart. Chiara, I didn't mean it. I didn't—"

She turned toward him. She was sobbing; her face was wet with tears.

"Baby," he whispered, and then she was in his arms.

CHAPTER ELEVEN

RAFE gathered his wife tightly in his arms, his heart soaring as she looped her arms around his neck and pressed her body to his.

He knew that his anger had been nothing but a pathetic attempt at hiding the truth. He wanted her, had wanted her from that first kiss in Sicily. And she wanted him.

He was not going to turn away from that tonight.

The bed was only a few steps away.

He could take her to it, strip her naked, tear off his own clothes and bury himself in her. One deep thrust and she would be his.

Some still-functioning part of his brain told him he owed her much, much more.

She was innocent. A virgin. And she'd been told things about what happened between men and women that had terrified her.

He had to make what came next perfect. As perfect as her innocence.

"Chiara," he said softly.

Slowly she opened her eyes. The pupils were enormous, deep and dark and filled with all the questions a man could ever want to be asked. With all his heart, Rafe hoped he had answers that would please her.

"Chiara," he said again, and kissed her. Once. Twice, his

lips brushing gently over hers, each time lingering just a little longer until she gave a sigh of pleasure and her lips parted.

"That's the way," he murmured. "Yes, sweetheart. Open for me. Taste me. Let me taste you."

He could feel her hesitation. Then, slowly, she let him in.

The need to tumble her onto the bed swept through him with such power that he felt his muscles constrict. His big, powerful body shuddered.

"Raffaele?"

"It's all right. I just— I want—" He framed her face between his hands, lifted it to him and kissed her, his mouth hot and open over hers, his tongue seeking the sweetness that awaited him.

Her taste filled him. Honey. Cream. Vanilla. And, mingled with it, the taste of a woman aroused.

He whispered her name. She moved closer. Her hands crept up his chest to his shoulders, and he lifted her into him. He felt the delicate weight of her breasts against the hard wall of his chest, felt the feminine convexity of her belly pressed against the taut flatness of his.

Felt his erection rise and swell until he groaned with the almost unbearable pleasure of it.

Chiara gasped. Clutched his shoulders. Said his name again, and he could hear shock, wonder, apprehension in the single whispered word.

He was like stone. And all of this was new to his wife.

He took his lips from hers. Held her by the shoulders. She whimpered, tried to move closer, and though it killed him to stop her, he did.

"Why—" Her voice was low and thready. "Why did you stop kissing me? Did I do it wrong? If I did—"

"No," he said quickly. "God, no! There's no right way or wrong way to kiss." Another deep breath. "But I don't want to hurry you, sweetheart, or frighten you."

"I am not afraid of you," she whispered. "It is the rest. The…the touching."

"We can stop now," he said, and wondered if a man who was a liar could still be a candidate for sainthood.

Her response was too soft to hear.

She looked up into his eyes. "I don't want to stop. I want to know what it is men and women do together."

"Not men and women," he said gruffly. "Us. You and me."

Her smile filled his heart. "*Sì.* You and me, Raffaele. Show me, please."

He brought her hand to his lips, pressed kisses to her fingertips, then brought her hand between them and laid it lightly over his erection. Her breath hissed between her teeth; her palm cupped the hard bulge in his jeans.

Rafe shuddered and Chiara snatched back her hand. "Did I hurt you?"

"No," he said gruffly, clasping her hand, putting it on him again. "No, you didn't hurt me. I—" he swallowed hard "—I love what you just did. Touching me that way… Do you know what it means, that I'm hard like that?"

He watched her teeth worry her bottom lip. He longed to do that for her. Bite gently into that delicate flesh.

"It means—" Her voice was so low he had to bend to her to hear it. "It means you…you want to do things to me."

Rafe swallowed an oath. "It means that I want to do things *with* you. To touch each other in ways that bring us both pleasure."

She nodded, dipped her head so that her curls became a curtain that hid her from him.

"Do it, then," she whispered.

Rafe took a long breath, expelled it slowly enough to give him time to think. Then he put his hand under Chiara's chin and lifted her face to his.

"Hey," he said gently, "this isn't a visit to the dentist." That bought him a smile, as he'd hoped it would. "Chiara. Sweetheart, we're not going to do anything you don't want to do."

"That's just it. I do not know what I want or do not want."

She lifted her hands to his chest. Could she feel the race of his heart? "I only know that…that something happens when you kiss me, Raffaele. I feel…I feel—"

"Tell me."

Her face colored. "I feel things. Sensations. In…in parts of me…" A laugh that was close to a sob caught in her throat. "I cannot talk about it. Talking about my body is—"

She gasped as he cupped her breast, gave a little cry, almost pulled back, but he slid an arm around her, held her while his fingers moved gently, unerringly over her nipple. He could feel it budding even through the harsh, unyielding cotton of her dress. She moaned. Her lashes drooped, became inky-black crescents against her cheeks.

"Do you feel something when I do this?" he said hoarsely.

She looked up at him, her face striped with color. "Yes. Oh *Dio*, yes. Like that. Just like—"

"Where do you feel it?"

"There. Where you are touching me. And…and elsewhere. Lower than my breasts, Raffaele. I feel it—"

She cried out as he ran his hand down her body, to the juncture of her thighs. He had touched her there before but all of that had gone too quickly. None of what would happen now would be quick. He would bring her slowly, slowly to pleasure, and never mind his own desires.

This first time, only her needs, her pleasure, her fulfillment mattered.

"Here?" he said thickly. "What do you feel, baby?"

"I feel—I feel—heat. A tingle. It is what happens during a storm, when you stand outside and the lightning strikes on the hills and you can almost feel the electricity in your bones. Do you know what I mean, Raffaele?"

He knew. It was how he felt now, as if a storm of incredible magnitude were building inside him, the tension almost more than he could tolerate.

He answered the whispered question by urging her thighs

apart, just enough so he could cup her over the stiff fabric of her dress. She gasped, her eyes wild. "I feel as if…as if I am melting. There. Where your hand is."

He could feel his muscles trembling. Her innocence was enough to send him to the edge of control, but he would not let that happen.

"Your body is readying itself for me, sweetheart. For us."

He moved his hand and she gasped again, then buried her face against his shoulder. "I never knew—"

"No," Rafe said with a little laugh, "neither did I." It was true. He'd been with a lot of women and enjoyed them all, but this, what was happening now, what he was feeling now…

"I think I am burning up," she whispered.

So was he. When she returned tomorrow morning, Mrs. O'Hara might well find this bedroom in ashes.

"I think—" He cleared his throat. "Why don't we get some of this clothing out of the way?"

"Is it time for me to…to undress?"

"Leave that to me," he said huskily.

Did everything she owned have a thousand buttons? Did the buttons always have to be so small, especially when his fingers were so big and clumsy? It took forever to undo the first button. The second. The third…

The dress began falling open, revealing her to him, and he forgot about buttons, buttonholes, the size of his fingers. He skimmed the back of his hand down her throat, then followed the same path with light kisses. Her pulse, in the tender hollow where her neck met her collarbones, danced beneath his mouth and he exulted at the feel of it.

At last the buttons were all undone. Rafe freed her of the dress and let it fall to her feet.

Her bra, her panties were white cotton, just as they'd been that first time. Except he hadn't undressed her then, he'd torn the dress from her body.

All the more reason to do this with the greatest care. He would touch her as if she were made of the most delicate crystal.

He would. He would—but the curve of her breasts above that modest bra was lush. And, God, he could see the dark outline of her nipples…

Rafe bent his head and closed his mouth around the tip of one cotton-covered breast. Chiara's cry of pleasure almost tore him apart.

On a low growl, he scooped her into his arms, carried her to the bed and laid her down. He kicked off his mocs, yanked his sweater over his head and tossed it aside. Chiara's gaze flew over him, as hot and urgent as a caress. He came down on the bed beside her and kissed her, his mouth drinking the honey from hers, his hands learning her body.

Her bra closed in the front, and he sent up a silent thank-you to whatever god had sent him that gift. She didn't try to stop him as he undid the clasp but when the bra came away, her hands fluttered up to cover her breasts.

He shook his head, gently caught her wrists and brought her hands to her sides.

"Let me see you," he whispered. "I need to see you, Chiara."

She lay back. She was breathing hard. He could feel her eyes on him as he looked at her.

Ah, she was beautiful. More beautiful than he had imagined. Her breasts were round, with dusty pink crests already peaking as they begged for the heat of his mouth.

He brought his gaze to her face, watched her eyes as he cupped one breast, groaning as he felt the perfect weight of it in his hand. Her pupils widened, then seemed to swallow her irises as he moved his thumb over the tip.

"Raffaele…"

Her voice was shaky. He stroked her nipple again, then captured it between his thumb and index finger, gently caressed it.

Chiara moaned.

SANDRA MARTON   139

"Do you like that?" he said thickly.

A sob broke in her throat. She moaned again as he increased the pressure of his caress, lowered his head, closed his lips around the straining nipple and drew it deep into the heat of his mouth.

She said something in Italian. He didn't understand the words, but the arching of her body, the feel of her hand clasping the nape of his neck as he sucked on her beaded flesh, told him all he needed to know.

He drew back. She made a sweet sound of protest.

"Don't leave me," she whispered.

"No," he said fiercely. "Never."

It took only seconds to unzip his jeans, get rid of them and his shorts. He saw her eyes flash to his genitals, then widen and fly to his face.

He'd never considered what a woman might feel the first time she saw a fully aroused male. Now he did. Could it be frightening? Maybe, especially if the woman was completely innocent. And if the guy was big.

He was.

He'd always taken a kind of arrogant male pride in his size. Now he realized that what might make an experienced woman smile with anticipation could make his Chiara feel terror.

He took her hand. Brought it to his lips, pressed a kiss into the palm. "Don't be afraid," he said softly. "This is just another part of me." He kissed her hand again, then slowly brought it to his erection. She hesitated and then he felt the first, cool brush of her fingers.

It took all the determination he possessed not to throw back his head and groan.

"See?" he said, fighting to keep his voice steady. Slowly her hand closed around his turgid length. Rafe bit his lip.

"You are so hard here," she said in wonder. "And yet, so soft."

"Not soft," he said, trying for a little levity. "Not—"

Ah. She moved her hand. Up. Down. Up...

He caught her wrist. "Don't," he said gruffly. "Or this will end too quickly." He pressed a light kiss to her mouth. "Besides," he whispered, "this isn't fair."

"It isn't?"

He smiled. "I'm naked. You're not."

He kissed her again, deeper, longer, and as he did, he slid her panties off. Then he traced the path they'd taken with his hand. The lovely indentation of her waist. The curve of her hip.

The delicate curls that guarded her feminine heart.

Her fingers clamped on his.

"I won't hurt you, Chiara," he said softly.

Slowly she took her hand away.

Rafe stroked those curls. Soothed her with soft words. Softer kisses. She was silken under his touch, warm and, yes, wet. Wet for him.

He drew back and looked at her. His throat constricted.

Naked, she was everything he had imagined. She was an El Greco painting come to life, Praxiteles's Aphrodite made all the more exquisite because she was flesh and blood, not cold marble.

"Chiara," he whispered, and he moved down her body and pressed his lips to that sweet, female delta.

Her hands flew to his shoulders. "No! You must not—"

He caught her wrists and went on kissing her. Gradually, her hands relaxed in his grasp. Her breathing quickened. And when he gently parted her delicate folds, she sobbed his name.

"It is too much," she said brokenly. "Too much…"

He knew it wasn't nearly enough. He wanted to see her fly into the sky, then fly into it again…with him.

"Open your legs for me," he said in a voice so rough it didn't seem his own.

"I can't," she said breathlessly. "People do not—"

"Open your legs, baby. For me."

Slowly she did as he'd asked. He touched her with reverence, parted her again, groaned when he saw the tender bud of her clitoris.

"Chiara," he said softly, and he put his mouth against her.

Wild little cries burst from her throat. She began to weep. He froze but then he felt her hands in his hair, holding him to her instead of pushing him away. As if he would ever take his mouth from her, he thought in wonder. From her taste. Her scent. She was everything a man could ever want or dream.

She was his.

He slipped his hands under her, lifted her higher into the passionate intimacy of his kiss. He felt her shudder and then she screamed his name and he knew she had glimpsed the burning rays of the sun.

Now, he thought, and he moved over her, positioned himself between her thighs and entered her, teeth gritted with the determination to do it slowly.

He didn't want to hurt her, didn't want to hurt her—

Her legs closed around his hips, urging him on.

Rafe flung his head back, thrust deep, flew over the edge of the earth and took his wife with him.

Chiara lay beneath Raffaele's hard body, her arms still holding him to her.

His heartbeat was slowing or maybe it was hers. They were so close that she couldn't tell the difference. And he was still inside her.

She closed her eyes.

A man, inside her. No. It was *this* man who was inside her. This man, who had taken her on a journey so intense she'd never wanted it to end.

This man.

Her husband.

The thought sent a sweet tremor through her. Raffaele stirred. Without thinking, she tightened her arms around him.

"Hey," he said softly, and she blushed as she realized he wanted to get off her. Of course he did. Her mother had told her some things that were obviously incorrect but some were surely accurate.

For instance, when a man finished with a woman, he had no further wish to remain in her bed. This was Raffaele's bed, not hers, but the principle was the same.

What an idiot I am, she thought, and let him go.

He rolled off her, but he didn't go anywhere. Instead he gathered her into his arms and drew her close. Surprised, she let him do it—she loved having him do it—but she wasn't foolish enough to think he'd hold her for very long.

"Are you okay?"

She nodded and burrowed a little closer, her nose just at the juncture of his shoulder and arm. She loved the smell of him there. Back home, there'd been times the very scent of a man's body made her belly knot and her throat clench but this was different. Rafe's scent was masculine and musky and exciting.

"Chiara?" He ran one hand into her hair as he cupped her cheek. "Did I hurt you?"

He had, at that last amazing moment, but she'd have died rather than have stopped him. The feel of him, deep inside her… It had been pleasure so incredible that even remembering it made her tremble.

"Damn," he said gruffly, "I did."

"No. It's all right. I did not mind."

"You didn't mind?" Suddenly she was no longer lying cradled against him, she was on her back and he was leaning over her. "Damn it, you have every right to mind," he said gruffly. "I tried to go slow but—"

"Raffaele." She smiled. "It was wonderful."

He grinned. Such a becoming grin! But then, why wouldn't it be? He was beautiful.

"Yeah?"

"Wonderful," she said softly.

"The next time we make love, it'll be even more wonderful."

Her heart filled. They had not had sex, they had made love. How wrong her mother had been!

"What?" he said, smiling at her.

She smiled back. "Nothing. I was just thinking…"

"Me, too." His smile tilted. "About next time."

"I am glad you are thinking that, Raffaele," she whispered. "Very glad."

Rafe kissed her. She sighed and opened her mouth to his. His kiss deepened, his hand cupped her breast and her nipple engorged at his touch.

"Oh," she said softly, "oh, yes…"

He slid his hand down her body. Cupped her. Slipped a finger inside those plump folds… And saw her wince. Cursing softly, he gathered her into his arms.

"See? I did hurt you. Forgive me, baby. It's much too soon."

"No." Her cheeks turned pink. "If you would like to…to make love again—"

"I would like to make love straight into tomorrow," he said solemnly. "But this is your first time and you need to take it easy."

She would have protested but he kissed her again, then rose from the bed. She sat up, the sheet drawn over her breasts, and watched him. Had he changed his mind? Was he leaving her now?

No. He was not. Unashamedly naked, he went into the connecting bathroom and shut the door. Chiara lay back against the pillows. She felt boneless and happy and exhausted. It was as if she had experienced a miracle. That sex—that making love could be like this…

But it was not really love. Love was not what Raffaele—what her husband felt for her, and that was all right because… because it was not what she felt for him, either.

Tears welled in her eyes. And what for? What reason was there to weep? Something that had begun as a disaster had turned into something, yes, wonderful. She was free of her father, of San Giuseppe. And she was with a man who had taught her that sex could be the most wonderful experience of a woman's life—

Even if he was not going to be in her life…

"Hey."

Raffaele's voice was soft. He was standing beside the bed, holding a small basin and a towel.

"Sweetheart. Why are you crying?"

"I am not crying. I am just— I am weepy. Did no one ever tell you that women get weepy when they are happy?" She sniffed back her tears and hurried to change the subject. "Thank you for the basin of water but—"

"But you're going to take care of things yourself."

"Sì. As I should. As I— Raffaele, that is not for you to do."

But he was already sitting beside her, the washcloth in his hand.

"Yes," he said softly, "it is for me to do." He brought the warm, wet cloth to her thighs, nudged them gently apart and began laving her with it. "I took your virginity."

She smiled a little. "Yes," she whispered. "You did."

Rafe rinsed the cloth in the basin, wrung it out again and carefully used it on her once more. There were tiny drops of blood on her thighs and on the cloth. The sight of her blood, the knowledge that his lovemaking had been the reason she had shed it, was almost overwhelming.

He put the cloth aside, gently dried her with the soft towel, got into the bed and gathered her in his arms.

"Shut your eyes, sweetheart. You've had a long couple of days."

"Mmm."

"Just…just let me kiss you first…"

His lips closed over hers. She sighed with pleasure. His mouth moved lower. Along her throat. She sighed again. His mouth found her breasts and her sighs became moans.

"Raffaele," she said, as he drew a nipple deep into his mouth. "Raffaele…"

"It's too soon," he said thickly, but she slipped a hand between them, touched him, caressed him, and he groaned and moved over her. "Are you sure?"

Her answer came not in words but in the stroke of her fingers, the arch of her spine, the mingling of her breath with his.

He drew away, took something from the nightstand drawer. Chiara knew what it was.

A condom.

He had not used one the first time. It was her safe time of month—Miss Ellis had taught her the basics of biology—but she thought she would not have cared if he had made her pregnant. This was her Raffaele.

Her husband.

She watched as he tore open the little pack and rolled the condom on. She wanted to do it for him. To touch him. To explore his hard flesh with her hands, her mouth...

She reached for him as he came back to her, and he entered her slowly, eased into her with such care that his muscles trembled until, at last, he was deep, deep inside her.

Could a woman die of pleasure? If she did, it would be worth what she felt now.

The rhythm he set was hard and urgent but she stayed with him, thrust for thrust. She cried out, arched from the bed and, seconds later, cried out again as her Raffaele took her with him into that place where the sun blazed forever.

"Chiara," he whispered. "My beautiful, beautiful bride."

Tears again rose in her eyes. She blinked them back and returned his tender kisses as he drew her close in his arms. Moments later his breathing was deep and even, but she lay awake for a very long time, torn between incredible joy and heartbreaking despair.

Raffaele was her husband.

Except, he was not. Not really.

And this, all of this, could not last.

CHAPTER TWELVE

Was there a specific protocol for a woman's behavior when she woke in a man's arms?

Did you lie motionless until he was awake? Slip free of his embrace, gather up your clothes and tiptoe from the room? What if all that shifting around woke him?

What did people say to each other after they'd spent the night making love?

They'd made love again and again, Chiara thought with a little shudder of pleasure. And each time had been different and even better than the last.

How could her mother have been so wrong? This was not pain or submission or humiliation. This was pure joy, a heart-stopping, breathless climb to the very top of a mountain and then a long, dizzying flight to the stars.

At least, it was when Raffaele Orsini was your lover.

During the night she'd awakened to his kisses. She'd shot from sleep with her heart pounding, struggling against the alien, male touch.

"No," she'd said sharply, and he'd framed her face with his hands.

"Chiara. Sweetheart, it's me."

Slowly she'd became aware of the familiarity of the hard body poised just over hers. His scent. His features. His skin, smooth and warm over taut muscle.

"Raffaele," she'd whispered.

"I'm sorry, Chiara. I didn't mean to frighten you."

"No. You didn't. I just… What time is it?"

"It's late. Very late. You should be asleep."

She'd smiled, lifted her hand, stroked it against the sexy stubble on his jaw. "Mmm. So should you."

"Soon," he'd whispered, between kisses. "But first, a kiss…"

One kiss. Then another. She'd lifted her arms and wound them around his neck. His kisses deepened. Her response intensified. That part of him she had so feared was already hard against her belly. Now it swelled even more.

Why had she ever been afraid of this? Being held so intimately. Being kissed as if you were a man's only hope of salvation. The stroke of a strong, callused hand.

The pulsing, aroused flesh that was so beautifully, fiercely male.

"Raffaele," she'd whispered.

Shamelessly she'd wrapped one leg high around his. He'd said her name in a voice so filled with desire that it had been like a caress, slipped a hand beneath her and raised her into him. When his erect penis had nudged against her, she'd caught her breath.

Instantly he pulled back. "Forgive me, sweetheart. You're sore."

"I ache," she'd whispered, "but not because I am sore, Raffaele, I ache for you. I want you inside me." Overcome with embarrassment, she'd buried her face against his shoulder. "Oh. I should not have said—"

"Yes," he'd said fiercely, cupping the back of her head, lifting her face to his until their eyes met. "You should. I love hearing you say that you want me."

"I do," she'd replied, "I want you, want you, want—"

Their mouths fused. Moments later he had been deep inside her.

Remembering, Chiara smiled. Actually, she was a little

tender, but it was a wonderful tenderness, a reminder of her husband's lovemaking…

Her smile faded.

Her husband. Her very temporary husband. How had she forgotten that? More to the point, how had she forgotten that, despite his gentleness, his kindness, her husband was in the same "profession" as her father?

She wanted to weep. Her mother had things wrong. Sex was not ugly. It was a drug to make a woman forget the truth.

Quickly she pushed the blankets aside and moved out of Raffaele's embrace. There was enough early-morning light in the room so she could see her clothes, discarded on the floor. If she was quiet…

"Hey."

She froze, her dress clasped against her body, her back to the bed.

"What time is it?" Raffaele yawned; the bedding rustled. She knew he must be reaching for the clock on the nightstand. "Chiara," he groaned, "it's barely six-thirty." His voice dropped to a husky purr. "Come back to bed."

She took a steadying breath, forced the mental image of her husband's muscled, beautiful body from her mind. The important thing was to speak calmly. She had behaved foolishly, but it would not happen again. He needed to understand that.

"Six-thirty is late for me. At home, I would already be in the kitchen, making coffee."

His chuckle was low and sexy. "We tried that, remember? I'm the one who makes the coffee around here."

"It does not matter who makes the coffee. What matters is that your housekeeper will be arriving soon."

"And?"

"And I do not wish her to find us like this."

More rustling. Was he getting out of bed? *Please, no. Let him stay where he is. At least, let him put on some clothes.*

"Not a problem, sweetheart. Mrs. O'Hara doesn't come in

today. Even if she did, she never comes into my bedroom. Well, into a bedroom with a closed door."

"Certainly not. I am sure she is under strict orders not to disturb you and whatever woman you have brought home for the—"

"Is that what's troubling you?"

"No. It is not. Why would it trouble me?" Why, indeed? Why had she even said such a foolish—

He came up behind her, dropped his hands lightly on her shoulders. "Are you trying to count all the women who've spent the night with me?"

"No," she said again. "I already told you that."

Slowly he turned her toward him. Her heartbeat quickened. Yes, he was naked. Beautifully naked, his shoulders and arms taut with muscle, a whorl of dark hair over his hard-planed chest, a flat abdomen leading down to his sex.

"I'm not going to lie to you," he said quietly. "There've been women here."

Why did the admission hurt? "Really, Raffaele, you owe me no explanation."

"Maybe not. But it's important to me that you understand. I've never spent a night like this one, sweetheart. And I've never awakened wishing the night had not yet ended."

She didn't answer. She wouldn't even meet his eyes. Something was wrong, but Rafe had no idea what that something was.

"Chiara."

He put his hand under his wife's chin and lifted her face to his. Yes. She was troubled. So was he. Something had changed inside him, during the long night. It had to do with their making love but there was more to it than that. He wished to hell he knew what it was, but whatever had changed, whatever he felt, was just out of reach.

He only knew that he was happy.

Incredibly happy.

He said Chiara's name again, bent his head and kissed her. At first she didn't respond. Then she sighed and kissed him back.

He smiled. "Good morning, sweetheart," he said softly.

Her smile was tremulous. "Good morning, Raffaele."

His eyes moved over her face. As always, it was bare of makeup and it hit him that he couldn't recall seeing a woman without makeup, even after a long night in bed. Falco joked about it. The 5:00 a.m. face, he called it, because it was always freshly painted on by the time a man opened his eyes. Women were programmed, Falco said, to wake at dawn so they'd have time to scrub off last night's war paint and put on today's.

Chiara had put nothing on her face. She hadn't fixed her hair, either, as women always did. It went with the 5:00 a.m. face—the perfect straight fall or the artfully tumbled curls.

Not his wife. Her hair was a dark nimbus of silk.

Rafe's gut clenched. It was tough to decide what he wanted most right now. To carry her back to bed and make love to her, or simply to hold her close in his arms.

And there it was again, that sad expression in her lovely eyes. Did she regret their long, wonderful night?

"Sweetheart?" He hesitated. "Are you sorry we made love?"

He'd expected a quick answer, a smile and a no, and maybe a touch of her lips against his. But the seconds slipped past, and just when he thought he was going to go crazy, she shook her head and melted against him.

"The thing is," she said, in a small voice, "the thing is, I do not understand any of this."

His sense of relief was enormous. He pulled back, just far enough so he could see her face, and flashed a wicked, sexy grin.

"Which part don't you understand, baby? I'll be happy to help."

"I am serious, Raffaele. I mean, we hardly know each other. Our marriage is not…" She couldn't say it, and wasn't that silly? "Our marriage is not a normal one. We are only together because you were my Sir Galahad."

"Sorry to disappoint you, but I doubt if Galahad's armor was as tarnished as mine."

"And that is another thing." Her voice was low. "Your… your occupation."

His eyebrows rose. "Well, I'll admit, lots of people don't think much of guys in my business right now, but—"

"You have been so good to me. So gentle." Her eyes searched his. "So how could you be one of them?"

"One of who?"

"You know. You are part of…of— What is it called here? My father's organization. Your father's. How could you be you and be part of that, as well?"

It took a couple of seconds before he figured it out. She still thought he was a hoodlum. He would have laughed, but he sensed that this wasn't really funny.

"Okay," he said briskly, "here's what we're gonna do. Shower. Get dressed. Then we'll go out for breakfast and after that, I'll show you what it is I do for a living. What I *really* do for a living, sweetheart, as opposed to what you think I do."

"I know what you do, Raffaele. Didn't I just tell you that?"

"Yes. You did." He kissed her. Just for good measure, he kissed her again. "And," he said softly, "I can see that it really matters to you."

"Of course it matters," she said with indignation. "I— You and I—we did things…"

"Amazing things," he said huskily. "Incredible things." He gave her a slow, tender kiss. "And we'll do them again, sweetheart, but first I'm going to show you who I really am."

"I keep telling you—"

He silenced her with another kiss. "I know you do," he said gently. "And now, I'm telling you, baby. Give me the benefit of the doubt, okay?"

Chiara nodded. "Okay," she murmured, because maybe she was wrong about him. She *had* to be wrong. How could she, of all people, have made love with a man who was as evil as her father? How could she have lain in his arms?

Most of all, she thought, most of all…

Most of all, how could she be falling in love with him?

Rafe wanted her to shower with him.

She refused.

He knew it would take him less than a minute to change her mind. His wife was the most responsive woman he'd ever been with. All he had to do was touch her, kiss her. But if they ended up back in bed, he'd feel even guiltier about how many times he'd made love to her during the night.

So he made do with a kiss. Well, a few kisses. Her eyelids. Her cheeks. Her delectable mouth and, finally, her breasts. She put up a little struggle, a couple of *You must not, Raffaele* whispers, but she moaned when he tugged away that ratty dress she clutched like a shield and touched his lips to first one delicate nipple and then the other.

Stopping was sheer hell, but knowing she didn't want him to stop was a gift that made it worthwhile.

"Later," he said softly, and then he spun her toward the door and told her to hurry up and get ready to go out.

She bristled.

"I do not take orders, Raff— Oh!"

It was the reaction he'd hoped for, the indignant "Oh" when he swatted her lightly on her naked butt—she was clutching her dress again and she seemed to have forgotten it only covered her front—and then a shocked gasp when he followed it up with a quick kiss on that same place.

She all but ran for the bathroom. He chuckled. He knew he'd pay for it later.

At least, he hoped he would.

Twenty minutes later he was showered and dressed.

Jeans. A dark blue sweater and a leather jacket, because the day looked bright but he could see the tops of the trees in the park swaying under the wind. He scooped up his keys and wallet, then headed downstairs. Chiara wouldn't be ready, of course. He knew women. She would need another twenty, thirty minutes. He'd wait for her near the elevator. It was safer than waiting for her upstairs where all he had to do was go down the hall, turn the doorknob to her room…

But his wife was waiting for *him*. She'd tamed her hair, damn it, pulling it back into another of those knots, and she was wearing one of those black dresses.

Something must have shown in his face. She blushed a little, brushed her hand down the length of the dress.

"I know this is not what New York women wear, but—"

Rafe wrapped his arm around her shoulders and kissed her. It was the kind of opening he'd been waiting for, and he wasn't about to let it go by.

"Breakfast can wait," he said. "First we'll deal with what New York women wear."

It was still early. Too early for Saks to be open but why would that stop him? He had a client who knew a guy who a guy…

By the time they'd reached the lobby, he'd made a couple of calls on his cell. And by the time they reached Saks, a polite gentleman in an expensive suit was waiting at a side door to let them in.

Chiara balked. "What are we doing here, Raffaele?"

"I told you," he said easily, "we're going to see what it is New York women wear."

She dug in her heels. "This must be an expensive store."

He shrugged. "Maybe."

Her jaw firmed. "I cannot afford it. I have not had time to find a buyer for my mother's jewels."

Did she actually think he'd let her sell those jewels? She was his wife. For now, anyway. And a husband supplied his wife's clothes.

"You can argue with me later," he said, and he took her hand and led her inside the store.

Her soft ooh's and aaah's made him smile as the man in the suit led them through displays of silk scarves and accessories, past endless counters of perfume and cosmetics until they reached the elevators. One was waiting, and the three of them stepped inside.

"Where do we get off?" his wife whispered.

A good question. He hadn't asked; he'd simply told the guy his client had put him in touch with that he wanted to buy a few things for a lady…

The doors opened. An acre of garments stretched ahead but—Rafe breathed a sigh of relief—a guide was waiting.

Well, a salesclerk. A saleswoman. An associate. Whatever you called an angel who greeted you with a smile and gave no sign that her newest customer looked like she'd stepped off the ancient streets of Sicily.

"Good morning," she said pleasantly. "My name is Nella. How may I help you?"

Rafe made his first mistake. He asked Chiara what she needed.

Her chin came up. "Nothing!"

He nodded. "And maybe that's just as well," he said, eyes wide with innocence. "I mean, even if you did need, oh, I don't know…let's say, some sweaters. Jeans. A jacket. A couple of dresses…"

"I just said, Raffaele, I do not need—"

"Right. And I said that was good because I don't think they carry your size here."

"Raffaele. Perhaps you did not—" Her brow furrowed. "Excuse me?"

"You don't, do you, Nella?" He looked at the saleswoman. "You don't have anything, well, um, anything in a size big enough for my wife?"

Nella's lips twitched. "Well, Mr. Orsini, I must admit, I'd have to check."

Chiara was bristling.

"I am a small size," she said coldly. "A very small size. I am not a stick, which is perhaps the way you prefer your women, Signor Orsini, but I can assure you—"

"What you are," Rafe said, pulling her into his arms, "is gorgeous." He kissed her. And kissed her. Nella bit back a smile and drifted toward a display of cashmere sweaters. When he finally ended the kiss, what he wanted more than his next breath was to tell Nella to go away, but he behaved himself, pointed his wife toward the saleswoman and stepped safely out of the line of fire.

It was a new experience, sitting on a sofa too small and dainty for a man his size, quietly asking himself what in hell he was doing.

He had bought things for women before. Necklaces. Bracelets. Flowers and perfume and chocolate. Okay, correction. He'd had his PA buy them. He had never been part of the selection process.

A new experience, absolutely.

He felt weird at first, sitting there like some kind of potentate, nodding each time Chiara appeared. *Appeared* was too generous a word. Nella sort of prodded her out of the dressing room. At the start, anyway.

After a while, though, as the parade of cashmere sweaters and jeans, wool trousers and silk blouses, long dresses and short dresses kept going, there seemed to be less prodding and more, well, more prancing.

She might never admit it, but his wife was enjoying this game of dress up.

So was he.

She looked spectacular in everything and when Nella began adding shoes and boots with heels high enough to make him salivate, he wondered why nobody had ever come up with an evening's entertainment called *Watching a Beautiful Woman Parade before Her Lover.*

Parade before her husband.

Well, he wasn't. Not really. He wasn't anybody's husband. He wouldn't be, not for a very long time, certainly not at the behest of his old man.

"...the last one, Raffaele."

Rafe blinked. His wife stood before him. Her hair had come loose of that abominable knot. It spilled over her shoulders like long waves of dark silk. She wore a cashmere sweater the color of garnets, tight jeans and black leather boots that could only look better than they already did if she'd worn them without the sweater and the jeans and, damn it, he was on the verge of embarrassing himself.

"What?" he said, and cleared his throat.

"I said, this is the last outfit. You must decide which one we should buy."

He knew there was only one correct answer. He also knew better than to offer it in front of her. Instead, he rose to his feet.

"This looks nice," he said, as casually as possible.

She beamed. "I think so, too."

He nodded and turned to Nella. "My wife will take these things. In fact, she'll wear them now. Just add a jacket. Leather, to match the boots."

Nella nodded and hurried off. Chiara leveled a look at him.

"Raffaele," she said, the single word filled with warning.

"What?" he said innocently. "New York's cool this time of year."

"I have a coat."

Nella hurried back with a leather jacket. "Just try this on," he said. "Please."

Knowledge of the night they'd shared was in his eyes. Chiara's expression softened. "I will try it on, but I am not promising anything."

She slipped into the jacket and turned to the mirror. Rafe watched her reflection in the glass, saw her lips form a perfect O, heard her little sigh of pleasure. It struck him that there had not been much pleasure in his wife's life. The realization made him want to return to Sicily and shake her father until his teeth rattled.

The saleswoman raised her eyebrows. "Don't you like the jacket, sir?"

Rafe took a steadying breath. "I like it a lot." Forcing a smile, he took his Amex Black card from his wallet and handed it to her. "We'll take everything," he said quietly.

Nella's eyebrows rose another inch. *"Everything?"*

"Everything," he said, putting his finger to his lips. "Have it all delivered to my home. Understand?"

The woman's smile was wide and gentle. "I most certainly do, Mr. Orsini."

Good. Excellent. At least someone understood, because he damned well didn't. He had a wife who wasn't really his wife. A wife he didn't want. A wife forced upon him by the machinations of her father and his.

And yet, just looking at her filled him with joy. With delight. With…with—

He frowned and barked Chiara's name. She spun toward him.

He knew what he had to tell her. That it was getting late. That they had things to do. That he had no idea why he'd said he'd show her how he actually earned his living because what he was going to do was phone Marilyn Sayers's office and demand an immediate appointment so they could get moving with this divorce thing.

"Raffaele? Did you want to tell me something?"

"Yes," he said gruffly. 'I wanted to tell you…to tell you—" A muscle knotted in his jaw. "I wanted to tell you that you look beautiful."

Chiara smiled. "It is the jacket. And the sweater. And—"

"The hell it is," he said, and then she was in his arms and he was kissing her with a hunger that exceeded anything he'd ever imagined.

CHAPTER THIRTEEN

HE MADE a call on his cell phone while Chiara stepped into the cab he'd hailed, told the doorman to expect a delivery from Saks, that the porter was to take everything to his penthouse and stack it all in the master bedroom.

Then he climbed into the cab, took his wife's hand and told the cabby to take them to Balthazar, a Soho bistro where the morning meal was as much a ritual as an art.

He was greeted warmly by name and led to his usual table. It offered a modicum of privacy, though privacy was in short supply here, but the crowds, the noise, were part of the charm.

The busboy brought their menus. Chiara said thank you, opened hers but didn't look at it. She was too busy looking around the busy room.

Rafe didn't look at his menu, either. He was too busy looking at his wife.

Lord, how beautiful she was! And it wasn't the new clothes; it was her. She was beautiful and filled with life. She'd chattered away almost nonstop once they left Saks, excited by the sights, the architecture, the crowds.

"Such a city," she'd said with delight. "So filled with people! Where can they all be going in such a hurry?"

Where am *I* going? Rafe had thought.

Not just out to breakfast. He was heading somewhere at the

speed of light, a place he had never been before, and if that made no sense, he was stuck with it. The only sure thing was that he was heading there because of his wife.

He knew it was foolish to think of her that way, but legally that was who she was. His wife. Mrs. Rafe Orsini. Mrs. *Raffaele* Orsini, and when had he come to prefer the sound of his actual given name? He'd never felt comfortable with it, maybe because it had always been a reminder of his ancestry and all he'd imagined went with it.

The way his wife said it, "Raffaele" was a benediction. His wife. His beautiful, bright, exciting wife…

"Oh, Raffaele, this is a wonderful place!"

Chiara was leaning toward him, smiling. He reached for her hand and brought it to his lips.

"I'm glad you like it."

"Do you come here often? It seems a long way from where you live."

The waiter hovered beside them. Rafe waved him off.

"It is, but my office is just a couple of blocks from here."

Her smile dimmed. "Your office."

"Yes. So I've gotten into the habit of stopping here for breakfast when I have the chance."

"You don't work from home like…like—"

"Like your old man or mine? No. My operation's too big for that, though there are times I wish I could."

"Oh."

Her "oh" sounded flat. He knew what she was thinking, that his "operation" must be even more powerful than her father's. Let her think it. It would only increase her surprise and, he hoped, her pleasure when she saw the Orsini Brothers building and his handsome office.

"So," he said briskly, "what would you like for breakfast?"

Chiara looked down at her menu. She could feel the joy in her heart draining away. All this—the night in her husband's arms, the shopping trip this morning…

A dream.

She must not forget that again.

No matter what Raffaele made her feel, he was part of a world she hated. He had come to San Giuseppe to do his father's bidding because he was a good soldier in the Sicilian sense of the word.

It was just as well this so-called marriage would end as soon as his attorney returned to the city.

Suddenly the thought of eating made her feel sick. Carefully she put down the menu.

"Actually, Raffaele, I am not very—I am not terribly hungry."

She tried to pull her hand free of his. He wouldn't let her. Instead he leaned close.

"Chiara," he said softly, "the day's just begun. Don't sit in judgment on me yet." He kissed her palm. "Okay?"

Their eyes met. Her husband looked handsome and earnest and…and, God oh God, she was not falling in love with him, she was already in love with him. Desperately in love with him, and suddenly she knew that it didn't matter if he was a soldier in his father's organization or not.

Heaven help her, she didn't care. All that mattered was that she loved him. And she was going to lose him.

"Chiara? Can you do that? Can you put your trust in me for this?"

She wanted to weep. Or rise from her chair and fling herself into her Raffaele's arms.

"*Sì,*" she whispered.

He smiled and said they had to be driving their poor waiter crazy, and would she like him to order for her? Chiara nodded because she didn't trust herself to speak.

If she did, she would say words he didn't want to hear, that she loved him…

That she would always love him, and treasure these days that she had been his wife.

* * *

Halfway through the meal, Rafe realized he'd never phoned his PA to tell her he'd be coming in today.

He'd ignored his schedule all week, but at least he'd phoned her each morning to say he wouldn't be in.

He hadn't even thought of phoning her today.

He'd had other things on his mind this morning, and just remembering those other things made him want to sweep Chiara into his arms, carry her off and make love to her. Make love with her. Make her come, and this time, when she cried out his name, he'd tell her—he'd tell her—

The floor seemed to tilt.

Tell her what?

All at once it seemed hard to breathe.

What had happened to all last night's resolutions? He was too old to let sex, even great sex, muddle his head. As for what he'd planned, taking Chiara to the Orsini offices… He had to be out of his mind!

What would he have said to his brothers? How would he have introduced her? Good morning, how are you guys today and, by the way, this is my wife?

Aside from anything else, what was the point? Why would it matter if she saw him as a respectable banker or went on believing he was a thug with a good wardrobe? Yes, he was…he was fond of her. He enjoyed being with her. But the whole arrangement, this supposed marriage, had the staying power of a dandelion in a windstorm.

Rafe blew out a long, hard breath.

Wow.

All that stuff about not digging yourself further into a hole? He'd come within inches of burying himself so deep that getting out would have required a bulldozer.

Thank God he'd come to his senses.

He'd hail a cab, have it drive by the office, point the place out to Chiara. She could reach whatever conclusion she liked about him and his choice of occupations. Then he'd kiss her because, yeah, the sex was great. But that didn't mean he had to explain himself to her. So he'd kiss her, step out of the cab, go to work, let the cabbie take her back uptown. Once he was in his office, he'd phone Sayers's office. If she was back, fine. If not, who gave a damn if her partner creaked when he walked? Hell, a divorce was just a divorce. Any attorney could handle it.

What a relief, that he could suddenly see things with such clarity. He'd been in a fog the past few days, but the fog had lifted, the sun was out—

"More coffee?" the waiter said.

"No," Rafe replied. Chiara looked at him in surprise. Had he sounded a little brusque? Maybe, but suddenly he was a man in a hurry. How could he have let things get so far out of hand? "I just realized," he told her, "that I have a couple of appointments later this morning."

She nodded. Her face lost a little of its animation but she put her napkin beside her plate and rose to her feet before he could even get to his.

"Or course," she said politely. "You must work today."

"Yes, that's right. So, we'll just drive by my place—"

"It is not necessary, Raffaele."

"No. We'll drive by. Then, uh, then you can go back to the apartment while I—"

His voice trailed away as he peeled off a bunch of bills and dropped them on the table, too much in a rush, now that he'd come to his senses, to waste time waiting for the check.

A taxi pulled to the curb as they stepped into the street. As soon as its passengers got out, Rafe reached for the door and motioned Chiara in. He got in after her, gave the driver the address and sat back. He'd held her hand all the way downtown. Now he sat with his arms folded, saying nothing.

Chiara was silent, too. He glanced at her once. She was pale. It made him feel lousy. The cab pulled to the curb. Rafe looked out the window at the familiar building. It had a cast-iron facade, typical of many of the old buildings in the area, adorned with graceful arches and friezes. He and his brothers had put hundreds of thousands of dollars into restoring it; it had been named a New York City landmark and featured in half a dozen architectural magazines after the work was completed. He was proud of it—they all were—and he realized now he'd been hoping Chiara would like it, hell, that she'd find it charming, but what did that matter? What did her likes, her dislikes, her thoughts about him have to do with anything?

She was not part of his life.

He didn't want her as part of his life.

He wanted out of this mess. This marriage. This ridiculous situation…

"Damn it all," he growled, and when Chiara looked at him, her eyes blurry with tears, Rafe pulled her into his arms.

He kissed her hard. Kissed her deep. She kissed him back the same way, her hands clutching at his shoulders, her tears salty on his lips.

The cabby cleared his throat. "Uh, you want to get out, mister? Or you want to keep going?"

Laughter bubbled from Chiara's lips. Rafe grinned and leaned his forehead against hers.

"See this building?" he said softly.

She looked out and nodded. "It is a beautiful building, Raffaele."

"Yeah, well, it's mine." His voice was gruff with the pride that comes of knowing you've forged a place in the world and that you did it on your own. "Ours. My brothers and me. Dante, Falco and Nicolo. We're in business together. See that brass plaque above the door? Orsini Brothers. We're private bankers. Financial advisors. Brokers. Not one of us followed in our father's footsteps. You understand?" He cupped her face in his hands. "You didn't marry a saint, Chiara, but you didn't marry a crook, either. You married—you married me."

Her smile lit her entire face.

"I am glad," she said softly.

"Yeah," he said gruffly. "Me, too."

Rafe drew her close in his arms, gave the driver his Fifth Avenue address, and took his wife home.

A private elevator was a fine thing.

It meant a man could kiss his wife as soon as the door shut, and by the time the door opened again, he could have her half-undressed. It meant he could lift her in his arms, carry her into his living room, tear off his own clothes and the rest of hers and then make love to her on a white silk sofa with the warmth of the midday sun on them both.

Rafe lingered over Chiara's every curve. No inch of skin went unkissed. He lavished attention on her breasts, sucking the nipples deep into his mouth, then gently spread her thighs and gave her clitoris that same intense care. And while she was sobbing from her first orgasm, he turned her on her belly, kissed the nape of her neck, the sensitive places behind her ears, stroked his hand down her spine, followed that same path with his lips, then cupped his hand between her legs, groaning with pleasure at how her body wept with desire for him, for his penetration.

"Please," his wife whispered, "Raffaele, please…"

He eased her onto her knees. Slid slowly, slowly inside her, his hands cupping her breasts, his breathing harsh as he fought for control. She cried out as her second orgasm took her. Then, only then, Rafe let go, let his control shatter, his emotions soar as the truth filled him with almost unbearable joy.

He was in love with his wife.

After, he opened a bottle of Châteauneuf du Pape and poured glasses of the rich, red wine for them both.

Though it was fall, it was not really cool enough for a fire. Still, he built one in the massive stone fireplace, dumped a couple of fat couch pillows in front of it, wrapped his wife and himself in a black cashmere afghan and sat holding her in his arms as they watched the flames and drank the wine.

The knowledge that he loved her weighed inside him.

He had not wanted Chiara, because his father had ordered him to want her. Now he wanted her with all his heart—but what if she didn't want him?

What if she wanted the quick divorce he'd promised her? Yes, that was before all the rest, the hours in each other's arms, but he wasn't a boy, he was a man. He knew damned well making love wasn't the same as being in love.

She'd lived the life of a fairy-tale Rapunzel, locked away in a castle. She'd been lonely. Innocent. Afraid of being given to a man who was an ogre. He'd come along and changed all that. If he told her he loved her, she might feel grateful enough to say she loved him, too, and gratitude was the last thing he wanted.

What if he wanted her…and she wanted her freedom?

When had things become so complicated?

He looked down at his wife, lying peacefully in his embrace, her head against his naked chest, her eyes half-closed, the dark lashes curved against her cheeks. His heart swelled with love.

Why was he trying to work this like an equation? He had to tell her what he felt, just say, "Chiara, sweetheart, I don't want a divorce. I want you. I need you. I love—"

The intercom buzzed.

Rafe frowned. Who could it be? He certainly wasn't expecting anyone.

Chiara looked at him. "Raffaele? What is that?"

"It's nothing, sweetheart. Just the intercom. It'll stop after a—"

Bzzzz.

Ah-ha. The Saks delivery. Rafe bit back a smile, kissed the top of her head and eased her off his lap. "It's the doorman. Must be a delivery. He's authorized to sign for me but…" He smiled. "I'll be right back."

But it wasn't a delivery. It was, the doorman said, his brothers. Two of them, anyway. They had their own elevator keys and they'd gone straight by him. In fact, they were pressing the call bell right now and considering that Mr. Orsini and his lady guest had, um, had gone upstairs rather hastily.

Rafe slammed down the phone. He could hear the gentle hum of the car starting its descent. Bewildered, he ran his hand through his hair. Two of his brothers. Nicolo and Falco, probably, unless Dante was back in town and—and what in hell did that matter? His brothers were on their way.

And Chiara was naked in his living room.

He ran to her. Took her hand and pulled her to her feet.

"Raffaele?"

"It's okay," he said as they raced up the stairs. "It's just that my brothers are here."

Her gasp almost suctioned all the air out of the stairwell. "*Dio mio!* Your brothers? But we are—"

"Right." He shouldered open the door to his room, almost broke his neck tripping over the dozens of boxes and shopping bags piled on the floor. "I haven't told them anything about— I haven't said a word to anyone about—" He took a breath. "Just get dressed, baby, okay? I'll handle the rest."

"Get dressed in what? This is not my room, it is yours."

"Yeah. Okay, but there's stuff here." He gestured at the packages. "The things you tried on this morning."

"You bought it all?"

"Yes. So just grab something and—"

"But I told you—"

"This is no time to argue!" Rafe hurried into his dressing room, yanked on a pair of jeans, tugged a T-shirt over his head and heard Nick's voice drifting up the stairs.

"Rafe? Are you up there, man?"

Chiara froze. So did he. "Raffaele?" she whispered.

Rafe shook his head, held up his hand. "I'll be right down."

"We'll come up if—"

"No! No, that's okay. I'm on my way."

"Raffaele." His wife was the color of cream. "My clothes... they are all over the living room!"

So were his. Damn. It was face-the-music time. A couple of minutes from now his brothers would know all about Chiara. That he had gone to Italy, that he had married her against his better judgment...

That he loved her.

The timing sucked. They'd know that last part before she did but what the hell, if there was one thing life had taught him, it was that you played the cards you were dealt even if they weren't the ones you'd have preferred.

He took a couple of breaths, then went to the door.

"Raffaele, wait!"

Chiara flew to him, wrapped her arms around his neck, rose on her toes and kissed him. He took her by the wrists and drew her hands to her sides.

"We have to talk."

He sounded more serious than she had ever heard him sound. The look in his eyes was serious, too. A chill swept through her.

"Talk about what, Raffaele?"

She saw his Adam's apple move as he swallowed.

"About us." He lifted his hand as if he might cup her cheek but he didn't. Instead he headed for the stairs.

CHAPTER FOURTEEN

FALCO and Nick were on the terrace, deep in conversation.

Rafe knew they were talking about him. He hadn't gone to the office in over a week. He'd shown up at The Bar and behaved like a crazy man, and today, again, he hadn't shown up at work.

Yeah. Well, okay. The sooner he told them what was going on, the better.

First he'd get rid of that telltale pile of clothes by the sofa. Maybe they hadn't noticed it. He could just grab the stuff, like this, open a door of the built-in sound system and jam it all inside.

Good. Excellent. Now take another deep breath—he was becoming an expert at those—and join them on the terrace.

"Hi," he said brightly.

His brothers turned toward him. They looked grim.

"Great idea, coming out here," he said so cheerfully that he felt like a TV commercial. "The sun, the blue sky—"

"What's going on?" Falco said.

"Going on?"

"You heard him," Nick said. "What's the deal with you?"

"No deal." This was going to be harder than he'd thought. "I just…I just—"

"You haven't come to the office in days."

Falco's tone annoyed him. "What, I need a note from Mama saying why I'm absent?"

"Are you sick?"

"Am I—?" Rafe shook his head. They were worried about him, was all. His expression softened. "No, Nicolo. I'm not."

Nick and Falco exchanged looks. Then Nick reached into the pocket of his suit jacket.

"You left this in the elevator."

He looked at what was in Nick's hand. Hell. Chiara's white cotton panties. He'd forgotten to tell the clerk at Saks to provide his wife with lingerie, but it didn't matter; there was something about all that innocent white cotton that—

"Rafe?"

His head came up. Nick's eyebrows were raised. So were Falco's.

"Yeah," he mumbled, and grabbed the panties from his brother.

"Either you've taken to cross-dressing," Falco said calmly, "or more than the elevator was going down."

Another time Rafe would have laughed. Now he was too busy trying to stuff the panties into his pocket.

"Very amusing."

"Does this have to do with that woman you said was staying here?"

"No. Yes." Rafe glared at Nick. "Hey, man, what is this? An interrogation?"

His brothers looked at each other again.

"It's called brotherly concern," Falco said wryly. "It's what happens when you have a brother who's always behaved a certain way and all of a sudden he begins doing stuff that doesn't make sense."

"Look, I'm fine. Okay? I'm not a kid. And—"

"We're worried about you, man."

Rafe's righteous indignation vanished. They *were* worried. He could see it. Besides, putting this off wouldn't make the telling any easier.

"Yeah." He cleared his throat. "Uh, anybody for a beer?"

"No," Falco growled.

Nick gave him a sharp elbow in the ribs. "Beer sounds good."

Falco glared at him. Nick shrugged his shoulders, raised his eyebrows, did everything he could to transmit the message. Back off. Give him time. Don't crowd him. Okay?

A muscle ticked in Falco's jaw. He was not good at backing off, but after a couple of seconds he nodded.

"Beer's fine."

The brothers marched into the kitchen. Nick almost tripped over a woman's high-heeled boot. He grinned, gave Falco another elbow. Falco looked, grinned, but then the two of them frowned.

The situation might have been funny, but it wasn't. They had come here worried that Rafe was sick. Now they knew whatever was wrong with him had something to do with a woman. A woman for whom he'd lost a week's worth of appointments. A woman he was so hot for he'd undressed her in his elevator. Okay, sure, each of them had done the elevator bit or something close to it, but for one of them to change the very pattern of his life...

Not good. Not good at all.

They took the cold, sweating bottles of beer Rafe took from the Sub-Zero fridge. Opened the bottles, drank, wiped the backs of their hands across their mouths, gave him time, gave him time, gave him—

"I got married."

Nick's beer bottle slipped through his hand. He made a last-minute grab and caught it, but not before half its contents spilled on his shoes. The bottle in Falco's hand tilted, sending a waterfall of beer down the front of his suit.

"You what?"

Rafe raised his shoulders, let them drop.

"I got married. A week ago."

Nick looked at Falco. "He got married."

Falco nodded. "The white underpants."

"He married a woman who wears white—"

"Okay," Rafe said coldly, "that's enough. We're not going to do a comedy riff on my wife's underwear."

Silence. Then Nick cleared his throat. "Fine. What we'd really like to discuss is your wife."

Rafe hesitated. Then he gave another of those shrugs. "Yeah. I just— The thing is, I don't know where to start."

"The beginning almost always works," Falco said quietly.

Rafe nodded. He put his bottle of beer on the counter. His brothers did the same. Then they wandered into the living room, sat down, and Rafe began to talk.

He did as Falco had suggested. Began at the beginning, at the meeting called by their father.

"The old man was at his best," he said grimly. "He didn't just talk about dying, he talked about his soul."

His brothers snorted. "What soul?" Nick said.

"I told him that, but he insisted he'd done something years ago, in Sicily, and now he had to make up for it."

"And what did that have to do with you? For that matter, what does it have to do with your getting married?"

"He said the only way to make up for what he'd done was for me to go to San Giuseppe—"

"Where he was born?"

"Right. He wanted me to go there and marry the daughter of a Sicilian *don*."

"And you told him what he could do with that request," Falco said.

"I did. I told him there was no way in the world I'd do it. Trouble was, I'd already given my word that I'd help him with the immortal soul nonsense." Rafe paused, tried to pretend his brothers weren't looking at him as if he'd lost his mind. "So I said, okay, I'd fly to Sicily but I sure as hell wasn't marrying anybody."

"Then, how'd you end up marrying this—this hoodlum princess?"

"She's not," Rafe said sharply. "She'd not anything like that."

"Sorry," Falco said coolly. "How'd you end up putting a ring on a stranger's finger?"

Rafe laughed. "Actually, I haven't. Not yet. It was—it was a kind of quick thing, you know? See, what happened was…"

Was what?

He thought about how Chiara had waylaid him on the road from Palermo. He thought of the first time he'd kissed her. They didn't need to hear all that. It was too personal, too much a part of what he and his wife had immediately felt for each other and tried to deny. Instead, he told them the only part that counted. The ultimatum handed down by her father, that if Rafe didn't marry her, he would give her to his brute of a *capo*.

Nick swore softly.

Rafe nodded. "I didn't have any choice. I said I'd marry her. And I did."

"You had a choice," Falco said. "You could have walked away."

"Would you?"

Falco gave him a long, assessing look. Then he shrugged. "Okay. You married her. Brought her to the States. And then what? Surely you told her you weren't doing this for real."

"Of course!" Rafe dug his hands into the back pockets of his jeans and began to pace. "Would I marry a woman I didn't choose for myself? Would I marry a woman because Cesare demanded it?"

"Hell, no."

"I made it clear this whole thing was temporary."

"You called your lawyer?"

"Sayers. Sure. I called her right away." Rafe shook his head. "She's been out of the country. She told me to call the guy covering for her."

"And you did."

"No. I didn't." Telling the story was almost as complicated as living it. "I thought I'd wait for Sayers to come home…but things began to change."

"The white-panties-in-the-elevator kind of change," Nick said mildly.

Rafe swung toward him, glaring. "I told you that wasn't up for discussion."

"Maybe it should be. You took the lady to bed. You turned a logistical problem into an emotional one," Falco said coldly.

"No. Yes. Damn it, it's not that simple!"

"Isn't it?"

"I knew what I had to do. Be supportive. Help her get started. Find her a place to live, that kind of thing."

"But?"

"But it was all easier said than done. I felt responsible for her." He paused. "And then, just a little while ago, I got it all sorted out."

"Thank God for small favors," Falco muttered.

"I realized I'd been dancing around, refusing to deal with reality."

Nick rolled his eyes. "Hallelujah."

"And now, I know exactly what I have to do."

"Then do it."

"I was going to. I was going to talk to Chiara, tell her the truth—but you two bozos showed up."

"So, you'll tell her after we leave."

"Of course I will. But, see, it isn't that easy." Rafe turned and paced the room again, then swung toward his brothers. "She knows I wanted out. I was up-front about it right from the start. Hell, I said it every chance I could. I didn't want her misunderstanding our deal. But—"

"But you've slept with her," Falco said bluntly. "And that complicated things."

"Did you hear what I said? It isn't that simple."

"Sure it is. You're worried about how she'll react when you tell her the truth."

"Damn it, of course I'm worried! What if she doesn't react the way I want her to react? What if she says no? What if she says, 'Raffaele, I married you. And now—'"

"And now," a female voice said, "and now, it is over."

The three men swung around. Nick and Falco blinked. The woman who stood halfway down the steps was dressed all in black. Her hair was pulled back in a bun and she was carrying a black overnight bag.

"Chiara." Rafe smiled and started toward her. "Baby. I'm glad you're here. I want you to meet my—"

"I have no interest in meeting these men."

Chiara's tone was frigid. A good thing, because her pulse was racing so fast that the room was spinning. If she sounded cold, sounded controlled, perhaps she would not weep. Perhaps her Raffaele would never know that he had broken her heart.

"Sweetheart. These are my broth—"

"I left the things I wore on the bed, Raffaele. I am sure you can give them to charity."

Rafe blinked. What in hell was happening? Why was his Chiara dressed like this? Why was she looking at him through such cold eyes? He'd just been about to tell his brothers that he was in love with his wife, that he was terrified of telling her he loved her because she might say that was all very nice but she wanted her freedom, just as he'd promised.

"Baby. What's this all about?"

"Do not call me that. And do not treat me as if I were stupid. I assure you, I am not."

Rafe stepped in front of her as she came down the rest of the steps. "Chiara…"

"Please get out of my way."

Her chin rose. Her eyes glittered with unshed tears. She was, once again, his tough yet vulnerable Chiara. And though he didn't understand the reason, she was making it clear she didn't want him.

His eyes narrowed. "What's going on here?"

"The truth. That is what is going on here. You and your brothers have no need to worry. I do not want this marriage. I never did. I want a divorce, as we agreed, and I want it as fast as possible."

"Chiara—"

"I heard everything," she said, and felt her composure slipping. "I heard every word, Raffaele!'

"You heard…? No. Wait a minute. See, you misunderstood. What I was telling my brothers was that… Chiara!" Rafe's voice rose as she swept past him and ran not to the elevator but to the kitchen.

Okay. At least she hadn't left. All he had to do was get rid of Nick and Falco and talk to her, get her to listen…

The kitchen?

"Damn it," Rafe said, "the service entrance!"

Falco grabbed his arm. "Raffaele. Let her go."

"Damn you, let go of me!"

"Rafe," Nick said. "Okay, she got the last laugh. So what? Who cares who made the first move? You wanted her gone. Well, she's gone. Give it a couple of days, a week, you'll forget this little scene ever—"

Rafe wrenched free of Falco's hand.

"You idiots," he roared. "I didn't want her gone! I love her. I'll always love her. She's my *wife*!"

Nicolo and Falco looked at each other as Rafe raced into the kitchen. The service door stood open. Beyond it the lights above the service elevator showed that it had already reached the basement.

"Cazzo!" Falco said.

"You got that right," Nick said.

Then they took off after Rafe, who was already pounding down the fire stairs.

* * *

Chiara burst into the street and stopped in confusion.

She was on an unfamiliar side street. Then she heard the blare of a horn, looked toward the corner and saw that she was a few hundred feet from Fifth Avenue and its taxis and buses. She had no money for either but that was a problem she'd handle when she had to.

She began to run.

What a fool she'd been! This afternoon, lying in Raffaele's arms, her heart filled with love, she'd indulged in a little fantasy, let herself think that what she saw in his eyes was more than desire, that it was love.

"Idiota," she said, and she ran faster.

He didn't love her. Why would he? She'd been an encumbrance that had changed into a sex toy. Very nice for him, but then, sex was what men were all about. She knew that, she had *always* known that. How could she have forgotten?

"Chiara!"

It was his voice. Her Raffaele was running after her, but he wasn't "her" Raffaele anymore, he wasn't "her" anything.

"Chiara! Wait!"

She had the advantage of a head start but his legs were longer. He would catch her; it was just a matter of time. She was on Fifth Avenue now. There were taxis whizzing by and she ran into the street, waving her hand wildly, but she might as well have been invisible. The cabs kept going.

"Chiara!"

She looked back. *Dio!* His brothers were just behind him. She had to do something!

Chiara dove into the snarl of traffic, ignoring the blasting horns, the squeal of brakes. She heard Raffaele shout after her again, and then, mercifully, she was in the park.

Running was easier here.

No cars. No buses. Pedestrians, but she raced past them. She was a good runner. She had strong legs from years of tromping the hills outside San Giuseppe. If she could just put some real distance between her and—

Raffaele grabbed her from behind.

She yelped, his legs tangled with hers and they went down in a heap. She tried to roll away but he had her on her back, his hips straddling hers, his hands clasping her fists. Now his brothers were there, too, disheveled and panting and looking down at her with anger in their eyes.

"Let me go!" she demanded.

Raffaele stood up and dragged her to her feet.

"I said, let—me—go!"

"Never," he growled, and the hard look in his face made her shudder.

"I will scream—"

"No. You won't," he said, and covered her mouth with his.

Chiara beat her fists against her husband's powerful shoulders. She nipped at his lip. And then, even though it was disgraceful to do it, she gave herself up to this one last kiss.

And then another. And another...

"Uh, Rafe? You need us, buddy?"

Rafe didn't answer. Instead he framed his Chiara's face with his hands, changed the angle of the kiss and felt his heart take a tentative leap when she gave one of those little moans.

"He doesn't need us," Falco said.

"No," Nick said, laughing, "he doesn't."

They wished him luck, said they'd really like to meet the little woman if the two of them ever came up for air—

And then they were gone.

"I love you," Rafe whispered against his wife's lips.

"No," she said brokenly, "you do not. I heard every word you said."

"You couldn't have, because I never had the chance to say the only words that mattered." Rafe held her away from him, just far enough so he could see her beloved face. "I love you, Chiara."

"But you said you didn't know how to tell me you wanted to end our marriage. You said—"

"I said I didn't know how to tell you I loved you. At least, that was what I was going to say." Rafe smiled. "You just didn't give me the chance."

"Oh, Raffaele. Be sure. Please, be sure…because I love you. I adore you. I—"

Rafe kissed her again. This was New York, and people were detouring around them, but even some of those hardened New Yorkers smiled.

"I love you," Rafe said. "I don't ever want to lose you. I want you to be my wife, forever." He swallowed hard. "That is, if you'll have me."

Chiara laughed, even though tears still shone in her eyes.

"I will have you for all the rest of our lives, my Raffaele," she said, and her husband swept her into his arms. Those hardened New Yorkers whistled and cheered, and Raffaele Orsini carried home his beautiful, tempestuous bride.

Not every man got to marry the same woman twice.

Rafe did.

When he broke the news of his marriage to his family, everyone went a little crazy.

His mother wept. His sisters, too. Falco and Nicolo, who, of course, already knew all about it, rolled their eyes at the unseemly commotion. Dante, who'd been clued in on his return from only he knew where, shrugged and flashed a cryptic smile.

Cesare just looked smug and said he had known it would happen. Rafe decided to leave it at that. His father had meddled in his life, not to benefit his son but to salve his own conscience. That things had worked out changed nothing.

"A wedding," his mother said, drying her eyes on her apron. "We must have a *real* wedding."

Rafe said they'd already had one, but his sisters took up the chant, and when he looked at his wife, he saw that her eyes were shining at the very idea. So he did what men always do in such situations.

He gave in.

The ceremony took place in the little neighborhood church Sofia Orsini had always loved. Either the Feds and the cops were kind that day or they simply kept a low profile, but there wasn't an agent or a police officer in sight.

Chiara wore a gown of antique French lace over silk. Tiny pink silk rosebuds adorned the train, and Sofia's wedding veil fell gracefully from a tiara of pink roses in her dark hair.

"Cesare and I eloped," Sofia said shyly, "but my mama knew our plan and gave me her veil. I would be honored if you wore it."

Chiara wept a little, kissed her mother-in-law and said it was she who would be honored.

Anna and Isabella were her maids of honor. Nick, Falco and Dante were Rafe's best men. It made for a crowd at the altar. The men grinned, the women giggled, but everyone grew solemn once the simple ceremony began.

"My Chiara," Rafe whispered when it was time to lift his bride's veil and kiss her.

She smiled into his eyes. "My Raffaele," she said softly, and kissed him with all the love in her heart.

Afterward, at the reception, Isabella and Anna happily agreed it had all been like a fairy tale.

There were no fairy tales, Dante thought grimly, not for him, anyway.... But he wisely decided to keep that bit of information to himself.

* * * * *

FALCO: THE
DARK GUARDIAN

SANDRA MARTON

CHAPTER ONE

THERE were those who said that Falco Orsini was too rich, too good-looking, too arrogant for his own good.

Falco would have agreed that he was rich, that he was probably arrogant, and if you judged his looks by the seemingly endless stream of beautiful women who moved in and out of his bed, well, he'd have had to admit that perhaps he had something going for him that women liked.

There were also those who called him heartless. He would not have agreed with that.

He was not heartless. He was honest. Why let a competitor buy an elite investment bank if he could scoop it up instead? Why let a competitor get the edge in a business deal if he could get it first? Why go on pretending interest in a woman when he no longer felt any?

It wasn't as if he was a man who ever made promises he had no intention of keeping.

Honest, not heartless. And in the prime of life.

Falco was, like his three brothers, tall. Six foot three. Hard of face, hard of body. Buff, women said. That was true but it had nothing to do with vanity. He was fit the way a man must be when he knows keeping himself that way could mean the difference between life and death.

Not that he lived that kind of existence anymore.

Not often, at any rate.

Not that he talked about.

At thirty-two, Falco had already led what many would consider an interesting life.

At eighteen, he'd grabbed his backpack and thumbed his way around the world. At nineteen, he'd joined the army. At twenty, he became a Special Forces warrior. Someplace along the way, he picked up a bunch of disparate university credits, a skill at high-stakes gambling and, eventually, a passion for high-stakes investing.

He lived by his own rules. He always had. The opinions of others didn't concern him. He believed in honor, duty and integrity. Men who'd served with him, men who dealt with him, didn't always like him—he was too removed, some said—but they respected him almost as much as women coveted him.

Or hated him.

It didn't matter.

Family was everything.

He loved his brothers the same way they loved him, with a ferocity that made the four of them as formidable in everything as they were in business. He would have given his life for his sisters, who would happily have returned the favor. He adored his mother, who worshipped all her sons as perhaps only Italian mothers can.

His father…

Who gave a damn about him?

Falco, like his brothers, had written off Cesare Orsini years ago. As far as his wife and daughters were concerned, Cesare owned a carting company, a construction firm and some of New York City's priciest real estate.

His sons knew the truth.

Their father was the head of something he referred to only as La Famigilia.

He was, in other words, the same as the thugs who had originated in Sicily in the last half of the nineteenth century. Nothing could change that, not the Brioni suits, not the enormous mansion in what had once been Manhattan's Little Italy and was now Greenwich Village. But, for their mother's sake, there were times Falco and his brothers put that aside and pretended the Orsinis were just another big, happy Sicilian-American family.

Today, for instance. On this bright, late autumn afternoon, Dante had taken a wife.

Falco still had trouble getting his head around that.

First Rafe. Now Dante. Two brothers with wives. And, Dante, it turned out, wasn't just a husband, he was also a father.

Nicolo and Falco had spent the day smiling, kissing their new sisters-in-law and grinning at Dante and Rafe. They'd done their best not to feel like jerks cooing at their infant nephew—not that it was difficult because the kid was clearly the world's cutest, most intelligent baby. They'd danced with their sisters and shut their ears to Anna's and Isabella's not-so-subtle hints that they had friends who'd make them perfect wives.

By late afternoon, they were more than ready to slip away and toast their bachelorhood with a few well-earned cold beers at a place the four brothers owned. Not their investment firm. This place was called, simply enough, The Bar.

Cesare headed them off before they could get to the door. He wanted to talk to them, he said.

Not again, Falco had thought wearily. One look at Nick's face and he knew his brother was thinking the same thing. For months now, the Don had been giving his "after I'm dead" speech. The combination to his safe. The names of his attorney and his accountant. The location of important papers. Stuff none of the brothers cared about; none of them wanted a penny of their father's money.

Falco's initial instinct was to ignore Cesare and keep walking.

Instead, he and Nick looked at each other. Maybe the long day had put them in a mellow mood. Maybe it was the champagne. What the hell, Nick's expression said, and Falco replied with a sigh that clearly said, Yeah, why not.

Their father had insisted on talking to them separately. Felipe, Cesare's capo, jerked his head, indicating Falco should go first.

Falco gave a moment's thought to grabbing the capo by his skinny neck, hoisting him to his toes and telling him what a slimy bastard he was to have spent his life as the Don's guard dog, but the family celebration was still going strong in the conservatory at the rear of the house.

So he smiled instead, the kind of smile a man like the capo would surely understand, moved past him and entered Cesare's study. Felipe shut the door behind him....

And Falco found himself in an endurance contest.

His father, seated at his desk, the heavy drapes behind him drawn so that the big room with its oversized furniture seemed even more gloomy than usual, looked up, nodded, waved a manicured hand toward a chair—a gesture Falco ignored—and went back to leafing through the contents of a manila folder.

According to the antique mahogany clock that hung on a wall, all but lost among photos of politicians, old-country ancestors and age-yellowed religious paintings, four minutes ticked away.

Falco stood perfectly still, feet slightly apart, arms folded, dark eyes locked on the clock. The minute hand ticked to yet another marker, the hour hand made its barely perceptible jump. Falco unfolded his arms, turned his back on his father and went to the door.

"Where are you going?"

Falco didn't bother turning around. "*Ciao,* Father. As always, it's been a pleasure."

The chair creaked. Falco knew the Don was pushing back from his desk.

"We have not yet had our talk."

"Our talk? You were the one who requested this meeting." Falco swung toward his father. "If you have something to say, say it—but I assure you, I recall your touching words the last time I saw you. Perhaps you don't remember my response so let me remind you of it. I don't give a damn about your safe, your documents, your business interests—"

"Then you are a fool," the Don said mildly. "Those things are worth a fortune."

A cool smile lifted the corners of Falco's mouth. "So am I, in case you hadn't noticed." His smile vanished. "Even if I weren't, I wouldn't touch anything of yours. You should know that by now."

"Such drama, my son."

"*Questa verità*, Father. Such truth, you mean."

Cesare sighed. "All right. You've made your speech."

"And you've made yours. Goodbye, Father. I'll tell Nicolo to—"

"What were you doing in Athens last month?"

Falco stood absolutely still. "What?"

"It's a simple question. You were in Athens. Why?"

The look Falco gave the older man would have made anyone else take a hurried step back.

"What in hell kind of question is that?"

Cesare shrugged. "A simple one. I asked you—"

"I know what you asked." Falco's eyes narrowed. "Did you have me followed?"

"Nothing so devious." Cesare moved his chair forward

and reached for an elaborately carved wooden box. "Pure Havanas," he said, opening the box to reveal a dozen fat cigars. "They cost the earth. Have one."

"Explain yourself," Falco said sharply, without a glance at the box. "How do you know where I was?"

Another shrug. "I have friends everywhere. Surely you know that by now."

"Then you also know that I was in Athens on business for Orsini Brothers Investments." Falco smiled again, even more coldly. "Perhaps you've heard of us, Father. A privately held company started without any help from you."

Cesare bit the tip off the cigar he'd chosen, turned his head and spat the piece into a wastebasket.

"Even in these bad economic times, we've made our investors wealthy. And we've done it honestly, a concept you couldn't possibly understand."

"You added a private bank to your stable when you were in Athens," Cesare said. "Nicely done."

"Your compliments mean nothing to me."

"But banking was not all you did there," the Don said softly. He looked up; his eyes met Falco's. "My sources tell me that during that same few days, a child—a boy of twelve— held for ransom by insurgents in the northern mountains of Turkey, was somehow miraculously returned to his fam—"

Falco was around the desk in a heartbeat. His hand closed on his father's shirt; he yanked him roughly to his feet.

"What is this?" he snarled.

"Take your hands off me!"

"Not until I get answers. No one followed me. No one. I don't know where you got all this crap but—"

"I was not foolish enough to think anyone could follow you and live to talk about it. Let go of my shirt and perhaps I'll give you an answer."

Falco could feel his heart racing. He knew damned well no one had followed him; he was far too good to let that happen. And, yes, though he would never admit it, there had been more to his trip to Greece than the acquisition of a bank. There were times his old skills came in handy but he kept that part of his life private.

Falco glared at his father. And silently cursed himself for being a fool.

He had not let Cesare get to him in years. Fifteen years, to be exact, on a night one of his father's henchmen had caught him sneaking back into the heavily guarded house at two in the morning.

The Don had been furious, not at where his seventeen-year-old-son might have been, not at how he'd defeated the alarm system, but at how he'd gotten by the silent men who kept watch from the shadows outside the front door and deep within the walled garden.

Falco had refused to explain. He'd done more than that. He'd smirked as only a badass teenage boy could.

Cesare had backhanded him, hard, across the face.

It was the first time his father had hit him, which was, when he'd had time to think about it, a surprise. Not the blow; the surprise was that it had not happened before. There'd always been a hint of violence in the air between father and son; it had grown stronger when Falco reached adolescence.

That night, it had finally erupted.

Falco had stood still under the first blow. The second rocked him back on his heels. The third bloodied his mouth, and when Cesare raised his hand again, Falco grabbed his wrist and twisted the Don's arm high behind his back. Cesare was strong, but at seventeen, Falco was already stronger.

He was also fueled by years of hatred.

"Touch me again," he'd said in a whisper, "and I swear, I'll kill you."

His father's expression had undergone a subtle change. Not fear. Not anger. Something else. Something swift and furtive that should not have been in the eyes of a powerful man who'd just lost a battle, physically as well as figuratively.

Falco's face was badly bruised the next day. His mother questioned it, as did his sisters. He said he'd fallen in the shower. The lie worked but Nicolo, Raffaele and Dante had not been so easy to fool.

"Must have been a pretty awkward tumble," Rafe had said, "to blacken your eye as well as give you a swollen lip."

Yeah, Falco had said calmly, it was.

He never told anyone the truth. Had the beating been too humiliating to talk about? Was it his shock at the intensity of the quicksilver flash of rage that had almost overcome him?

Eventually, he understood.

Power had changed hands that night. It had gone from Cesare to him…and then back to Cesare. What he'd seen in his father's eyes had been the knowledge that despite Falco's vicious threat, he, Cesare, had actually won the battle because Falco had let emotion overtake him. He had lost control of his emotions and somehow, he had no idea how or why, that loss of control gave the other person power.

And now, here he was, fifteen long years later, losing control all over again.

Carefully, he unfisted his hand, let go of Cesare's starched white shirt. Cesare fell back into his chair, his jowly face red with anger.

"If you were not my son…"

"I'm not your son in any way that matters. It takes more than sperm to make a man a father."

A muscle knotted in the Don's jaw. "Are you now a philosopher? Trust me, Falco, in many ways, you are more my son than your brothers."

"What's that supposed to mean?"

"It means that what you so self-righteously claim to hate in me is what is also inside you. The lure of absolute power. The need to control." Cesare's eyes narrowed. "The willingness to shed blood when you know it must be shed."

"Damn you, old man!" Falco leaned over the desk and brought his angry face within inches of the older man's. "I am nothing like you, do you hear? Nothing! If I were, God, if I were…"

He shuddered, drew back, stood straight. What was he doing, letting his father draw him deeper into this quagmire?

"Is this what you wanted to talk about? To tell me you've come up with absolution for yourself by pretending your genes are my destiny? Well, it won't work. I am not you. And this so-called discussion is at an—"

Cesare took something from the folder on his desk and pushed it toward Falco. It appeared to be a glossy page, an advertisement, torn from a magazine.

"Do you know this woman?"

Falco barely spared the picture a glance.

"I know a lot of women," he said coldly. "Surely your spies have told you that."

"Indulge me. Look at her."

What the hell did it matter? Falco picked up the photo. It was an ad for something expensive. Perfume, jewelry, clothing—it was hard to tell.

The focus of the page, though, was clear enough.

It was the woman.

She was seated crossways in an armchair, one long leg on the floor, the other draped over the chair's arm, a shoe with the kind of heel that should have been declared lethal dangling from her toes. She wore lace. Scarlet lace. A teddy. A chemise. He had no idea which it was, only that it showed almost as much cleavage as leg.

A spectacular body. An equally spectacular face. Oval. Delicate. The essence of femininity. High cheekbones, eyes as amber as a cat's, lashes long and thick, the same ebony color as her long, straight hair.

She was smiling at the camera. At the viewer.

At him.

It was, he understood, a deliberate illusion. A damned effective one. Her smile, the tilt of her head, even her posture, dared a man to want her. To be foolish enough to think he could have her. It was a smile that offered as much sexual pleasure as a man could want in a lifetime.

Something hot and dangerous rolled through Falco's belly.

"Well? Do you recognize her?"

He looked up. Cesare's eyes locked on his. Falco tossed the photo on the desk.

"I told you I didn't. Okay? Are we done here?"

"Her name is Elle. Elle Bissette. She was a model. Now she is an actress."

"Good for her."

Cesare took something else from the folder. Another ad? He held it toward Falco, but Falco didn't move.

"What is this? You expect me to spend the next hour playing Name the Celebrity?"

"*Per favore*, Falco. I ask you, please. Look at the photo."

Falco's eyebrows rose. Please? In Italian and in English. He had never heard his father use those words or anything close to them. What the hell, he thought, and reached for the photo.

Bile rose in his throat.

It was the same ad but someone had used a red pen to *X* out her eyes. To trace a crude line of stitches across her lips.

To draw a heavy line across her throat and dab red dots from her throat to her breasts. To circle her breasts in the same bright, vicious crimson.

"Miss Bissette received it in the mail."

"What did the cops say?"

"Nothing. She refuses to contact them."

"She's a fool," Falco said bluntly, "if she won't go to the authorities."

"The parents of the Turkish boy went to you, not the authorities. They feared seeking official help."

"This is America."

"Fear is fear, Falco, no matter where one lives. She is afraid or perhaps she does not trust the police. Whatever the reason, she refuses to contact them." Cesare paused. "Miss Bissette is making a film in Hollywood. The producer is, shall we say, an old friend."

"Ah. I get it now. Your pal's worried about his investment."

"It concerns him, yes. And he needs my help."

"Send him some of your blood money."

"Not my financial help. He needs my help to safeguard Miss Bissette."

"I'm sure your goons will love L.A."

Cesare chuckled. "Can you see my men in Beverly Hills?"

Falco almost laughed. He had to admit, the idea was amusing—and, suddenly, it all came together. The talk of what had happened in Turkey, this conversation about Elle Bissette...

"Okay."

"Okay?"

Falco nodded. "I know some guys who do bodyguard work for celebrities. I'll call around, put you in touch—"

"I am already in touch," Cesare said gently. "With you."

"Me?" This time, Falco did laugh. "I'm an investor, Father, not a bodyguard."

"You did not say that to the people you helped in Turkey."

"That was different. They turned to me and I did what I had to do."

"As I am turning to you, *mio figlio*, and asking that you do what must be done."

Falco's face hardened. "You want some names and phone numbers, fine. Otherwise, I'm out of here."

Cesare didn't answer. Falco snorted, turned on his heel, headed for the door again, changed his mind and decided to exit through the French doors hidden by the heavy drapes. The mood he was in, the last thing he wanted was to risk running in to his mother or his sisters.

"Wait." His father hurried after him. "Take the folder. Everything you need is in it."

Falco grabbed the folder. It was easier than arguing.

By the time he'd taxied to his mid-sixties town house, he'd come up with the names of four men who could do this job and do it well. Once home, he poured a brandy, took the folder and his cell phone and headed outside to his walled garden. It was close to sunset; the air was chill but he liked it out here, with the noise of Manhattan shut away.

There was nothing of much use in the folder. Stuff about the movie; a letter from the producer to Cesare.

And the pictures. The one with her in lace. The marked-up duplicate. And another that his father had not shown him, a photo of Bissette standing on a beach, looking over her shoulder at the camera. No lace. No stiletto heels. She was dressed in a T-shirt and shorts.

Falco put the three pictures on the top of a glass table and looked from one to the other.

The one of her sexy and mysterious was a turn-on if you liked that kind of thing. He didn't. Yeah, he liked crimson and lace and stiletto heels well enough; was there a man who didn't? But the pose was blatantly phony. The smile was false. The woman looking at the camera had no substance. She might have been looking at a million guys instead of him.

The mutilated picture made his gut knot. It was an outright threat, crude but effective.

The third photo was the one that caught him. It was un-selfconscious. Unposed. A simple shot of a beautiful woman walking on a beach, needing no artifice to make her look beautiful.

But there was more to it than that.

She'd sensed someone was watching her. He'd been the watcher often enough in what he thought of as his former life to know how subjects looked when they suspected the unwelcome presence of an observer. He could see it in her eyes. In the angle of her jaw. In the way she held her hair back from her face. Wariness. Fear. Distress.

And more.

Determination. Defiance. An attitude that, despite everything, said, Hey, pal, don't screw with me.

"Goddammit," Falco growled.

Then he grabbed his cell phone and arranged for a chartered plane to fly him to the West Coast first thing in the morning.

CHAPTER TWO

ELLE HAD spent most of the morning in bed with a stranger.

The stranger was tall and good-looking and maybe he was a good kisser. She didn't really know.

The thing was, she didn't like kissing. She knew less about it than, she figured, 98 percent of the female population of the United States over the age of sixteen, but that didn't mean she didn't know how to make kissing seem fantastic, especially with a guy who looked like this.

Kissing, the same as walking and talking, laughing and crying and all the other things an actress did, was part of the job. She had to remember that. This was a movie. Kissing the man in whose arms she lay was, yes, part of the job.

No question that women everywhere would change places with her in a heartbeat. Fans, other actresses... Chad Scott was world-famous. He was box office gold. And, for this scene, at least, he was all hers.

Elle knew how lucky she was. She hated herself for not being able to get into character this morning. Love scenes were always tough but today...

Today, things were not going well at all.

It wasn't her co-star's fault. She'd worried he might be all walking, talking ego, but Chad had turned out to be a nice guy.

He'd shaken her hand when they were introduced days ago, apologized for arriving after everyone else. She knew he hadn't had to do that. They'd spent five minutes in small talk. Then they'd run their lines. Finally, they'd shot their first scene, which was actually a middle scene in the film. Movie scenes were rarely shot sequentially.

Today, they were shooting their first love scene. It was, she knew, pivotal to the story.

The set was simple, just a seemingly haphazard sprawl of blankets spread over the sand near a big Joshua cactus. She was wearing a strapless slip; the camera would only catch her head, her arms and her bare shoulders, suggesting that she was naked. Chad was shirtless and wearing jeans. They were surrounded by a mile of electrical cable, reflectors and boom mikes, and the million and one people it took to film even the simplest scene. Antonio Farinelli, as hot a director as existed, had told the two of them he hoped to do the scene in one take.

So far, there'd been four.

A sudden gust of wind had ruined the first shot but the three others... Her fault, every one. She'd twice blown her lines; the third time she'd looked over Chad's shoulder instead of into his eyes.

Farinelli sounded angrier each time he yelled, "Cut."

Elle sat up, waiting while the director spoke with the lighting guy. Her co-star sat up, too, and stretched. Chad had been really good about all the delays. He'd obviously sensed she was having a problem and he'd made little jokes at his own expense. She knew they were meant to put her at ease. *Heck*, he said, *I'm pretty sure I shaved this morning. And don't feel bad, kid, my wife once told me the ceiling needed paint at a moment just like this.*

Everyone who heard him laughed because he was not just a hot property, he was a hot guy. Elle laughed, too. At least, she did her best to fake it. She was an actress. Illusion was everything.

In real life, she could never have lain in a man's arms and gazed into his eyes as he brought his mouth to hers, but then, reality was a bitch.

And reality was the phone call that had awakened her at three o'clock that morning.

"Darling girl," the low male voice had whispered, "did you get the picture? Did you get my note?" A low, terrible laugh. "You're waiting for me, aren't you, sugar?"

Her heart had slammed into her throat. She'd thrown the telephone on the floor as if it were a scorpion that had crept in under the motel room door. Then she'd run to the bathroom and vomited.

Now, all she could hear was that voice in her head. All she could see was that mutilated ad from the magazine, the note nobody knew about. Bad enough Farinelli knew about the ad. If only he hadn't walked into her on-set trailer just as she'd opened the innocent-looking white envelope she'd found propped against the mirror of her makeup table.

"Elle," Farinelli had said briskly, "about tomorrow's schedule…"

But she wasn't listening. The blood had drained from her head. She'd been as close to fainting as she'd ever been in her life.

"Elle?" Farinelli had said, and he'd plucked the envelope and what she'd taken out of it from her hand.

"Madre di Dio," he'd said, his words harsh with fury. "Where did this come from?"

She had no idea. Once she got her breath back, she told him that. A crazy person must have sent it. She'd had nasty little notes before, especially after the Bon Soir lingerie ads, but this marked-up photo…

Still, anything was possible. Her face was out there. In those two-year-old ads and now in stuff the publicity people for *Dangerous Games* had started planting. It was nothing, she and Farinelli finally agreed, but if she received any more things like this, she was to tell him and they'd go to the police.

Elle had agreed. She'd told herself the photo was a one-shot. Whoever had sent it would surely not contact her again.

Wrong. A few days later, a note arrived in her mail. Its message was horrible. Filthy. Graphic. And it was signed. The signature stunned her but it had to be a hoax. She told herself she would not let it upset her. She was an actress, she could pull it off.

Evidently, she was not as good an actress as she thought.

Farinelli had taken to asking her if she was okay and though she always said yes, certainly, she was fine, she knew he didn't believe it. He'd proved it two days ago when he stopped by her trailer during a break. Was she ill? No, she assured him. Was she upset about her part? No, no, she loved her part. Farinelli had nodded. Then he could only assume that the photo he had seen was still upsetting her because she was most assuredly not herself.

Elle had tried telling him he was wrong. He silenced her with an imperious wave of one chubby hand. He had given the situation much thought. The photo had been *of* her but it had been meant for him. She had been in, what, two, three films? She was almost unknown. He, however, was famous. He was taking a big chance, starring her in *Dangerous Games*. Obviously, someone understood that and wished to ruin his film.

But, by God, he would not permit it. He had millions of his own money tied up in this project and he was not going to let someone destroy him. He was going to contact the police and let them deal with the problem.

Elle couldn't let that happen. The police would poke and pry, ask endless questions, snoop into her past and find that the story of her life that she'd invented had nothing to do with reality.

So she'd resorted to high drama. She pleaded. She wept. She became a *diva*. A risky gambit but she had not come as far as she had by playing things safe. No guts, no glory. Trite and clichéd, maybe, but true. Besides, really, what did she have to lose? A police investigation would destroy the burgeoning career she had worked so hard for. She was twenty-seven, a little long in the tooth to go back to modeling....

More to the point, she could not face her ugly, ugly past all over again.

In the end, Farinelli had thrown up his hands. *"Basta,"* he'd said. "Enough! No police."

A disaster avoided. She'd forced herself to forget the ad, the note, to keep focused on the movie. And then that phone call at three this morning...

"Okay, people" Farinelli said. "Let's try it again."

Elle lay back. Chad leaned over her, waiting for the camera to roll. She felt his breath on her face....

"Hey," her co-star said softly. "You okay?"

"I'm fine," she said, with no conviction at all.

Chad sat up and looked at Farinelli. "Tony? How 'bout we break for lunch?"

The director sighed. "Why not? Okay, people. Lunch. Half an hour."

Chad stood up, held out his hand and helped Elle to her feet. One of Farinelli's gofers rushed over and held out an oversized white terrycloth robe. Elle snugged into it and Chad squeezed her shoulder.

"Sun's a killer, kid," he said softly. "Some shade, some water and you'll be fine."

Her smile was real this time. He truly was a nice man, a rare species as far as she was concerned.

"Thank you," she said, and she knotted the belt of the robe, slid into the rubber thongs the gofer dropped at her feet and made her way quickly to the half-dozen Airstream trailers clustered like Conestoga wagons awaiting an Indian attack a couple of hundred yards away.

Chad Scott was right, she thought as she went up the two steps to the door of her trailer. Cool air, cool water, some time alone and she'd be fine.

"Absolutely fine," she said as the door swung shut...

A man was standing against the wall just beyond the closed door. Tall. Dark-haired. Wraparound sunglasses. Her brain took quick inventory...and then her heart leaped like a startled cat and she opened her mouth to scream.

But the man was fast. He was on her, turning the locking bolt, one hand over her mouth before the scream erupted. He gripped her by the shoulder with his free hand, spun her around and hauled her back against him.

She could feel every hard inch of his leanly muscled body.

"Screaming isn't going to help," he said sharply.

A waste of time.

Falco could damned near feel the scream struggling to burst from her lips.

To say this wasn't exactly the reception he'd expected was an understatement. He'd spoken with the director, Farinelli, on his cell from the plane. He'd told him when he'd be arriving, more or less, and the director had said that was fine, it gave him lots of time to brief the Bissette woman and that it would be best if he, Falco, met with her in private because she'd probably want his presence on the set kept quiet, so—

"Hey!"

She had kicked him. Useless, as kicks went, because she

was kicking backward and wearing ugly rubber beach thongs, but it told him what he needed to know about whether or not she'd calmed down.

Okay. He'd try again.

"Ms. Bissette. I'm sorry if I startled you but—"

She grunted. Struggled. Her backside dug into his groin. It was a small, rounded backside and under different circumstances, he'd have enjoyed the feel of it—but not when the backside might as well have belonged to a wildcat.

"Dammit," Falco said. He swung her toward him, one hand still clasping her shoulder, the other still clamped over her mouth. "Pay attention, okay? I. Am. Not. Going. To. Hurt. You."

Mistake.

She slugged him. Two quick blows, one to the chest, one to the jaw. He was damned if he knew what to do with her now. He had only two hands and she was already keeping both of them occupied.

"Okay," he said grimly. "You want to play rough? That's fine."

He shoved her, hard. She stumbled back against the door and he went with her, pinned her there with his body. Her hands were trapped against his chest; her legs blocked by his. She was tall but he was a lot taller; her head was tilted back so that she was staring up at him with eyes even more tawny than they'd seemed in the defaced magazine ad.

Eyes filled with terror. And with what he'd seen in the candid photo that had brought him out here.

Defiance.

Okay. Instead of saying to hell with this and walking out the door, he'd try and get through to her one last time.

"Ms. Bissette. My name is Falco Orsini."

Nothing. Still the hot blend of fear and defiance shining in those eyes.

"I'm here to help you."

Fear, defiance and now disbelief.

"Trust me, lady. This isn't my idea of a good time, either. I'm here as a favor. And if you don't calm down and talk to me, I'm gonna walk straight out that door and leave you to handle this thing on your own."

She blinked and he saw confusion sweep across her face. Yeah, but she couldn't be any more confused than he was, unless—unless—

Oh, hell.

"Didn't Farinelli tell you I was coming?"

Another blink. A delicate vertical furrow appeared between her dark eyebrows.

"He said he would. He said you'd want to keep this private and that I should wait for you here, in your trailer."

Her eyes widened. "What?"

It sounded more like "wmf" because his hand was over her lips but there was no mistaking her surprise. Everything was starting to come together. She, a woman who'd been sent a picture defaced by a madman, walks into her trailer and finds a stranger waiting for her….

Merda! That fool, Antonio Farinelli, had never told her he was coming.

"Okay," Falco said, "here's the deal. Somebody sent you a picture." She began to struggle again. He shook his head. "Just listen. You got a picture. A bad one. Your boss wanted to call the cops. You refused. Am I right?"

He could see he was. So far, so good.

"So your boss contacted someone I—someone I know, and that someone contacted me. I agreed to talk to you, check things out, see if there were a way to deal with this so it all goes away quietly. No muss, no fuss. Yes?"

She exhaled sharply. He felt the warmth of her breath flow

over his hand, just as he could feel a fraction of the tension ease from her body. Her eyes were still locked to his, bright and distrustful, but now, at least, curious.

"My name," Falco said, "is Falco Orsini. I, ah, I sometimes do what you might call security consulting. That's why I'm here. I know about the picture, I know that you're worried about it, I know you don't want the authorities involved. I'm here to discuss the situation and offer some advice. That's the only reason I'm here—and the only reason I scared you is because your boss was too stupid to tell you about me." He tried for what he hoped was a reassuring smile. "I'm going to take my hand off your mouth. And maybe we can have that talk. Does that work for you?"

She blinked. Nodded. Now she was wary—but she was ready to listen.

He took his hand from her mouth.

She didn't scream.

Instead, the tip of her tongue came out and slid lightly over her bottom lip. Falco watched its progress. His gaze fell lower, to the rise of her breasts in the vee of her bulky terrycloth robe. He knew what she had under it; he'd watched the scene Farinelli had been filming at a safe distance before he'd slipped into the trailer. What she had on was a slip. Plain. Unadorned. Not like what she'd worn in that ad.

This slip was plain. Sexless.

Not that she was.

She was gorgeous. That hair. Those eyes. That mouth. Still, even with theatrical makeup on, there was another quality to her that he had not seen in the ad. A kind of innocence.

Which was, of course, ridiculous.

She was an actress. She played to the camera. To men. She could be whatever a particular part called for. Maybe she'd decided this part called for wide-eyed and innocent. Not that he gave a damn. He was only interested in her problem, and every problem had a solution.

"Antonio shouldn't have hired you," she said.

"He didn't."

"But you said—"

"I'm doing someone a favor."

"Whatever you're doing, I don't want you here."

Her voice was husky. Shaken.

"Listen," Falco said, "if you want to sit down—"

"I can handle this myself."

"The hell you can," he said bluntly.

Her chin rose. "You don't know what I can and can't do."

"I saw that picture. You can't handle that. No woman can. And there'll be more."

Her gaze sharpened. "What's that supposed to mean?"

Her answer, her body language, gave her away. Falco took off his sunglasses.

"There's been more already," he said grimly. "Hasn't there?"

"No," she said, but far too quickly.

She turned her head away; he reached out, cupped her chin, gave her no choice but to meet his eyes.

"What was it? Another picture? A letter? A phone call?"

No answer, which was answer enough. Her mouth trembled; Falco fought back the illogical desire to take her in his arms and comfort her. It was an uncharacteristic reaction for him in this kind of situation and he didn't like it.

"Have you ever seen a cat play with a mouse?" he said. "He'll keep things going until he tires of the game."

Elle shuddered. "You mean, until he does the things he drew on the picture."

"Yes," he said bluntly.

She nodded. And said, in a low voice, "And you think you can stop him?"

Falco's lips curved in what nobody would ever call a smile. "I know I can."

She stared up at him. "You can keep him from—from doing anything to me?"

"Yes."

"A man of few words," she said, with a little laugh. "How can you be so sure?"

"It's what I do. What I used to do," he said evenly. "I can find him and keep him from hurting you."

Elle stared at this stranger with eyes so dark they resembled obsidian. Why should she believe him? The answer was agonizingly simple.

Because, otherwise, she might not have a life.

Perhaps this man, this Falco Orsini, really could help her.

"If I agreed to let you get involved," she said slowly, "you won't—you won't contact the police?"

"No."

"Because, uh, because the publicity," she said, scrambling for a reason he'd accept, "because the publicity—"

"I told you. I'll handle this alone. No cops."

"What would you do, if I hired you?"

"You can't hire me. Remember what I said? I'm here as a favor. As for what I'll do… Leave that to me."

"The thing is…I wouldn't want anyone to know I had a-a bodyguard. There'd be talk. And questions. And questions are the last thing I want."

"I already figured that."

"So, how would we do this, then? I mean, how could you watch over me, go after whoever this is, do whatever you need to do without people knowing?"

Falco had considered that dilemma during the six-hour

flight from New York. There were lots of ways to move into someone's life to provide protection and search out information without raising questions. The idea was to assume a role other people would accept. He could pass himself off as her driver. Her assistant. Her personal trainer.

Personal trainer was pretty much what he'd decided on. Hollywood was filled with actors and actresses who worked on their bodies 24/7. He was fit; he'd look the part. And it would give him access to her no matter where she went.

Okay. Personal trainer it would be…

"Mr. Orsini?"

"Falco," he said, looking down into her eyes. He saw the rise and fall of her breasts, remembered the soft, lush feel of her against him, and he knew he wasn't going to pretend to be her trainer after all.

"Simple," he said calmly. "We'll make people think I'm your lover."

She stared at him. Then she gave a little laugh.

"That's crazy," she said. "No one will believe—"

"Yeah," he said, his voice low and rough, "yeah, they will. Falco reached out, gathered Elle in his arms and kissed her.

CHAPTER THREE

THE FEEL of her mouth under his was incredible.

Warm. Silken. And soft. Wonderfully soft.

Not that he cared about that.

He was kissing her only to wipe that smug little smile from her face. To show her, in no uncertain terms, that they sure as hell could play the part of lovers, fool anybody who saw them.

Did she think she was the only one who could stick to a script?

Or did she think a bodyguard was too far out of her class to seem a convincing lover for a woman like her?

She was fighting him. Trying to twist free of his arms, to drag her lips from his. To hell with that. That who-do-you-think-you-are attitude of hers deserved a blunt response. She was wrong and he wasn't going to let her go until she knew it.

"No," she gasped against his mouth, but she might as well have saved her breath. Falco speared his fingers into her hair, tilted her face to his and kept on kissing her.

So what if she tasted of honey and cream? If she felt warm and soft against him? Those things were meaningless. This was about nothing else than teaching her that she couldn't laugh at Falco Orsini and get away with it.

He nipped lightly at her bottom lip. Touched the tip of his tongue to the seam of her mouth. With heart-stopping suddenness, she stopped fighting, stopped struggling.

She leaned into him, sighed and parted her lips. His tongue plunged deep.

The taste of her made his mind blur.

And his body react.

In an instant, he came fully erect, not just aroused but hard as stone, so hard it was painful. Desire pulsed hot and urgent in his blood. He slid his hands to her shoulders, cupped them, lifted her to her toes, drew her so close he could feel the race of her heart against his.

This was what he had wanted since he'd seen her in that first, unaltered ad. The eyes and mouth that promised passion, the made-for-sex body—

The knife that pressed against his belly caught him fully unaware.

Falco went absolutely still.

Where she'd gotten the knife was irrelevant. The feel of it wasn't. With instincts and sharp reflexes honed by his time in Special Forces, he locked one hand around her forearm and grabbed her wrist with the other, bending it back until the knife clattered to the floor. He kicked it into a corner, saw that it wasn't a knife at all but the slim plastic handle of a hairbrush. Not that it mattered.

It was the intent that counted.

"Let go of me!"

Her hands clawed for his face. He grunted, shoved her back against the unyielding door, used his weight to keep her in place. The only way she could hurt him was if she managed to throw him off and that was about as likely as the trailer sprouting wings. He had at least seven inches in height on her and probably eighty, ninety pounds of muscle.

"Stop it," he snarled.

That only made her fight harder. Falco tightened his grasp on her wrists, brought her hands to her sides and pinned them to the door.

"I said, stop it! You want me to hurt you, I will."

She made a choked sound but it wasn't of rage, it was of terror. Her face, bright with color a moment ago, blanched. Those enormous topaz eyes turned glassy.

He'd flown out here to protect this woman. Instead, he was scaring her half to death. Kissing her had been a straight and simple matter of ego and he wasn't into BS like that. He was who he was; he didn't need anybody's applause to do whatever job he set out to do, certainly not a client's. He'd let his pride, whatever you wanted to call it, get in the way.

And he didn't like it, not one bit.

"Listen to me."

She wouldn't. She was lost in her own world, fearing the worst.

"Ms. Bissette," he said sharply. "Elle. Pay attention. I'm not going to hurt you."

Her eyes met his.

Hell. He'd seen a dog look at him like this once, years back when he was just a kid. He'd found the animal wandering an alley not far from the Orsini mansion in Greenwich Village. Its ribs had showed; there were marks he hadn't wanted to identify on its back. *Come on, boy*, he'd said, holding out his hand, but the creature had looked at him through eyes that said it damned well knew his soft voice didn't mean a thing.

He'd won the dog's trust by squatting down, holding out his arms, showing his hands were empty. What was the human equivalent of that kind of message?

Falco cleared his throat.

"Okay. Here's what happens next. I'll let go of you and step back. You stay where you are. No hands, no fists, no weapons. And we'll talk. That's it. We'll just talk."

He gave it a couple of seconds. Then he did what he'd told her he'd do. Another couple of seconds went by. She didn't move. Neither did he. That was some kind of success, wasn't it? A little color had returned to her face. Another plus. Finally, she took a deep breath.

"I want you to leave."

Her voice was low but steady. Her eyes had lost that terrified glitter. Good. Maybe now they really could talk.

"Look, Ms. Bissette—"

"I said—"

"I heard you. But we need to discuss this."

"We have nothing to discuss."

She was back. He could see it in the way she held herself, in the lift of her chin, the steadiness of her gaze.

"Actually, we do. I'm sorry if I frightened you but—"

"Frightened me?" Her eyes narrowed. "You disgusted me!"

"Excuse me?"

"Putting your hands on me. Your mouth on me." Her chin went up another notch. "Men like you are…you're despicable!"

Falco felt a muscle jump in his cheek. He'd been called similar names, a long time back, though they'd been names that were far more basic. It happened when you were a kid and your old man was Cesare Orsini.

He'd learned to respond to such remarks with his fists.

Not this time, obviously. This time, he flashed a cold smile.

"Trust me, Ms. Bissette. The feeling is mutual. I'm not into women who look into a camera as if they want to screw the guy behind it. I was simply making a point."

"You made it. You're contemptible."

Falco gave an exaggerated sigh. "Disgusting, despicable, contemptible. Yeah, yeah, yeah. I've heard it all before."

Elle Bissette folded her arms. "I'll bet you have."

"You said we couldn't fool anybody if we pretended we were lovers. I figured I could save us ten minutes of talk by showing you that you were wrong."

"Well, you didn't. And I wasn't. I'm an actress but playing at being your lover would take more talent that even I possess."

Her insults almost made him laugh. From poor little victim to haughty aristocrat in the blink of an eye. Damned right, she was an actress.

But he was willing to bet that her terror a little while ago had not been an act.

"Look," he said in as conciliatory a tone as he could manage, "why don't we start over? We'll go somewhere, have a cup of coffee, you'll fill me in on why you need a bodyguard—"

"I do not need a bodyguard. Are you deaf? I want you out of here, right now."

She pointed an elegant hand at the door and tossed her head. Her hair, a mane of jet black, flew around her face. He'd bet she'd practiced the gesture in front of a mirror until it looked just right.

"Get out or I'll scream so loud it'll bring half the world running."

Enough, Falco thought grimly. He took a step forward and clasped her elbows.

"That's fine," he said coldly. "Go right ahead. Scream your head off."

"You think I won't? I will! And five minutes after that, you'll be in jail."

"You left out a step. The part where the cops show up." He tightened his hold on her and hauled her to her toes, his head lowered so their faces were inches apart. "They'll want to have a nice, long chat with you, baby. Are you up for that?"

She stared at him. The color drained from her face and she became still.

"What's the matter, Ms. Bissette? Don't you like that idea?" She didn't answer and he flashed a smile as cold as a New York winter. "Maybe, if we're really lucky, the paparazzi will come by along with the cops. Then you can talk to the whole world."

Whatever fight was left in her was gone. She went limp under his hands, her head drooped forward and all at once he thought, to hell with this! He had not flown 3,000 miles to play games. She found him disgusting? Her prerogative. She had a reason to keep the cops away? Her prerogative again. She was not his problem, none of this was. How he'd let himself be drawn into the mess was beyond him but no way was he going to get drawn in any deeper.

The lady had said "no," and "no" it was.

"Relax," he said, his tone flat as he let go of her and stepped back. "You don't need to scream to get rid of me. Just move away from the door and I'm out of here."

She didn't move. He rolled his eyes, shouldered past her and reached for the knob.

"Wait a minute."

Falco looked over his shoulder. Elle Bissette swallowed; he saw the muscles move in her throat. Which color were here eyes? Amber or topaz? The thought was so completely inappropriate, it made him angry.

"What now?" he growled.

"Mr. Orsini." She hesitated. "This is your—your line of work? You're a bodyguard?"

He smiled thinly. "I am any number of things, Ms. Bissette, but it's a little late to ask for my CV."

"The thing is...I didn't ask for a bodyguard."

"Here's a news flash, baby. I didn't ask for the job."

"But you said someone sent you."

"I said someone I know told me you had a problem and asked me to check it out." His mouth twisted. "And here I am."

"Look, it's not my fault you agreed to do a favor for a friend and—"

"He isn't a friend and I don't do favors for anybody." Falco heaved out a breath. Why get into any of that? How he'd come to be here didn't matter, especially since he was about to leave. "It's a long story and it doesn't change the facts. I came here because I was under the impression you needed help." Another thin smile. "I was wrong."

"You *were* wrong," she said quickly. "You can see for yourself, I'm just fine."

He thought of the terror that had shone in her eyes a little while ago. Well, maybe it was true. Maybe she was fine. Maybe all that fear had been strictly of him.

"Really, I'm fine. I'm just wondering why you...why someone would have thought otherwise."

Falco dug his hands into the pockets of his flannel trousers. "You posed for a magazine ad," he said. "A provocative one."

Her chin rose again. He'd seen pro boxers with the same habit. It wasn't a good one, not if you didn't want to end up in trouble.

"It was a lingerie ad, Mr. Orsini, not an ad for—for Hershey's chocolate."

He grinned. "No argument there, Ms. Bissette." His grin faded. "Fifty thousand lovesick idiots went out and bought their girlfriends whatever it is you were wearing in that ad, then wondered why it didn't look on them the way it looked on you."

She stiffened. He could almost see the gears working. She

was trying to figure out if what he'd said was a compliment or an insult.

"For your information," she said coldly, "statistics show that women are the target audience for lingerie ads."

"Great. So fifty thousand broads went out and bought that outfit, put it on, looked in the mirror and wondered what the hell had gone wrong."

For a fraction of a second, she looked as if she wanted to laugh. Then that chin rose again.

"Is there a point to this, Mr. Orsini?"

"Damned right. All those people looked at an ad and saw an ad." His voice became chill. "One sicko saw something else and decided to—what's today's favorite psychobabble term? He decided to 'share' what he saw with you."

A flush rose in her cheeks. "You've seen what that—that person sent me."

Falco nodded. "Yes."

He expected a rant. Indignation, that Farinelli had sent the thing to someone. Instead, she shuddered.

"It was—it was horrible," she whispered.

A fraction of his anger dissipated. She looked tired and vulnerable; she was frightened even though she was determined to claim she wasn't, but she wasn't going to do anything to protect herself. It made no sense.

"It was worse than horrible." He waited a beat. "Why won't you go to the cops?"

"You said it yourself. It was just the work of some—some crazy."

"Crazies can be dangerous," Falco said. "He should be found."

She stared at him, her eyes suddenly filled with that same despair he'd seen in the photo of her on the beach.

"That would mean publicity."

"Publicity's better than turning up dead."

His blunt statement was deliberate. He'd hoped to shock her into telling him the real reason she didn't want to go to the police—he'd have bet a thousand bucks there wasn't an actor or actress on the planet who didn't want publicity, good or bad—but he could see that wasn't going to happen.

"It's just a prank," she said, very calmly. "Stuff like that happens. I mean, this is Hollywood."

"Has he contacted you again?"

"You already asked me that. I told you, he hasn't."

She'd lied again. So what? So what if there was more to this than she was letting on? Fifteen minutes from now, he'd be on a plane heading back to New York.

"Just that one thing?" he heard himself ask. "Nothing else?"

"Isn't that what I just said?" A smile as false as the one she wore in that lingerie ad curved her lips. "Look, I'm not worried. Really. There's security on the set. I have an alarm system in my house." Another smile. A toss of the head. Forget despair. What he saw in those topaz eyes now was dismissal. "At any rate, thank you for coming to see me."

Falco shrugged. "No problem."

She held out her hand. It was a queen's gesture. She was discharging him, her subject.

Something flickered inside him.

Had that softening of her mouth under his, that barely perceptible sigh, really all been an act? Had she been diverting him so he wouldn't expect that phony knife at his belly? Or had it been real? That sudden, sexy little sound she'd made. The way she'd parted her lips beneath his.

One step forward. One tug on those slender fingers extended toward him. Then she'd be in his arms, her breasts soft against his hard chest, her thighs against his, her lips his for the taking. And he would take them, he'd kiss her again and again, taking each kiss deeper than the last until she moaned and rose to him, whispered her need and her hunger against his mouth…

Dammit, was he insane?

She didn't go for men like him. Hey, that was fine. He didn't go for women like her. And he sure as hell wasn't turned on by women who flaunted their sexuality, who all but invited a faceless sea of men to get off on thinking what it would be like to take her to bed.

Falco ignored her outstretched hand.

"Goodbye, Ms. Bissette," he said, and he opened the door of the trailer and stepped briskly into the heat of the desert.

The afternoon's shoot began badly and went downhill from there.

It made the morning's attempts look good.

Everybody was unhappy.

The heat was awful; they'd been breaking early because of it but Farinelli announced that they were going to get this scene filmed or, *per Dio*, nobody was leaving!

Elle just could not get the scene right. Not her fault, she kept telling herself. The encounter with Falco Orsini had shaken her. She'd done her best to be polite to him at the end but it hadn't been easy. Finding him in her trailer, a stranger so tall, so powerful that he'd seemed to fill the space…

And the way he'd kissed her, as if he could make her want to kiss him back.

Some women might; even she knew that. Not her, though. She hated the whole sex thing. It was like a bad joke, a woman hired for her sex appeal in an ad, but it wasn't a joke, it was the terrible truth. A man's wet mouth, his rough hands…

Falco Orsini's mouth had not been wet. It had been warm

and hard and possessive but not wet. And his hands…hard, yes. Strong. But he hadn't touched her roughly….

Elle gave herself a mental shake.

So what? The point was, he'd had no right to kiss her even though he'd done it in response to her telling him she and he could never pretend they were lovers. Besides, it didn't matter. He would not be her bodyguard. Nobody would. Nobody would poke and pry and ask questions she had no intention of answering….

"…listening to me, Elle?"

She blinked. Antonio was standing close to her while everyone waited. "This is a love scene. A very important one. You must convey passion. Desire. Hunger. And you must do it with your eyes, your hands, your face. There is no kissing in this scene, *si*? There is only teasing. Of your character, of Chad's character, of the audience." He took her arm, looked up at her, his expression determined. "You can do this. Relax. Forget the cameras, the crew. Forget everything but whatever brought that look to your face in the advertisement you did for Bon Soir."

Elle almost laughed. She'd had small movie roles before but that ad had gotten her this big part. What if people knew that "that look" had been the lucky result of an unlucky sinus infection? A heady combination of aspirin, decongestant and nasal-and-throat spray had miraculously translated to glittering eyes, slumberous lids and parted lips.

Better not to mention that, of course.

"One last try," Farinelli said softly. "I want you to imagine yourself in the arms of a man whose passion overcomes your most basic inhibitions, a man who stirs you as no other ever could. Imagine a flesh-and-blood lover, *bella*, one you have known and never forgotten. Put Chad out of your mind."

Chad rolled his eyes. "Damn, Antonio. You really know how to hurt a guy."

The joke was deliberate. A tension reliever, and it worked. Everybody laughed. Elle managed a smile. Farinelli patted her hand, stepped away, then raised his hand like the Pope about to give a benediction.

"And, action!"

Elle lay back in her co-star's arms. Her heart was racing with nerves. What had she been thinking, letting her agent convince her to take this part? What Antonio wanted of her was impossible. She couldn't do it, couldn't look into a man's eyes and want him not even when it was make-believe.

Having a man's hands on her. His wet mouth on her mouth. God, oh, God...

"Look at me," Chad's character said. It was a line of dialogue he'd repeated endless times today. Elle looked up, just as *she* had done endless times today....

And saw not his movie-star handsome face, but the beautiful, proud, masculine face of Falco Orsini.

Obsidian eyes. Thin, aristocratic nose. Chiseled jaw and a hard, firm mouth—a mouth that she could still remember for its warmth, its hunger, its possessiveness.

An ache swept through her body, heat burned from her breasts to low in her belly...

"And, cut!"

Elle blinked. She stared at the man looking down at her. Chad, her co-star, who flashed a toothy grin.

"Elle, *mia bella*!" Antonio Farinelli hurried toward her. She heard a smattering of applause, a couple of whistles as he held out his hands and helped her to her feet. "*Brava*, Elle. That was *perfetto*!" He brought his fingers to his lips and kissed them. "The screen will sizzle!"

Chad rose beside her and winked. "I don't know who you were thinkin' about, honey, but he is sure one lucky guy."

* * *

A quarter of a mile away, half-concealed by a Joshua tree, Falco Orsini slammed a pair of high-powered binoculars into a leather case and tossed it into the front seat of his rented SUV.

What a hell of a performance! Elle Bissette and a cameraman. Elle Bissette and an actor. And when this movie hit the theaters, Elle Bissette and a couple of million faceless men.

She was hot for every guy in the world.

Except him.

No that he gave a damn.

What got to him was that he'd flown 3,000 miles and she'd sent him packing. Her choice, but he couldn't stop thinking about that look in her eyes in the beach photo and again in the trailer, a look that spelled FEAR in capital letters.

Something was happening and no way was he leaving until he knew what it was. Falco got into the SUV and settled in to wait.

CHAPTER FOUR

AN HOUR passed before he saw her. She was heading for the cars parked near the set. He'd figured her for something bright and expensive. He was right about the bright part, but expensive? He smiled. The lady drove a red Beetle.

He'd been wrong about her destination, too. He'd figured her for a rented house in Palm Springs or maybe a glitzy hotel but she headed northwest. To L.A.? It was a fairly long drive but this was Friday. She was probably heading home for the weekend.

Following her wasn't a problem. There was plenty of traffic, plus she turned out to be a conservative driver, staying in the right-hand lane and doing a steady 65 miles per hour.

He settled in a few of cars behind her.

After a while, her right turn signal light blinked on. She took an exit ramp that led to the kind of interchange he was pretty sure existed only in California, a swirl of interlocking roads that looked as if somebody had dumped a pot of pasta and called the resultant mess a highway system.

Freeway. That was what they called them here. He remembered that when the Bissette woman took a freeway headed north.

Still no problem but where was she going?

Another thirty minutes went by before her turn signal

came on again. This time, the exit led into a town so small he'd have missed it had he blinked. Following her wasn't so simple now, especially after she hung a couple of lefts and ended up on a two-lane country blacktop.

Traffic was sparse. A couple of cars, a truck carrying a load of vegetables, that was about all.

Dusk had fallen. There was no other traffic now. Bissette's taillights came on. Falco kept his lights off and hung farther back.

They'd been on the road a long time and the passing minutes had only made his suspicions sharpen. Why was she so determined to handle the mess she was in all by herself?

Why was she so smugly certain nobody would buy into him as her lover?

Did she want him to believe she could convince a million horny guys looking at her in an ad or in a movie that they turned her on, but that she couldn't play the same act one on one with him?

His hands tightened on the steering wheel.

Was that the real reason he was tailing her? To confront her again, show her what could happen if he wanted it to happen, if he kissed her not to make a point but to make her damned well admit she wanted to respond to him, that it wouldn't take any acting at all for her to come alive in his arms?

"Merda!"

Falco slowed the SUV to a crawl. Was he going nuts?

It was years, hell, it was more than a decade since he'd cared about proving himself to anybody. And it had never, ever involved a woman. "The Orsini Stud," his brothers had laughingly called him when they had been in their teens. They'd all done just fine in that department but yeah, some of the local girls had burned extra hot for the neighborhood bad boy.

It had been like that as he got older, too; it still was.

Women, beautiful women, were easy to come by. Women even more beautiful than Elle Bissette. Women who didn't play games. So, what was he doing following her into the middle of nowhere?

It wasn't logical, and it wasn't like him.

Okay. It had been a long day. He needed to kick back, have a drink, a meal…

Yes, but what was Bissette doing in the middle of nowhere? Maybe that was the real question. This all but empty road, curving now like a snake as it climbed into the mountains, tall trees on either side. It wasn't a good place to be if some crazy was after you. Crowds. Bright lights. People. There was safety in numbers. A cliché but also a fact.

Falco frowned.

Maybe the whole thing was a lie.

Maybe it was her idea of publicity. Or the director's. He didn't think so, after talking with Farinelli, after seeing that mutilated ad, but anything was possible.

Or maybe she was all the way out here to meet some guy. A lover. A woman like this, lush and sensual, sure as hell would have a man around. A weekend of sex, of lying in her lover's arms, of giving him what she had made clear she would never give Falco, her body naked under his, her hands on him, her mouth…

His body reacted so quickly, so completely, that it was embarrassing.

Forget needing a drink. What he needed was a run, a long one. Or a workout. Better still, he needed both. He'd been in L.A. before, he knew a couple of gyms where he could sweat whatever this was out of his system and—

Falco blinked. Bissette's taillights, two dots of crimson bleeding far into the distance, flashed brightly, then disappeared.

Had she made him?

He picked up speed. Slowed when he reached the approximate location where she'd seemingly vanished. Without headlights, it was difficult to see much of anything, but, yeah, he spotted something, a pair of old wooden posts to the left of the road and between them, a rutted track barely wide enough for a car. The VW had taken it; he could see its taillights and, in the sweep of its headlights, the murky outline of a house in a small clearing.

The lady had reached her destination.

A muscle flickered in Falco's jaw.

A strange place for an actress to rendezvous with her lover. A dangerous place, if she wasn't meeting anyone and would be here alone, but hey, not his problem...

"Dammit," Falco said. He pulled to a cleared space fifty feet ahead, parked and got out of the SUV.

Elle sighed with relief as her headlights picked up the shape of the cabin.

She parked her VW under a soaring pine, stepped out and shut the door after her. The clearing was dark; there were stars overhead but the moon had not yet risen.

No matter. She knew every foot of the clearing and the cabin by heart.

And loved all of it.

She'd rented it for a while and she'd been heartbroken when the owner decided to sell it or tear it down. She couldn't blame him. The cabin was small, it needed lots of work, and the ski resort that had once been planned a few miles away had never materialized.

Nobody wanted the run-down cabin but her. It was her sanctuary but she couldn't afford to buy it.

And then, a miracle. She'd signed with Bon Soir. Her contract called for more money than she'd ever imagined she might earn and she'd taken the entire check and plunked it down on the cabin.

Now, it was hers.

She was still fixing it up. It needed a new porch, a new roof, but what did that matter? It belonged to her. Nobody else. No one knew about it, either. It was the one place where she could relax, be herself...

Be safe.

She'd always felt safe here, despite the isolation. The cabin, the surrounding woods, took her back to her childhood. Part of her childhood, she thought quickly, the only part she ever wanted to remember, when her mother was still alive and there'd been just the two of them living in a cabin like this in a woods like this...

An owl called from the trees.

Elle jumped. Silly. The woods were home to lots of creatures, none of them frightening. It was the day that had left her feeling unsettled, she thought as she climbed the porch steps. The scene that just wouldn't end, the movie role she should never have taken...

The man.

Falco Orsini.

Elle took her keys from her pocket and unlocked the door.

How dare he show up the way he had? Without warning, without permission.

She stepped inside the cabin, shut the door behind her.

Part of it was Farinelli's fault. The director had no right going behind her back; he should have told her he was going to hire a bodyguard and she'd have told him to do no such thing. But that man. Orsini. Entering her trailer. Waiting for her there. Acting as if he owned her. Kissing her. Forcing her into his arms, forcing her to endure the feel of his hands, his body, his mouth.

A tremor went through her.

Awful, all of it…

It *had* been awful… Hadn't it?

She could still feel his embrace. The strength of his arms. The hardness of his body. The warmth of his mouth. And—and the sudden, incredible quickening of her blood.

No. That was impossible. What she'd felt had been disgust. What else would a woman feel when a man touched her? She knew all she needed to know about men and their needs, their appetites, their hunger. Some women endured it all, some pretended to like those things. Not her. She knew. She had always known, and what did that matter?

Falco Orsini had burst into her life and now he was gone.

All that talk about protecting her… Elle tossed her purse aside. Baloney, her mama would have said. He had his own agenda; hadn't he proved it by trying to kiss her? Men always had their own agendas. Her co-star acted like Mr. Nice Guy, but, really, it was only because he wanted to get this movie over with. Her director wanted the same thing and had proved he'd do anything to have it happen, including hiring a bodyguard that he had to know she would not want.

Especially a bodyguard like Falco Orsini.

The hard, handsome face. The powerful body. The low, husky voice. The veneer of good manners laid over the persona of a street tough.

Elle shook her head, reminded herself she'd come all the way up here so she could spend the weekend ridding herself of all those thoughts and reached for the nearest light switch.

Nothing.

Click. Click. Click.

Dammit, the light wasn't coming on. Moving carefully, feeling her way, trying to ignore the sudden unease tiptoeing up her spine, she made her way to a table and reached for the lamp centered on it.

Click. Click. Click.

The hair rose on the nape of her neck. Two bulbs dying at the same time? Coincidence? Yes. It had to be. Hadn't she just thought about the fact that nobody even knew the cabin existed? She'd kept it as her secret hideaway from the start. She had an apartment in Studio City, but this was where she came to restore her soul. Mama would have said that, too. The woods were like a cathedral where you went to find peace.

Coincidence, absolutely.

Briskly, she moved forward, hand outstretched, feeling for the little round table beside the sofa. Yes. There it was. Her fingers found the slender column of the lamp centered on it, skated up its cool surface, closed around the switch.

The light came on.

Elle breathed a sigh of relief...

And saw what had been hung on the planked pine wall beside the fireplace.

A scream rose in her throat but she couldn't get it out. It seemed to take forever before it burst, full-blown, into the dark silence of the night.

Falco was standing on the edge of the woods that surrounded the cabin, asking himself—for the third time—just what, exactly, he was doing here.

He'd come out of curiosity or maybe out of anger and a slightly dented ego, and none of that justified following her here. Elle Bissette didn't want his help. She didn't want any part of him. Fine. End of story. By now, he should have been on a plane, halfway to New York.

His mouth thinned. Hell, he thought, and he turned and started jogging toward the road.

He'd already made a fool of himself, trying to protect this woman. Why would he do it again? She wanted to spend the night in a place that looked like a leftover from a *Friday the 13th* movie? Her business, not—

Her scream tore apart the night.

Falco turned and ran to the house. He charged up the porch steps. This was not the textbook response to trouble. He had no weapon, no knowledge of what awaited him, but that scream…

The door opened and Elle flew through it, straight into his outstretched arms.

"No," she shrieked, "no, no, no…"

"Ms. Bissette. Elle. It's me. Falco Orsini."

He knew she couldn't hear him, not in the state she was in, eyes wide with terror, face white with it. Panting, sobbing, she beat at him with her fists but he had no time to worry about that. Instead, he shoved her behind him, braced himself to take on whoever was in there…

Nobody.

The cabin, brightly illuminated by a lamp at the far end, was empty.

Falco turned to Elle, huddled in the corner of the porch. Her breath was coming in desperate little gasps. Her teeth were chattering. She was cold and shaking and he cursed, reached for her and gathered her into his arms.

"Elle. You're safe. You're with me."

Slowly, she raised her head and focused on his face. "Mister—Mister Orsini?"

"Yes. That's right. Tell me what happened. Was someone waiting for you here?"

She shook her head. "N-no."

"But something scared you. What was it?"

"I saw—I saw…" Her expression changed, her voice was still weak but not it was tinged with suspicion. "What—what are you doing here?"

"I followed you."

"You followed…?" Her hands flattened against his chest. She pushed back a couple of inches. "Why?"

Why, indeed? "We can talk about that later. Right now you need to tell me what frightened you."

Her eyes clouded; she dragged them from his and looked down. "It's—it's nothing. A—a spider."

Falco's mouth twisted. "That's bull and you know it." He cupped her face, forced her to meet his steady gaze. "Here's the bottom line, lady. You won't call the cops? I will."

"No. You have no right—"

"You need help. If not from me, then from the police."

"All right!" She took a breath. "Someone—someone left something here. Something for me."

He felt his belly knot. "Another picture?"

She shook her head. Her hair whispered across his hands like ebony silk. "Not a picture. An—an animal. A dead animal."

Falco nodded. "Okay. Here's what you're going to do. My SUV is parked on the road about fifty feet up. Here are the keys. Go to it, get inside, lock the doors and—"

"No!" Her fingers curled into his jacket. "I don't want to be alone."

Falco put his arms around her again. She stiffened but she let him hold her. He could feel her heart racing. She felt fragile and female and hell, any man would show a woman compassion at a moment like this.

"All right. Forget the SUV. You stay here while I check things out."

"Okay."

Her voice was low and shaky. He'd have liked it better if she'd given him a hard time. She was tough, he already knew that, and this show of obedience told him, even more than her pallor and her trembling, that she was far too close to shock.

"Good girl." Her eyes had not left his. Instinct took over. He bent his head and brushed his lips gently over hers, told himself it was simply another way of offering her the reassurance she needed. Her mouth trembled at the touch of his; the warmth of her breath was a shocking contrast to the icy feel of her skin. "I'll be right back."

She nodded. He stroked a strand of hair back from her cheek. Then he took a deep breath and stepped inside the cabin.

It wasn't much. Anybody expecting the palatial digs of a movie star would have been disappointed. One room, simply furnished. A couple of small tables. A couple of chairs. A door to his left stood open and led into a no-nonsense bathroom. Sink, shower, toilet. An alcove to the right held an apartment-sized stove, refrigerator and sink.

The lamp at the far end of the cabin burned as brightly as the sun.

There was a light switch by the door. A lamp on a table a couple of feet away. Why would Elle have ignored both, made her way through a dark cabin to reach the most distant light source in the room?

He tried the wall switch. The table lamp. Got useless clicks both times. Coincidence? He doubted it. A quick look confirmed it. There was no bulb in the wall fixture, none in the lamp.

Someone had set things up so Elle would be drawn farther into the room.

To the wall beside the fireplace.

To something he could see hanging on that wall.

Falco moved forward slowly. The thing on the wall became easier to identify. His belly knotted. Yes, it was an animal. A possum? A squirrel?

A cat. Yes, but not a real—

"Falco?"

He spun around. Elle stood in the doorway, hands clasped at her waist, face a pale oval against the darkness behind her. Her gaze was fixed on the wall.

"Is it—is it dead?"

"It's okay," he said, but she shook her head. Falco moved toward her. "Honestly, baby, it's okay. It isn't a real animal, it's a toy. A toy cat."

Elle made a little sound. She began to sway. Falco cursed and got to her just before she went down in a boneless heap.

CHAPTER FIVE

IT COULD have been an act.

Bissette was an actress, wasn't she? Maybe she thought she could play him for sympathy if she did an old-time swoon.

But the light-as-air feel of her limp body in his arms, the way her head lolled back against his shoulder, was all too real. She was out like the proverbial light.

Falco cursed under his breath and carried her to the futon. "Elle," he said urgently. "Elle, can you hear me?"

Nothing. Her face was devoid of color. For all he knew, she was going into shock.

The cabin was cold. And damp. There was wood and kindling on the fireplace hearth but no way was he going to let her remain here long enough for a blazing fire to matter. The time for her to make her own decisions was over.

When he left this place, so would she.

A patchwork quilt, almost translucent with age, was neatly folded across a ladder-back maple chair. He shook open the quilt, drew it over her then lay his fingers against her throat.

Good.

Her pulse, though rapid, was strong and steady. She'd stopped shaking and now tinges of color were starting to stain her cheeks.

His throat tightened.

God, she was beautiful. Even now, with no makeup, her hair wild, she was the most beautiful woman he'd ever seen.

And what did that matter at a time like this?

He had to get Elle Bissette up and moving and out of this dreary, isolated place. She might not want a bodyguard but she was in no condition to make that determination. She was his responsibility. For the moment, anyway.

A man didn't turn his back on his duty.

Falco went quickly to the alcove that passed for a kitchen, pulled a dish towel from a rack, checked the minuscule fridge, found a bottle of water. Halfway to the futon he made a quick detour, ripped the toy cat from the wall and put it aside.

Elle gave a soft moan.

He squatted next to her, opened the bottle of water, poured some onto the towel and patted it over her forehead and cheeks.

"Elle," he said firmly. "Open your eyes."

A sigh. A murmur. A flutter of lashes so long they seemed to curve against her cheekbones. Her eyes opened. Confusion glittered in their amber depths. Then she gave a hoarse cry, jerked upright and went for his face.

"Dammit," he said, and caught her wrists. "Elle. Take it easy. You're all right. It's me. Falco."

She stilled. Her eyes cleared. "Falco?" she whispered.

He let out a breath he didn't know he'd been holding.

"Yeah," he said gruffly. "It's me."

She fell back against the futon. "What—what happened?"

"You fainted."

"That's impossible. I've never fainted in my life."

Her voice was thready but the determination was there just the same. He would have laughed if he hadn't figured that would only send her into attack mode again and there wasn't time for that.

"Yeah," he said, "well, there's a first time for everything."
He leaned forward, wrapped a strong arm around her shoulders,
drew her toward him and held out the water bottle. "Drink."

"What is that?"

Falco rolled his eyes. "Gin and tonic with a slice of lime.
It's water, babe. H$_2$O."

"But I'm not—"

"Thirsty. Do you ever do anything without an argument?"

She gave him the glare he figured the Medusa had used to
turn men to stone. That was good, considering she'd been out
cold only a few minutes ago. Then she snatched the bottle
from his hand, put her head back and took a long drink. He
watched the play of muscle in her throat, watched a trickle of
water make its way over her bottom lip.

All he had to do was lean in, put the tip of his tongue to
that tiny bit of moisture…

Falco shot to his feet. "Okay," he said brusquely. "Are you
ready to tell me what just happened?"

"What do you mean, what just happened? I passed out."

"Somebody that knows about this place broke in to it and
left something for you."

"Oh, God." Her voice turned thready. "The cat."

Idiot, he said to himself, and squatted beside her again.

"It was a toy, Elle. It wasn't real."

"I know. You said so."

He nodded. "But you fainted anyway."

Her gaze met his, then skittered away. "From relief."

"Or because that toy has some meaning to you."

"No," she said quickly. Much too quickly.

"I saw you, Elle. You thought the cat was real… That was
bad." A muscle knotted in his jaw. "But finding out it was a
toy was even worse." His eyes drilled into hers. "Why?"

Elle gave him another of those cold glares. He could see

the defiance, the tough independence coming back, but he knew enough this time to recognize it for what it was.

A shield.

She knew something. And she wasn't about to let him in on it.

Still, he couldn't demand answers now. He wanted her out of here. He didn't like the cabin's seclusion, the impenetrable wall of tall trees that surrounded it, the fact that he had no idea what, or who, might be hiding within those trees.

Most of all, he didn't like the fact that whoever had wanted to scare the bejeezus out of her had damned near done it. If she'd been alone when she saw that thing on the wall…

"Okay," he said, as he stood up, "the questions can wait."

"I'm not answering any questions, Mr. Orsini—but I have one for you. Exactly what are you doing here?"

"I see we're back to formalities."

"We're back to the fact that I didn't hire you as a bodyguard."

"Nobody hired me. I told you that. Consider me a volunteer."

"This is not a charity," she said coldly. "I don't accept volunteers."

Despite everything, he laughed. She didn't. She just fixed him with that look again. He figured it had surely sent other men running. Too bad she was wasting it on him.

"You followed me." Her tone was as sharp as a well-honed blade. "Why?"

He thought of taking her in his arms and giving her a graphic answer to the question, kissing her until she responded to him—and he could make that happen, he was certain—but it was a crazy idea. Besides, everything had to take a backseat to getting her the hell out of this place. They'd already been here too long.

Whoever had tacked that stuffed animal to the wall could still be outside. Okay, it was doubtful, but why take chances?

"Answer me, Mr. Orsini. Why did you follow me?"

"Maybe I like red VWs."

Elle rose to her feet. "Maybe I don't like smart answers."

"Look, baby—"

"Do not call me that!"

"Look, Ms. Bissette, you want conversation, fine. But not here."

"I am not the least bit interested in conversation. What I want are answers."

"So do I, but not here."

"On second thought, forget the answers. All I want is you out of here."

Falco narrowed his eyes. "Is it me, or do you just like giving men a tough time?"

"I don't give men anything," she snapped. "Why would I?"

Why, indeed. Was she into women? No way. That kiss in the desert assured him of that. Was she a woman who used men to suit her purposes, then discarded them when it was time for a change? Did she change lovers as often as some women changed hair color?

Not that it mattered. He had nothing to do with her life. Somebody was out to get this woman. The obscenity of it was not just wrong, it was vicious.

"Look," he said, trying hard to sound reasonable, "you can't stay here."

She laughed. It made his fists clench.

"Did I say something amusing?" he said.

"I don't know how to break this to you, Mr. Orsini, but I can do whatever I want."

"Somebody broke into your cabin. Left you a—a message."

"Oh, please! Break-ins happen in wild country like this. It was vandalism. Kids, plain and simple."

Falco smiled thinly. "Did kids nail that toy to the wall and send you that marked-up advertisement, too?"

It was a low blow. He knew it, wanted to feel guilty about it but if it forced her to see reality, it was worth it. He waited for her to retaliate. To his surprise, she didn't. Instead, she swung away from him, wrapped her arms around herself, and that did it. Falco clasped her shoulders and turned her toward him.

"Don't you see, Elle? These two things must be related."

She shook her head. "No," she whispered, "they aren't."

"And the sun won't set in the west."

She swallowed hard. "That's different."

"Yeah, it is. The sun isn't interested in hurting you."

For a few seconds, nothing happened. Then her eyes filled with darkness. "Oh, God," she whispered, "God…"

Falco muttered an obscenity, reached for her and gathered her close against him. A sob broke from her throat and he cupped her face, lifted it to his.

"I'll protect you," he said softly. "I swear it."

"I don't need anyone to protect me," she said, her voice breaking, and instead of arguing and telling her she was wrong, he drew her to him again and held her.

She felt warm and soft against him; the fragrance of her skin and hair was delicate and clean. He wanted to kiss her. Undress her. Take her to bed. Make love to her until she forget fear, forgot sorrow, until he was all that mattered.

Carefully, he cupped her shoulders, took a step back, waited until her eyes met his. Her nose was red and running. It made him want to hold her close again. Instead, he reached into his pocket, took out a pristine white handkerchief and handed it to her.

"Thank you," she said, and mopped her eyes, blew her nose.

He nodded.

"So. I'm assuming you don't live here full-time."

"I don't, no."

"Is this a rental?"

"It's mine." Her voice was low; he had to strain to hear it. "I bought it with my first big paycheck."

"From that lingerie company?"

Damn, he hadn't meant to sound accusatory. What did he care if she smiled and pouted for the eyes of every man on the planet? But she simply nodded and said yes, that was right.

"I'd always wanted a place like this. Quiet. Tucked away."

The cabin was definitely both. Still, someone had found it. A lover she'd brought here one weekend? The very possibility made him furious. That a man would violate a woman with such calculated cruelty. That a man would violate this particular woman—

Falco frowned. He was wasting precious time.

"Okay," he said briskly, "here's the plan. Get together anything you think you'll want. We'll leave your car. I'll arrange to have—"

"No." Elle shook off his hands. No more tears. No shaky voice. She was the portrait of composure.

"No, what? Your car will be fine. I'll arrange to have somebody pick it up and—"

"I'm not leaving."

"Dammit, woman, be reasonable."

"I'm being totally reasonable. If anybody—if anybody had wanted to—to do anything to me, they'd have been here, waiting."

"That's one way to look at it."

"It's the only way to look at it."

It wasn't, but telling her about similar situations that had ended in blood and disaster wasn't on the agenda right now. She thought she was being reasonable? Okay. He'd appeal to that.

"Look, there's nothing complicated about this, okay? Pick a friend. I'll drive you there and you can spend the night."

"I don't have friends."

His eyebrows rose. She made the announcement without drama, the way another woman might say she didn't have a potted geranium.

"It doesn't have to be a bosom buddy. Just somebody who'll put you up until tomorrow while I check things out."

Her expression went from composed to icy.

"Have I asked you to, as you so brilliantly put it, 'check things out' for me, Mr. Orsini?"

"Dammit, woman—"

"No. I have not. That's because I am perfectly capable of making my own plans."

"Then make some." Falco narrowed his eyes. "Otherwise I'll make them for you."

"You are an arrogant man, Mr. Orsini. That may impress some of your clients but it doesn't do a thing for me."

"I don't have 'clients,'" Falco said, each word dipped in ice. "And if there's anybody here who's arrogant, baby, it's not me."

"My name is not 'baby.' And I am not going to explain myself to you."

Forget arrogant, forget determined. Her tone, her posture, the look on that gorgeous face was downright hostile.

"I have a car. If I want to go somewhere, I'll drive myself."

"Fine. You take the VW. I'll follow you."

"Are you hard of hearing, Mr. Orsini? I'm staying right here."

The hell she was, Falco thought grimly. She was not staying here—and neither was he. It was too late, too dark to check the woods. Somebody was stalking her; why she refused to acknowledge that was a question that needed answering but he'd screwed around here much, much longer than was prudent.

And he wasn't about to waste more time arguing with a woman who gave new meaning to the word *mulish*.

"Don't you get it, Mr. Orsini? You are dismissed."

That did it. Falco scooped Elle Bissette off her feet and dumped her over his shoulder. She was an egotistical, irritating, obstinate witch, but no way would he leave her in a place like this.

She punched, kicked, shrieked. None of it mattered. He walked straight through the cabin, along the dirt track to the road, right to where he'd left the SUV, its ebony surface lit by a newly risen ivory moon.

"Son of a bitch," Elle huffed. "You no-good, no-account—"

"Do us both a favor," Falco said, "and shut up." He shifted her weight, yanked open the passenger door and dumped her in the black leather seat. She responded by trying to scramble out, but he'd expected that and he put one big hand in the center of her chest and unceremoniously shoved her back. "Stay put," he warned, "or so help me, I'll tie you up and stuff you in the cargo compartment."

She looked up at him, starlit eyes hot with fury.

"You bastard! For all I know you—you pinned that—that thing to the wall in there."

Okay. She knew he hadn't but the look on his handsome, arrogant face was worth the stupid taunt.

"Right." His voice dripped with sarcasm. "I figured out where you were heading, got here before you, hung kitty up, drove away, hid out and waited until you arrived." His mouth twisted. "Man, I am one clever dude!"

"You have no right to—to kidnap me."

He laughed. Laughed, damn him, as if she and the entire situation were amusing.

"Is that what you're going to tell the cops? You are one lucky lady. I mean, two chances to call the cops in one day?" His laughter died; his voice turned cold and he leaned down until their eyes were almost level. "Go on, baby. Use your mobile. Call the cops, tell them how you found that message in your cabin—"

"What message?" she said and, once again, her words tumbled out too fast.

"Oh, it was a message, all right. We both know that. The difference is, I don't understand it—but I have a feeling you sure as hell do."

Her chin lifted. "That's ridiculous."

"Good. So call them. Tell them what you found, tell them how I dragged you out of the freaking middle of freaking nowhere to save your pretty ass. Tell them that's what you call a kidnap, and I'll stick around for the laughs."

Pay dirt. He could see it, see the fight drain out of her.

"Bastard," she hissed.

"If only," Falco said with a quick, dangerous smile.

"I hate you!"

"And that breaks my heart."

"It couldn't. You have no heart, Orsini."

"I've been told that before."

"Oh, yes, I'll just bet you have."

Her mouth was trembling, that soft-looking mouth. He remembered the taste of it, the hint of sweetness she had not given him time to savor and then he thought, what the hell, she might as well hate him for cause and he leaned in, captured that sweet mouth with his, kissed her, swept his hands into her hair when she tried to turn away...

And heard the soft catch of her breath, the whisper of acquiescence that told him all he needed to know.

The need burning hot inside him burned inside her, too.

"Elle," he said, and her lips softened. Parted. Clung to his.

He said her name again and she moaned, curled her hands around his wrists as he took the kiss deeper and deeper.

The world fell away.

He could have her.

Everything in him knew it, knew as well that having her would be like nothing he'd ever known before. There had been women all his life but there'd never been a woman like this.

All he had to do was lift her from the SUV, carry her back into the cabin, undress her, bare her to his hands, his eyes, his mouth, take her again and again until he stripped her of that cold arrogance…

An owl hooted from the forest.

Falco pulled back.

Elle's eyes opened.

They were pools of deepest, darkest amber, shining with bewilderment. He could hardly blame her. Kissing her, wanting her, made no sense.

Neither did leaning in and kissing her again, his lips featherlight on hers.

"I'm in charge," he said in a low voice. "I'll take care of you. Nothing will happen to you, Elle, I swear it."

Then he slammed the door shut, went around to the driver's side, got behind the wheel and took the SUV away from the cabin fast enough to make dust rise into the moonlight.

CHAPTER SIX

THE NIGHT was magnificent, the ebony sky shot with silver starfire, the cool air fragrant with the tang of pine and fir.

The isolation, the beauty of the coastal mountains and the ever-present sound of the Pacific, beating against a rocky beach, were what had drawn Elle here in the first place.

In some ways, it reminded her of home and her earliest, happiest memories. No ocean, of course. She had grown up in a secluded valley hundreds and hundreds of miles from anything, least of all the sea. It had been a wonderful place, a wonderful life....

And then it had ended.

Elle frowned.

Why think of that now? She hadn't, for years. Until a few weeks ago. Until the ad torn from the fashion magazine...

"Are you cold?"

Startled, she turned to Falco Orsini.

"What?"

"You were shivering. If you're cold—"

"No. No, I'm fine. I just..." She bit her lip. "I'm fine," she said again, and looked down at her hands, tightly knotted in her lap.

Why had she let him carry her off? He'd given her little

choice, but the truth was, she could have stopped him. Could have made the attempt to stop him, anyway. But she hadn't. She'd let this stranger stuff her into the SUV and drive away with her.

And she'd let him kiss her.

Elle closed her eyes against the unwanted memory. She'd let him kiss her, force a response from her...

Liar!

He hadn't "forced" anything. He'd put his lips on hers and something had happened deep inside her, something she had never believed could possibly happen if a man kissed her.

But it had.

She'd kissed him back, kissed him and wanted to go on kissing him.

Which only proved what bad shape she was in.

She did not respond to—to that kind of thing. Why would she? She knew women did but she'd never been able to understand it. And what impression had she made with that one moment of irrational behavior? Did the man beside her think she would repay him for coming to her rescue by having sex with him?

Not that he'd come to her rescue.

He'd turned up, unwanted, uninvited. Not once. Twice. In the trailer. At the cabin. Yes, she'd flown into his arms when he'd burst through the door but she'd have been fine if he hadn't been there. She'd have gotten over her fear.

She would have.

Absolutely, she would have.

"Elle. If you're cold, just say so."

"I told you, I'm—"

He reached out, touched a button. The windows went up; a whisper of warm air drifted through the vehicle. He looked at her.

"Is that better?"

It was, actually. She hadn't realized it until now but he was right, she felt chilly.

"Yes. Thank you."

He nodded. Looked back at the windshield.

More silence.

They'd been driving for the better part of an hour, virtually alone on the narrow road. She'd never been on it this far past her cabin, hadn't even been curious where it led. Falco had turned onto it going fast, no signal light, checking and rechecking the mirrors. After a while, he'd settled into a steady, what, sixty, seventy miles an hour? They'd seen only two other vehicles, both heading toward them and then, a little while ago, headlights had come up behind them.

Falco had known it well before she did. She knew because she'd been watching him from the corner of her eye. That hard, handsome profile. The long fingers of one hand splayed over the steering wheel, the others lying loose on the gearshift lever.

Both hands had suddenly tightened.

A long minute later, the pinprick of headlights had illuminated the interior.

Logic told her his eyesight was better than hers. Instinct told her it had nothing to do with eyesight. He had sensed the presence of the other vehicle. He was like a predator, sleek and alert to every nuance of what might be prey, or what might prey on him.

Such a breathless analogy from a woman not given to breathless analogies, but she suspected it was accurate. Falco Orsini was different. At this point, nothing about him could surprise her.

Well, yes, she thought. Something could. Or, rather, something had. The way he'd kissed her.

The way she'd responded.

Back to that.

Elle turned her face to the window and stared blindly into the night. She responded to music. To art. That didn't come close to describing how she had reacted to that kiss. The quick, reflexive sense of disgust. Of revulsion. The shock at the feel of a man's mouth on hers...

And then, oh, God, and then the incredible explosion of heat that had swept through her thighs, her belly, her breasts...

"Take the ramp, on right, in four-point-eight miles."

Startled, Elle swung toward him. "What was that?"

"My navigator."

"Your what?"

"My navigator," he repeated. "She says we turn off just ahead."

Was she losing her mind? "Who says?"

Falco flashed a quick grin. It was so unexpected that she was half-afraid her mouth had dropped open.

"The GPS," he said, jerking his chin toward the dashboard. "The Voice of the Robot Queen. She has all the charm of a machine but she's generally right on the money."

The global positioning system. Of course. Elle looked at the lighted panel. Was she so far gone that she hadn't noticed it glowing like a TV monitor?

"I turned it on only a few minutes ago," Falco said, as if he'd read her thoughts. "I don't know this area and I don't want to just keep driving without doing some reconnoitering."

"Reconnoitering?" she said blankly.

"Checking things out. Making some plans."

"What plans? As soon as we get to Los Angeles—"

"Is that where you live?"

"In Studio City. Yes. The street is—"

"We're not going there."

Elle cocked her head. "What do you mean, we're not going there?"

Falco shifted his weight. "I told you before. I want you someplace safe."

"And I told you—"

"Turn right in point-three miles."

"I know what you told me." Lights glowed faintly in the distance ahead; a sign flashed by. The name of a town she'd never heard of, logos for food, for gas, for motels. "Remember? I asked if you had a friend who'd take you in for the night and you told me that you didn't."

He was right. He'd asked and she, idiot that she was, had stupidly said she had no friends. It was true enough but she hadn't meant he could take her wherever it was he was taking her.

"Look, Mr. Orsini—"

"I'd think, after all this, we could give up the 'Mister' thing, don't you?"

She looked at him, felt the rush of color climb her face until she realized he hadn't meant the remark the way she'd taken it. His tone was level, his concentration still on the road. He'd been referring to what had happened in the cabin, not to the kiss.

The kiss hadn't meant anything to him. Why would it? He'd probably kissed more women than he could remember. She wasn't a fool, she knew that most women would be eager to be kissed by a man like him.

She also knew the reason he'd kissed her. To show control. He'd even told her that. Not that it had been necessary. She knew all about that kind of thing.

The SUV slowed, took a right.

"Pick one."

Bewildered, she swung toward him. "One what?"

"A motel. Your choice." He slowed the SUV and now

she saw the line of motels fronting what had become a four-lane road.

Her belly knotted.

What she'd feared was happening. He had taken that kiss as permission to take her. A bitter taste filled her mouth. Despite everything she knew about men, a tiny part of her had hoped he was different.

She should have known better.

None of them were different, she thought coldly, and sat up straight in the leather seat.

"Forget it," she snapped.

"Yeah, I know. They're not up to your usual standards but it's the best we're going to do."

"You've miscalculated, Mr. Orsini."

Her voice was cold enough to turn water to ice. What now? Falco thought wearily. He was bone tired; the last thing he wanted was another battle.

"Look," he said, "it's late. I told you, I don't know this area. I punched in a request for a place to stay the night, the GPS came up with this as the closest loc—"

"I am not sleeping with you."

Her tone was quick and sharp. Another time, another place, he might have seen her reaction as having some logic to it. She was a movie star; she was paid to turn men on. Maybe that was a crude way to put it, but, basically, it was what women like her did. He was a stranger, a man who had shown up, uninvited, in her life and now he'd told her they were going to spend the night at a cheap motel.

So, yes, maybe her attitude bore some semblance of logic.

Unfortunately, he wasn't in the mood to see it.

For starters, he didn't like Elle Bissette. She was a gorgeous package on the outside, but on the inside, she was the worst kind of snob. She'd taken one look at him and decided he wasn't in her league. He despised that kind of thinking; he'd never be interested in a woman who made judgments like that, not even for a night's worth of sex with a woman most men would crawl over each other to reach.

Besides, sex was the last thing on his mind.

He was tired and hungry and what he wanted was a shower, a hot meal, enough strong coffee to keep him awake while she told him what in hell was going on because, come hell or high water, she was going to tell him.

Then he wanted to fall into bed and sleep.

And all Elle Bissette could think of was that he was going to jump her bones?

Anger rose inside him, quick and hot. At her, at himself. He slammed on the brakes and pulled into the parking lot of the nearest motel, stopping the engine and swinging toward her even as he did.

"Has anybody ever told you that you have one incredibly overblown idea of where you stand on the desirability scale?"

Elle undid her seat belt and reached for the door handle. "Good night, Mr. Orsini. It's been—"

Falco's hand wrapped around her elbow. He spun her toward him.

"You really think that's what this is all about? That I took one look at the famous Elle Bissette and began plotting a way I could get my hands on her?"

Color shot into her face. "You're disgusting!"

"Or maybe you think that's the way I get women into my bed. Wander around, find one who looks as if she needs a little help, then tell her she owes me."

"Let go of my arm!"

"Well, let me set the record straight. I'm not interested. Have you got that, or you want it spelled out?"

"Damn you! I said—"

"I heard what you said." Falco, eyes glinting, mouth hard, leaned forward. "You are nothing I would ever want."

"And nothing you could ever have!"

"You don't get it. A man would have to be crazy to put up with an egotistical psycho like you."

"Thank you for the personality analysis," she said coldly. "Be sure and add the cost to your bodyguarding bill."

"Trust me, honey." Falco's lips twisted. "My services cost nothing. The whole thing is free of charge."

"Fine, because that's exactly what your services are worth."

"I'd sooner go to bed with a block of ice than with you."

She flashed an ice-queen smile. "Whatever turns you on, Orsini."

"Not you, babe, that's for sure."

Elle recoiled. His words were like a slap in the face and that was ridiculous. She had no wish to turn anybody on, certainly not a man like him, all that overbearing arrogance, that swaggering masculinity...

All that strength, the courage, the sudden hints at tenderness...

Qualities he didn't have, she thought grimly. Qualities she'd assigned him because she had the imagination that went with being an actress.

Elle raised her chin. "Are you done?"

"I'm done, all right." Falco lifted his hand from her arm. "You want out?"

"Damned right I do."

"Fine." He dug in his pocket, hauled out his wallet. "You'll need cash."

"I won't need anything from you."

"Yeah, you will. Or did you remember to grab your purse before I hauled you out of that cabin?"

That stopped her. Her eyes narrowed.

"Hauled me out, is right. Carrying me out of there as if—as if I were a recalcitrant child."

Dammit, how could she do this? How could she accuse him of being the worst kind of bastard? And how could she be so beautiful?

Her eyes blazed. Her mouth was set in a sulky pout. She was full of passion and life and no matter what he thought of her, the fact that some crazy wanted to hurt her made his belly knot.

"Exactly as if I were a recalcitrant child, if you even know what the word means!"

"That's enough." His voice was low, rough, filled with warning.

"You think you can—you can pretend you want to protect me when all the while, all the while you just want to—to overpower me—"

"Elle." He grasped her wrists. "You know better than that."

"Oh, I know better, all right. I know all about men like you…"

Her voice broke. Falco was looking at her as if she were crazy and perhaps she was. Everything he'd said was true. He'd done nothing but offer her kindness and she—and she—

Tears rose in her eyes and spilled down her cheeks. Falco cursed and reached for her. She gave a little mew of protest, but when he pulled her into his arms, she burrowed against him.

"I didn't mean—"

"I know." And he did know; she was terrified and doing one hell of a job of not showing it. Beautiful as well as brave, he thought, and drew her closer.

"I just— Everything seems so out of control—"

"It isn't," he said with more conviction than he felt. "You're safe and I'm going to keep you that way."

She gave a wet sniffle. "I know you didn't bring me here to—to seduce me."

"No," he said, trying for a light touch as he held her, rocked her gently in his arms. "I'm more a hot sheet motel man myself."

She gave a hiccupping laugh. It was a start. He went on rocking her, his lips pressed lightly to her hair. It smelled of the night and, incongruously, of roses. After a few seconds, she lifted her head from his shoulder. "Falco?"

"Yeah?"

"I know—I know you didn't bring me here looking for—for payment."

"Damned right, I didn't," he said gruffly.

"But—but you have the right to know that—that it isn't you. I mean, I'm just not— I'm just not—"

"That's okay," he said, and wondered why the words sounded hollow. A few seconds went by. Then he cleared his throat. "Is it that make-believe cowboy actor?"

"Chad?" Elle gave a low laugh. "He's got a wife he's crazy about and six kids. No. It's not him. It's just—it's just that I don't do that."

"Sleep around." Why did that admission make him feel so damned good? "I'm glad."

"No. I mean—I mean, I don't—I don't do the—the sex thing."

She felt a stillness suddenly settle over him. What in the world had made her make such an admission? Sex was not something she thought about, much less talked about, not in any way, not with anyone.

"The sex thing," he said, as if he'd never heard those words before.

Elle winced. What he'd never heard were those three words infused with such special meaning. How could she have shown such little discretion? Irritation at herself made her tone turn cool.

"Is that a problem?"

Yes, Falco thought, it damned well was. That a woman should not like sex, because that had to be what not "doing" the sex thing meant, that a woman, especially one who looked like this, who felt warm and soft in a man's arms, whose mouth tasted of honey, should feel that way about sex was, well, unfortunate.

But was it a problem for him?

No.

He was, okay, attracted to her. Never mind all that stuff he'd told himself a little while ago. She was incredibly easy on the eyes and she needed help.

His help.

Whatever mess she was in had *Danger* written all over it. That kind of thing upped the ante. A maiden in distress. A knight on a white charger, and never mind how tarnished his armor might be. Add it all together and you had a hot thing going.

Hell, he'd been there enough times to know.

But there were other women. There would always be other women. That was the cold, honest, down-and-dirty truth. Women liked to think the world was full of kindred souls searching for each other.

Men knew better.

He did, anyway.

At seventeen, he'd made out with Cathy Callahan in the backseat of her father's Buick. A month later, Cathy was history and he'd repeated the performance with Angie Baroni under the creaky stands of a high school on Staten Island where he'd won an "away" football game with a last-minute touchdown and she'd waved her pom-poms and cheered.

Of course, he'd polished his style over the ensuing years but even his brothers, no one man/one woman forever enthusiasts themselves—though that seemed to have changed recently for Dante and Rafe—had laughed and said it would be a day at the beach in Antarctica when Falco Orsini decided he needed one woman to the exclusion of all others.

"Mr. Orsini?"

Falco frowned, focused on the lovely and suddenly composed face inches from his.

"Just in case you see this as a challenge to your masculinity…"

Her voice had become cool. It irritated him, the sudden change from tender to tough, but, hell, he admired it, too.

For a couple of seconds, he wondered how she'd react if he said yes, that was exactly how he saw it, that she'd melted in his arms a little while ago and was he really expected to believe she wasn't in to, as she put it, "the sex thing"?

But none of this was about sex. It was about keeping her safe.

That was all that mattered.

Time to lighten the mood again, he decided. He put a serious look on his face and drew back. She sat up straight, her eyes wary as they met his.

"Here's my best offer," he said politely. "You stop calling me 'Mr. Orsini,' I'll try and survive the blow to my ego. How's that sound?" He almost laughed at the expression on her face. Clearly, his answer was not what she'd expected. "Deal?" he said, holding out his hand.

He watched her think it over. Then she gave a quick smile and put her hand in his. "Deal."

And just the brush of her palm against his, the touch of her fingers, made every muscle in his body leap to attention.

Something told him celibacy wasn't going to be as easy as he'd made it sound.

He left her in the SUV while he got them a room.

The clerk must have been asleep. He showed up at the desk

looking bleary-eyed. Falco signed the register as E. Presley, 10 Blue Suede Lane, Memphis, Tennessee, and ignored the line where you were supposed to enter your license plate number. He didn't mention there was anyone else with him, paid cash, took the room key card—he suspected it would turn out to be the most up-to-date feature in the place—and asked if there was somewhere nearby to get a meal.

"Diner's one block that direction," the clerk said, smothering a yawn.

Falco nodded, thanked the guy and strolled out to the parking lot. Elle was still there. She was sound asleep, her head resting on the seat back.

He got behind the wheel and watched her for a couple of minutes. She looked exhausted, incredibly young…and there it was again, that sweet vulnerability that had brought him to Hollywood in the first place.

A muscle knotted in his jaw.

He drove to the rear of the two-story building. He'd requested a corner room on the first floor and the parking space directly in front of it was empty. Most of the spaces were; it didn't take much effort to figure out that the world had long-ago bypassed this little town.

He got out of the SUV, went around to the passenger door, opened it.

"Elle."

Nothing. Not even a flutter of her lashes.

"Elle," he said more loudly, "come on, wake up. We'll get washed, then go get something to eat and have a long talk." He sighed. "Okay, we can talk tomorrow. Showers, food, and then you can climb into a real bed."

Still nothing. Falco leaned into the car, touched her shoulder.

"Elle, come on. Open your eyes."

She murmured something and turned her face toward him. Her hair brushed over his fingers. Her breath caressed his cheek. The muscle in his jaw knotted again. Okay. Let her sleep. He'd carry her into the motel room, give her a few minutes, then wake her.

Lifting her was simple. One arm under her, the other around her. He stepped away from the car, kicked the door shut. It was easy enough to shift her weight, carry her to the room and maneuver the key card into the lock. The door opened to a dark room that smelled of disinfectant and disuse. He used his elbow to feel around for a wall switch, found one and hit it.

A dull light came on.

The room was small, shabby but clean. The furnishings were utilitarian. One window. One chair.

One double bed.

Her carried her to it, stood her on her feet while he kept one arm clamped tightly around her. She slumped against him like a rag doll as he drew back the patterned bedspread, pulled down the thin top sheet and equally thin blanket.

"Come on, baby," he said softly. Slowly, gently, he eased her down on the mattress.

She gave a deep sigh. So deep, he thought, so weary. It was a sigh of exhaustion.

He took off her shoes. Thought about taking off her clothes and getting her down to her underwear and just as quickly decided against it. Instead, he pulled up the covers, tucked them around her shoulders, all his movements brisk and businesslike…

Yeah, but brisk and businesslike didn't keep him from thinking of how much he wanted to bend down and brush her lips with his. Just that. A light kiss. A way to repeat his pledge to keep her safe.

"Hell," he muttered.

He checked the window lock, pulled the curtain. Double-locked the door. Located the heating unit and turned it to high.

Okay. To the john next. He used the facilities, washed his hands, his face, tore open the plastic pack that held a plastic cup, filled it with a tepid mix of water and chlorine from the tap and rinsed his mouth. It wasn't the best hygiene in the world but it would have to do.

In the bedroom again, he turned out the light, waited a few seconds until his eyes adjusted to the dark. The single chair looked as if it might support a dwarf but not a man who stood six-three. And the last time he'd weighed himself at the gym near the Orsini Brothers Investments building in Manhattan, he'd been at 220.

There was always the floor, but he needed a night's rest.

"Okay," he said, as if there were someone there to hear him.

Falco toed off his mocs and lay down on the bed as far from Elle as he could. The mattress sagged, the heater was making noise though it wasn't producing much heat, but he'd slept in places that made this look like a palace.

Elle Bissette, Hollywood actress, surely had not. That cabin she owned wasn't luxurious by any means but she'd made it clear it had sentimental value to her as her first big purchase.

Her day-to-day home, in L.A., was certain to be movie-star impressive.

Shabby motel room or not, she had not awakened. But she'd started dreaming, making little noises, arms and legs twitching. Not a good dream, whatever it was.

"Elle," he said softly. "You're okay."

She whimpered. Her lovely face contorted.

The hell with it.

Falco moved closer and gathered her in his arms, whispering reassurances. He felt the tension ease from her body. After a minute or two she sighed, turned toward him and lay her head on his shoulder, her hand over his heart. Her breathing went from choppy to relaxed.

He told himself he could let go of her now.

He could...

But he didn't. Instead, he drew her closer. Shut his eyes as he inhaled the clean, sweet fragrance of her skin.

And followed her into sleep.

CHAPTER SEVEN

ELLE CAME awake slowly, rising from the depths of a deep, dreamless sleep.

It was the first time in longer than she could remember that she hadn't spent the night trapped within fragmented dream landscapes…

Unless she was dreaming right now.

She felt the sudden leap of her heart.

Yes. This had to be a dream. How else to explain coming awake in a strange bed in a strange room, the half light of dawn visible behind the curtain?

How else to explain coming awake in the warm, strong arms of a man?

"Morning," a husky male voice murmured into her hair, and Elle knew it wasn't a dream at all.

Frantic, she tried to pull free of Falco's embrace. That didn't work. His arms only tightened around her.

"Don't panic," he said softly. "It's me. Falco."

If that was supposed to calm her, it didn't. Elle's struggles increased.

"Elle," he said quietly, "we shared the bed, that's all. Nothing happened. Absolutely nothing."

They'd shared the bed. Shared a night's rest. Elle stopped struggling, took a long breath.

"We're both still fully dressed." His words took on a touch of light humor. "If we'd done anything except sleep, trust me, honey, we wouldn't be."

He was right. She was wearing all her clothes. So was he. But his arms were around her... His arms were around her, and she was safe.

Elle let out a breath and went still in his embrace.

"Okay?"

She nodded and slowly, carefully, looked up at him. Her heart gave another leap but it had nothing to do with fear. What a beautiful man he was! Instinct told her he'd laugh at hearing himself described that way but it was true. His face had the elegant bone structure of Michelangelo's *David*: the strong nose, chiseled lips, firm jaw. His eyes were very dark, all obsidian pupils in the dusky early morning light; his lashes were long and enviably thick.

Beautiful, indeed.

The night had brought the shadow of morning stubble to his cheeks. Male models often cultivated that look to give them a macho aura but it never quite worked.

It did on Falco Orsini.

He looked masculine and beautiful and dangerous.

And sexy. Incredibly sexy. It was just a reasonable conclusion. A woman didn't have to like sex to admit a man looked sexy.

"What are you thinking?"

Falco had a little smile on his lips. It was intimate and knowing, as if he'd read her thoughts, and it brought a rush of color to her cheeks.

"Nothing," she said quickly. "I mean—I mean, I was trying to remember what happened last night. The last thing I can recall, we were sitting in the car."

"Yeah." He caught a strand of her hair in his hand, let it

trail through his fingers. Her hair felt like silk. How could a woman look so beautiful after what she'd gone through last night, and without a drop of makeup? For years, he'd joked about what he called the 5:00 a.m. face, the one he swore women put on while a man was still sleeping rather than let him see her as she really was. This, what he saw now, was Elle's true five-in-the-morning face and it was spectacular. Skin as creamy as satin. Eyes bright with intelligence. Cheekbones washed with light color. And that mouth. That lovely mouth, so pink, so soft, so perfect…

Falco forced himself to breathe normally, dragged his thoughts away from entering what could only be dangerous territory.

"I left you in the SUV, booked this room…" He smiled. "When I got back, you were sound asleep. So I carried you inside." He smiled again. "You missed your chance to get a first look at our deluxe, six-star accommodations. Does that do it?" He could see that it didn't. "No, huh? You're wondering what you're doing here, in bed with me."

She felt her face fill with heat. Falco nodded.

"Well, it never occurred to me to ask the character in the front office what the sleeping arrangements were. Turned out we have only the one bed. I put you on it. Then I looked around and saw that I had a couple of options. I could sack out on the Aubusson on the floor—"

Okay. That had helped. Elle's lips curved in a smile. It was faint, but yes, it was a smile.

"Definitely an Aubusson," she said.

"My other option was that very comfortable Eames chair."

She peeped over his shoulder. Eames, indeed. The battered chair reminded her of one in a shelter where she and her mother had once stayed. Something of the memory must have shown on her face because Falco put his hand under her chin and tilted her face to his.

"Hey," he said softly, "are you okay?"

"Yes, of course." She forced a smile. "Lucky man, to have had two such great choices."

He grinned. "I thought so, too. That's why I went for option numero three. Share the bed by taking the far side of it." His smile faded; his eyes turned dark again. "But you started dreaming. It didn't take much to see it wasn't a good dream so I got you out of it and you sort of turned toward me and I figured if I pushed you away you'd fall back into that dream so I stayed where I was and you—you settled in."

She wanted to tell him she didn't believe him, that she'd never, as he'd called it, "settled in" a man's arms and never would. But his tone was calm, his gaze steady. And the way they were lying, she in his arms, her hand on his heart, was proof that he was telling the truth.

How could she feel safe with this man? With any man, but especially one this big, this strong, this sure of himself?

He was watching her with an intensity that would have sent her running just twenty-four hours ago, but now—

Now, she found herself wondering what the stubble on his jaw would feel like under the brush of her fingers. Would it be bristly or soft? She could find out in a second. All she had to do was lift her hand, touch his face and then—then, maybe that tingle in her breasts, her belly would go away.

"Elle."

His voice was low. Rough. The sound of it thrilled her.

"Baby. You keep looking at me like that and—"

She knew what she had to do. Stop looking at him. Move away. Get up from the bed.

"And what?" she said in a voice she hardly recognized as her own.

Falco groaned, bent his head and kissed her. It was the lightest of kisses, just the soft brush of his lips over hers.

And it wasn't enough.

She heard the sharp intake of her own breath and then her hands were lifting, lifting, moving up his chest, over his shoulders, capturing his face and yes, oh, yes, that stubble on his cheeks felt incredible. Soft, like his mouth. Rough, like his voice when he'd said her name.

He said it again now, whispered it against her mouth, and then he groaned and rolled her onto her back, came down over her, cupped her face as she was cupping his and his lips moved against hers, his kiss changed, hungry now, hot and wild and she yielded to it, more than yielded, wanted it, wanted his kiss, wanted him.

She moaned and flung her leg over his. He made a rough sound, slid his hand under her shirt, cupped her breast. A cry broke from her throat. She put her hand over his, felt her nipple swelling, beading, felt a liquid heat forming low in her belly…

Felt a wave of sheer terror sweep through her.

"No!"

Her cry of fear was fierce. She tore her mouth from Falco's and at first she thought he wasn't going to let go of her but then his big, hard body went still and he rolled away from her and got to his feet.

Silence filled the dingy room. She wanted to say something, anything. But he spoke first.

"It's getting late," he said brusquely. "I want to be out of here ASAP."

Elle scrambled up against the creaking headboard. Falco's mouth was a flat line, his eyes were cold. She knew she owed him an explanation but how could she offer one when she couldn't even explain what had happened to herself?

"Falco, I'm sorry. I didn't mean to—to lead you on."

He looked straight at her. What she saw in his face made her breath catch.

"It was my mistake."

"No, it was me. I don't even understand why—"

"No," he said coldly, "neither do I. I'm responsible for your safety. I lost sight of that but it won't happen again." He swung away from her. "I'm going to take a shower. When I'm done, you can do the same."

"Falco…"

"Five minutes," he said curtly. "Then we're out of here."

He was impossible.

Caring one minute, unfeeling the next.

She knew she'd hurt him. Not him. His pride. She'd had a couple of minutes to think and she was pretty sure she knew what had happened. She was frightened, she'd reacted in the most primitive way to a primitive man.

No. Falco was a lot of things but "primitive" wasn't one of them despite the long, muscular body, the quick reflexes, the ability to think and react like a predator.

And he wasn't a man who'd take advantage of a woman's emotions.

He wouldn't have to.

Elle took her turn in the bathroom. She stood under the lukewarm spray—that was as hot as the water would get—and wondered what twist of fate had sent him into her life. The better question was, how would she get him out of it?

That arrogant declaration. *I'm responsible for your safety.* The hell he was! Nobody was responsible for anything about her except her.

Was that true? What about what she'd found waiting at the cabin last night? What if Falco hadn't been there to take her in his arms and ease her terror?

She shut her eyes, lifted her face to the tepid spray.

The toy cat had frightened her more than the marked-up Bon Soir ad, more than the note, more than anything she could have anticipated. The toy cat, her toy or one that was its absolute image, pinned to the wall of a cabin nobody knew existed except her...

Ever since this started, she'd told herself she didn't know the reason for it or who could do this to her. A lie. She knew. At least, she had a very good idea. And she could no longer avoid admitting it to herself, but, dear heaven, not to anyone else.

A fist banged on the bathroom door. "One minute, Bissette. After that, we'll pass on breakfast."

Elle's eyes narrowed. Forget caring. Falco Orsini was a bullying dictator. She didn't want him poking his nose into her life. She couldn't afford to let him poke his nose into her life!

Once they returned to the real world from wherever this place was, she'd get rid of him. *Here's a check for your time, a handshake, and goodbye, Mr. Bodyguard.*

As for that ridiculous threat about passing on breakfast... Did he really think he could scare her with such nonsense?

Her stomach growled.

Elle rolled her eyes, shut off the water and reached for a towel.

Falco worried that someone might recognize her. Her face was famous. The last thing he wanted was to have word go out that Elle Bissette was in whatever in hell you called this town.

Once they were in the rented SUV, he grabbed the pair of sunglasses he'd left on the dash and handed them to her.

"Put them on," he said curtly.

She looked at them as if she'd never seen dark glasses before.

"I don't need them," she said, "but thank you for the offer."

He almost grinned. The thank-you was as close to being a four-letter word as anyone could have managed. The lady had balls, he had to give her credit for that.

"Put them on anyway."

"I just said—"

"You want a meal? Or you want some truck driver spotting the famous Elle Bissette and calling the local news station?"

She glared at him, obviously hating that he'd out thought her. Then she snatched the glasses from his hand and plopped them on her nose.

Better, but not perfect.

Falco made a quick left and pulled in to a gas station. He pumped the tank full, went into the minuscule office to pay and came out with a red ball cap emblazoned with the oil company's logo.

"Put your hair up and wear this."

She looked at the cap, gave a little shudder—a shudder that would have been lots more dramatic had she seen the guy who'd been wearing the thing before Falco bought it for twenty bucks. But she twisted her hair into something like a ponytail, held it at the crown of her head, then pulled on the cap and yanked it low over her eyes.

Definitely better. You could still see her nose, her mouth and her chin, all delicate, all beautiful, all pure Elle Bissette, but he knew damned well that the only man who'd realize that was the one who'd held her in his arms through the night, who'd awakened long before she had and imagined what might happen if he woke the sleeping princess with a kiss.

He was a damned fool.

He stepped hard on the gas even though the diner was only a couple of hundred feet ahead and lurched into a parking slot.

"I know it's not what you're accustomed to," he said coldly, "but we all have to make sacrifices."

She shot him a look. "You have no idea what I'm accustomed to," she said, and before he could respond, tell her he damned well did and that third-rate motels, greasy-spoon diners and stuck-up females were not what he was accustomed to, either, she was out of the car and striding toward the door.

What had happened this morning was what had to happen when a man woke up tenting the sheets. Elle had been handy, that was all. He hadn't liked her from the start and the more time he spent with her, the more that assessment was validated.

As for that heart-wrenching little story about not "doing the sex thing"... Bull. What she did understand was how easy it was to use men. A little teasing, then pull back. It probably kept guys on the edge of sanity until she got things her own way.

She was almost at the front door. Falco went after her, grabbed her wrist, jerked her against his side.

"I can walk without your help, Orsini," she snapped.

"Not while you're with me," he snapped back, and the way she looked up at him said, as clearly as words, that being with him was a situation that wasn't going to go on much longer.

And that was just fine with him.

She didn't open the menu.

"I'm not hungry," she said and when the waitress showed up, she ordered coffee. Black.

"The house special," Falco said. "Do the eggs over easy, make sure the bacon's crisp. Hotcakes, not French toast, extra syrup on the side." He looked up at the girl and smiled. "Please."

Please was all it took, Elle thought coldly. The waitress's answering smile made it clear she'd have walked on burning coals to provide whatever this particular customer wanted.

"Toast?"

"Rye. And do the whole thing twice."

Elle waited until the girl hurried away. "I hope you didn't order the extra meal for me. I told you, I'm not—"

"Hungry. I'm not deaf. Just let the food sit there if you don't want it."

They waited in silence until the waitress brought their breakfasts, one gigantic platter for him, one for Elle. He spread a napkin in his lap, picked up his fork and dug in. He could feel Elle's eyes on him. After a couple of seconds, she put her napkin in her lap, too, and reached for her fork.

He raised an eyebrow. She flashed him a murderous look, but when she spoke, her voice was surprisingly young, almost childlike.

"It's a sin to let food go to waste."

Then she dug in.

She ate everything.

He wondered about that. Was it because she believed leaving it would have been wrong? Or was she starved for a solid meal? Despite what she obviously thought about him, Falco had dated a lot of models, a couple of actresses and a well-known Broadway star. All of them had moaned about having to watch their weight; they'd order endless courses, then poke at them.

Not Elle.

She ate as if it mattered. Then she slugged down two mugs of black coffee, made a quick trip to the ladies room and they were on their way again.

"Where are we going?"

"To your cabin."

"Good. I'll get my car—"

"I want to see if anyone's been there since we left. Assuming they didn't, you can pick up your handbag and anything else you can't do without. Then you're going to tell me where you live and we'll go there."

"That's ridiculous. I am perfectly capable—"

"That's how we're going to do it," he said in a take-no-prisoners tone. "You don't agree, we'll bypass the cabin and head straight for your place."

He felt her eyes on him. "I really dislike you intensely, Mr. Orsini."

Back to square one. "That breaks my heart."

"Such a childish attitude. Just because I didn't—I didn't succumb to your pathetic attempt at seduction…"

Elle gasped as Falco turned the wheel hard, brought the SUV to the shoulder of the road and shifted into Park.

"Is that what you think this is all about?"

"I know that's what this is all about."

"You seem to know everything you need to about me," he said coldly. "Well, here's a flash. I wasn't the one who started things this morning."

"Not true," she said, even as a small voice inside her said *He's right, it was all your doing.*

His smile made her wedge herself as far into the corner as her seat belt would permit. "You're good, I'll give you that. The dramatic little scene about not doing 'the sex thing'— and then, the next second, you're looking up at me with big, innocent eyes and asking me to make love to you—"

"I didn't do anything of the sort! I never asked you to—"

His fingers flew, undoing his seat belt, then hers, and he hauled her into his arms.

"Do you think that's the way to keep a guy like me in line?"

"What are you talking about?"

"Play that kind of game again, baby, I can promise you how it will end."

"No. It wasn't a—"

He kissed her, his lips taking hers, parting hers, possessing hers. She formed a hand into a fist, pounded it against his shoulder but he was ruthless, determined—and suddenly she felt fire ignite in her blood, felt it rush from her breasts to her belly.

Falco lifted his head.

"No more games," he said gruffly. "Not unless you're prepared to play straight to the end."

Calmly, as if nothing had happened, he closed the latch of her seat belt, then his, turned on the engine and pulled back onto the road.

The cabin stood silent, the door open as he'd left it and stirring idly in the soft breeze.

He could tell no one had been there since they'd left but he wasn't about to take chances. He took a long look before he opened the car door.

"Stay," he commanded.

Elle smiled sweetly. "Woof woof."

He couldn't help it. He laughed.

"Good girl," he said, and laughed again when she bared her teeth.

He checked the cabin. Nobody. Elle's purse and car keys were where she'd left them. He grabbed them, did another walk-through, then went back to the SUV.

"Has anyone…"

Her laughter was gone. Her eyes were big and filled with anxiety.

"No," he said. "The place is untouched."

She let out her breath. "That's good. That's very good. And since that's the case, Mr. Orsini—"

Falco raised his eyebrows.

"Since that's the case, Falco, you can surely leave me here."

"Forget that."

"I'm not going to stay." She shuddered. "I'm never going to stay here again. I'll just get into my car and drive myself home."

"To find what? Something similar to what you found here?"

"Oh, for God's sake," she said, no more dulcet tones wrapping the words in sugar, "I'll be absolutely fine!"

"That's the way it's going to be, Elle. I'll drive you to your place. Check it out. If everything's okay, I'll leave."

Her eyes searched his. "Promise?"

"Promise," he said, but why spoil things by adding that he'd first telephone a guy he knew out here who did excellent body-guard work because he wasn't about to leave Elle on her own and he sure as hell wasn't about to go on guarding her. He had a life to go back to. Anyone could do this job; it didn't have to be him. He didn't have to like his clients or whatever you wanted to call them, but he had to at least get along with them.

He and Elle were not getting along, that was for sure—especially in those moments when he crossed the line he always kept between himself and those who needed his help. He'd never done that, until now. And he didn't like it...

"Promise," he said again, and crossed his heart, but with his fingers crossed the way he and his brothers used to when they were kids lying to each other. "So, if there's anything you want inside..."

She hesitated. Then she nodded, her face expressionless. She stepped from the SUV and headed for the cabin. He started after her but she held up her hand.

"It's just one thing. I can handle it by myself."

He waited, leaning against the SUV, arms folded while she went up the porch steps and into the cabin. The "one thing" was probably a sack full of cosmetics. Or jewelry. Or clothes. Just because she wasn't wearing makeup or jewelry, just because she was dressed like a couple of million other American women her age didn't mean—

How wrong could a man be?

She came out of the cabin a minute later, a small silver-framed photo in her hand.

"That's it?" he said in disbelief.

"That's it," she said.

He had questions. A thousand questions. But the expression on her face—sorrow, distress, despair so profound it made him forget his anger—kept him from voicing them.

"Okay," he said, and because it was too late to think, he leaned down when she reached him and kissed her. It was a soft kiss. Tender. And, for just long enough to make his heart kick against his ribs, she fitted her lips to his and kissed him back.

Then she got into the SUV, put the picture in her purse, told him her address in L.A. as if nothing had just happened and they made the two-hour trip in silence.

She lived, as she'd already told him, in Studio City.

A condo. The area was pleasant, the building was well-maintained, but Falco knew something about property costs out here and though prices in this part of Los Angeles might be astronomical by the standards of the American heartland, it didn't have the feel of super-priced real estate.

He went in alone, left Elle in the car.

"Stay put," he warned, but this time, he didn't get a sarcastic "woof" in response. She seemed remote. Was it because of that kiss? Or was she hoping everything would be okay here?

Part of him wanted to think it was because he'd told her he'd be leaving and that she was anticipating that and wishing it wouldn't happen, which was ridiculous. They were like oil and water; besides, he had work waiting back East, a tough meeting Monday with a banker from Indonesia, lunch Tuesday with a contingent of money men from Zurich.

As soon as he'd finished checking the condo, he'd put in a call to a guy he'd served with. Rick lived out here, he was top-notch at what he did.

Elle would be well-protected.

Her place was small, just a living room, small dining room, kitchen and lavatory on the lower level, all of it spotless and undisturbed. The rooms were nicely furnished but walking into it was pretty much like walking into a high-end hotel suite.

Falco climbed the steps to the upper level. A bathroom. Fine. A small room that seemed to be a home office. Also fine. The last door had to open on Elle's bedroom...

"Merda!"

Someone had taken the place apart. Drawers had been flung open, the contents dumped on the pale birch floor. Clothes had been yanked from the hangers. Words, ugly words describing women, had been scrawled on the pristine walls in what he at first thought was blood, but when he touched it, was red paint.

Worst of all was Elle's bed. Someone had gone at it with something sharp. A knife. A big knife. Nothing else could have left such devastation behind...

"Omigod!"

Falco whirled around. Elle stood in the doorway, her face white.

"My God," she said, "my God, my God, my God—"

He went to her, scooped her into his arms, carried her down the stairs to the SUV, got inside with her on his lap, his lips against her hair, his hands sliding up and down her spine, whispering words of reassurance.

Her arms were tight around his neck. She was shaking, sobbing, repeating "Why? Why? Why?" like a litany.

"Shhh, baby," he said, his arms tightening around her, holding her, rocking her, wanting to turn back the clock so she would not see what someone had done as much as he wished he'd been here when it happened so he could have killed the bastard who had done it with his bare hands.

At last, her trembling stopped. She took a couple of deep, shaky breaths. He felt her heartbeat slow. "Elle," he said softly, framing her face with his hands, drawing back so he could look into her eyes. "Elle. Who did this, honey? Who wants to hurt you?"

Her lips parted. She started to speak. Then she made a sad little sound and buried her face against his throat.

"I can't stay here," she whispered.

Falco nodded. "No," he said calmly, "you can't."

"There's a—a hotel on—"

"You can't stay there, either."

He was not only calm, but he also was possessed by a deadly quiet. His brothers, anyone who'd ever had anything to do with him, would have recognized it.

"I told you, there's no one I can impose on."

"It wouldn't matter. I don't want you in L.A." His mouth thinned. "Hell, I don't want you in California."

"Falco. That sounds good but—"

"Hawaii," he said. "Hawaii's perfect."

Elle sat back, Falco's arms enclosing her. She gave what might have been a laugh.

"Hawaii is six hours away. I've never been there. I don't know anything about it. I don't know anyone who lives there. I don't have a plane ticket. And then there's the movie. My contract. Antonio will expect me on the set Monday morning."

He smiled. "Details," he said softly, and when she parted her lips to tell him that going to Hawaii was impossible, he drew her close and kissed her until she sighed, leaned into his protective embrace and kissed him back.

CHAPTER EIGHT

DETAILS, Falco had said.

That turned out to be an interesting way to describe things.

As soon as they were in the SUV and heading for the freeway, he flipped open his mobile phone and hit a speed dial number. Elle fought back the desire to tell him using a phone while driving was illegal. She had the feeling the man beside her never cared too much about legalities.

The thought should have been worrying.

It was, instead, reassuring. While she was trying to figure out how that could be, she heard him say, "Farinelli? Falco Orsini here."

He was talking with Antonio. Her director. He would not be thrilled to hear Falco didn't want her on the set Monday. An understatement. He would not permit it; she was certain of it. They were on the freeway now and the roar of traffic drowned out Falco's side of the conversation, only the end of it when he said, "Yes, that's correct, I'll be in touch."

Surprised, she looked at him. "Antonio said it would be all right?"

Falco shrugged. "He'll shoot around you."

"Yes, but—"

He reached for her hand and brought it to his mouth.

His lips brushed her fingers. His breath whispered over her skin.

"Stop worrying, okay? I told you, I'll handle everything."

He put her hand back in her lap, flipped his phone open again. She could still feel the electric tingle of his lips on her flesh.

Her heart raced.

She was turning control of her life over to this man. How had that happened? She certainly hadn't given him permission to take charge—but then, she couldn't imagine him ever asking for permission to do anything.

Being with him, putting herself in his hands, was like riding a roller coaster. The nervous anticipation of the long climb to the top, the sharp bite of fear that began at the moment of descent and then the rush, the breathless realization that you'd let go of everything solid and real in favor of the transcendent excitement of just being.

Elle swallowed hard. She didn't like roller coasters. Then, why go on this particular ride? She swung toward Falco, ready to tell him she wouldn't go along with his plans.

"Falco—"

He raised the index finger of the hand that held the phone in acknowledgement.

"Right," he said. "On the ocean. Very private. Limited access. Top-notch security system. Yes, Maui would be perfect. And I'll need a car waiting at the airport. No, I don't care about the make. Just something with lots of horses. And black. Yes, fine. That will do."

Do for whom? No one had made decisions for her in years, especially not a man. Why was she letting such a thing happen now?

"Falco," she said sharply. "We need to discuss this. I've been thinking it over and I'm not at all sure I want to go to Haw—"

But he was already deep in call number three.

"Yes," he said, "that's correct. Immediately. To Hawaii. Just two people."

"Two people?" she blurted.

Falco shut the phone and glanced at her.

"You and me," he said. "Or did you think I'd let you go alone?"

She stared at him. The truth was, she didn't know what to think.

Not anymore.

He drove to LAX, parked at a section new to her and walked her quickly through doors marked ReadyServe Charter Flights.

"We're renting a plane?"

"How long do you think it would take for the world to know Elle Bissette is going to Hawaii if we took a commercial flight?"

"They'll know anyway, once they see my credit card."

"We're using mine."

"But a chartered flight will cost…" She bit her lip. She didn't want to insult him but surely he had to realize that this would run to thousands of dollars. "I mean, my card has no—"

"No dollar limit. But neither does mine."

Did her reaction show on her face? It must have, because he squeezed her hand.

"Trust me," he said quietly. "Can you do that, do you think?"

A better question was, did she have a choice?

There was a counter ahead of them, staffed by a young woman. Falco tugged the ball cap lower on Elle's forehead.

"Keep to the side," he said in a low voice. "Let me do all the talking." Then he let go of her hand, strolled to the counter and flashed a sexy, dazzling smile.

"Hi," he said. "I'm Falco Orsini. I phoned a little while ago."

"Oh, Mr. Orsini. Of course, sir. I have your paperwork all ready."

Elle was all but invisible. The girl hardly glanced in her direction, but then, why would she when Falco was flirting with her?

Not that it mattered.

He was her bodyguard. Their relationship was strictly business. When had she ever wanted any other kind of relationship with a man?

"Never," Elle said under her breath as Falco caught her elbow and began hustling her toward the double doors at the rear of the office.

"Never what?" he said mildly. "Or don't I want to know?" She would have jerked away but his fingers clasped her elbow more tightly. "Just keep moving."

"Don't you want to say goodbye to your little friend?"

Falco chuckled. "Why, honey, I do believe you're jealous."

"You wish."

A sleek silver jet was waiting on the tarmac. Falco walked her toward it.

"When we get to the plane, go up the steps, straight into the cabin."

"Why? Do you expect your fan club to follow you onto the field to say goodbye?"

Falco chuckled. "Nicely done, don't you think?"

"You mean, how you turned her head? Very nicely done, indeed."

"The idea was to keep her eyes from you."

"Yes, well you managed that." Dammit, why did she sound so irritated?

"And without a card from Actor's Equity, either."

She shot him a cold look. His face was expressionless

but amusement danced in his dark eyes. That annoyed her even more.

"Or maybe you'd have preferred it if she'd asked you for your autograph."

Elle narrowed her eyes. "Don't be an ass!"

"An ass." He arched one eyebrow. "Very nice."

"You know what I mean. Of course I didn't want that."

"So, what's the problem?"

The man was infuriating! "There is no problem."

"Yeah, there is." They'd reached the plane. Elle went up the steps, Falco close behind her, and they entered a handsomely appointed cabin. "You're ticked off because I kept that kid from noticing you."

"She wasn't a kid. And there were other ways you could have kept her from noticing me instead of—instead of flirting with her!"

A grin angled across his chiseled mouth. "Ah."

"Ah, what?" Elle folded her arms. "It was wrong, that's all. For all she knew, you and I were—we were—"

"Together," Falco said, a sudden roughness in his voice.

"Yes. No. I only meant—"

He caught her face between his hands and kissed her. Hard. Deep. Kissed her until she moaned into his mouth and wound her arms around his neck. Then, only then, he put her from him.

"I know exactly what you meant," he said, his voice still rough, his eyes hot, his hands slipping to her shoulders. Then he took a long breath and let go of her. "Sit anywhere," he said, as calmly as if nothing had happened. "I'm going to talk to the pilot."

She stared after him, watching that very male walk, that arrogant and, yes, incredibly sexy I-own-the-world swagger. Her heart was beating so hard she could hear it.

What was she doing, going to Hawaii with this man? What

did she know about him, really, beyond the fact that he could talk Antonio Farinelli into changing a shooting schedule, that he was as at ease checking into a cheap motel as he was chartering a flight that had to cost twenty thousand bucks or more?

Was she going from one kind of danger to another?

Logic told her to get off the plane. There was still time.

Falco strolled back into the cabin. "All set," he said. He took a seat and reached for a magazine.

Elle hesitated. Then she sat down as far from him as she could get.

Moments later, they were in the air.

She slept most of the flight, awakening once as Falco draped a light blanket over her.

"Mmm," she whispered, and she must have dreamed that he smiled, leaned down and pressed a kiss to her temple because she surely would not have permitted that to really happen.

She woke to the impersonal touch of his hand on her shoulder.

"We'll be on the ground in twenty minutes," he said briskly. "If you need to use the facilities, now's the time."

Great. Now he was taking charge of her bathroom habits. Elle unsnapped her seat belt, used the lavatory, shuddered at her reflection over the sink. Her hair was lank, her face was pale, she hadn't changed her clothes in, what, almost two days.

As soon as they touched down, she was going to find the nearest mall.

That turned out to be a foolish hope.

The plane landed, taxied to a stop at the terminal. Falco clasped her elbow as if he expected her to bolt and led her to a low, gorgeous shiny black Ferrari. You didn't have to drive one to recognize one, not when you lived in LaLa Land where driving anything that cost less than the national budget of a small nation was evidently against the law.

Falco gave the car a glance, held out his hand so the teenaged kid who'd delivered it could give him the necessary papers to sign. He handed the papers back along with a bill that made the kid's grin spread from ear to ear.

"In," he said brusquely to Elle.

The kid looked at her. Hidden safely behind the ball cap and dark glasses, wanting to stay that way, she had little choice but to obey the command. Still, she couldn't resist clicking her heels and saluting.

"Yessir!"

The kid started to laugh, saw Falco's face and thought better of it.

"All the house stuff—the keys, the gate opener, the paperwork—is in an envelope on the seat."

But Falco had already found the envelope, handed it to Elle and put the car in gear.

Forty minutes later, they pulled up at a massive iron entrance gate.

They had passed no one since leaving the main road. Now, a seemingly endless tangle of grasses and palm trees stretched ahead. If there was really a house here, it was well-hidden.

Elle peered through the windshield. "Are you sure this is it?"

"The GPS says it is." Falco aimed the control device at the gate and depressed the button. There was an audible click and then it swung open.

"Here we go," he said.

The narrow road beyond, bordered by tall native plants, twisted in a series of lefts and right. Whatever lay ahead of them was obscured by the foliage. Then, gradually, the heavy growth cleared, revealing a long shell drive lined with stately palms.

And a house.

Elle caught her breath.

It was an amazing house, all angles and planes standing on a low promontory overlooking a sea so blue it could have been a stage set, except for the white froth of waves breaking against the sand of an equally white beach.

She had spent the flight telling herself whatever Falco had arranged for them here would not matter.

A lie.

This house, this beach, this magic mattered. How could it not? The place was magnificent and secluded and like nothing she had ever seen or imagined.

She must have made some little sound because Falco looked at her as he stopped the Ferrari a few yards from the house.

"Not bad," he said.

Elle swung toward him. "Not bad? It's—"

She saw his face. The big grin. She grinned, too.

"It's not bad," she said, and he laughed, got out of the car and came around to her side, but she was already out of her seat, out of the car and staring at the house. "How did you find it?"

He shrugged and reached for her hand. "I didn't. I called a realtor we've used in the past."

"We?" Elle said carefully.

Falco looked at her. "I'm not involved with anyone."

Her cheeks blazed scarlet. "I didn't mean—"

"Yes," he said, "you did."

He waited for her to deny it. She didn't. She just stared at him, those incredible eyes filled with a variety of emotions. Anger. Embarrassment. And something more, something that made him want to take her in his arms and kiss her.

He closed the distance between them. Said her name. Reached out toward her…

And, as if Fate were the director and this was a movie set, a fat drop of rain hit his head, another hit her nose. In seconds, they'd be caught in a tropical deluge.

They ran for the house.

Just as well, Falco told himself, absolutely just as well. The last thing he needed was to get into this any deeper than he already was.

They went through the house together.

Falco wanted to see how it was set up.

The alarm system was at the top of his list. It was good, maybe very good but he could see ways, low-tech ways, to tweak it. As the realtor had promised, there were absolutely no other houses nearby.

Everything else was fine, too.

The house was built around an atrium. Glass-enclosed. An infinity pool, complete with waterfall. All the rooms opened onto it, and the rooms seemed endless.

Four bedrooms. Six bathrooms. Two half baths. A dining room, a kitchen, a wine storage room, a den, a media room. A living room the size of a basketball court with one entire wall that could be completely opened at the press of a button. A teak terrace wrapped around the part of the house that faced an empty stretch of private, white sand beach. Two miles of beach, according to a cheerful note the realtor had left stuck to the Sub-Zero fridge with a hula dancer magnet.

And, of course, there was the incredibly blue Pacific stretching to the distant horizon.

Elle stood on the terrace and threw her arms wide, as if to encompass all 10,000 or so square feet of the house.

"My God," she said, "it's huge!"

Falco, lounging, arms folded, in the door to the den,

watched her. For a movie star, the lady was surprisingly easy to please.

"Well, yes," he said, "but you never know when you're gonna need some extra space."

She laughed. It was, he thought, a lovely thing to hear.

"When I was growing up, in Beaufort Creek…"

She bit her lip, flashed him a look that could only mean she'd said more than she'd intended.

Falco said, very softly, "Beaufort Creek?"

"Just a place," she said brightly. "Where did you grow up?"

A neat change of subject, but he went with it. "New York. Greenwich Village. Or Little Italy."

She raised her eyebrows. "Which was it?"

"Well, it was Little Italy when my old man bought the first house, maybe even when he bought the second. By the time he'd bought the third, real estate mavens were calling the neighborhood part of the Village."

"I don't understand. You grew up in three different houses?"

Falco grinned. "Three houses, side by side, that he converted into one big house. Believe me, there were times so much construction was going on, we didn't understand it, either."

"We?"

"My brothers and my sisters," he said, and frowned.

How had she managed that? Getting him to talk about himself, especially about his family? He never discussed his family with anyone. Besides, he was the one who was supposed to be getting information from her.

It was just that she was easy to talk to…

"It must be nice," Elle said in a soft voice. "Having brothers and sisters."

"Didn't you?" he said, seeing a way to way to change directions and going for it. "Grow up with brothers and sisters, back in Beaufort Creek?"

She looked at him. "I'm not going to discuss my life with you," she said calmly.

Yes, he thought as she walked back into the house, oh, yes, she would. She was hiding something and she had to tell him what it was. She had to talk to him, and soon.

She had to, if he was going to keep her safe.

The kitchen was clearly a woman's dream.

It was only that he hadn't figured this particular woman was into things like that. But she was, he thought, suppressing a smile as she poked into cabinets and oohed and aahed over the appliances, the dishes, even the flatware.

"Don't tell me you can cook," he said.

She tossed her head. "If you don't want me to tell you I can, then don't ask."

He laughed as he poked into cabinets, too, though his interests were not in dishes but in food. All he came up with was the realtor's idea of a gift basket. A tiny box of crackers. A wedge of cheese. A split of champagne. Two small bottles of Fiji water and a note that said Welcome to Maui.

"Welcome to a tea party for dolls," Falco said glumly. "Okay, we'll head for town. Get some supplies." He made a face. "And clothes. I don't know about you, Bissette, but I'm starting to want to stand upwind of myself."

Elle gave up ogling the Viking range long enough to look at him. "I saw a Walmart on the way here."

He grinned. "You, in a Walmart?"

"There's nothing wrong with Walmart."

"No," he said quickly. Good God, was she actually bristling? She was. There were glints of fire in her eyes. "Absolutely not. Walmarts are, uh, they're great."

"I worked in one."

"Ah. The famous 'what I had to do before I got my first acting break,' huh?"

"I worked in one long before that. And I bought my clothes there, too."

Amazing. A town called Beaufort Creek, and now this. She'd told him more about herself in the past half hour than she had since they'd met…and from what he could remember, there hadn't been a word about Walmart or Beaufort Creek in the studio-scripted story of her life he'd found tucked within the folder his old man had given him.

"Well," he said, with a little smile, "here's your chance to buy some again. How's that sound?"

"Perfect," she said.

Wrong, Falco thought.

The only perfect thing he knew was her.

They drove to town, made a stop at a gas station.

"Pit stop," Falco said, with a quick smile.

There was no need to tell her he'd made a call on the plane while she slept, to a guy who'd served with him and lived here, in the fiftieth state.

"I need a weapon," Falco had said. "Something powerful, not big, easily carried."

The gun was waiting for him there, in bottom of a full wastebasket in the men's room. Falco retrieved it, got behind the wheel of the Ferrari and headed for Walmart.

"It's safer," he said. "It'll probably be more crowded than a regular store and—"

Elle touched a fingertip to his lips. It scalded him. He fought back the desire to suck that sweet finger into his mouth, told himself it was enough that she had touched him without him first touching her, added it to the list of amazing things that had already happened since they'd gotten to Maui.

"Honestly," she said, "I really am fine with Walmart. I can get everything I want here."

She did. Shorts. Tees. Sandals. Jeans. A zippered hoodie for cool evenings. Underwear—white, plain, utilitarian but that didn't keep him from imagining her wearing it and nothing else. Toothpaste, toothbrush, toiletries. Falco dumped similar things into the cart.

They loaded a second cart with groceries. Falco picked up wine, steaks and chops, eggs and bacon, butter and cream and coffee. Elle added vegetables, fruit, whole grain bread and yogurt. She read the labels with the attentiveness of a doctoral student in a chemistry lab.

Amazing, he thought. She didn't just seem comfortable doing this mundane stuff, she seemed to be enjoying it. He knew part of it was probably that they had, at least for the moment, left whomever was stalking her behind. Then again, maybe it was more than that. Maybe it was that she enjoyed being with him...

"All done," Elle said. She smiled at him and that was all it took. He looked into that lovely face, all but hidden by the brim of her cap and the oversized sunglasses, and right there, surrounded by cookies and snacks, he took Elle in his arms and kissed her.

What made it even better was that she sighed and kissed him back.

She was quiet on the drive back to the house.

So was Falco.

Why had he kissed her? He wasn't given to impulsive acts, not in public, especially when they involved women. There'd just been something about the easy way she had of making the best of things, the motel and now the shopping trip. He couldn't imagine any of the women he'd been involved with pushing a cart up and down the aisles of a big box store, picking out plain clothes without complaint.

Ahead, the light turned red. He eased the Ferrari to a stop, glanced idly at the mall across the way. It was small but clearly upscale. That figured, considering the price of real estate once you got along the coast. A Starbucks. A jewelry store. A hair salon.

A place called La Boutique.

There was only one thing in the window. A long gown. Slender straps, supple, softly clinging silk in a color that could only be called topaz.

Or maybe amber. The color of Elle's eyes.

A horn beeped behind them. Falco blinked, put the car in gear, made a sharp turn into the mall and pulled to a stop.

"Forgot to buy coffee," he said briskly.

"But we bought coffee," she said, but he pretended not to hear her and headed for the Starbucks.

He went in. Bought coffee. Mocha Java Bliss, Heavenly Espresso, Capriccio Cappuccino. It didn't matter. He paid for it, then went out the door, gave the Ferrari a quick glance. Elle's face was turned to the road.

Quickly, he slipped inside the boutique.

Five minutes later, he returned to the car and tossed the Starbucks bag into the rear seat. Did Elle notice its bulk? Probably not, because she was silent the rest of the way.

And, once again, so was he.

CHAPTER NINE

OKAY. Maybe he was losing his grip on reality.

First he'd kissed her in a crowded store. An impulsive act he'd quickly regretted. So, how had he made up for it?

Falco's jaw tightened.

By doing something not just impulsive but insane. Why had he bought that gown? Shoes, too. Hey, how could a woman wear a fall of silk the color of autumn leaves with flat leather sandals?

He was out of his mind.

He thought about turning around, going back to the little shop where he'd felt as out of place as snow on a Hawaiian beach, but what would he say to the sales clerk? Sorry but I shouldn't have bought this stuff? The way she'd looked at him, he figured she'd thought he was weird to start with, a man who looked as if he'd slept in his clothes because he had, a two-day stubble on his face...or was it three?

"I want that gown," he'd said, "size six or eight. And shoes to go with it."

The woman hadn't moved until he pulled out his wallet and his black Amex card. That won him a big smile.

"Of course, sir," she'd chirped.

No. Falco blew out a long breath. No, he wasn't going back

there. He'd just hustle the gown and the shoes into the trash and nobody would be the wiser.

Certainly not Elle.

He glanced over at her. The folded arms, the taut profile, eyes straight ahead, chin raised. Thinking about it, it was clear she'd enjoyed the shopping excursion because she'd seen it as a game.

He was, without question, out of his mind.

She wanted this situation to be over with ASAP. And so, absolutely, did he.

What was Falco thinking?

Elle could feel his eyes on her every few minutes but she kept her own focused straight ahead, as if the road that led out of town, then down toward the ocean, required her complete concentration.

Falco knew the way and he was a competent driver. Competent? An understatement. The car was like a growling jungle cat; he handled it with easy self-assurance, one hand on the wheel, one resting lightly on the shift lever.

How could the sight of a man driving a car be sexy?

Elle rolled her eyes.

It wasn't. He wasn't. Not to her, anyway. The word, the very concept, was foreign to her unless she was wearing a designer's creation on a runway or inside character on a film set. Even then, she was pretty much a disaster.

Something was happening. Something was changing. Inside her. Between them. Whatever it was, she didn't understand it, didn't like it, didn't want it…but it was happening just the same.

That kiss. In, of all places, a crowded aisle in a crowded store. Falco's lips moving lightly against hers; hers clinging to his. She'd done nothing to stop it. She hadn't wanted to stop it. He hadn't touched her. No hands. No embrace. Just that hot, sweet, electric fusion of lips until a grumpy female voice said, "Excuse me!" and they'd sprung apart, each of them grabbing a shopping cart, and made for the registers as if their lives depended on it.

It there hadn't been all those people around...

Her throat constricted.

Stress. That's what it was. That, or incipient insanity. There was no other explanation, no reason for that kiss or for her to wonder how it would feel if the house ahead of them—this beautiful, isolated, romantic house Falco had rented—had nothing to do with safety and expediency and had, instead, everything to do with his wanting to be alone with her....

Elle folded her arms.

What on earth was she thinking? She didn't want him wanting that. He was her bodyguard. She was his client. His not altogether willing client, when you came down to it, and that was it.

Why would she ever be stupid enough to want more?

They'd reached the house. She reached for the door handle before he'd brought the car to a complete stop.

"Hey!" He grabbed her arm and jerked her back into her seat. "Didn't anybody ever tell you it's a good idea to wait until a car stops before you get out?"

His tone was curt. It would be. Mr. Orsini didn't like anyone doing something he hadn't given them permission to do. Too bad. She wasn't in the mood to take orders.

Maybe that was the problem.

He'd stormed into her life, uninvited, and taken over. He made decisions without a word or a question, and when had she said he could do that? Never, and that was the point. He had taken over and now she was paying the price for letting him do it. That "woof" she'd barked when he'd told her to stay put today or yesterday or whenever in hell it had been, was no longer a joke. She was behaving like a well-trained dog. Compliant. Obedient. Malleable. And, she was tired of the act.

"Thank you for that helpful information," she said coldly. "I'm sure I'd never have figured it out for myself."

"You have a problem accepting advice?" he said, just as coldly.

"When I need your advice, I'll let you know."

"Do us both a favor, baby, and—"

"That's another thing. I've asked you not to call me that."

His eyes narrowed. From that soft, sweet kiss to this? Never mind that he regretted the kiss. Obviously, so did she. But why? Why should she? That had to be what this was all about, that she'd kissed him in the middle of a store, and whose fault was that? She'd wanted him to kiss her. She'd melted straight into him.

It was time to take a step back. Reassess things. He already knew he'd violated his own rules. What had become of his commitment to keeping things professional? Well, he was returning to that, right now. And she needed to know it.

"Okay," he said briskly, "here's the way things are going to be from now—"

"We need a change in plans."

His eyebrows rose. "Meaning?"

"Meaning, starting now, you're to consult me on decisions."

A cold knot was forming in his gut. "Consult you," he said calmly.

"Yes. You made all these plans—the plane, the house, Hawaii—as if I weren't involved. I don't want that to happen again."

"And I'm to do this because…?"

"Because this is my life!"

"That last I checked, you were standing in a bedroom that had been turned inside-out, wringing your hands and trying to figure out what in hell to do with that life."

She looked as if she wanted to slug him.

"I did not wring my hands. And you didn't give me the chance to figure out anything!"

Falco's lips drew back in a dangerous smile.

"This is all about that kiss."

Elle started to answer. Then she thought better of it and reached again for the door. Falco's hand closed around her wrist.

"You kissed me," he growled. "Now you're behaving as if it was a crime. Would you like to explain that?"

"I kissed you?" She laughed. "Funny, but I don't remember it that way."

"We kissed, okay? So what?"

Pointedly, she looked from him to her wrist.

"Let go of me, Orsini."

"I want an explanation, Bissette. What's this all about?"

What, indeed? She was so angry that she was shaking. He knew damned well what this was all about. He had kissed her. For some reason, she had let it happen. And, yes, she'd let it happen several times and she didn't understand it but she didn't have to.

All that mattered was that it would not happen again.

She knew how these things went.

A man came along, he offered his help, he made you feel safe and then—and then—

Falco's hand tightened on hers. "Answer me, dammit. What's going on?"

Elle raised her chin and looked into his anger-filled eyes.

"What's going on is that you are here solely to protect me."

"You have complaints about how I've been doing that?"

"Yes, I have. You seem to have forgotten your place."

God, where had those horrible words come from? She saw Falco's eyes cloud with rage. She wanted to call back what she'd said, not because she feared him but because it was a lie. She never, ever thought that way about people and she wasn't going to start now, especially with someone like Falco, an honorable, decent man whose only crime was—

Whose only crime was that he had somehow turned her world upside down.

"I've forgotten my place," he said, repeating her words in a low, dangerous voice.

"No," she said quickly, "that isn't what I meant!"

It was too late. He flung her hand from him, opened the door and got out of the car. She scrambled out, too.

"Falco! Please. I didn't mean—"

"Yeah. You did." He swung toward her. She stumbled back. "And you're right. I did forget my place."

"No. I swear, I didn't—"

"Get in the house."

"Falco—"

"I'm going to take a look around."

"What for? We already—"

"It's part of what I have to do to protect you." He reached inside the car, rifled through the bags until he found the one from Starbucks. "You're one hundred percent correct, Ms. Bissette. That's why I'm here."

Elle shook her head. "Listen to me. Please."

"Don't worry about getting the rest of the stuff inside. It's probably within my job description to haul in the groceries, but I'll get your things inside, too, even though some might call that fetching and carrying. But I'll oblige and do it—if you approve, of course. I mean, consider this a consultation."

"You're twisting everything I said!"

"Yes or no? You want me to deal with this stuff or not?"

Shaking with anger, she glared at him over the roof of the Ferrari. "A decent man would accept an apology."

His smile was quick and cold. "But I'm not a decent man. Isn't that pretty much what you just told me?"

"You can go straight to hell!"

"Sounds like a plan," he said, and he turned his back and walked away.

It took her three trips to get the all the things they'd bought into the house, including the groceries, but leaving them for Falco was not an option.

She didn't need anything from him, didn't want anything from him, not even his services as a bodyguard. She'd been doing just fine, handling things on her own.

And she'd handle things on her own, again.

Letting the all-knowing Mr. Orsini into her life had been a mistake, one she'd remedy right away. First thing in the morning, she'd call the airport, call for a taxi, get out of here so fast it would make his head spin. She'd have done it now but she wasn't even sure what time it was.

All she knew was that she needed a bath and a meal and a solid night's rest.

Choosing a bedroom was easy. She took the first one she came to, dumped the bags that held the things she'd purchased on the bed and locked the door behind her.

Falco Orsini was an infuriating, heartless bully. Her temper outburst was his fault. Kissing her, then trying to blame the incident on her...

Elle stalked into the attached marble bathroom, flicked on the light and turned on the hot water tap in the deep soaking tub.

Wait. She'd forgotten something. She hurried into the

bedroom, emptied the contents of her purse on the bed. There it was. The silver frame that held the picture of her and Mama. Tears burned behind her eyes as put her index finger to her lips, then to the picture. She gazed at it for a while. Then she took a deep breath, found the toothbrush and toothpaste she'd bought and returned to the bathroom.

She sniffed at little packets and bottles of oils and bath salts, chose an oil called Tranquility and a matching bar of elegantly wrapped soap. Elle brushed her teeth, stripped off her clothes, made a face and stuffed the clothes into a wicker basket.

The bath was steaming and fragrant. She climbed into the tub, moaned with pleasure and lay back.

Falco Orsini was impossible. He was not a knight in shining armor; he was a man like all other men. That she'd let that slip her mind, even briefly, proved how exhausted she was. The mutilated picture, the note, the mess at the cabin and the condo… All of that had worked against her, had made her vulnerable to letting a man make decisions for her.

And what would you have done if he hadn't made the decisions? If he hadn't followed you to the cabin, or hadn't refused to let you return to your place that night?

Elle gave herself a mental shake. She'd have done what had to be done, that's what. She didn't need the high-and-mighty Mr. Orsini, the police or anyone else. And she'd make that clear tomorrow. Not that Mr. Orsini needed or deserved an explanation. She was taking her life back in her own hands and that was her choice, not his.

She sank lower in the tub. The bath was wonderful. Absolutely wonderful, she thought, closing her eyes as the water lapped against her breasts. Its touch was gentle. Soothing. How would Falco's hands feel against them, instead? His palms cupping their weight. His thumbs moving over her nipples. Lightly. Gently. Then harder as he bent his head to her, pressed his lips to her throat.

Her breasts tingled. A heaviness made its slow way from them to a place low in her belly.

His hands would make their way there, too.

Elle's thighs fell open. The scented water brushed against her flesh. She could feel a pulse beating deep inside her. Beating. Throbbing. Her hand drifted over her belly. Falco's hand would follow that same path and then his mouth. He would stroke her. Part her. Touch her...

She shot upright in the water, heart racing, mind whirling, bile rising in her throat as she shoved the ugly images away. Not just ugly. Horrible. Painful. She knew that, she'd known it forever.

Quickly, she pulled the drain plug and traded the tub for the shower stall, where she scrubbed her skin until it was reddened, washed her hair and made quick work of it.

To hell with the shampoo and conditioner she'd bought. All she wanted now was to get dressed.

The clothes she'd bought lay on the bed. The clothes Falco had bought. He'd used his credit card as if the shopping trip was his to control.

Control was what he was all about. What men were all about. Whatever security company he worked for would, she knew, pick up the tab, but to hell with that. Before she left tomorrow, she'd write him a check for the chartered flight, the house, the shopping trip...

How could an hour in a faceless store have been so much fun?

"What kind of cereal do you like?" she'd said, and he'd answered by plucking a box of sugar-sweetened junk from the shelf. "Yuck," she'd said, grabbing it and putting it back, laughing at the way he'd groaned when she added a box of unsweetened granola to the cart instead, laughing just before he'd kissed her, before he'd made her heart almost stop with that sweet, sweet kiss….

"Stop it," Elle said firmly.

Hell. She'd forgotten to buy pj's. No matter. She dressed quickly: underwear, T-shirt, white jeans, everything clean and fresh against her skin. She'd caught Falco biting back a smile at her choice of underthings. It had made her blush. Would he smile if he saw her wearing them? Not that he ever would but…

Her breath caught. "Stop it," she said again, her voice sharp and a little raw.

Her thoughts were wandering across a wild landscape that had nothing to do with reality. She was tired, was the problem.

And hungry.

Her belly gave a monumental growl.

Breakfast seemed a lifetime ago. There was lots of food in the kitchen. They'd bought cheese and ham, and peanut butter and jelly because Falco had said—with a straight face—that PB and J on white bread was a staple of life.

Elle eased the door open.

The house was silent. Falco's plans had probably mirrored hers. A hot shower, then a nap. She could picture him now, that long, leanly muscled body sprawled naked across the bed.

A frisson of heat shimmered through her body.

Enough. She needed a meal and then some sleep. No. Not a meal. A sandwich would be quicker. She could be out of the kitchen before Falco so much as stirred.

She moved down the hall quickly, silent on bare feet. The kitchen was just a couple of feet away….

Damn, damn, damn!

Falco had beaten her to it. Shirtless, barefoot, wearing only jeans, his dark hair damp and glittering with drops of water, he stood with his back to her at a long granite counter. The loaf of white bread was beside him, the opened jars of peanut butter and jelly next to it. From his motions, she figured he was making a sandwich.

She watched, transfixed, as the muscles in his shoulders and triceps flexed. Her eyes swept downward. He had a powerful-looking back, a narrow waist. His jeans were low on his hips. Was the top button undone? Was that why they hung that way?

And what did it matter?

Why this sudden dryness in her mouth? The equally sudden leap of her heart? Elle took a quick step back.

"Want one?" he said casually.

Falco had sensed her presence and asked the question without turning around. A peace offering? Well, why not. They had hours to get through before she could leave, Elle reminded herself, and she moistened her lips with the tip of her tongue.

"I, ah, I… Yes, thanks. I'd love a sandwich."

He motioned toward one of the counter stools to his left. She shook her head, even though she knew he couldn't see her.

"There must be something I can do to help."

"You can pour us some milk. I'm not usually a milk kind of guy but when it comes to PB and J…"

"The drink of choice. I know."

Elle searched for tall glasses, found them, poured the milk. She put the glasses on the counter, added napkins and silverware and plates.

There was nothing left to do except sit down and watch him put the finishing touches on the sandwiches.

"Kind of like being at one of those sushi restaurants," he said. "You know, where you sit at the counter and get to watch guys wielding knives like homicidal jugglers."

She laughed. "I'm always surprised they end their shifts with five fingers still on each hand."

Falco turned toward her, reaching for the plates. The breath caught in her throat. She'd guessed right. Yes, button at the waistband of his jeans was undone. And, yes, the faded denim hung precariously low on his hips. And yes, oh, yes, he was a magnificent sight, all those sculpted muscles in his shoulders and arms, the cut abs, the dark whorl of hair on his chest that arrowed down and disappeared under the waistband of the jeans…

"What I think," he said, "is that I owe you an apology."

Elle's gaze flew to his. "It was my fault," she said quickly. "I don't know what made me say such an awful thing."

He nodded, his eyes on hers.

"We were both quick on the trigger. And some of what you said was right. I have made a lot of decisions without checking with you first. I shouldn't have done that."

"You made necessary decisions. I know that. It's just that—"

"You're accustomed to making your own decisions."

"Yes."

"Sure. I understand." He hesitated. "And about that kiss…"

She felt her face heat. "Really, there's no need to—"

"I was the one who initiated it. I've initiated every move I've made on you, baby, but they weren't 'moves,' not the way you think. I…hell, I never get involved with the people I'm helping, never step over the boundaries." He snorted and ran a hand through his hair. "There I go again. Calling you 'baby' when you've specifically asked me—"

"Don't stop."

His eyes met hers. "What?"

"I said—I said, don't stop calling me 'baby.'" By now, she knew her face was blazing. "I—I like it. The way you say it. As if—as if it means something to you."

His eyes turned black. "You mean something to me," he said in a low voice.

"You don't have to say—"

He came toward her, put a finger gently over her still-parted lips. His skin was warm; all she had to do was ease the very tip of her tongue between her lips and she could taste him.

"That's one of my flaws," he said. "I tend to say the things I mean. And I mean that, Elle. You—you've become important to me."

She sighed. Her breath was warm against his finger. A shudder went through him as he slid his hand into her hair.

"I want to kiss you," he said roughly. "Hell, I'm going to kiss you. And if that isn't what you want—"

Elle made a little sound, leaned forward and brought her mouth to Falco's. He didn't move, not for a long minute. Then he groaned, wrapped his arms around her and lifted her from the stool. Her arms went around his neck; her legs closed around his hips and he kissed her again, the kiss deepening and deepening until she was moaning into his mouth.

"Elle." He leaned his forehead against hers. "Honey, I want to make love with you."

"I know."

He gave a gruff laugh. Of course, she knew. His erection was enormous and her pelvis was pressed hard against it.

"Tell me it's what you want, too."

He could feel her heart, racing like a tiny bird's against his. She was trembling, breathing fast. He drew her even closer.

"Baby. What is it? Are you afraid of me?"

"No," she said quickly. "Never of you."

"What, then? The—" He hesitated. "The 'sex thing'? Have you had a bad experience? Because if you have—"

"It's—it's something like that."

Who had done this to her? How? What had some bastard done to this beautiful, intelligent, amazing woman? His arms tightened around her.

"I've never—I've never wanted to be with a man before. I can hardly believe it's what I want now. At least—at least, I think it's what I want. But if it's not… I wouldn't want to disappoint you."

"You could never disappoint me," he said fiercely. "If it's not what you want, we'll stop." And I'll die, he thought, but he'd do that rather than do anything to hurt this woman.

She gave a watery laugh. "Men don't stop."

Falco fought to control his fury.

"I am me, honey. Falco Orsini. I am not 'men.' I'd never do anything to hurt you, Elle. I swear it, with all my heart."

She drew back a little and looked at him.

"Just what a guy wants, I'm sure," she said, with a sad attempt at a smile. "To talk a moment like this straight into the ground."

"What this guy wants is to hold you. To kiss you. To sleep with you in my arms. And maybe that's all we should even consider tonight." He gave a little laugh. "Assuming it is night," he said. "I seem to have lost track of time."

Elle stared at him. "Do you think you could really do that?"

What he thought was that by morning he might be dead from the aching need to make love to her, but if being held in his arms was all she wanted, that was all that would happen.

"Remember what you said," she told him solemnly, "about only saying what you really mean."

Falco sighed. "I want to make love to you, baby. To change whatever it is you think you know about sex. If that's not what you want, I'll just hold you while we sleep." He paused. "Or you can trust what I said. About making love and stopping if you want to stop." He smiled. "Your decision to make, Ms. Bissette."

A day ago, an hour ago, she might have said no man could manage sleeping with a woman without sex, but if Falco said

he could do it, she believed him. If he said he could stop—
stop doing the things men did if she asked him to stop doing
them—she believed that, too.

So—so maybe she could let him kiss her. Caress her. And
he'd stop when she told him to stop. Because she would tell
him to stop. Absolutely, she would.

"Elle?" He cleared his throat. "There's a third option,
honey. I'll let go of you, we go to our separate rooms—"

Elle leaned forward and stopped his words with a kiss.

"Take me to bed, Falco," she whispered. "Please. Take me
to bed and make love to me."

CHAPTER TEN

ELLE'S WHISPERED words raced through Falco's blood like a fast-moving drug.

If someone had asked, he'd have said he knew all the sexy things a woman could whisper to a man.

Wrong.

Elle's simple words were the most erotic he'd ever heard.

His answer was in his kiss as he carried her through the silent house, not to the bedroom he'd chosen only because it had been the nearest at hand, but past it, to the master suite. Its walls were almost entirely glass, open on one side to the sea and on the other to the cascade of water that tumbled into the atrium pool.

The bed, a four-poster, hung in sheer white lace, dominated the room.

He imagined taking her to it, laying her on it, baring her to his eyes, his hands, his mouth.

But he didn't.

Elle's lips trembled beneath his. Her heart raced against his palm. She wanted him but she was frightened.

Falco was determined to replace that fear with joy even if it took every bit of self-control he possessed.

He kissed her again. Then, slowly, he put her on her feet.

She made a little sound when her breasts brushed his bare chest, caught her breath when the heavy thrust of his erection pressed against her belly. When she would have stepped back, he gathered her in his arms, kept her close.

"That's just my body telling yours how much I want you." His voice was low and rough but the hand he put under her chin was gentle. "Don't be afraid, baby. I won't hurt you. I promise."

He kissed her, soft kisses that belied the hunger inside him until finally he felt her lips soften and cling to his. He took the kiss deeper little by little, touching the tip of his tongue to the tender inside flesh of her bottom lip. He knew he had to go slowly, that everything that came next hinged on it.

And he could do it.

He was a man who had built his life on self-discipline.

Surely, he could carry that ability into this. Into holding back. Into being content just to taste her. Into keeping from cupping her face, parting her lips with his, plunging deep, deep into the honeyed sweetness of her mouth…

Falco groaned.

Elle tensed. "What?" A quick, uneasy breath; she put her hands on his chest. "Am I doing this wrong?"

His throat constricted. He wanted to groan again. Or maybe curse, not at the woman in his arms but at whatever—whomever—had left her feeling this way. Instead, he forced a quick smile.

"No, honey. No, you're doing it just right. It's just that you taste so good…." The hell with it. He could cup her face, lift it to his, kiss her gently. Like that. Exactly like that. Again and again and suddenly she was on her toes, her hands locked around his neck, her lips open to his.

"Yes," he whispered, "yes, that's the way."

"Falco," she said, just that, and he gathered her against him, kissed her mouth, her throat, and she was trembling again but he knew it wasn't with fear, it was with what was happening, what she felt, what he was making her feel, and then he stopped thinking, stopped planning, and his kisses deepened, his hands moved over her, stroking, cupping, caressing until she was making soft little cries and clinging to him as if he was all that could keep her from falling.

He slid his hand under her T-shirt. Up her back, along the sweet, silken warmth of her skin. His palm spread over the side of her breast. She caught her breath and he waited, waited...

His thumb brushed over her nipple.

She sighed against his mouth.

He stroked her again. Felt the nub of flesh harden, felt it press against his thumb. Another sigh. A moan. Falco moved his hand, cupped her breast, bit back a groan at the delicate weight of it in his hand.

She moved.

Moved against him.

Her hips. Her thighs.

A shudder went through him.

He drew back. Put an inch of space between them but it wasn't enough, how could it be when it felt as if an entire room wouldn't be enough to keep his erection from pressing into her belly? He was harder than he'd ever been in his life, so hard that he hurt...and she wasn't leaving space between them anyway, she was moving closer, clasping his shoulders, raising herself to him.

On a low growl, Falco caught Elle's elbows and put her from him. She swayed, blinked her eyes open and stared up at him.

"Falco?"

He dragged air into his lungs.

"I can't," he said. "Honey, I'm sorry. I thought I could do this. I really thought..." Another harsh breath. "But I can't."

Tears rose in her eyes. "Yes. I mean—I mean, no. Why should you?" Elle stepped back, wrapped her arms around herself. "Of course, you can't. I shouldn't have asked—"

"Dammit!" He grabbed hold of her shoulders, lifted her to her toes. "What I'm trying to tell you is that I can't go slow and easy. I want too much. Do you understand?"

Elle swallowed hard. "You want to—to go to bed. Straight to bed. I should have—"

"Hell, no. I don't want to drag you into bed. I want to touch you first. See you. And you're not ready for that."

"See me, how?" Her eyes flew to his. "You mean, undressed?"

Her voice was low. In any other set of circumstances, her answer, the look she gave him, might have made him laugh, but laughter was the last thing in his mind at that moment. Instead, her expression, the response…both filled him with an awful combination of anger and sorrow.

"Undressed," he said gruffly. "Yes."

She nodded. He could almost see her processing his words. Then she crossed her arms, grasped the hem of her T-shirt. Falco caught her wrists, brought her hands to his lips and kissed them.

"No. I don't want you to do anything just for me, baby. That's not what making love is all about."

"I want you to see me," she whispered.

"Are you sure?" She nodded. "Then," he said, "then, let me do that."

Her hands fell to her sides. Falco reached for the hem of her T-shirt, drew it over her head and tossed it aside. God, she was beautiful. Honeyed skin. Demure white cotton bra. He'd watched her buy it, watched her bypass lace and satin for this. It had made him smile.

Now, it made his body tighten with hunger.

He waited, mentally counted to ten before he spoke again.

"I'm going to take your jeans off, too." His voice was rough as sandpaper. He cleared his throat. "Is that okay, Elle?"

"Yes," she whispered, her face bright with color.

His hands felt huge and clumsy as he reached for the button, then the zipper of her jeans. The hiss of the metal teeth parting seemed inordinately loud, but then, maybe not.

Maybe it wasn't half as loud as the hammering beat of his heart.

Slowly, he slid the jeans down her hips. Her legs. He wanted to squat down, lift her foot, ease the jeans all the way off, but he didn't trust himself, he knew the temptation to put his face against her belly might be more than he could handle. He let the jeans slither to the bamboo floor, took her hands, held them to steady her as she stepped free of them.

Then he looked at her.

Long, dark hair, falling over her shoulders. A face free of makeup. The plainest possible bra and panties. And a beauty so pure it stole his breath away.

Falco's heart kicked against his ribs as he drew her into his arms and kissed her. Lightly. Gently. Told himself to keep it that way but she moved closer to him, framed his face with her hands. Opened her mouth to his and he slid his hands behind her. He hadn't had trouble opening a bra since high school, but now his fingers felt huge and clumsy and, it seemed forever but, thank you, God, at last, the bra opened.

Elle's reaction was to clasp it to her.

Falco's hands closed over hers.

"I want to see you, baby," he said thickly.

A heartbeat's hesitation. Then she let go of the white cotton and it drifted to the floor. His eyes held hers. Then, slowly, he let them fall to her breasts. Ah, they were perfect. Small. Round. Nipples a pale, seashell pink. He raised his eyes to her face, watched her as he traced the outline of one perfect nipple with the tip of his index finger.

"Do you like that?" he whispered.

She moaned. It was all the answer he needed. His hands went to the waistband of the innocent white cotton panties; slowly, he eased them down her long legs. He bent, steadied her as she stepped free of them, fought back the desire to kiss his way up those long legs and bury his face in the soft, dark curls between her thighs and, instead, stood up straight and reached for her again.

Elle shook her head.

"I want…" Her tongue swiped across her bottom lip. "I want…" The rest was an inaudible whisper.

"Honey. I don't know what you said. I couldn't hear—"

"I said—I said, I want to see you, too."

He swallowed. "What?"

"I want to see you naked. That's all. Just to see you."

Sweat beaded on his forehead. He was never going to survive this. Why had he thought he could?

"Falco? Could I—could I see you? Please?"

His hands fumbled at the zipper of his jeans. He took a breath, got it open, pushed the jeans down. He had not put on underwear after he'd showered and now his swollen penis sprang free. His sense of relief was profound.

Profound, but short-lived because—

Because, she was looking at his aroused flesh. Just looking, not touching, and if this kept up, he was going to disgrace himself.

Where was his self-control? That control he prided himself on, that control that always, always kept him in charge of what happened, in bed and out.

"Dammit," he growled, and when she looked up at him he thought, the hell with this and he gathered her into his arms and kissed her, kissed her hard, one hand in her hair, the other holding her tightly against him. He'd do this, kiss her, feel her, let her feel him and then he'd tell her he'd been crazy to think he could pull this off, that he was too old to play doctor.

But how could he do any of those things when Elle was rising on her toes, winding her arms around his neck, meeting his kisses with kisses of her own?

"Please," she sobbed against his lips, "Falco, please, please, please…"

His heart thundered.

Whispering her name, he scooped her up, carried her to the bed. Tumbled onto it with her. Kissed her mouth, her throat, her breasts, exulting in her cries, her sobs.

And tried, one final time, to hang on to sanity.

"Elle…"

There was warning in his voice. She heard it but instead of frightening her, it filled her with ecstasy. She wanted this, wanted him, wanted everything he was, everything he had to give.

"Falco," she said softly, and she touched him. Danced her fingers the length of his rigid flesh, closed as much of her hand around him as she could, felt the throb of life within that part of him that was all male.

"Elle!" The breath hissed from his lips. He took her hand, brought it to her side. "Elle…I'm not a saint…"

She reached up. Kissed his mouth. Kissed him long and deep and sweetly until he groaned and parted her thighs.

She sobbed as he entered her. Slowly. God, so slowly.

Her head fell back against the pillows. She was coming apart. Coming undone. She was flying, blazing across the sky like a shooting star.

"Falco," she sobbed and he said her name, threw back his head and flew into the heavens with her.

* * *

She awoke hours later.

At least, it felt like hours later. Time had lost all meaning.

Perhaps they'd slept the day away. Or the night. Whichever it was, Elle came awake draped over Falco like a blanket, her face buried against his throat, his arms holding her close.

It should have been uncomfortable. He was hard, muscled, lean. And his embrace made it almost difficult to breathe.

But it wasn't uncomfortable. It was wonderful. Her lips curved in a smile. She had never felt this happy, this safe. It was as if she belonged here, with this man, as if she'd been created for this.

Her smile faded.

What was she thinking? This, being here, being with Falco…it was all a fantasy. It was worse than that. Falco had only come into her life because the past was finally catching up to her.

If he knew that past, if anyone knew it…

"Hey."

He was awake. She shut her eyes, opened them again, lifted her head and forced a smile.

"Hey, yourself," she said, and her heart turned over. He was so beautiful! She knew he'd groan if she told him that but it was true, he was beautiful. His dark hair was mussed, he had even more of that five o'clock shadow she'd always thought made a man look grungy but made him look almost unbearably sexy. There were laugh lines at the edges of his eyes and a tiny little white line she'd never noticed until now….

"It's a scar," he said softly.

"Was I staring?" She blushed. "Sorry. I didn't mean to—"

"No, it's cool." He smiled. "I like it when you stare at me." His hand slid into her hair; he brought her face to his and kissed her. "Are you all right, baby?"

"Yes." She could feel her color deepening. "I mean—"

"I know what you mean. And I'm happy to hear it."

His words were spoken in a tender whisper. "Tender" was something she couldn't afford. She couldn't let him get too close. For her sake—

And, she thought with a shudder, for his. How come that hadn't occurred to her before?

She took a breath, drew back as far as his encircling arms permitted and flashed a bright smile.

"Yes," she said, "and thank you for that."

His eyes narrowed. "For what?"

"For, you know, for helping me, ah, for helping me get past my, ah, my problem."

She squealed as he rolled her onto her back. He lay above her, his body pinning hers to the mattress, his hands wrapped around her wrists, cold fire in his eyes.

"Thank you?" he said in an ominous whisper.

"Yes. You know. For—"

"Maybe you're going to recommend me to your friends."

"No!" Her breath caught. "I didn't mean that as an insult, I only meant—"

His mouth swooped down and captured hers, his kiss hard and merciless until, despite her best intentions, she moaned his name in a way that made him let go of her hands. His arms went around her; she wrapped hers around him and the kiss changed, became soft and yes, tender, so tender that she wanted to weep.

"I'm sorry," she whispered. "Falco, I'm so sorry. What happened just now—"

"You and me," he said gruffly, "making love."

"Yes. It was—it was—"

"Yeah." A cheeky grin tweaked the corners of his mouth. "It damned well was."

Elle snorted. "Did anyone ever tell you that you have an oversized ego?"

He moved against her. "I'm just an oversized guy."

She didn't want to laugh but she couldn't help it. He was impossible. She told him so.

"You are impossible," she said, trying for stern and not even coming close.

Falco smiled. He kissed her. Kissed her again. Soft, teasing kisses that lengthened and deepened until her bones had absolutely melted.

"So is this," he whispered, "impossibly wonderful." And then he was inside her again, moving inside her, taking her up and up and up and within seconds, nothing else mattered but him.

She wouldn't shower with him.

She wouldn't even leave the bed as long as he was still in the room.

She knew it was foolish, that he knew her body with shocking intimacy, but that didn't mean—it didn't mean she could walk around in front of him without clothes on.

He didn't argue, not once he saw that she meant it. Instead, he kissed the tip of her nose, rose from the bed and strolled toward the adjoining marble bathroom. She tried to avert her eyes. Yes, they'd been intimate, but seeing him, seeing him naked, that part of him naked...

"I would never hurt you, Elle," he said softly.

She looked up. He was standing in the bathroom doorway, not just unashamedly naked but unashamedly beautiful.

Tears rose in her eyes.

She blinked them back, took a deep breath, tossed back the duvet and went to him. He gathered her against him.

"What happened to you?" her knight in shining armor said, so ferociously that it almost broke her heart.

She shook her head, burrowed closer. After a very long time, he brushed his lips lightly over hers.

"Okay," he said, as if nothing had happened, "shower time."

The peanut butter and jelly sandwiches he'd made hours ago were still on the counter.

Elle touched one with a fingertip and winced. "Hard as stone." She looked up and smiled. "I don't think the *P* in PB and J is supposed to stand for 'petrified.' They must have sat here for hours…."

She realized what she'd said and blushed. Lord, he loved the way she blushed, Falco thought as he drew her into his arms.

"Hours," he said softly. "But not half long enough."

He kissed her. Sweet kisses that grew deeper. Quick kisses that grew longer. Kisses that made their breathing quicken until he groaned and leaned his forehead against hers.

"If we don't eat something soon," he said huskily, "the realtor's going to come by one morning and find us as petrified as those sandwiches."

Elle laughed and gave him a gentle push. "I'll cook something. What would you like?"

"Hey, you think I've waited for peanut butter and jelly all this time only to give up on them now? Let's go, woman. Same as before. You pour the milk, I'll make the sandwiches."

They worked side by side and wolfed down their meal while sitting on stools at the granite kitchen counter. Four for Falco, two for her.

"The wardrobe mistress will kill me," Elle said mournfully.

He grinned. "That's how I got this scar," he said, touching his finger to the little white line she'd noticed earlier. "Defending myself against a PB and J attack."

Elle raised her eyebrows.

"My brother, Nick. We were maybe four and five, something like that. He made himself a sandwich. I stole half of it and he came after me. We'd been playing *Star Wars*, you know, the lightsaber thing? Anyway, Nick swung, got lucky and got me. I retaliated, of course—"

"Of course," Elle said. She didn't really accept the story. She suspected the truth was something much darker, but she smiled, picturing him as a little boy.

"And we both went down in a heap. Well, Rafe had left a Tonka Payloader on the floor and—"

"You have two brothers?"

"Three. Nicolo. Raffaele. And Dante." Falco ate the last bite of his sandwich. "And two sisters. Anna and Isabella."

"Oh, that's nice. To have such a big family, I mean."

Falco laughed. "It's nice most of the time. Sometimes, it's a pain in the, ah, in the butt. How about you?"

Elle's smile faded. "How about me, what?"

"Do you have sisters? Brothers?"

"No."

"No, what?"

"No," she said, "there's just me."

Her tone had become cool. Falco cocked his head. "And?"

"And, what?" Elle slid off the stool and put her plate in the sink.

"And, why is talking about family such a big deal?"

"It isn't," she said, even more coolly.

"Trust me, honey. It isn't always my favorite topic, either. I mean, Izzy and Anna, Nick and Rafe and Dante… They're great. So is my mom. But anybody mentions my old man—"

"Don't tell me," Elle said, her voice not cool but frigid. "You and your father have—what's the current term? You have 'issues.' What, he didn't let you borrow the family car when you were seventeen?"

Falco narrowed his eyes. "My father's a thug," he said carefully. "His name is Cesare Orsini. Maybe you haven't heard of him, but, trust me, the cops sure have."

"Oh." Elle reached out her hand. "Falco. I didn't mean—"

"I know you didn't, baby. So, whatever it is about your family that upsets you—"

She laughed. At least, he thought it was a laugh. But it wasn't. She was weeping.

"Ah, honey, I'm an idiot. Come here. Let me hold you."

She shook her head and pushed past him. He thought about stopping her but he didn't. Instead, he watched her go through the atrium doors and on into the starlit night, watched as she padded barefoot through the sand, to the beach. Then he went after her. They were as safe here as he'd been able to make it: the gates, the alarm system, the little touches he'd added of his own, but no way would he let her out of his sight until he got the son of a bitch who was stalking her.

A chill danced down Falco's spine.

He knew a lot of people who had what Elle had called "issues" with their families. It was, more or less, a sign of the times. Hell, he had his own thing about his father. So did his brothers.

But Elle's reaction just now…

His steps quickened.

He had held off asking her what she knew about her stalker though he suspected she knew something. He hadn't pushed her on why she didn't want the cops involved, either; she was a celebrity and maybe she just didn't want that kind of press. He hadn't pressured her because she'd been through a lot in the past few days. He'd figured on giving her a little time before asking more questions.

Some seventh sense, some instinct told him that the time for asking them was now.

He caught up to her at the surf line, fell in beside her as she walked. She shot him a poisonous look but he ignored it.

"What's going on?"

"I don't know what you're talking about."

"Elle," he said firmly. He caught her elbow, turned her toward him. "You have to tell me. You know you do."

"Go back to the mainland, Falco. Just—just leave me alone."

"The hell I will! I can't protect you without knowing what you know about this maniac."

Her eyes flashed. "Is that what you call taking me to bed? Was that about protecting me?"

She was deliberately trying to make him angry. He knew it, but that didn't make it any easier.

"Answer the question. Tell me what you know."

"What I know is that that we had sex."

He wanted to shake her. Or kiss her. Instead, he grabbed her by the shoulders and hauled her to her toes.

"Dammit, woman! We made love."

"It was sex," she said bitterly. "And I should have known you'd think that grants you some kind of ownership—"

Falco cursed, pulled her against him and captured her lips with his. She struggled, tried to twist free—and then she sobbed his name, wound her arms around him and kissed him back with all the hunger in her heart. He swept her into his arms, carried her to the house and to bed. They made love again and again, until she wept with joy. One last kiss and then she fell asleep in his arms.

Falco remained awake, eyes fixed on the ceiling.

He had violated the principles by which he lived, giving in to his emotions, letting them take him deep into uncharted waters—but he didn't care. If he had to, he would give his life for the woman beside him.

He had only known her a few short days but she had come to mean more to him than he'd ever imagined possible....
And more than he wanted to define.

CHAPTER ELEVEN

HE ASKED no more questions.

His time with Special Forces had taught him the importance of knowing as much about the enemy as he could. Later, doing clandestine work for private clients, he'd adhered to that rule. The Turkish couple he'd recently helped had accused him of indifference because he'd demanded they bare their souls to him, but what he'd ultimately learned had been instrumental in helping him find, and save, their son.

The bottom line was that the one stipulation he always required was full access to information. A client either gave it up freely or Falco would go after it.

This was different. There wasn't a way in hell he'd do that to Elle.

It made his job more difficult but he cared too much about her to force her to divulge whatever dark secrets she possessed. And he cared more and more about her as the days, and the nights, slipped by.

Time had become as fluid as the ocean. There was no beginning, no end. There were only long, sweet days and long, hot nights. The hours blurred into each other, every one of them filled with pleasure.

Not that they did anything special.

Long walks on the beach, with Elle plucking what Falco would have sworn was every shell they saw from the sand. Lazy hours by the pool. They played poker after Falco taught her the game, betting with the shells she'd collected, then with play money filched from a Monopoly set they found on a shelf in the den.

He let her win most of the hands and then, to make it interesting, he said, he suggested betting with the clothes they were wearing.

Surprisingly enough, he began winning.

"You lost all those other times on purpose," she said with mock indignation when she'd been reduced to only an oversized white T-shirt and her panties.

"Hey," he said, eyes filled with innocence, "are you calling me a liar?"

"I'm calling you a cheat, Orsini," she said, squealing as he tossed his cards aside and grabbed her.

They laughed and tussled, and gradually the laughter became sighs and the tussles became touches, and they forgot all about poker and made love until Falco thought his heart would burst with happiness.

Because, God, he was happy. Not that he hadn't been happy before but never like this, doing such mundane things. He was not a man who enjoyed mundane things, at least, he never had before. He lived for risk, for danger, for walking on the edge. And there was nothing risky about those long walks or lying in the sun or driving to the little farm stand they'd discovered, buying fresh mahi mahi and grouper, dew-covered fruits and vegetables.

He'd found condoms there, too, and he bought an amount he figured would have made Elle blush if she knew, but the simple truth was, he wanted to make love with her all the time and to his joy, she wanted the same thing.

And then, one night as he grilled their meal in the atrium and Elle emerged from the house with the salad he looked at her and he thought maybe there was something a little dangerous about this, about what he felt when he looked at her....

Something must have shown on his face.

"What?" Elle said.

"I, ah, I was just thinking that, uh, that my brothers would be proud if they could see me now."

Smiling, she poured two glasses of chilled Prosecco and handed him one.

"Because?"

"Because I've turned into a world-class chef." He grinned at the look on her face, cut off a tiny bit of the grilled fish with a fork and held it out. "Taste this and tell me it isn't the best grilled mahi mahi you've ever eaten."

She leaned forward. Parted her lips. Falco moved fast, pulled back the fork and put his mouth against hers.

Elle sighed. "Delicious," she said softly.

He kissed her again, then popped the bite of fish into her mouth.

"Mmm. That's delicious, too."

"What did I tell you? Falco Orsini, master chef. Don't laugh. Compared to the last fish-type dish I cooked, this is fancy stuff."

"'Fish-type dish,' huh?" Elle smiled as she propped her hip against the table. "I'm almost afraid to ask."

"Oh, ye of little faith." Falco slid a spatula under the fish and flipped it onto a platter. "Tuna."

"Ahi tuna?"

His lips twitched. "Bumble Bee. Chicken of the Sea. I'm not particular about the brand."

"You mean, canned tuna?"

"Toss in some penne pasta, cream of mushroom soup..."

"Yuck."

"Okay, then." He drew out a chair for her. She sat down, and he sat opposite. "The tuna, parmesan cheese, frozen peas—"

"Double yuck." She paused. "You want a gourmet meal, it's macaroni and cheese."

He laughed.

"Go on, Orsini, laugh. But until you've cooked up a box of mac and cheese, maybe add some diced ham if you want to be fancy…" She laughed, too. "No, huh?"

Falco spread his napkin in his lap. "My mother already figures I have the eating habits of a barbarian."

"Is she a good cook?"

"Is she a…" He rolled his eyes. "She's Sicilian. Of course, she's a good cook. Well, she is just as long as you don't balk at what she thinks you like to eat."

"Thinks you like to eat?"

"Yeah. She's got these ideas. For instance, my sister, Izzy, went on this vegan kick one time and Mama said no problem, she'd cook vegan."

"But?"

"But, she thought 'vegan' meant adding vegetables to things. There was no convincing her that chicken and pork and steak, vegetables tossed in or not, wasn't 'vegan.'"

Elle forked up some salad. "Uh-oh."

"Uh-oh, is right. It was interesting."

"I'll bet."

"And then there's Dante, who can't stand the sight of pesto. Somehow, Mama got the idea he loves it." He chuckled. "You cannot imagine all the ways she's come up with to serve my poor brother what she's sure is his favorite dish."

Elle's smile was soft and wistful. "It must be nice, having a big family."

They'd had this conversation before. It hadn't gone well.

Falco figured it was worth another try. He knew, in his gut, whatever Elle wasn't willing to talk about was somehow connected to the topic of family.

"So," he said casually, "you didn't, huh?"

She shook her head. "No."

"Just, what, you and your mom and dad?"

"My dad died when I was little."

"Ah. Just you and your mom, then."

There was a slight pause. Then Elle shrugged. "Yes."

"She never remarried?"

Another pause. "She did, after a while."

Her voice was suddenly tight. Falco felt a tingling on the nape of his neck.

"Nice. That she met somebody, I mean, and fell in love."

"Very nice," Elle said in a flat voice.

"It wasn't?"

"He said he'd take care of us. See, we were dirt poor."

That surprised him. "But your bio—"

She looked up. "You've read that nonsense?"

"On the plane flying out to L.A. It said—"

"I know what it said. That I grew up in San Francisco. That I had private tutors."

"Not true, huh?"

She shook her head, kept her eyes on her plate as if it were the most interesting thing she'd ever seen. "I grew up poor."

"In a place called Beaufort Creek."

She looked up. "Yes. That's where I was born. But I lived in different places after that before I finally moved to New York."

"Moved to New York, and started modeling."

"And started modeling," she said, her tone flat again. "You have a problem with..." She sighed. "Sorry."

"No," he said quickly, reached for her hand and held it

tightly in his. "I'm the one who's sorry. I guess I seemed a little, you know, a little hinky about the lingerie stuff."

The breath sighed from her lungs. "I didn't want to sign that contract. But I knew it was a big chance, that it could lead to bigger and better work—"

"Elle." Falco put down his fork. "Honey, you don't owe me or anybody else an explanation."

"If I'd never posed for that last damned picture, he might never have found—"

She fell silent. Falco's hand tightened on hers.

"Who?" he said softly. "Who is he?"

"I only meant—you know, I meant 'he' as in—as in the man stalking me."

She was lying. Her eyes were dark with despair. Her mouth was trembling. Now, when she was so vulnerable, was the time to pursue the topic. She'd break in five minutes….

Instead, Falco shot from his seat, went to her and wrapped her in his arms.

"I can't," she whispered. "Please, please, don't ask me to talk about it…."

"Hush," he said, and he tilted her face to his, kissed her until the darkness in her eyes faded and despair died in the flame of passion.

They went for a drive a couple of days later. On the way home, Falco pulled in to the big mall where they'd bought food and clothes, and stopped outside a FedEx store.

"FedEx?" Elle said, puzzled.

"Man does not live by mahi mahi alone."

She laughed. "Seriously, Orsini…"

"Seriously, Bissette," he said, dropping a light kiss on her mouth. "Just stay put. I'll be right back."

He returned with a package, dropped it in the rear seat

and pretended he didn't hear her questions. After a while she gave up.

"Nap time," he said, once they'd returned to the house.

That made her smile. Nap time had become an important part of their day, not that it actually involved napping. This time, however, after they made love—long, sweet, incredibly tender love—she fell asleep, curled against her lover's side.

And awoke, alone, in the bed.

She sat up, yawning. What time was it? It felt late. A glance at the clock proved that it was almost seven. Where was Falco? She loved waking with him in their bed. Not that this was actually "their" bed. It was so easy to fall into the fantasy, to let herself think that this would go on forever, that what he seemed to feel for her was…that it was real.

It wasn't, of course.

He was attracted to her. And concerned about her. But then, that was his job. Falco was her bodyguard. Her guardian. Yes, he'd developed some feeling for her, but it was sexual and that was okay because her feeling for him was the same and that was enough, that she'd gone from terror at the thought of a man touching her to wanting to be touched.

By Falco. Only by him. Always by him…

"Hello, sweetheart."

Elle looked up—and blinked at the apparition in the doorway. "Falco?"

He grinned. "Nobody else."

Nobody else, indeed. Her bodyguard wore a black tux with black silk lapels, black trousers that emphasized his narrow hips and long legs, a white shirt, a black bow tie…

He was beautiful.

"Am I dreaming?" she said, as he came toward her.

He laughed softly. "Close that gorgeous mouth, baby," he said, putting a finger lightly under her chin. "On second thought…" He bent down and kissed her, ran the tip of his tongue lightly over the sweet surface of her bottom lip. Then he straightened up and struck a pose. "Well? What do you think?"

Elle sat up against the pillows, the duvet drawn to her chin. If this was a dream, it was lovely.

"I think," she said, "that neither Walmart nor FedEx sells custom-made tuxes."

"Good conclusion."

"But?"

"But, FedEx is a wonderful thing, especially when a guy can call at least one brother with a key to his town house."

"You called your brother and had him send you a tux?" Elle laughed. "Because…?"

"Because, of course, we're going out to dinner."

"Out? You and me? But you said I had to keep a low profile."

"We're going to a very private place, baby."

"But—"

"Trust me."

Trust him? With all that she was, all she would ever be…

"Come on, Bissette. Get yourself all dressed up and meet me in the atrium."

Get dressed up. In what? Shorts? A T-shirt? Rubber thongs? He was more handsome than any actor in Hollywood, any male model in New York, and she was going to look like—

"Oh. One last thing." He smiled. "You might want to check the closet."

"For what?"

He cupped the back of her head, bent to her again and gave her a long, lingering kiss.

"What did I say, baby? Just trust me."

The instant the door shut after him, Elle scrambled from the bed and flung open the closet door….

"Oh," she whispered, "oh, Falco…"

A gown of amber silk hung before her. It was beautiful, the kind of thing she'd have picked for herself to wear for an evening with him. There were shoes, too, as delicate as if they'd been spun from gold. The only possible word for them was sexy. Narrow straps. Slender, spiked heels…

Tears rose in her eyes. Silly, to weep over something so sweet, so generous, so thoughtful…

Even more silly, to weep at the realization that she had fallen deeply, deeply in love with her bodyguard.

She showered.

Washed her hair.

Dried it, brushed it until it shone, then let it flow down her back. She put on mascara and lip gloss, which was twice the makeup she'd worn all week. Then she went back into the bedroom.

The gown lay across the bed. She didn't know how Falco had bought it; maybe his brothers had sent it. It was exquisite but there was a problem. She had no undergarments to go with it. The white cotton bras had straps that would show; the panties would be outlined under the softly clinging silk.

Elle shut her eyes.

She could wear it without underwear.

No. No, she couldn't. No underwear? Just the kiss of cool silk against her skin? The knowledge, all evening, that she was naked beneath it?

Her breath hitched.

She let the bath towel fall to the floor, picked up the gown and slipped it over her head. The silk slid down her body. It did, indeed, feel cool.

And she felt sexy. Wicked. Wonderfully, gloriously wicked. Wicked in a way that had nothing to do with Madison Avenue photo shoots or the artful fakery of Hollywood movie sets. She felt wicked the way a woman would surely want to feel for her lover.

She stepped into the sexy shoes and adjusted the straps. Ran her hands through her hair. Took a quick look at herself in the mirror and then, knowing she was a breath away from losing her courage, opened the door that led to the atrium and stepped outside.

Stepped into a world of glittering, shimmering candle-light.

There were dozens and dozens of candles. All shapes, all sizes, all glowing as brightly as stars.

A round table, draped in ivory linen and set with delicate china and gleaming sterling flatware, stood near the pool. There were candles on the table, too, elegant pink tapers on either side of a crystal vase overflowing with pink and white orchids. A serving cart laden with silver chafing dishes stood nearby; a bottle of champagne stood chilling in a silver wine cooler. Music played softly from hidden speakers, something soft and romantic and perfect....

But most perfect of all was Falco.

He stood beside the waterfall, watching her, and when she saw the look on his face, her heart soared.

"Elle," he said softly, "my beautiful, beautiful Elle."

His Elle. Yes. That was what she wanted to be. Smiling, she turned in a graceful circle.

"It's the gown. The shoes. How did you—"

"Magic," he said.

She laughed. "Magic, indeed."

He came slowly toward her, arms outstretched. "May I have this dance, Ms. Bissette?"

"Most assuredly, Mr. Orsini. My card is reserved for no one but you."

He gathered her to him. She looped her arms around his

neck. He made a sound deep in his throat. Had he realized she had nothing on beneath the gown? Surely he must have: her nipples were beaded against his chest, his hand lay at the very base of her spine. But he said nothing, simply held her as they began moving to the music.

"I was afraid the gown wouldn't do you justice," he said softly.

She leaned back in the circle of his arms and looked up at him. "The gown couldn't be more beautiful."

"Neither could you."

He meant it. She was, without question, the most beautiful woman he'd ever known. If only he'd bought her something else, something more to bring out the topaz fire of her eyes….

"Diamonds," he said. "Canary-yellow diamonds."

She laughed. "What?"

"It's what you need. One perfect heart-cut stone that would lie right here." He bent his head and kissed the hollow of her throat. He could feel her trembling against him, could feel her heart beating as fast as the wings of a hummingbird.

His heart lurched. He said her name, drew her closer and they began moving again, lost in the music and in each other.

"Falco." His name was the softest whisper on the still night air. "Falco," she said again, "Falco…"

He kissed her.

He wanted to take her inside, strip away the gown, bury himself deep inside her, but had planned this night for her. Nick, who had sent the tux, had started to ask questions but he'd cut them off with a terse, *I'll explain when I see you…*

Except, how could he explain what he didn't understand himself? When had this gone from being a mission to something else, something even more dangerous than the violence he knew he would eventually face? When had Elle become everything that mattered in his life?

What did all of that mean?

Falco cleared his throat, laced his fingers through hers and led her to the table. He seated her, took the chair across from hers and took the bottle of champagne from the silver bucket. The cork made a soft pop when he eased it free. He filled two flutes, gave Elle one.

"To this night," he said, touching his glass to hers.

"This perfect night," Elle said, smiling at him.

Her lover had thought of everything. Vichyssoise. Lobster. Asparagus. Chocolate mousse. Kona coffee with heavy cream, all as perfect as the night. At least, Elle assumed it was perfect. She couldn't taste anything. Her senses were all centered on him.

He poured the last of the champagne. Then he took her hand and brought it to his lips. "I wish we could have really gone out to dinner." He smiled. "Someplace where every man in the room would have cheerfully killed to change places with me."

She laughed. "What a wish!"

Falco flashed that gorgeous, macho grin. "What can I tell you, baby? Under all the smooth veneer, a cave is a guy's natural habitat."

"Well, for a caveman, you clean up pretty good." Elle looked around them, at the candles, the serving cart, and shook her head. "How did you manage all this?"

"I told you. Magic."

He was the magic. She came within a heartbeat of telling him that.

"Nobody ever…nobody in my entire life ever did anything like this for me."

He pushed the flowers aside, leaned forward and kissed her. "Part of me wishes someone had," he said softly. A smile of blatant male satisfaction angled over his mouth. "But the part that's living in that cave is glad I was the first."

She touched her hand to his face.

"You were the first for so many things," she whispered. "Especially about—about making love. I never…until you, I thought…I always thought—"

Her admission filled him with pleasure as well as pain. He hated knowing she'd feared sex…and yet, he exulted in the knowledge that he was the man who'd freed her of that fear.

"Hush," he said gruffly. "You don't have to explain."

"I didn't mean to embarrass you."

He turned his head and pressed a kiss to her palm.

"You could never embarrass me," he said roughly, "especially if you talk about what I make you feel."

Elle took a deep breath. "And me?" she murmured. "How do I make you feel?"

She waited for his answer, asking herself what had ever made her foolish enough to ask him such a question….

"As if you and I are alone on this planet," he said huskily. "As if nothing matters but us." He rose to his feet, drew her to hers, his eyes hot as fire. "As if the only thing under that gown is you."

Her heart leaped as he reached behind her for the zipper. He had undressed her many, many times over the past days and nights, but never like this. A week ago, this would have terrified her. Now, it sent waves of hot excitement through her blood.

The zipper opened. The thin straps of the gown fell from her shoulders and the slender column of amber silk drifted sensuously over her naked skin and became a discarded chrysalis at her feet.

Falco groaned. "Elle," he said, "God almighty, Elle…"

She trembled as his eyes swept over her. The look on his face… Her body's response was swift. She felt her breasts lift, her nipples bud. Heat pooled between her thighs.

"Falco," she whispered.

"Yes," he said, and he kissed her eyes, her mouth her throat.

Then he dropped to his knees and did what he had longed to do since the first time he'd made love to her, put his face against the soft curls that guarded her femininity.

Elle gasped. "No! You can't—"

His hands closed on her wrists as she reached out to stop him.

"I can," he said. "I have to."

Gently, he gently nuzzled her thighs apart. And kissed her.

Her cry tore through the night and he kissed her again, licked her, tasted her. Her orgasm raced through her, shattering her, turning her bones to liquid. He rose to his feet, scooped her into his arms, carried her to a *chaise longue* beside the pool and tore off his clothes. He entered her on one hard, deep thrust and she screamed as she came again. And again.

"Elle," he said, watching her face as he rode her, knowing that what he had told her the night they'd quarreled was the truth.

This wasn't sex.

It was far more than that.

It was—it was—

"Falco," she sobbed, and he flung back his head and let go.

They fell asleep wrapped around each other.

The night grew cool. A breeze swept in; the candles sputtered and went out. He woke with a start.

Elle was gone.

Falco shot to his feet…and saw her, at the far end of the atrium, wrapped in an oversized pool towel and staring blindly at the thin white line of surf beating against the sea.

He pulled on his trousers and went to her, slid his arms

around her and tried to pull her back against him but she stood stiff and unresponsive within his embrace.

"What's wrong, honey? Are you cold?"

"Falco. I have—I have to tell you—"

The words were heavy with meaning. A coldness that had nothing to do with the night went through him.

"You were right when you said I knew who's stalking me. I do know. I've known, all along." She swallowed, the sound audible in the silence of the atrium. "I just—I just don't know how to tell you…."

Falco held her closer. "Just tell me," he said softly. "Whatever it is, we'll deal with it together."

"His name is Willy Joe Johnson. He is…he was my stepfather." Elle drew a shuddering breath. "I told you that my real father died, remember? He was a coal miner. We lived in a little town in West Virginia and—and one day, there was an accident in the mine. My daddy and ten other miners didn't make it out."

Her voice had undergone a subtle change. It had taken on an accent, the softness of vowels he associated with small town girls from places where men risked their lives in the bowels of the earth.

"Go on," he said softly.

"My mama wasn't well. She hadn't been for a long time. With Papa gone, it was worse. We had no money. We got a little money from the union, but—but mostly, we lived on charity."

Falco shut his eyes, trying to block out the vision of a little girl with dark hair and topaz eyes, living on the kindness of strangers.

"Mama had a sister in Ohio. We moved there. But her sister had her own troubles. So we moved again, to Kentucky. Mama got a little better and she took a job but then she got sick again. We started going to this storefront church where there was a soup kitchen." She paused. "And a preacher."

Falco's gut knotted. Whatever came next would be dark and ugly. He wanted to turn Elle toward him, tell her she didn't have to say any more, but she did. What came next was at the heart of what had been happening to her.

"Willy Joe liked Mama. He seemed nice. And he said—he said he'd always wanted a little girl of his own. So, when I was thirteen, Mama married him. She did it for me. So I'd have food to eat and a roof over my head and—and—"

Falco turned her to him and set aside everything he knew about maintaining distance between himself and a client.

"You don't have to do this tonight, honey. It can wait until morning."

"No. It can't. It's waited too long as it is. You need to know. You have the right to know." Her voice broke. "I—I want you to know, do you see?"

So he let her talk.

She told him that she knew, almost right away, something was not right. Her stepfather barked at her mother, shouted at her. Even the house was unpleasant. It was dark and dirty. It had a bad feel to it.

And the walls were thin.

"They were very thin. I could hear what was happening in the next room, his and Mama's room, at night. Mama crying, Willy Joe grunting, but when I asked Mama, she said everything was fine. I knew it wasn't but I couldn't do anything to help her."

Falco cursed, swept Elle into his arms and carried her into the house. He sat down in an overstuffed living room chair and held her close.

"Mama got sick again. Real sick. And that was when—it was when Willy Joe started looking at me. Watching me. He'd brush against me as if it was an accident, come into the bathroom—the lock didn't work—and say he hadn't known I was in there. And then, one night, he came into my bedroom."

Falco said something ugly. Elle kept talking.

"He—he came every night after that. And he—he did things. But I wasn't there. Not really. I had this little stuffed animal my daddy had given me—"

"A toy cat," Falco said, because by now he knew, he knew.

Elle nodded. "I'd hold on to that cat and hold on to it, no matter what happened. I didn't scream, I didn't cry, I didn't tell anybody anything because Willy Joe told me what he'd do to Mama if I did."

And then, one morning, she said, her mother didn't wake up. The day of the funeral, her stepfather put his meaty hand on Elle's shoulder. He said that now, she really belonged to him.

He moved her into his room. Into the bed he'd shared with her mother. And that night—that night...

Elle began to sob. Falco went on holding her, rocking her, but his heart had become as cold as ice.

"I went to school the next morning," she said raggedly. "It was safer than staying home. But something must have showed because Miss Toner, my English teacher, asked if I was okay." She dragged in a breath. "'You can tell me, Ellie,' she said, and it was like a light coming on because she was right, I didn't have to protect Mama anymore. So I told her everything."

The rest of the story was straightforward. The teacher took her to the principal; the principal called the sheriff. Her stepfather was arrested. Elle, sixteen by then, was scheduled to testify at his trial but she didn't have to. Willy Joe pleaded guilty. He said only his God had the right to judge him.

"They sentenced him to fifty years and my teacher said he could never hurt me again...."

"But she was wrong," Falco said tonelessly. "When did he get out?"

"Six months ago. He found out where I lived. Sent me that—that horrible picture. He wrote to me. He told me I was going to pay for defying him and God. And then—and then, right before you showed up, he telephoned me…."

"Ah, baby. My sweet baby. Why didn't you go to the police?"

"Don't you see? Nobody knows what happened to me, Falco. Nobody but you. To have the whole world know—and it would be the whole world, this time—to have them stare and whisper, to have to live through the nightmare again…" She shuddered. "I was Ellie Janovic until Willy Joe was sentenced. The next day, I took a bus to New York. I became Elle Bissette. And I'm never going to be that other person again."

"Yes," he said, "yes, baby, I see."

And he did. Elle's scars went deep. She had survived a horrendous ordeal but if the media got hold of the story, she'd be victimized all over again.

He held her for hours, stroking her, comforting her, telling her that he would never let anything hurt her. Gradually, she stopped weeping and fell asleep, safe in his arms.

He wanted to hold her forever, but he couldn't. The monster had to be dealt with. To do that, he had to contain his anger. Hell, his rage. He had to formulate a plan.

Discipline. Self-control. Logic. Those had always been the bastions of his life.

Until he caught the bastard who'd done this to his Elle, he needed them more than ever.

CHAPTER TWELVE

A MAGICAL evening.

But everything changed, the next day. Everything including Falco.

He became…removed.

Elle couldn't think of another way to describe his behavior. He was there but he wasn't, not in the ways that mattered. There were no more long walks on the beach, no easy laughter, no drives along the back roads.

Something was wrong. The question was, what?

The change had been painfully abrupt. He'd been so wonderful that night. So tender, holding her in his arms until she slept, soothing her with whispers and caresses. At dawn, she'd felt him slip from the bed. She'd assumed he was going to use the bathroom but then she heard the rustle of cloth and she'd looked from under her lashes to see him putting on a T-shirt and a pair of denim cutoffs.

Come back to me, she'd almost said, but there'd been such caution in the way he moved that she'd remained silent. Silly, because he probably only wanted to make sure he didn't wake her, but when he left the room without at least dropping a light kiss on her lips, the first tendrils of doubt crept in. Had the things she told him changed the way he saw her?

No. That was crazy. He wasn't that kind of man, Elle told herself as she dressed and went looking for him. He wasn't in the kitchen or the atrium, he wasn't anywhere in the house. He was on the beach, making one call after another on his cell phone. When he was done, he stripped off his T-shirt and began exercising. One hundred push-ups. One hundred squats. And then what appeared to be a wild combination of kickboxing and kung fu and tae kwon do.

After a while, sweat glistened on his body. A beautiful body she'd come to know with heart-stopping intimacy and yet—and yet, even his body seemed different. Beautiful, of course, but now she saw it could be a tool of violence.

She went back into the house and waited for him.

"Hey," she'd said as lightly as she could manage when he finally came in, "what's going on?"

"I've let things go," he'd answered. "Now I'm making up for it."

No kiss. No smile. Just those cool words as he headed for the shower.

By now, four days had gone by. Falco's morning workout routine became more intense. He seemed to be always on his phone. He spoke to her in short, clipped phrases. The most difficult thing to accept was that they didn't go to bed at the same time. They always had, since becoming lovers. Not anymore.

"You go ahead," Falco would say when it grew late. "I'll be a little while."

She fell asleep alone. Or didn't fall asleep, but it didn't matter. When he finally came to bed, he didn't touch her. Didn't hold her. And yet, during the darkest hours of the night, she'd awaken to his hard body against hers, to the drugging heat of his mouth, the skill of his hands moving over her and then the almost savage power of his possession.

No words. No whispers. Just that stunning, exciting joining of flesh to flesh.

In the morning, no matter how early she awoke, he was already gone.

At first, she wept. Not where he could see. Never that. Her heart ached; she longed for the man she'd come to know as Falco Orsini. Then tears gave way to anger. What was the point to self-pity? If she'd given in to that kind of defeatist behavior years ago, Elle Bissette would not exist.

What had created Elle Bissette was determination, guts and, yes, anger. Anger at her stepfather and then anger at herself for not getting on with her life. Anger was a strong, safe emotion. And by day four, it consumed her.

If Falco had a problem accepting the truth about her, why in hell had he insisted on hearing it? Why had he been so caring after she'd told him everything? Given time to think things over, had he regretted making love with a woman who, face it, Elle, was damaged goods?

Did he think he could have sex with her under cover of darkness and reject her when daylight came? If so, he had another think coming.

Elle glared out the window. She could see him down by the water, doing those ridiculous martial arts moves.

"Enough," she said through her teeth, "is enough."

She went out the door and strode toward him. If he heard her coming, he didn't show it. He went on grunting and straining, whirling around on one foot, kicking and jabbing. She snorted. He looked ridiculous....

Except, he didn't.

He looked graceful and almost dauntingly masculine, and for one desperate moment she almost flung herself into his arms to tell him that she wasn't angry or ticked off, she was in pain because he was breaking her heart...

"What do you want?"

She blinked. Falco stood glaring at her, his hands on his hips.

"Elle. If you have something to say, spit it out. I'm busy here."

Elle narrowed her eyes and slapped her hands on her hips, mimicking his posture without realizing it.

"I want to know what's going on."

"I'm working out. That's what's going on."

"You know what I mean. Where have you been all week?"

He stared at her. She thought she saw awareness in his eyes, but then he grabbed a towel and rubbed it over his face. When he looked at her again, his eyes were blank.

"I've been doing what I should have been doing from the start. A bodyguard's not much use if he's not in shape."

"And this occurred to you because…?"

Falco struggled to remain unmoved. She was angry. Her color was high. Her voice was sharp. She'd obviously tumbled out of bed and put herself together in a rush because her hair was tangled and she hadn't bothered with a bra; he could see the pout of her nipples against the thin cotton of her tank top.

She was, in other words, mouth-wateringly delicious. She always was.

Going to bed without enfolding her in his arms each night was agony. Leaving her each morning was just as tough. He didn't think about it so much during the day because he was busy from morning until night, getting back in shape, talking with the guy who'd gotten him the gun here in Maui and another guy he knew and trusted back in L.A., planning every move a dozen times over because if he made a mistake, his Elle was the one who would pay.

Even so, there'd been times the last few days she'd walked by him and he'd wanted to grab her. Haul her into his arms.

Tell her he was doing this for her, that this was the only way he knew to pull off something so dangerous, that it was the most important thing he'd ever undertaken because of what he felt for her.

He didn't, of course.

Control. Containment. Discipline. Making plans and reviewing them until they were part of him. It had to be handled like this.

That he lost all that control and containment and discipline in the dark hours of the night, that he was too damned weak to keep from turning to her, taking her in his arms, seeking comfort in her warmth, her silkiness, her almost pagan response to him…

That he permitted that to happen was wrong.

How could he prepare for what came next unless he kept his mind and body separate? And that was the problem. He couldn't seem to keep them separate anymore. Something inside him had changed; he didn't just want to touch Elle, he wanted to think about her. All the time. To make her part of him. To tell her—to tell her that he—that he—

His cell phone beeped. Falco almost groaned with relief as he snatched it from his pocket and shot a look at it. It was the guy from L.A.

"Yes?"

"Bingo," the guy said. "My contact at the *L.A. Times* came through. The article reads…" There was the rustle of paper. "It reads, 'Everybody can stop wondering why Elle Bissette walked off the set. She's been spotted canoodling with her latest at a private estate off Paradise Road on the beach at Maui.' Plus, his wife works for *Entertainment Tonight*. She got the same item online and on TV yesterday."

"Perfect. And the rest?"

"Well, you already know I located your man three days back, and that I've been on him ever since."

Falco looked at Elle, then swung away from her. "And?"

"And, he's getting ready to make his move. In fact, I'm standing a few feet away from him right now. He bought a ticket to Maui at the American Airlines counter. His flight's due to land at midnight, your time."

Falco nodded. "Good work," he said softly. "And Rick? Thanks."

"*De nada*, dude. Feels like old times, right?"

"Right." Falco disconnected, hit a speed dial button. Jack, the guy in Maui, picked up on the first ring.

"Yeah?"

"Time to rock and roll, Jack."

"I'm ready, man. I'll be there in an hour."

Falco closed his phone and turned to Elle. This would be the hardest part of all.

"Who," she said coldly, "was that?"

"A couple of friends." He paused. "I need their help so I can take care of your problem."

Elle saw something cold and primitive flicker in his eyes. All her anger drained away.

"Oh, God," she whispered, "Falco—"

"Your stalker is on his way here. You and I both know what he intends to do." A muscle tightened in his jaw. "Except, things won't go exactly the way he figures."

"Falco." Elle took a step toward him. "What are you saying?"

He tucked his phone in his pocket, draped the towel around his neck, grabbed his shirt and started for the house. Elle had to run to keep up.

"Answer me," she said. "What are you going to do?"

"Whatever needs doing."

"No!" She caught his arm, swung in front of him. "He'll kill you!"

Falco laughed. Elle shook her head.

"Falco. Please. Call the police."

"You gave me good reasons why the police shouldn't get involved in this," he said, shaking her off and continuing towards the house.

"I've changed my mind. If you get hurt—"

"I won't."

"Dammit, nobody's immortal!"

He stopped and swung toward her again. "I told you. I'm not going to get hurt."

"But—but if—if you should…" Her eyes searched his. "I'd be—I'd be—"

"What?" he said in a low voice.

"I'd be—" She stared at him. Heartbroken, she thought. Devastated. Lost for the rest of my life because I love you, love you—

Did the words spill from her lips? All she knew was that Falco cursed, grabbed her by the shoulders, hauled her to him and took her mouth in a bruising kiss. Elle sobbed his name, all but jumped into his arms, wrapped her arms and legs around him and kissed him back. His hands snaked under her tank top; he said something she couldn't understand as he tore it from her. Her shorts and panties followed.

Naked, she moaned his name as he backed her against the house, fumbled at his fly and then he thrust into her, hard, deep, all of him hot and rigid within her wet, welcoming heat. She screamed with pleasure, screamed again and again until he had emptied himself into her. He held her for a long moment, her face against his throat, his arms tight around her. Then, slowly, he lowered her to her feet.

"I'm not going to let you do this," she said in a shaky whisper. "You don't know what he's like. He'll—"

"I know precisely what he's like." Falco scooped up her clothing and handed it to her. He didn't want to see her naked

like this. It made him want to take her in his arms and hold
her to his heart and there wasn't a way in hell he was going
to let that happen. "Put your clothes on," he said roughly.

Color swept into her face but, she went right on facing him,
the clothes held to her breasts.

"Falco. I beg you. Listen to me—"

"Do you hear me, dammit? Go inside. Get dressed. Pack.
There'll be someone here soon to fly you to Los Angeles."

"Fly me…? No! I won't go. If you're going to be so—so
pigheaded, I'll stay. I'm not leaving you."

His mouth twisted as he moved past her, into the coolness
of the house.

"I'm not giving you a choice, Bissette."

"Wait a minute. Wait just one damned minute!" Elle rushed
after him, grabbed his arm. Tears of anger and frustration
streaked her face. Looking at her made his throat constrict.

"I love you," she said. "Do you understand? I love you!
I'm not going to let you do this. I love you. And you—and
you love—"

His heart turned over. She was right about part of that. He
loved her. Why deny the truth to himself? He loved her with
every fiber of his being and that made it all the more impera-
tive to get her out of here. He could not do what he had to do
if he worried about her stepfather somehow getting past him
and putting his filthy hands on her.

There was only one way to make sure she left, and he took
it.

"You're wrong," he said, fighting to keep his emotions
from showing. "You don't love me."

"Dammit, Orsini, do not tell me what—"

"And I sure as hell don't love you. You're beautiful and de-
sirable and sexy but wanting you isn't loving you."

Her face paled. "Falco. You don't mean—"

"You needed a knight errant. And there I was, riding in to save you."

Elle shook her head. "That's not how it was. It was more than that. It was—"

"It was sex," he said bluntly. "Great sex." She tried to look away from him. He caught hold of her and forced her to meet his cool gaze. "Yeah, we made love. But making love isn't the same as being in love."

A moan escaped her lips. He knew he would never forget this moment just as he knew that at least part of what he'd told her was true. She didn't love him. For all her sophistication, his Elle was an innocent. She'd never loved a man, never lain in a man's arms, and she'd damned well never had a man do battle to save her.

Add it all up, she was confusing gratitude with love. He knew it and, once she got a little distance from what had happened, so would she.

"So…" She paused. "So, you were just doing your job?"

"And it isn't over."

She nodded. "But we are," she whispered.

Falco shrugged his shoulders. "You've got it."

She took a step back. Her nose was running; she swiped at it with the clothing balled in her hand. She had forgotten she was naked and he let his eyes sweep over her one last time.

She thought she saw something flash in those eyes…until he simply turned and walked away.

Then she knew, for sure, what they'd had—what she'd let herself believe they'd had—was finished.

CHAPTER THIRTEEN

JACK, THE Maui guy, showed up.

Falco introduced him to Elle. Elle said nothing. Not to his old pal, not to him. Well, sure. What was there left to say after you'd said it all?

Elle got into Jack's car and they left for the airport. Falco had chartered a plane to take them to L.A. He watched until the car was just a spot of dust. His heart was heavy but he knew Elle would be safe. Back in the day, he and Jack had trusted each other with their lives. They still did.

It was time to prepare for Willy Joe Johnson's arrival.

He checked the house, its perimeter, touched up a couple of refinements he'd made to the security system. An hour later, Rick, the L.A. guy, phoned. Willy Joe's plane had taken off on time. Elle's stepfather was on his way to Maui.

Falco ate a light meal. Checked his weapon. He looked at his watch, set it for midnight, lay down on a bed—not the one he'd shared with Elle—and slept. He woke a minute before the watch beeped, threw cold water on his face, went into the dark living room and settled in to wait.

Jack phoned. He and Elle were in L.A., in the suite Falco had reserved at the Four Seasons. Everything was fine, except Elle still wasn't talking to him.

That made Falco smile. What a tough lady she was.

Midnight came and went…one a.m., two a.m. Still nothing. Time was dragging.

He thought back over the last few days, thought about Elle. Sending her away had been the right thing, the only thing. She'd fallen in love with the idea of love, not with him.

And he—he would forget. The taste of her mouth. The warmth of her in his arms. The exquisite feel of her closing around him as they'd made love for the very last time.

That had been wrong. Terribly wrong. He'd known that even as he'd slipped deep inside her, but having her that one last time had been as vital as drawing breath….

The lights on the silent alarm console blinked to life. Falco felt his pulse start to race.

Elle's stepfather had arrived.

In the end, much of Falco's planning hadn't been worth a damn.

He'd expected a stealthy attack. The rear door. The front door. The door to the atrium.

Instead, there was a horrendous crash.

Johnson, evidently not given to subtlety, had smashed his way into the atrium. Moonlight illuminated him, six feet six inches of lard laid over prison-honed muscle.

He had a knife in his hand.

"Where is she?" Willy Joe shouted. "Where is that heathen bitch whose lies sent me to prison?"

Falco stepped into the atrium, gun drawn.

"She's where you can't hurt her," he said in a low, hard voice. "You're never going to hurt her again."

Willy Joe spat on the terrazzo floor. "She lured me to her. Seduced me. She's a whore, just like her mama." He curved his body forward, spread his feet apart. It was the stance of a man who knew how to use the silvery blade he held. "Now she's your whore, Orsini. But not for long. I'm going to kill you and then I'll kill her." He smiled, the smile of a maniac. "Get ready to meet your maker."

Willy Joe took a shuffling step forward. All Falco had to do was pull the trigger and a bullet traveling at better than 1,000 feet per second would stop this hulking mountain of vile flesh.

Instead, he tossed the gun aside.

He had no knife. No other weapon. What he had was the hot, blazing rage a man can only feel when the woman he loves has been violated.

"Come on and try it, you son of a bitch," he growled, and Willy Joe cackled and came at him.

The stalker was as big as a mountain but Falco was fast. And he was all muscle, no fat laid over it. He lunged to the left, feinted to the right and struck out. The first blow staggered Willy Joe but he shook it off, rushed Falco again and closed his massive arms around him. They wrestled. Struggled. Fell to the glass-strewn floor and rolled. Suddenly, the knife was driving down toward Falco's throat.

"Whore-master," Willy Joe shouted, but all Falco could hear was the sound of Elle weeping, the night she'd told him what she'd endured.

Falco roared. Grabbed his attacker's wrist. Slowly, slowly, grunting with the effort, he forced the hand holding the knife backward, toward Willy Joe.

The blade sank in.

Willy Joe gasped, then froze. And rolled onto his back, dead.

Falco shook his head to clear it, got to his knees and looked down at the stalker.

"Give my regards to the devil," he said hoarsely.

Then he staggered to his feet and took out his cell phone, which was when he realized he'd been cut. It didn't matter.

The monster who had caused the woman he loved years and years of pain was no more.

The police arrived, then a crime scene crew and a pair of detectives.

The detective in charge took Falco's statement, took notes, poked Willy Joe's body with the shiny toe of one black brogue.

"Mean SOB," his partner said. "Checked him on the computer soon as we got the call from the local guys."

Falco nodded. The EMTs had cleaned his wounds. He needed stitches but that could wait.

"So, you were staying here, on vacation, and this mother turned up from out of nowhere?"

Falco nodded again. "He must have figured the house was empty and filled with expensive stuff he could steal."

"Not his M.O.," the first detective said. "Guy was arrested and did time years ago for raping a kid."

"Well," Falco said, "I guess he decided to try something different."

"And you were here, alone. Big place, for one man."

Falco forced a smile. "I had some company for a couple of days," he said, knowing that if they checked, the best anybody would do was give a vague description of a woman.

The second detective cleared his throat. "You know, I mentioned you to my captain, Orsini. Says he knew you, back a ways in the Middle East. Knew of you, anyway. Says you were involved in some nasty stuff, says it's a damned good thing Johnson happened to choose this place to rob, that he'd surely have killed anybody else who'd tried to stop him."

Falco shrugged. "The luck of the draw."

The detectives looked at each other. "Yeah," the one in charge said with a quick smile, "that's what it must have been. The luck of the draw."

* * *

Elle read about it in an L.A. newspaper.

She knew things had gone the way Falco had intended because his friend, Jack, got a call from Falco, smiled and told her she could leave the hotel anytime. He wouldn't say more than that.

It was a small article, just a few lines. An ex-convict had broken into a house on Maui and attacked the vacationer staying there. The vacationer had killed him. No names mentioned; it wasn't an important enough news item for that.

A clear case of self-defense, said the police, but it would be up to the district attorney to make the final decision.

Elle put the paper down. Her hands were trembling.

Her tormenter was dead. Her lover had killed him. The man she loved—because, yes, she loved Falco and always would, despite the fact that he didn't love her—the man she loved had risked his life, even his freedom, for her.

And what had she done for him except run away?

He'd forced her to leave but the truth was, she could have bolted once his friend got her to the airport. What would the man have done about it? Tie her up? Drag her, kicking and screaming, onto the waiting chartered plane? Not hardly.

She had let Falco drive her away because she couldn't bear the thought that he didn't love her, that he would never love her, that she had been a job and sex and nothing more.

But what about all the rest?

He had brought her out of a lifetime of darkness. He had shown her that sex, that making love, could be joyful. He was her knight and he'd slain the dragon—and she'd abandoned him.

What if the D.A. didn't agree with the police? What if he brought Falco up on charges? Surely there could be consequences. Assault? Manslaughter? Murder?

Tears rose in her eyes. All her life, all the past months, she had thought only of herself. Now, it was time to think of someone else. The one man she would always love.

Her dark knight. Her Falco.

Falco sat in his office in the Orsini Brothers building in downtown Manhattan.

He had a stack of papers on his desk; he knew his e-mail box was stuffed. He'd blown off a meeting this morning and he was in no mood for one scheduled for this afternoon, either.

He leaned forward, hit the button on his intercom.

"Yes sir, Mr. Orsini?"

Falco sighed. His P.A. was new. He'd told her, a dozen times, to call him Falco.

"Cancel my three o'clock, please. Make it for next week."

As if anything would change by next week. As if anything would ever change, he thought, and tilted back his chair.

All he could think about was Elle.

He missed her. He ached for her. He thought of her each morning when he woke up, thought of her last thing at night, dreamed of her.

His brothers sensed something was up. They were about as subtle as elephants in a Victorian parlor. He knew they'd been talking about him. Last night, they'd badgered him into having beer and burgers at The Bar, the place they owned in SoHo. He hadn't wanted to go. The last thing he was in the mood for was fun and games but he'd figured it was easier to agree and then cut out early.

Not early enough, as it had turned out. The burgers hadn't even arrived when Raffaele flashed a phony smile and said, "So, Falco, how're things going?"

"They're going fine," he'd replied.

"Because," Dante had said, "well, you know, if anything's wrong…"

"Why would anything be wrong?" he'd said.

He'd changed the subject, talked some inane nonsense about baseball and they'd let him do it but sooner or later, they'd start pushing. And when they did—

"Falco?"

He looked up. Raffaele, Dante and Nicolo had cracked the door. They were peering in at him and, dammit, they had that look, the look they all got, him included, when they were worried about each other.

Well, hell. He didn't want anyone worrying about him.

"Hey, guys," he said, flashing a big smile, "I'd love to hang around and talk but—"

The three of them stepped into his office. Rafe shut the door.

"But what?" Dante said.

"But, I have a three o'clock appointment. And—"

"The hell you do," Rafe said. "You just cancelled."

Falco sighed. "That new P.A. is never going to work out."

Nick cleared his throat. "What's going on? And don't tell us nothing's going on. We know that's not true."

Falco looked from one of his brothers to the other. For one wild second, he almost blurted it out, almost said, *I met the only woman I'll ever love and I destroyed any possible hope she might have cared for me—*

"Whatever it is," he said coolly, "I don't need the Three Musketeers busting into my life."

"Think of us more as the Spanish Inquisition." Rafe grinned. "We have ways of making you talk."

Falco shoved back his chair and rose to his feet. "Okay, gentlemen, that's it. This meeting is—"

"Do your amazingly high spirits have anything to do with that errand our old man laid on you?"

Falco's eyes narrowed. "What'd you do, Nick? Put your ear to the door?"

Nick grinned. "Hey, I wasn't even there. I got tired of waiting and I took off."

"Yeah, well, good for you. Now, if you'll all excuse me—"

"Dammit, Falco," Dante said, "what's happening with you?"

Falco glared at his brothers. "I'll tell you what's happening with me," he snarled. "I met a woman, okay? And I—I got involved. And I told her I didn't give a damn for her. And—and, hell, it was a lie."

His brothers looked at each other. They were almost as shocked as Falco by his admission.

"So," Rafe said, "so, ah, go tell her. Tell her you—"

The intercom buzzed. Falco slapped the talk button. "Dammit," he roared, "what do you want?"

"I just…someone is here to see you, Mr. Orsini. Sir. I told her you were busy but—"

"But," Elle said as she opened the door and stepped into the office, "I told her I'd only take a minute of your time."

Falco blinked. "Elle?"

She nodded, looked around and bit lightly into her bottom lip. "You must be Falco's brothers."

Rafe and Nick and Dante nodded. Introduced themselves. Shook her hand. Looked at Falco, waited for him to say something…

"Go away," he said, and the three of them rushed for the door and shut it behind them.

"Elle." Falco could feel his heart racing. "You look—you look wonderful."

"Thank you. I guess I should have called first…"

"No," he said quickly, "no, I'm—I'm glad to see you."

Elle's mouth had gone dry. This was her Falco. The man

she adored. She wanted to run into his arms but that wasn't why she'd come here.

And it wasn't what he wanted.

She swallowed hard. "I read about—about what happened."

Hell, Falco thought, she'd hated Johnson but who knew how she felt now, knowing that he had killed him.

"The paper didn't say much, just that Willy Joe—that he broke in and—"

"We scuffled. I lucked out."

"He could have killed you!"

"No way," he said with a smile meant to be reassuring, "you know what they say about guys who were born to be hung."

"Falco." Her eyes blurred. She came toward him, lightly touched the small scar above his eyebrow. "Oh," she whispered, "did he—did he—"

"It's nothing." But the cool touch of her hand was almost more than he could bear. He caught her hand and laced his fingers through hers. God, he wanted to take her in his arms...

"The paper said that the police called it self-defense but that the final decision would be up to the district attorney."

"Right. It always is. And—"

"And," Elle said, hurrying the words together, "and if he decided it wasn't, you'll have to stand trial."

"No. I mean, yes, but—"

"I won't let that happen! I'm going to fly to Maui."

"What?"

"I said, I'm going to Maui. I'll tell the D.A. exactly what happened. How—how Willy Joe abused me. How he was sentenced to prison because of me and how he hated me for it and stalked me and—and—"

Falco felt the first flutter of hope. "Why would you do that?" he said softly.

"Because—because it's the right thing to do. I can't let you go to prison because of me."

He reached out and touched her hair. He couldn't help it. The need to stroke those dark strands one last time was too strong.

"I won't go to prison, honey. The D.A. reached a decision a couple of days ago. There won't be any charges."

Elle let out her breath. "Oh, I'm so glad!"

"You'd have done that, for me? Gone to the D.A.? Let your story go public?"

She nodded.

"Because?"

"I told you. It's the right thing to—"

Falco had lived his life taking risks. Now, he took the greatest risk of all.

"Tell me the truth," he said huskily. "Why would you do all that for me?" She didn't answer and he took her in his arms. "Is it because you love me, baby? Because you love me the way I love you?"

Tears spilled from her eyes. "Do you mean it? That you love me? Because I love you, Falco, I adore you. And—and I'd do anything for you, my knight, anything, anything—"

He kissed her. She gave a little cry, rose on her toes and wrapped her arms around his neck.

"Are you sure?" she said, against his lips. "Please be sure!"

"I love you with all my heart," he said huskily. "I love Ellie Janovic and I love Elle Bissette. With all my heart, all my soul. I'll love you until the end of time. Don't you know that by now?"

Elle made a sound that was half laugh, half sob. "You said you didn't. And you said I didn't love you. You said—"

"Hush," Falco said, and kissed her again. "I said a lot of things that day, every one a lie." He smoothed his thumbs over her cheekbones, felt the warmth of her tears against his skin.

"I loved you then. I love you now. I was just afraid you'd fallen for the man you thought I was—"

"I did. I fell for my knight in shining armor."

"I'm no knight, honey. I'm a lot of things but not that."

Elle smiled. "How little you know, Orsini. Of course you're a knight. My knight. And you always will be."

He smiled back at her. "You are one tough broad, Bissette. There's no arguing with you when you're sure you're right, is there?"

"Not about this," she said. "Never about this."

Falco drew her closer. "Still, there are things about me you don't know."

"For instance."

"For instance, your knight's old man is a crime boss."

"You already mentioned that." Elle laid a light kiss on Falco's lips. "So it's a good thing I'm not in love with your old man. What else?"

"Well," he said, straight-faced, "the other thing is even worse. I'm not a bodyguard."

"I sort of figured that when I looked in the Manhattan directory and found the listing for Orsini Brothers."

"Yeah. I'm an investor, along with those three idiots who just stumbled out the door."

"An investor." She smiled. "You're right. Considering everything, that might be even worse." She kissed him again. "But I'm willing to survive it if you can."

"Elle." Falco's expression grew serious. "Elle, will you marry me?"

Her eyes filled with happy tears. "Just try and stop me, Orsini," she said, and Falco reached past her, locked the door and kissed her.

EPILOGUE

THEY were married in the same little church in Greenwich Village that had so recently been the setting for Dante's and Rafe's weddings. Mercifully, no police cars were parked outside and only one photographer showed up. He beat a quick retreat after the Orsini brothers had a little talk with him.

Elle wore ivory silk; she carried a trailing bouquet of white orchids and wore her new mother-in-law's wedding veil, which made Sofia beam with delight. A heart-shaped canary-yellow diamond glittered in the hollow of her throat; another adorned the ring finger of her left hand.

Falco was gorgeous in the same tux he'd worn on what Elle called their first date, back in Hawaii. Isabella, Anna, Chiara and Gabriella were her bridesmaids, all of them beautiful in gowns of pink silk. Her new brothers-in-law kissed her and told her how happy they were to have her in their family.

The reception was held in the conservatory of the Orsini mansion. Everyone laughed, drank champagne, ate lobster and caviar and even managed bites of the huge wedding cake.

By late afternoon, things were getting quiet.

The bride and groom slipped away. They were going to Hawaii, though not to Maui, on their honeymoon. Dante and Gaby left with their son, Daniel, asleep in his daddy's arms.

Rafe and Chiara left, too. Chiara was pregnant, glowing with happiness, as was Rafe.

Nicolo kissed his mother goodbye, avoided his father as he'd done all day. Avoiding Cesare was habit; he didn't like the Don any more than his brothers did and besides, Nick was very aware of the fact that he had, thus far, avoided the talk Cesare had wanted to have with him a few months ago on the day Dante and Gabriella had married.

He and Falco had both been told their father wanted to see them. Falco had gone in first, Nick had waited outside for a few minutes and then he'd though, *Eff this*, which was exactly what he'd said to Felix, his father's *capo*, had put out a hand to stop him from leaving.

"I am not one of the Don's soldiers," Nick had said coldly. "He wants to see me, let him call and make an appointment."

But there'd been no call and Nick had figured he'd escaped his father's latest "after I'm dead" speech.

"Nicolo."

Nick, halfway to the front door of the big house, groaned. He took a deep breath and turned around.

"Father," he said politely.

"We must talk."

"I have an appointment. And you and I have nothing to talk about."

Cesare smiled around the fat, unlit Havana cigar clutched between his teeth.

"But we do. Besides, you owe me a few minutes. Did you think I had forgotten how you slipped out the last time?"

"I didn't 'slip out', Father, I just got tired of cooling my heels like one of your men."

"Exactly. You are not one of my men, you are my son. Surely, you will give me the courtesy of a chat just as your three brothers have done before you."

Nick's jaw tightened. His father was right. Dante, Raffaele and Falco had all gone through the wringer. It was his turn now, and he wasn't a man to walk away from a responsibility.

"Five minutes," he said brusquely. "That's it."

"Of course, Nicolo," Cesare said smoothly. "In my study, *per favore*. Yes?"

Nick strode toward the dark, overfurnished room from which Cesare ruled his empire.

"Whatever speech you've prepared, Father, had better be good."

The Don's *capo*, silent as a cat, stepped out of the shadows. Cesare motioned him aside and followed his son into the study.

"I assure you, Nicolo," he said as he shut the door, "it is."

NICOLO: THE POWERFUL SICILIAN

SANDRA MARTON

CHAPTER ONE

THE wedding at the little church in lower Manhattan and then the reception at the Orsini mansion had made for a long day, and Nicolo Orsini was more than ready to leave.

A naked woman was waiting in his bed.

She'd been there when he left his Central Park West triplex at ten that morning.

"Must you go, Nicky?" she'd said, with a pout almost as sexy as the lush body barely covered by the down duvet.

Nick had checked his tie in the mirror, checked the whole bit—the custom-tailored tux, the white silk shirt, even his wing tips, spit-polished the way he'd learned to do it in the corps. Then he'd walked back to the bed, dropped a light kiss on her hair and said yeah, he did.

It wasn't every day a man's brother got married.

He hadn't told her that, of course, he'd simply said he had to go to a wedding. Even that had been enough to put a spark of interest in her baby blues, but if he'd said it was one of his brothers doing the deed...

Talk about the Orsini brothers and weddings was not a thought he cared to leave bouncing around in any woman's head.

"I'll phone you," he'd said, and she'd pouted again—how come that pout was becoming less of a turn-on and more of an irritation?—and said maybe she'd just wait right where she was until he returned.

Nick lifted his champagne flute to his lips as he thought back to the morning.

Damn, he hoped not.

He had nothing against finding beautiful women in his bed, but his interest in this one was definitely waning and the female histrionics that sometimes accompanied the end of an affair were the last thing he wanted to deal with after a day like this. Much as he loved his brothers, his sisters, his mother, his sisters-in-law and his little nephew, there was such a thing as too much togetherness.

Or maybe it was just him. Either way, it was time to get moving.

He looked out the glass-walled conservatory at the garden behind the Orsini mansion. The flowering shrubs his sister Isabella had planted a couple of years ago were still green despite the onset of autumn. Beyond the shrubs, stone walls rose high enough to block out the streets of his childhood, streets that were changing so fast he hardly recognized them anymore. The Little Italy that had been home to generations of immigrants was rapidly giving way to Greenwich Village.

Trendy shops, upscale restaurants, art galleries. Progress, Nick thought grimly and drank some more of the champagne. He hated to see it happen. He'd grown up on these streets. Not that his memories were all warm and fuzzy. When your old man was the don of a powerful crime family, you learned early that your life was different. By the time he was nine or ten, he'd known what Cesare Orsini was and hated him for it.

But the bond with his mother and sisters had always been strong. As for the bond with his brothers...

Nick's lips curved in a smile.

That bond went beyond blood.

All day, his thoughts had dipped back to their shared childhoods. They'd fought like wolf cubs, teased each other unmercifully, stood together against kids who thought it might be fun to give the sons of a *famiglia* don a hard time. Barely out of their teens, they'd gone their separate ways only to come together again, their bond stronger than ever, to found the investment firm that had made them as wealthy and powerful as their father but without any of the ugliness of Cesare's life.

They were part of each other, Raffaele, Dante, Falco and him. Close in age, close in looks, in temperament, in everything that mattered.

Was that going to change? It had to. How could things remain the same when one after another, the Orsini brothers had taken wives?

Nick tossed back the rest of his champagne and headed for the bar that had been set up at one end of the conservatory. The bartender saw him coming, smiled politely as he popped the cork on another bottle of vintage Dom Pérignon and poured the pale gold liquid into a Baccarat flute.

"Thanks," Nick said.

Unbelievable, he thought as he watched Rafe dancing with his wife, Chiara. His brothers, married. He still couldn't get his head around it. First Rafe, then Dante and now even Falco. I-Am-An-Island-Unto-Myself Falco…

Absolutely unbelievable.

His brothers had fallen in love.

"So will you, someday," Rafe had said last night, as the four of them had toasted Falco's coming nuptials in The Bar, the Soho place they owned.

"Not me," he'd said, and they'd all laughed.

"Yeah, my man," Dante had said, "you, too."

"Trust me," Falco had said. "When you least expect it, you'll meet the right woman and next thing you know, she'll have your poor, pathetic heart right in the palm of her hand."

They'd all laughed, and Nick had let it go at that.

Why tell them that he'd already been there, done that—and no way in hell was he going to do it again.

Sure, it was possible his brothers would end up on the positive side of the grim statistics that said one in four marriages wouldn't last. Their wives seemed sweet and loving, but that was the thing about women, wasn't it?

They played games.

To put it bluntly, they lied like salesmen trying to sell ice to Eskimos.

Nick scowled, went back to the bar and put his untouched flute of champagne on its marble surface.

"Scotch," he said. "A double."

"I'm sorry, sir. I don't have Scotch."

"Bourbon, then."

"No bourbon, either."

Nick narrowed his dark eyes. "You're joking."

"No, Mr. Orsini." The bartender—a kid, maybe twenty-one, twenty-two—swallowed hard. "I'm really sorry, sir."

"Saying you're sorry isn't—"

A muscle ticked in Nick's jaw. Why give the kid a hard time? It wasn't his fault that the only liquid flowing today was stuff that cost two hundred, three hundred bucks a bottle. Cesare's idea, no doubt. His father's half-assed belief that serving a classy wine would erase the stink that clung to his name.

Forget that. Falco would have paid for the wedding himself, same as Dante and Rafe had done. That was the deal, the only way any of them had agreed to hold the receptions in what their mother insisted would always be their home. Isabella had done the flowers, Anna had made the catering and bar arrangements. If he wanted to bite somebody's head off, it would be hers.

That did it. The thought of taking on his fiery kid sister—either one of them, actually—made him laugh.

"Sorry," he told the kid. "I guess I only thought I was all champagned out."

The kid grinned as he filled a flute. "No problem, Mr. Orsini. Me, I'm all weddinged out. Did one yesterday afternoon, another last night and here I am again. Comes my turn, my lady and I are definitely gonna pass on this kind of stuff."

Nick raised his glass in a mock salute. It was the appropriate reaction but what he really wanted was to say was, *Hell, man, why get married at all?*

Still, he knew the answer.

A man made his mark in the world, he wanted to make it last. He wanted children to carry on his name.

So, yeah, he'd marry some day.

But he wouldn't pick a wife by fooling himself into thinking it was love.

Outside, visible through the walls of glass, the sky was graying. Rain, the weatherman had said, and it looked as if he'd got it right for a change.

Nick opened the door and stepped onto the patio.

When he was ready to choose a wife, he would do it logically, select a woman who'd fit seamlessly into his life, who would make no demands beyond the basic ones: that he support her comfortably and treat her with respect. Respect was all he would ask from her in return.

Logic was everything, in making business decisions, in planning a marriage. He would never make an emotional decision when selecting a bank to take over, or a stock to ride out. Why would he do it in selecting a wife?

Relying on emotion was a mistake.

Once, only once and never again, he had come dangerously close to making that error.

At least he hadn't been fool enough to tell anybody. Not even his brothers. He hadn't planned it that way; he'd just kept what was happening to himself, probably because it had all seemed so special. As a result, there hadn't been any "Oh, man, we're so sorry this happened to you" bull. Not that his brothers wouldn't have meant it, but there were some things a man was better off keeping to himself.

Things like learning you'd been used.

It had happened four years ago. He'd met a woman on a business trip to Seattle. She was smart, she was funny, she was beautiful. She came from a family that was as close to royalty as you could get in America but she'd made it in business on her own as the CFO of the small private bank he'd gone to the Northwest to buy.

To consider buying.

And that had turned out to be the key to everything.

She'd been in his bed by the end of the first day. And he'd wanted to keep her there. Before he knew it, they'd set a pattern. He flew to Seattle one weekend, she flew to New York the next. She said she missed him terribly when they weren't together; he admitted he felt the same way.

He had been falling in love, and he knew it.

A month into their affair, he decided he had to tell her about his father. He'd never done that before. A woman either knew his old man was a crook or she didn't. Who gave a damn? But this was different. This was—he'd avoided even thinking the word in the past—a relationship.

So, one night, lying in her bed, he told her.

"My father is Cesare Orsini." When she didn't react, he told her the rest. That Cesare was the head of a notorious *famiglia*. That he was a gangster.

"Oh," she purred, "I already knew that, Nicky." A sexy smile. "Actually, it's a turn-on."

A muscle knotted in his jaw.

The revelation should have set off warning bells. But the part of his anatomy with which he'd been thinking didn't have the luxury of possessing bells, warning or otherwise.

A long holiday weekend was coming. He'd asked her to spend it with him. She said she couldn't. Her grandmother, who lived in Oregon, was ill. She'd always been Grandma's favorite; Saturday morning, she'd fly out to spend the weekend with her, just the two of them, alone. She smiled. And she'd tell Grandma about the wonderful man she'd met.

Nick said he understood. It was a sweet thing to do.

And then, Friday night, he thought, what if he went with her? He could meet Grandma. Tell her how important her granddaughter had become to him.

He decided to make it a surprise.

He took the Orsini jet to Seattle, rented a car, drove to his lady's town house, took the key she'd given him and slipped quietly inside.

What came next had been like a punch in the gut.

His lady was in bed with her boss, the bank's CEO, laughing as she assured him that Nicolo Orsini was absolutely, positively going to make an offer for the bank that far exceeded its worth.

"An Orsini and you, babe," the man had said. "It's a classic. The princess and the stable boy…"

The delicate champagne flute shattered in Nick's hand.

"Merda!"

Champagne spilled on the jacket of his tux; a tiny drop of crimson oozed from a small cut on his hand. Nick yanked a pristine white handkerchief from his pocket, dabbed at his tux, at his finger…

"Hey, man," an amused male voice said, "the champagne's not that bad."

It was Rafe, coming toward him with a bottle of Heineken in each hand. Nick groaned with pleasure and reached for one.

"You're a miracle worker," he said. "Where'd this come from?"

"Ask me no questions, I'll tell you no lies." Rafe frowned, jerked his head at Nick's hand. "You okay?"

"Fine. See? The bleeding's stopped already."

"What happened?"

Nick shrugged. "I didn't know my own strength," he said with a lazy smile. "No problem. I'll get something and sweep it up."

"Trust me, Nick. One of the catering staff is bound to come out of the woodwork before you can—" A woman appeared, broom and dustpan in hand. "See? What did I tell you?"

Nick nodded his thanks, waited until the woman was gone, then touched his bottle to his brother's.

"To small miracles," he said, "like brothers with bottles of beer at just the right moment."

"I figured it would do away with that long face you were wearing."

"Me? A long face? I guess I was—ah, I was thinking about that Swiss deal."

"Forget business," Dante said, as he joined them. He, too, had a bottle of beer in his hand. "It's a party, remember?" He grinned as he leaned closer. "Gaby says that little caterer's assistant has been eyeing you all afternoon."

"Well, of course she has," Nick said, because he knew it was expected.

His brothers laughed. They talked for a few minutes and then it was time to say goodbye to the bride and groom.

Finally, he could get out of here.

He went through the whole routine—kisses, hugs, promises to his mother that he'd come to dinner as soon as he could. His father wasn't around. Perfect, he thought as he made his way down the long hall to the front door. He never had anything to say to Cesare beyond a perfunctory "hello" or "goodbye," and if the old man got hold of him today, it might take more than that because—

"Nicolo."

Hell. Think of the devil and he was sure to turn up.

"Leaving so soon, *mio figlio?*" Cesare, dressed not in Brioni today but in an Armani tux, flashed a smile.

"Yes," Nick said coldly.

Cesare chuckled. "So direct. A man after my own heart."

"You don't have a heart, Father."

"And you are quick. I like that, too."

"I'm sure I should be flattered but you'll forgive me if I'm not. Now, if you'll excuse me—"

"Have you forgotten you were to meet with me the day of Dante's wedding?"

Forgotten? Hardly. Cesare had cornered Falco and him; Nick had cooled his heels while Falco and the old man were closeted in his study and after a few minutes Nick had thought, *What am I doing, waiting here like an obedient servant?*

Besides, he'd known what his father wanted to tell him. Safe combinations. Vault locations. The names of lawyers, of accountants, everything the don felt his sons had to know in case of his death, when truth was none of them would ever touch the spoils of what the media called the Orsini *famiglia.*

"Five minutes," Nick said brusquely. "Just so long as you know in advance, Father, that whatever speech you've prepared, I'm not interested."

Freddo, Cesare's capo, stepped out of the shadows as father and son approached the don's study. Cesare waved the cold-eyed hoodlum aside, followed Nick into the room and shut the door.

"Perhaps, Nicolo, I will be able to change your mind."

Ten minutes later, Nick stared at his father.

"Let me be sure I get this. You want to invest in a winery."

Cesare, seated behind his oversized mahogany desk, hands folded on its polished surface, nodded. "Yes."

"The Antoninni winery in Florence, Italy."

"In Tuscany, Nicolo. Tuscany is a province. *Firenze* is a city within it."

"Spare me the geography lesson, okay? You're investing in a vineyard."

"I have not made that commitment yet but yes, I hope to invest in the prince's winery."

"The prince." Nick laughed, but the sound was not pleasant. "Sounds like a bad movie. *The Prince and the Don,* a farce in two acts."

"I am pleased you are amused," Cesare said coolly.

"What'd you do? Make him an offer he couldn't refuse?"

The don's expression hardened. "Watch how you speak to me."

"Or what?" Nick leaned over the desk and slapped his hands flat on the surface. "I'm not afraid of you, old man. I haven't been afraid of you since I figured out what you were two decades ago."

"Nor have you shown me the respect a son owes a father."

"I owe you nothing. And if respect's what you want from me—"

"We are wasting time. What I want from you is your professional expertise."

Nick stood straight, arms folded. "Meaning what?"

"Meaning, I need to know the true value of the vineyard before I make a final offer. A financial evaluation, you might call it."

"And?"

"And, I am asking you to make the evaluation for me."

Nick shook his head. "I evaluate banks, Father. Not grapes."

"You evaluate assets. It is your particular skill at the company you and your brothers own, is it not?"

"How nice." Nick's lips drew back from his teeth in a lupine smile. "That you noticed your sons own a business so different from yours, I mean."

"I am a businessman, Nicolo." Nick snorted; Cesare's eyes narrowed. "I am a businessman," he repeated. "And you are an expert on financial acquisitions. The prince offers me a ten percent interest for five million euros. Is that reasonable? Should my money buy me more, or will I lose it all if the company is in trouble?" The don picked up a manila envelope and rattled it. "He gave me facts and figures, but how do I know what they mean? I want your opinion, your conclusions."

"Send an accountant," Nick said with a tight smile. "One of the *paesano* who cooks your books."

"The real question," his father said, ignoring the jibe, "is why he wants my money. For expansion, he says, but is that true? The vineyard has been in his family for five hundred years. Now, suddenly, he requires outside investors. I need answers, Nicolo, and who better to get them for me than my own flesh and blood?"

"Nice try," Nick said coldly, "but it's a little late for the 'do it for Dad' routine."

"It is not for me." Cesare rose to his feet. "It is for your mother."

Nick burst out laughing. "That's good. That's great! 'Do it for your mother.' Right. As if Mama wants to invest in an

Italian vineyard." Nick's laughter stopped abruptly. "But it's not going to work, so if you're done—"

"There are things you do not know about your mother and me, Nicolo."

"Damned right, I don't. For starters, what in hell possessed her to marry you?"

"She married me for the same reason I married her." Cesare's gruff voice softened. "For love."

"Oh, sure," Nick said sarcastically. "You and she—"

"We eloped. Did you know that? She was betrothed to the wealthiest man in our village."

Nick couldn't keep his surprise from showing. Cesare saw it and nodded with satisfaction.

"That man is the father of Rafe's wife, Chiara."

"Chiara's father? My mother was engaged to...?"

"Your brother knows. He kept the information to himself, as is proper. Sì, Sofia and I eloped." Cesare's expression softened. "We fled to Tuscany."

Nick was still working on the fact that his mother had run away with his father, but he managed to ask the obvious question.

"Why? If you were both Sicilian..."

"Tuscany is beautiful, not harsh like Sicily but soft and golden. There are those in Italy who think Tuscany is the heart of our people's culture while Sicily and Sicilians..." The don shrugged. "What matters is that it was your mother's dream."

Nick felt the story drawing him in.

"Then, why did you emigrate to America?"

A small tic danced under Cesare's left eye.

"I had no skills other than those I acquired as a boy," he said in a low voice, "skills that had a use in Sicily. And here, in this country, as well. I knew this, you see, just as I knew that if I wanted to give your mother more than a life of poverty—"

Nick leaned over the desk and slammed his hands on either arm of his father's chair. "How dare you use my mother as an excuse for the things you've done!"

"I have done what I have done," Cesare said flatly. "The decisions were mine and I offer no apologies or excuses." His tone softened. "But if I could give Sofia this—this bit of Tuscan soil, this only thing she ever asked of me—"

"It's a hell of a story," Nick said coldly, "I'll grant you that."

But was it true? The only way to know was to ask his mother, and there wasn't a way in hell he was about to do that.

What it came down to was simple. Cesare might be using him...but so what? A couple of days out of his life was all it would take.

"Okay," Nick snapped. "I'll give you two days. That's it. Two days in Tuscany. Then I head home."

Cesare held out the manila envelope. "Everything you need is here, Nicolo. *Mille grazie.*"

"Don't thank me. Thank your wife for having eloped with a man unworthy of her forty years ago."

Nick took the envelope, turned on his heel and walked out.

"Two days, Alessia," Prince Vittorio Antoninni said. "That is all I ask."

Alessia Antoninni kept her gaze on the moonlit grape vines that stretched toward the softly rolling Tuscan hills. It was fall and the vines, long since stripped of their fruit, seemed lifeless.

"I told you, Papa, I have work waiting for me in Rome."

"Work," the prince scoffed. "Is that what you call running around with celebrities?"

Alessia looked at her father. They stood on the verandah

that spilled from the rear of the centuries-old villa that was her ancestral home.

"I work for a public relations firm," she said evenly. "I do not 'run around,' I deal with clients."

"Which means that handling public relations for your very own father should take you no effort at all."

"It is not a matter of effort. It is a matter of time. I don't have any."

"Perhaps what you do not have is the wish to be a dutiful daughter."

There were endless answers to that but the hour was late. Alessia decided to let the gauntlet lie where her father had thrown it.

"You should not have agreed to a visit from this American if you knew you would not be available for it."

"How many times must I explain? Something's come up. I cannot be here for *Signore* Orsini's visit and it would be impolite to cancel it."

"You mean, it would be dangerous to disappoint a gangster."

"Cesare Orsini is a businessman. Why believe the lies of the tabloid press?"

"Your staff can handle things. Your accountants, your secretary—"

"And what of the dinner party I arranged?" The prince raised an eyebrow. "Would you have my housekeeper assume the role of hostess?"

"I have not been your hostess for years. Let your mistress play the part. She's done it before."

"*Signore* Orsini was born in this country."

"He was born in Sicily," Alessia said, with all the disdain of a Tuscan aristocrat.

"And Sicilians often cling to the old ways. Being entertained by my mistress might offend him." The prince's eyes turned cool. "Did you expect me to deny that I have a mistress? You know of your mother's condition."

Alessia looked at him in disbelief. "My mother is in a *sanatorio!*"

"Indeed." The prince paused. "A very expensive *sanatorio.*"

Something in her father's tone sent a chill down Alessia's spine. "What are you saying?"

The prince sighed. "Without an infusion of capital, I am afraid I will have to make some difficult choices. About your mother and the *sanatorio.*"

"There are no choices." Alessia could feel her heart pounding. "There is the *sanatorio,* or there is the public hospital."

"As you say, my dear. There is the one—or there is the other."

Alessia shuddered. She knew he meant it. Her father was a man with no heart.

"I see the condemnation in your eyes, daughter, but I will not lose what has been in our family for five centuries."

"You should have thought of that before you brought the vineyard to the edge of bankruptcy."

The prince made an impatient gesture. "Will you do as I ask or not?"

Was there a choice? Alessia thought bitterly.

"Two days," she said. "That is all I can give you."

"Grazie, bella mia."

"A blackmailer does not thank the person he blackmails, Papa."

It wasn't much of a rejoinder, she thought as she went into the villa, to the room that had once been hers, but it would have to do.

CHAPTER TWO

THERE was no woman waiting in Nick's bed, but she'd left a note.

Call me.

Nick sighed and tossed the note aside. He'd call, but not until he'd returned from this pointless trip. Call, send flowers and say goodbye. It was definitely time to end things.

He stripped off the tux, showered, put on a set of well-worn Marine Corps sweats and went into the kitchen. It was a decorator's dream but he pretty much used it only for making a sandwich or a pot of coffee, as he was now, spooning the stuff into a French press, putting the kettle on to boil, then settling in to wait.

The more he thought about it, the more certain he was that he'd been suckered into going to Italy. That story about his mother... Even if it were true, and that was a stretch, why would his father have waited forty years to give her, as he'd put it, a little bit of Tuscany?

Not that it mattered.

He'd said he would do this thing. A man was nothing if he broke his word.

The kettle whistled. Nick made the coffee, gave it a few minutes, then poured some into an oversized mug. Too much champagne or maybe too much Cesare. Either way, a couple of sips and he felt the caffeine kicking in as he emptied the contents of the envelope his father had given him onto the polished stone counter.

He picked up a document, read a couple of paragraphs, then shook his head in dry amusement. He was due to meet with Prince Vittorio Antoninni the next day.

"Would have been nice if you'd consulted me first, Father," he muttered, but a quick meeting would serve his purpose. The sooner this was behind him, the better.

He drank a little more coffee, then reached for the phone. The Orsini jet was taking Falco and his bride on their honeymoon. No problem. The company used a travel agent; Nick had the guy's home phone number. It was one of the perks of doing seven figures worth of business with him every year.

To his surprise, there were no nonstop flights from Kennedy Airport to Florence. He would have to change planes in Rome. That meant the travel time would be longer than he liked, but still, two days for this would be enough. He arranged for a first-class ticket that would get him into the city by 2:00 p.m., arranged for a suite at the Grand Hotel and a rental car he'd pick up at the airport.

Okay.

Nick punched a speed-dial number, ordered *pad thai* from a little place a few blocks away. While he waited for it to arrive, he went through the rest of the Antoninni Vineyard papers, but he learned little more than he already knew. The Antoninni family had owned the land and the winery for five centuries. Prince Vittorio had taken over from his father; his daughter would eventually take over from him, though she seemed disinterested in anything to do with business.

Alessia Antoninni was a party girl. She called herself a publicist but she spent her time in Rome, running with a fast crowd of people too rich for their own good. He knew what she was like without half-trying. Self-centered. Self-indulgent.

And bored out of her empty mind. New York was filled with young women like her.

Not that it mattered to him.

His business was with her father. Without question, the sooner it was over with, the better.

There was a note in the envelope, on heavy vellum adorned with a royal crest. *Signore* Orsini was to telephone the prince's secretary when he knew the exact time of arrival. The prince would not simply send a car, he would, himself, be at the airport to greet *Signore* Orsini. And, of course, *Signore* Orsini would be his guest at the Antoninni villa in the hills outside *Firenze*.

Nick made the call. It was the middle of the night in Italy by then so he ended up leaving a voice mail message in what he suspected was terrible Italian because he'd never picked up more than the basics, confirming he'd be arriving the next day, as planned, but omitting the time and flight information, and politely refusing the offer that he stay at the villa.

He preferred being on his own when he was checking out possible investment properties.

The bell rang. It was the doorman with the *pad thai*. Nick settled down with his dinner and his laptop and went through the Antoninni Vineyards paperwork again.

By midnight, he had lots of questions and not many answers. He could only hope the prince could provide them.

The prince, Nick thought, and laughed. This entire thing was like a bad joke.

Alessia paced the waiting area in the Peretola Airport, the last of her patience rapidly fleeing.

This was like a bad joke, she thought grimly. If only she could see enough humor in it to laugh.

The Orsini gangster had left a voice-mail message in

the middle of the night. Did he not realize there was a time difference between America and Europe?

Probably not.

He was a hoodlum. He would have the IQ of a snail. The message was delivered in incredibly bad Italian. Delivered? Barked, was more like it, in Sicilian-Italian. Such a lower-class patois…but what else would such a man speak?

He had an interesting voice, she had to give him that. Low-pitched. Slightly husky. A young voice for an old man.

What counted was that the message was pointless. He would arrive today. Alessia bit back a snort of derision. Of course he would! That was the arrangement he had made with her father. Then there'd been something about hotel arrangements when he surely knew he would stay at the villa. As for his arrival time, the airline he was flying…

Nothing.

She'd had to waste time scanning for all the incoming flights that he could take from London or Paris or who knew where. She'd ended with a list of arrivals that ranged from early morning to this last one due in now, from Rome.

She had been pacing these grimy floors for hours. An entire day, wasted.

An unladylike word slipped from her lips. A nun, hurrying by, gave her a shocked look.

"You try putting yourself in my place," Alessia said to the nun's retreating back, and then she thought, *I am losing my mind!*

A message blinked on the arrivals board. *Grazie a Dio!* The plane from Rome had landed. Orsini had to be on it. Five minutes for the passengers to disembark. Ten for them to collect their luggage. Another ten to clear passport control…

Her feet were killing her.

She had worn Dior heels. Heels? They were more like stilts. Foolish to have done so but they went well with her ivory

Armani suit. She had dressed with care, not to impress this Cesare Orsini but to remind him of who she was and who *he* was and if that seemed wrong, so be it. Heaven only knew what her father had led the man to think about this unholy deal, but since going to work in Rome, she had seen enough deals go sour to know that it was important to establish one's position as soon as possible.

This gangster wanted to buy into the Antoninni Vineyards? She would set the rules. That was her right, now that her father had dumped the situation in her lap. And the first rule was that if it had been left to her, the American thug would never have thought to set foot on Tuscan soil.

Ah. Finally. The passengers from Rome were starting to trickle into the hall. A trio of priests. A middle-aged woman, wheeling a suitcase. Two teenaged boys with backpacks. A harassed-looking mother clutching a wailing child. An elderly man, leaning on a cane. A young couple, hands tightly clasped.

And a man.

Tall, dark-haired, impeccably dressed in what was surely a custom-made suit, his stride long and fluid, the look on his face one of such controlled anger that Alessia took an unthinking step to her left.

A mistake, because he took one to his right.

They collided.

No. Too strong a word. His body simply brushed hers....

An electric shock seemed to jolt through her.

He looked at her. He must have felt the same thing, judging by the sudden narrowing of his eyes. Such dark eyes, the color of the strongest, richest espresso. The rest of his features were strong, too, she thought on a little inrush of breath. The narrow nose, with just the slightest dent near the bridge. The square jaw. The firm mouth.

It was a hard, masculine face. A beautiful face...

"Excuse me."

Alessia blinked. The man's voice was as cold and hard as his expression. And the words were a lie. "Excuse me," he'd said, but what he meant was, "Why don't you get out of my way?"

Her eyes narrowed, the same as his.

She took a step to the side. "You are excused," she said, her tone as frigid as his.

His dark eyebrows rose. "Charming," he muttered, and strode past her.

Charming, indeed. The rudeness of him! He had spoken in English; without thinking, she had answered in the same tongue. He was, without question, an American, and everyone knew how *they* were….

Wait.

Had there been something familiar in his voice? Deep. Husky. Silken, despite its sharpness…

A bustle of noise and motion jerked her back to the present. More passengers had just appeared. It was an interesting parade of humanity but when it ended, it had not included Cesare Orsini. There was no short, rotund figure wrapped in a dark overcoat, an old-fashioned fedora pulled low over his eyes.

To hell with this.

Alessia turned on her heel, marched through the terminal and out the exit doors. Her black Mercedes had acquired two more parking tickets. She yanked them from under the wiper blades, opened the car and tossed them inside.

Her father could deal with this nonsense.

She had had enough.

She got behind the wheel. Turned the key. Opened the windows. Started the engine. The Mercedes gave a polite but throaty roar. It had no effect on the pedestrians swarming past the hood. Crossing without acknowledging traffic was a game in Italy. Pedestrian or driver, you could not play if you showed fear.

Slowly, she inched the Mercedes forward. The crowd showed reluctance but, gradually, a narrow tunnel opened. Alessia pressed down harder and harder on the gas....

And struck something.

She heard the tinkle of glass. Saw the crowd part.

Saw the broken taillight of the Ferrari ahead of her.

Dio, what now? she thought as the driver's door flew open. A man stepped out, strode to the rear of the Ferrari—dammit, of all cars to hit, a Ferrari—looked at the shattered glass, then at her...

Cavolo!

It was him. The tall, dark-haired American. He didn't just look angry, he looked furious. Alessia almost shrank back in her seat as he marched toward her. Instead, she took a long, deliberate breath and stepped from her car, her professional easing-the-tension smile on her face.

"Sorry," she said briskly. "I didn't see you."

"You didn't see me? Am I driving a slot car?"

She almost asked him what a slot car was and caught herself just in time. All she wanted was to get home—to the villa, which was not really home but would have to do—and kick off her agonizingly painful shoes, peel off her wrinkled suit, pour herself a glass of wine...or maybe two glasses—

"Well? Do you have anything to say for yourself?"

His tone was obnoxious, as if this were her fault. It wasn't. He'd been parked in a no-parking zone. Yes, so had she, but what had that to do with anything?

"First you try to walk through me. Now you try to *drive* through me!" His mouth thinned. "Did you ever hear of paying attention to what you're doing?"

So much for easing the tension. Alessia drew herself up. "I don't like your attitude."

"*You* don't like *my* attitude?"

He laughed. The laugh was ugly. Insulting. Alessia narrowed her eyes.

"There is no point to this conversation," she said coldly. "I suggest we exchange insurance information. There has been no injury to either of us and only the slightest one to your vulgar automobile. I will, therefore, forgive your insulting attitude."

"My car is vulgar? My attitude is insulting, but you will forgive it?" The man glared at her. "What the hell is with this country, anyway? No direct flights from New York. A layover in Rome that's supposed to take forty minutes and ends up taking three hours, three endless hours because some idiot mechanic dropped a screwdriver, and when I made a perfectly reasonable attempt to charter a private plane instead of standing around, killing time…"

He was still talking but she couldn't hear him. Her thoughts were spinning. He had come from New York? A layover in Rome? A longer layover than planned?

"Do you speak Italian?" she blurted.

Stopped in midsentence, he glared at her as if she were crazy. "What?"

"I said, do you—"

"No. I do not. A few words, that's all, and what are you, an adjunct to passport control?"

"Say something. In Italian."

He shot her another look. Then he shrugged as if to say, *Hey, why not accommodate the inmate?* And said something in Italian.

Alessia gasped.

Not at what he'd said—it was impolite and it had to do with her mental state but who cared about that? She gasped because what he'd spoken was not really Italian, it was Sicilian. Sicilian, spoken in a deep, husky voice…

"Your name," she whispered.

"Excuse me?"

"Your name! What is it?"

Nick slapped his hands on his hips. Okay. Maybe he'd stepped into an alternate universe.

Or maybe this was the old-country version of Marco Polo. Kids played it back home, a dumb game where they bobbed around in a swimming pool, one yelling "Marco," another answering "Polo." It made about as much sense as this, an aggressive, mean-tempered babe—if you could call her a babe and, really, you couldn't—who had first tried to walk through him, then tried to run him down....

"Answer the question! Who are you? Are you Cesare Orsini?"

"No," Nick said truthfully.

"Are you sure?"

He laughed. That made her face turn pink.

"I think you are he. And if I am right, you've cost me an entire day."

"Meaning?"

"Meaning, I have been here for hours and hours, waiting for your arrival."

Nick's smile faded. "If you tell me you're Vittorio Antoninni, I won't believe you."

"I am his daughter. Alessia Antoninni." Her chin jutted forward. "And, obviously, you are who you say you are not!"

"You asked if I was Cesare Orsini. I'm not. I'm Nicolo Orsini. Cesare is my father."

"Your father? Impossible! I know nothing of a change in plans."

"In that case," Nick said coldly, "we're even, because I sure as hell don't know about a change in plans, either. Your father was supposed to meet me. If I'd let him meet me, that is, which I had no intention of doing."

"I have no idea what you're talking about."

"That makes things even. I don't understand anything you're babbling about, lady, and—"

"Where have you been all these hours?"

"Excuse me?"

"It is a simple question, *signore*. Where were you while I paced the floor here?"

"Where was I?" Nick's jaw shot forward. "In the first-class Alitalia lounge in Rome," he said sharply. "And trust me, princess, it loses its charm after a while."

"The title is no longer accurate."

Nick looked Alessia Antoninni over, from her falling-apart chignon to her wrinkled Armani suit to the shoes she seemed to be trying to ease off her feet.

"Yes," he said, "I can see that."

She flushed. "I was expecting—"

"My father. Yeah. I get that part. What I don't get is what you're doing here. Where are your old man and his driver?"

"So. You admit you knew that someone would be waiting for you. And yet, you left no word of your arrival time, of the airline you would be flying. You did not spend so much as a second looking for my father or his chauffeur inside the terminal, and you did not trouble yourself to telephone the villa when you did not see them. If you had, someone would have called me."

"Yeah, well, I'm sorry this didn't go according to royal protocol, princess, but life doesn't always do what you want."

"I repeat, I am not a princess. And this has nothing to do with protocol. If you had left your arrival information as part of that useless voice-mail message—"

"If I had, your father would have met me. Or, as it turns out, you'd have met me. And I'm not interested in being taken by the hand and shuttled to your villa while somebody tells me how lucky I am to be given the chance to invest in what's probably a disaster of a vineyard."

"I thought it was your gangster father who would be investing. And to so much as suggest the vineyard is a disaster—"

Alessia caught her breath as Nicolo Orsini stepped closer. With him this near, she had to tilt her head back to see his face. Even in these shoes of medieval torture, he towered over her.

"I'm here as my father's emissary," he said in a cold, dangerous voice. "And I'd advise you to watch what you say, princess. Insult one Orsini, you insult us all."

Nick frowned even as he said it. Where had that come from? Insult his brothers or, even worse, his mother or his sisters, and, of course, you insulted them all. But the old man? The don, who was part of something ancient and ugly and immoral? Was an insult to him an offense to all the Orsinis?

"Your father is what he is," Alessia Antoninni said with dogged determination. "If you expect me to pretend otherwise, you are wrong."

He looked down into her face. Her hair was an unruly mass of streaked gold, long tendrils dangling free of what had once been some kind of ladylike knot. Her eyes flashed defiance. There was a streak of soot on a cheekbone high enough to entice a man to trace his finger across its angled length.

The rest of her was a mess.

Still, she was stunning. He could see that now. Stunning. And arrogant. And she was looking at him as if he were beneath contempt.

His jaw tightened.

She had pegged him for the same kind of man as his father. He wasn't—but something in him rebelled at denying it. She was an aristocrat; his father was a peasant. Nick had once delved into the origins of *la famiglia*, enough to know that though some scholars traced the organization solely to banditry, others traced it to the rebellion of those trapped in poverty by rich, cruel landowners.

It didn't matter. Whatever the origins of his father's way of life, Nick despised it.

Still, there was a subtle difference between viewing that way of life from the comfort of America and viewing it here, on such ancient soil. It brought out a feeling new to him.

"Your father is also what he is," he said, his voice rough. "Or do you choose to forget that your vineyard was created by the sweat of others?"

"I do not need a lesson in socioeconomics! Besides, times have changed."

"They have, indeed." Nick smiled coldly. "You and your father must now come to me, an Orsini, to beg for money."

Alessia stiffened. "The House of Antoninni does not beg! And you forget, we come to Cesare Orsini, not to you."

She was right, of course. His only function was to report back to his father....

"Why, *signore*," she all but purred, "I see I have silenced you at last."

She smiled. It made his belly knot. There were hundreds of years of arrogance in that smile; it spoke of the differences between commoners and kings, and in that instant, Nick knew the game had changed.

He smiled, too, but something in it made her expression lose a little of its upper-class defiance. She began to step back but Nick caught her by the wrist and tugged her toward him.

"There's been a change in plans, princess."

"Let go of me!"

He did, but only to slip his hand around the nape of her neck. Tendrils of the softest gold tumbled over his fingers.

"I'm the potential investor," he said softly, "not my old man."

"That is not what my father told me!"

A muscle knotted in Nick's jaw. She was staring at him through eyes so deep a blue they were almost violet. He'd stunned her, he could see that. Hell, he'd stunned himself.

He might be a peasant, but he was also a man. And she was a woman. A woman who needed to learn that this was the twenty-first century, not the sixteenth.

Nick's gaze dropped to her lips, then rose so his eyes met hers.

"Trust me, princess," he said in a voice as rough as sandpaper. "The only Orsini you're going to deal with is me."

Alessia Antoninni, the Princess Antoninni, shook her head. "No," she said, and he silenced her the only way a man could silence a woman like this.

He thrust his hands into her hair, lifted her face to his and kissed her.

CHAPTER THREE

TIME seemed to stop.

Alessia was too stunned to react.

A stranger's powerful arms around her. His mouth on hers. The heat of his body, the leanly muscled male strength of it…

Then she gasped. Fury and indignation transformed her into a virago. She twisted her head, slammed her hands against his chest, knotted those hands into fists when he failed to let her go.

A mistake, all of it.

His hand slid up into her hair so that there was no way to turn away from his kiss. One big palm slid down her spine, stopped at its base and brought her tight against him.

Was he insane?

He was kissing her as if he had the right to do it. To take whatever he wanted because of who and what he was, and to hell with propriety or their surroundings or the fact that they'd met only minutes ago and already despised each other.

Her hands flattened against his chest again. She pushed at that wall of hard muscle and when that had no effect, she tried to squirm free.

Another mistake, worse than the first one.

Instantly, she felt the thrust of his aroused flesh against her belly.

Her heart thudded.

She began to tremble, and his lips moved on hers, the angle of the kiss changing so that she had to tilt her head back. Was that why she suddenly felt dizzy and the ground took a delicate tilt beneath her feet?

She heard a sound. Was it she who'd made it, an almost imperceptible whimper overlaid by Nicolo Orsini's raw, ragged groan?

Her hands moved. Slid to his shoulders. Into his hair. Her lips began to part....

And then it was over.

He clasped her arms with such force that her eyes flew open, and as they did, he set her away from him.

She stared at him. His face was all harsh planes and angles; his eyes were slits of obsidian beneath thick, black lashes. Faint stripes of color ran beneath his high cheekbones as a muscle ticked in his jaw.

Alessia wanted to slap his face. More than that, she wanted to run.

But she wouldn't. She knew better than to show fear to a predatory animal. It was a lesson she'd learned when she was twelve, hiking the golden Tuscan hills alone late one afternoon and suddenly coming face-to-face with an enormous wild boar. Its long, razor-sharp tusks could easily have torn her open.

Despite her terror, she'd stood her ground. After what had seemed an eternity, the creature had snorted, stepped back and faded into the brush.

Now, as then, she forced herself to stand still. Not only wild animals but men, too, measured power in the fear they could engender.

That was why Nicolo Orsini had kissed her, and why she would not run from him. Instead, she drew a steadying breath and then slowly, deliberately, wiped the back of her hand across her mouth.

"If that was meant to impress me," she said in a steady voice, "it failed in its purpose."

The slightest smile curved his mouth.

"Did it," he said.

His tone made it clear the words were not a question. Alessia decided to ignore the implications.

"And I warn you, *signore,* if you do anything like that again—"

"Spare me the threats. You're in no position to make any."

Dio, the man was hateful! Alessia's chin lifted. *"Sei un barbaro!"*

"I'm a barbarian, huh?" He grinned. "Come on, sugar. Don't hold back. Say what you're thinking." His phony smile vanished. "What I am is the man who holds the purse strings. Remember that and we'll get along just fine."

Alessia stared at the hateful American and the last of her composure slipped away.

"We will not get along at all, *signore.* There has been a change in plans. The Antoninni Vineyard is not available for investment. You have made a long trip for nothing."

Nick narrowed his eyes. The *principessa* stood tall, shoulders back, head lifted in an attitude of defiance. She despised him, which was fine. He didn't think any better of her. All that was clear and up-front. The only question was, why had he kissed her?

To put her in her place?

A lie.

He didn't deal with women that way. He had faults, sure, but using sex as a weapon wasn't one of them. And he was not a man who'd ever take anything a woman wasn't eager to give.

Aside from all that, if putting her in her place had been what he'd intended, it had backfired. She wasn't shaken by what had happened; she was as cold and disapproving as ever. He must have imagined that something had changed in the last seconds of that kiss. That her mouth had softened. That her body had yielded to his. That she had parted her lips for him, that she had moaned...

Or had the moan been his?

"Do you understand me, *Signore* Orsini? Go home. Go back to your people. You have no further business here."

Nick looked at her. The message was clear. He was not only a barbarian, but he was also a Sicilian thug. An Orsini. And that was more than sufficient for a woman like her.

"We shall, of course, reimburse you for any expenses you've incurred."

The imperial *we*. The princess, addressing one of her subjects. Nick smiled, folded his arms and leaned back against the side of the Ferrari. It was a smile that those who'd faced him in boardroom battles or desert combat would have known enough to fear.

Hell, he thought coldly, *why not live down to her expectations?*

"Such a generous offer," he said softly.

"Yes. It is." She shot a look at the Ferrari's bumper. "I see some simple damage. Send us the bill."

"Shall I send it at the same time I send you a list of...how did you put it? The expenses I've incurred?"

"As you prefer. And now, *signore*..."

"And now, you assume, *arrivederci.*"

"Assume?" she said, her tone one of elegant disdain.

But she didn't look elegant. Nick's gaze made a slow circuit again, from the shoes that seemed to make her wobble to the wrinkled silk suit to the drawn-back hair. Wispy strands the color of winter sunlight fell around her oval face.

There was a bedraggled look about her.

And maybe *bedraggled* was the right word.

She looked as if she'd just tumbled out of a man's bed. His bed, he thought, and felt the immediate response of his body to the image of what it would be like to strip the arrogant princess of her clothes and do whatever it took to turn all that frosty hauteur to hot passion.

He did a mental double take. Why would he even think of something like that? Alessia Antoninni was beautiful in the way statues were beautiful. There was nothing soft or warm or welcoming about her. She wasn't a challenge, she was a turnoff. That he'd even imagined bedding her—hell, that he'd actually kissed her—made him furious.

Dammit, he thought, and he took his anger and put it where it rightly belonged.

"You were right," he said brusquely, "my trip was lengthy. Eight hours flying to Rome from New York, then a three-hour delay at the airport added up to lots of time to kill."

"And you expect compensation for that time immediately."

She said it as if it were a given. Nick watched as she opened her purse, rummaged through it and finally extracted a checkbook. "If you can provide me with a figure—"

She gasped as his hand closed around her wrist. His fingers were biting into her flesh. He was probably going to mark that tender, upper-class skin. Not only didn't he give a damn, but he was also grimly pleased to do it.

"Are you always so sure of yourself, princess? Or is it only with me?"

Her eyes flashed.

"Let go of me, Mr. Orsini."

Nick smiled tightly. "What happened to *signore?* Don't I even rate that much now that I'm about to call your bluff?"

"I don't know what you're talking about. And if you don't unhand me—"

"Another threat, *principessa?*" His smile twisted. "Maybe you need to listen before you make threats."

"Listen to what?" She looked as if she wanted to kill him. Fine, he thought grimly. The more certain she was of herself, the more he'd enjoy the sight of her taking a metaphoric tumble right on her icy ass. His grasp on her tightened until they were a breath apart. "I repeat, I had lots of time on my hands. I spent it going through the material your father sent about your precious vineyard. It was detailed. Very detailed… but there was lots missing."

"I have no knowledge of what material you saw and it is of no interest to me. You are—"

"Dismissed? A while ago, I was excused. Now I'm dismissed." Nick's smile was as frigid as his tone. "Antoninni Vineyards is on the verge of ruin."

"That is not your concern."

"Four years of bad weather damaged the grapes. Your old man chose new plantings that turned out to be a mistake. He made lousy marketing decisions. I don't know a damned thing about viniculture—"

"How nice to hear you admit it."

"But I do know about investments. I added up some figures, added them up again and figured out, real fast, that what your father neglected to list in that report is at least as meaningful as what he did."

"I don't know what you're talking about," she said, but Nick could hear the lie in the words.

"I think you do. Papa Prince took more cash out of those vineyards than he put in. Where did it go, sugar? The horses? The casinos? Women?"

Alessia yanked furiously on her imprisoned hand. "This conversation is over!"

"Without money—and we both know it's going to require more than the five million euros Daddy requested—without it, your family's business will be a thing of the past."

"You are a fine one to talk about family businesses," she said, her face filling with color.

It was a nicely placed jibe. Dead wrong, but she had no way of knowing that and Nick had no interest in pointing it out. She thought he was a *famiglia* heavy? Let her think it. Hell, he wanted her to think it. There was a sweet pleasure in a woman like this believing she was on the receiving end of help from the man she believed him to be.

"The bottom line," he said, "is that you need my money. I'd bet my last dollar your father will be more than happy to remind you of that."

"I need nothing from a man such as you!"

"Five hundred years of royal living, gone in the blink of an eye?"

"Do you think that matters to me?"

"I think it matters enough so that you were willing to show up today to greet a commoner."

"You're wrong, Mr. Orsini. I only, as you put it, showed up today because—because—"

She blinked. Nick could almost see her processing what was happening. She'd been sent to greet him. She was the prince's reception committee. She was an Antoninni, unaccustomed to dealing with the peasants, but she didn't have the power to get rid of him.

No wonder she was staring at him as if she'd just remembered something she'd all but forgotten.

He was sure he knew what that "something" was.

The princess had been flexing muscle she didn't have. She had no power. To all intents, she might as well have been a chauffeur, sent to meet the plane of the visiting banker.

"What's the problem?" Nick smiled thinly. "Thinking twice

about telling me to leave?" When she didn't answer, he took his cell phone from his pocket and offered it to her. "Here. Call Daddy. See what he says about sending me home."

Alessia looked at the sleek bit of plastic as if it might bite her. Then she looked at the man holding it toward her.

Bastardo insolente!

He knew damned well she wasn't about to make that call. He just didn't know why.

Mama, she thought, *Mama, how could I have forgotten you?*

For a few moments, anger at this horrible man had blinded her to reality. Now, it was back. She'd made a bargain with the devil. If she wanted her mother to remain in the *sanatorio,* she could not get rid of Nicolo Orsini. She had to deal with him, no matter what.

He was vile.

His macho arrogance. His brutal occupation, if you could call being a hoodlum an occupation. And that kiss, the assumption that he was irresistible, that the male domination of his world extended to hers...

Vile was not a strong enough word.

It didn't matter.

She was stuck with him. He was her problem, and she knew how to handle that. Problems were her specialty. Let her father think that the public relations business was nothing but an excuse for protecting people with too much money and ego. Perhaps that was a reflection of what he knew of Rome and Romans.

That was not her world.

Alessia had put endless days, weeks and months into learning how to deal with the people her firm represented.

Having a royal title helped, though she loathed the idea that titles should exist at all in today's complex world. The rest? Damned hard work.

Preventing clients from making asses of themselves was part of what she did. Cleaning up after they'd done so anyway was another part, as was making sure they did what they were supposed to do without veering from an accepted plan.

Some clients were pleasant, talented people. Some were not. And still some, admittedly a small percentage, thought that money and power and, often, good looks made them gods.

There was no question as to which category Nicolo Orsini belonged, nor was there any question that she could handle him. The truth was, given the circumstances, she had no choice.

"A problem, princess? Have you forgotten Daddy's phone number?"

She blinked, looked up at him. Barbarian though he was, gangster that he was, Nicolo Orsini was also—there was no other word for it—magnificent. The epitome of masculinity. Alessia met a lot of very good-looking men in her work. Actors, industrialists, men whose money bought them the clothes, the cars that could turn a nice-looking man into a good-looking one.

The American's clothes were obviously expensive, his haircut as well. But he was also—could you call a man *gorgeous?* Because that was what he was. Gorgeous, and it was not what he wore or how he was groomed.

It was him.

The thick, espresso-brown hair. The eyes the color of night, the strong, straight nose set above a firm mouth and chiseled jaw. Even that little depression between nose and mouth, what was it called? A philtrum. That was it. How could something with such a foolish name be sexy?

The truth was, all of him was sexy. The long, leanly muscled body. The hard face. The sculpted lips. Perfect in design, in texture. She knew that. Knew the warmth of that mouth, the feel of it against hers. If she'd parted her own lips a little when he'd kissed her, she'd even know his taste…

"Take a good look, princess. Let me know if you like what you see."

Alessia's gaze flew to his. His tone was as insulting as the heat in his eyes.

She felt her face redden.

That she could find him physically attractive was shocking. She didn't understand it. A man's looks meant nothing; she had never been taken in by such superficial things. No matter. Living with her father, dealing with his careless verbal and emotional cruelty, had taught her the benefits of a quick recovery.

"I was thinking," she said coolly, "that you do not look like a savage, *Signore* Orsini, but that only proves that looks can be deceiving."

He hesitated. Then, he shrugged.

"Your father is what he is, as is mine, *principessa*. As for me—I am precisely what you see."

Alessia's eyebrows rose. It was, at first, a disconcerting answer. Then she realized he was simply saying that she was right. He was the son of a don, a man from his father's world, venerated in some dark corners of old Sicily but despised by decent Italians everywhere.

And yes, she would have to deal with him.

So. A tour of the vineyard tomorrow. The formal dinner tomorrow night. He'd be gone the following day, out of her life, forever.

She could manage that.

As for what her father had intended, that she act as Orsini's driver, that he stay at the villa… Out of the question. He'd made it easy. He'd already told her he preferred to be on his own. The Ferrari, which would be a rental, was proof of it. Good. Excellent. As for his being a guest at the villa—she would suggest a hotel, if he hadn't already arranged for one, and pick him up there in the morning.

Easier and easier, she thought, but before she could say anything, Orsini punched a button on his cell phone and began speaking in English. There was no mistaking the conversation. He was talking with the agency from which he'd rented the Ferrari, telling a clerk in brisk tones of command that they could pick up the car here, at the curb. There was some minor damage; they could contact his insurance company. No, the car was fine except for that. It was simply that he would not need a car, after all.

"But of course you'll need it," Alessia blurted. "To drive to your hotel. You did make hotel reservations, didn't you?"

He smiled tightly. Eyes still locked to hers, he hit another button on his phone. She listened as he canceled a reservation at the Grand. Then he flipped the phone closed.

"Your father intended that I stay at your villa and that you be my tour guide. Isn't that right, princess?"

"Don't call me that!"

"It's what you are, isn't it? The princess who commands the peasants?"

Alessia thought of responding, then thought better of it. Instead, she jerked her head toward her Mercedes, still just behind the Ferrari.

"Get in," she said brusquely.

"Such a warm and hospitable invitation."

She strode around the car, got behind the wheel, sat stiffly as he folded his long legs under the dashboard. Then she slammed the car into gear, backed up just enough to avoid hitting the Ferrari again and pulled into traffic.

"Two days," she said through gritted teeth.

"Sorry?"

Dio, she hated him! The pleasant tone, the polite manner that was about as real as…as fairies at the bottom of the garden. Ahead, a green light turned red. She slowed the Mercedes, pulled to the light and stopped.

"I said, I can give you two days. That's more than enough time for you to tour the vineyard, see the wine-making operation and meet with my father's managerial staff."

Nick found the control next to his seat, pushed it and eased the seat farther back. Two days had been exactly the amount of time he'd intended to be in Tuscany...but things had changed.

"Really," he drawled. "Two days, hmm?"

"Two days," Alessia repeated briskly. "As I said, that's more than sufficient time to—"

"Two weeks," he said. "I'll need that much time to make a decision. And, of course, I'll expect you to be available to me 24/7."

She looked at him. The look of disbelief on her face made him want to laugh, especially considering that he'd just changed all the plans he'd so carefully made but, dammit, the woman needed to be taught a lesson in humility.

"Are you *pazzo?* There is no way in hell I am going to endure two weeks of—"

Nick leaned over. Put his mouth on hers. Kissed her, and when she tried to jerk away, he curved his hand around her jaw and went on kissing her until she made a little sound and when she did, he parted her lips with his, bit lightly into the exquisite softness of her bottom lip...

A horn honked impatiently behind them.

Nick let go of Alessia and sat back.

"Two weeks," he said in a gruff voice. "If you want that money badly enough, that's how long it's going to take to get it."

He folded his arms and stared straight ahead. He could feel her eyes on him. The horn behind them beeped again, this time joined by a growing chorus.

Alessia exploded, said the word that had horrified the nun at the airport but only made him laugh.

Then she stepped on the gas and the Mercedes all but flew down the highway.

CHAPTER FOUR

NICK was not a man who enjoyed letting someone else take the wheel of a car.

Life was all about control. It was a lesson all Cesare's sons had learned.

You could count on a microphone or a camera being shoved in your face anytime your old man hit the news and the only way to deal with the idiots who thought it was okay to invade your privacy was to keep your mouth shut and maintain your self-control.

The simple practice had served him well, not just on the streets of Little Italy but in the war zones where he'd seen action as a marine and, more recently, in the plush boardrooms where he negotiated billion-dollar deals. He'd never thought much about how his reliance on self-control impacted other parts of his life but now, sitting beside Alessia Antoninni as she drove the Mercedes along a busy highway, he knew he was in trouble.

They'd been on the road for maybe twenty minutes. Twenty more, and Nick figured he was either going to put a hole through the floorboard from constantly trying to stamp on a brake pedal that didn't exist or maybe he'd just pluck the princess from behind the steering wheel and take over.

She was, what, twenty-five? Twenty-six?

He looked at her, the stony profile, the set mouth, the fists gripping the steering wheel. It was too dark by now to see but he'd have bet a bundle her knuckles were white.

Whatever her age, she had a long way to go before she'd qualify for all those jokes that began, "There's this little old lady driving down a highway…"

Forget that. He had an aunt who was eighty-five. Even she didn't drive like this. Besides, he was long past being amused. What he was rapidly working up to was being scared spitless.

Not a good thing for a man who had never come up against anything he truly feared.

Until now.

Until this.

Alessia had managed to push the speed to a dazzling twenty miles an hour when the other cars were whipping by at one hundred. Okay, so that was an exaggeration. Maybe the others were doing ninety and she was doing half that. The point was, she was a road hazard.

Either she didn't know it or she didn't give a damn.

Cars zoomed up behind them, horns blasting. Swerved by them, and because the princess favored staying in the center lane, there was lots of opportunity for drivers passing on the right to put down their windows and scream the necessary invectives, complete with accompanying hand gestures.

And yes, it seemed as if the same one-fingered salute that worked in Manhattan worked equally well in Tuscany.

Alessia, oblivious, drove on.

Okay, Nick thought grimly, okay, there had to be something he could say. Or do. Carefully, searching for the right words, he cleared his throat.

"Ah, is something wrong with the car?" He waited a beat. "I mean, if that's the reason you're going so slow—"

"I am at the proper speed."

"Yeah, well, actually, I don't think you are."

"Actually," she said coldly, "I do not care what you think."

So much for subtlety. "Actually," Nick said, emphasizing the word, "I'm certain that you don't. What I'm trying to tell you, politely, is that it's a mistake not to keep up with traffic."

"The mistake is that of the traffic."

"The mistake is that of the traffic?"

"That is what I said. This is the proper speed for the hour and the road conditions."

"What conditions? The weather's fine. The road's smooth and straight. Traffic's moving the way it should except for—"

"*I* am driving, Mr. Orsini. Not you."

Mr. Orsini. She was even more angry than before; he'd already figured out that her mood dictated whether he was "mister" or *"signore."*

"Yes. You are. But—"

A big truck flew past them, so close he could have reached out and touched it. Nick found himself trying to jam his right foot through the floor again.

"Listen, princess—"

"This is my car. My country. I know how fast I must go. And I would prefer it if you would not address me that way."

"As princess?" Nick frowned at her. "It's what you are, isn't it?"

"Not really. The Italian monarchy ceased to exist in 1946 so, to be accurate, titles have no meaning here anymore. They are a relic, a remnant, a—"

Beeeep! Beep beep beeeep!

"Merda," Nick shouted. "That car almost—"

"The driver is going too fast."

"He is not going too fast!" Nick hunkered down in his seat

and folded his arms over his chest. "I'd love to meet whoever taught you to drive," he muttered.

Alessia glanced at him, then back at the road.

Perhaps that was the problem, she thought nervously.

No one had taught her to drive. Not the way he meant. Of course, she wasn't going to tell him that. He was angry enough already, though why he should be was beyond her. She was driving carefully. Safely. It was how she always drove. Was it her fault that Italian drivers treated speed as a national pastime?

Besides, the truth about how she had learned to drive was too humiliating. No one need know she had only accomplished that feat a couple of years ago, that until then, her father's wishes had ruled her life.

This tough American gangster could not possibly under-stand what it was like to grow up the child of a father more interested in his own pleasures than in his family.

At sixteen, when she had asked to take driving lessons, her father had said driving a car was inappropriate for her status. At eighteen, away at a demure college in Rome, there had been no reason to learn to drive, not when public transportation was readily available. Besides, it was easier not to argue.

At twenty, she received her useless degree and took the slip of paper with her on a visit to her mother at the *sanatorio*. Her mother was having one of her lucid days. She looked at the heavily engraved bit of nonsense, looked at Alessia and said, "Do something with your life, *mia bambina*. Do not let him crush the spirit within you."

There was no question who that "him" was.

It was an epiphany. Alessia had returned home, packed, moved out. She took an apartment in Rome with three other girls. Her father was furious. How dare she disobey him?

He cut off her allowance.

She went to work as a waitress. It was all her expensive

education had prepared her for, aside from marrying a rich man, which was, naturally, what her father had hoped she would do.

One morning, she awoke thinking that it was pitiful to be living on her own and still not know how to drive. So she convinced one of her flatmates who owned an ancient Fiat to take her outside the city and let her get behind the wheel.

It had been a harrowing day—her friend had babbled prayers throughout—but when it was over, Alessia could drive. More or less. She'd managed to pass her licensing exam but she'd never learned to enjoy driving or to feel comfortable in heavy traffic.

And having a stranger seated beside her didn't help, especially when that stranger was Nicolo Orsini.

How could one man seem to fill the car with his presence, his irritation, his masculinity?

If only she had taken her father's car and driver to the airport to meet Orsini. Her father had urged her to, which was precisely why she had not done it. It was her own fault that she was trapped in what had suddenly become a too-small vehicle on a too-busy road with a too-macho male breathing fire beside her...

"Figlio di puttana!"

Nicolo Orsini's cry was almost as loud as the blast from the horn of a huge truck in the next lane. How had the Mercedes drifted so close to it? Alessia gave a shrill shriek; Nicolo leaned in, slapped his hands over hers and steered the car back into the proper lane. She knew the entire incident could not have taken more than a second to play out but in that second, she saw her life flash before her.

"That's it," the American roared. "Pull onto the shoulder."

Yes, she thought, yes, pull over, pull over, pull—

Nick wrested full control of the Mercedes from her. They

veered into the right-hand lane, then bounced onto the narrow shoulder, accompanied by a frenzied chorus of horns.

"The brake," he yelled, and, thank God, she responded. The car shuddered to a stop and he shut off the engine.

For a heartbeat, neither of them moved. Then Nick let go of the steering wheel. Alessia's hands dropped into her lap. Silence settled over the vehicle, broken only by the *tick tick tick* of the cooling engine.

Nick could feel his pulse tick-tick-ticking, too. He waited, fought for composure. Still, when he finally spoke, his voice was a hoarse croak.

"Get out of the car, Alessia."

She looked at him. "I beg your—"

"Do as I say! Get out of the damned car!"

Do as he said? She bristled. "I do not take orders from anyone!"

Nick let fly with a string of Sicilian obscenities he hadn't used or even thought of since he was a kid. He flung open his door, stalked around the automobile, yanked open her door, all but tore open her seat belt and physically lifted her from the car.

"What do you think you are doing?" Her voice rose; she wiggled like an eel, struck out at him with tightly balled fists. "Damn you, Nicolo Orsini! You have no right—"

"You almost got us killed."

"I did nothing of the sort. That truck driver—"

"The truck driver is probably heading for a place where he can change his underwear."

"You are not only rude, you are crude!"

"At least I'm not a danger to every poor soul who gets within a hundred miles of me!"

Alessia wanted to weep. He was right. She was terrified, horrified, appalled by what had almost happened but why would she admit that to such a man as this?

"Let go of me," she said sharply.

"Try that imperious tone on someone you haven't tried to kill. Now, get into the passenger seat and behave yourself!"

"I do not take orders! I am not...Mr. Orsini! *Signore!*" Alessia's voice climbed as Nick lifted her off her feet and slung her over his shoulder. Tears of rage rose in her eyes; she knotted her hands into fists and beat at his shoulders and back as he strode around the car. "You cannot do this!"

"Watch me," he said grimly, depositing her on her feet and reaching for the door.

"Bastardo," she hissed. *"Siete come tutti i uomini!* You are the same as all men! You think women are incapable of taking care of themselves, that they need men to think for them—"

Enough, Nick thought, and he hauled Alessia to her toes and kissed her.

She gasped. Struggled. Fought him.

He went on kissing her.

And wondered, with almost clinical interest, why he was doing it.

Kissing her made no sense. A man kissed a woman because he liked her. Wanted her. Desired her and, God knew, he didn't like or want or desire the slippery-as-an-eel creature in his arms. Was he kissing her because he was angry? Hell, no. He had never kissed a woman out of anger. He didn't understand why a man would. Kissing wasn't about rage, it was about taste and texture....

And then Alessia stopped struggling and he stopped thinking and the kiss turned into something hot and raw and primitive, and she went up on her toes and thrust her hands into his hair and he groaned, slid his hands under her jacket, under her blouse, felt the silky warmth of her skin and she said something against his mouth and he slid the tip of his tongue between her lips and...

A horn bleated.

A male voice yelled something into the night. Nick didn't understand the words, his Italian wasn't good enough for that, but he didn't have to be a linguist to figure it out.

His hands clasped her shoulders.

He lifted his head.

A shudder went through him.

He was standing by the side of a busy road holding a woman he didn't know and didn't like in his arms, maybe a heartbeat away from shoving her against the side of the car, pushing up her skirt, tearing off her panties and burying himself inside her.

Holy hell, he thought, and Alessia opened her eyes and stared at him, her expression blank.

"Easy," he said, and knew as soon as he said it that the word was inadequate.

The blank look on her face gave way to shock and then horror. She said something under her breath. His Italian wasn't good enough for him to understand that, either, but once again, he got the gist.

"I know," he said. "I'm sorry. I don't know what—"

She slapped him. Hard. His head jerked back at the force of the blow.

"Okay," he said, "if that made you feel bet—"

She slapped him again, or she would have, but he saw it coming and wrapped his hand around her wrist.

"That's enough," he said in a warning voice.

"You—you bastard! You pig! You—you brute!"

As obscenities went, he'd heard far worse. But that wasn't the point. He'd initiated the kiss, yes, but she'd been into it, all the way.

"Calm down, princess."

"Calm down? After what you did?"

Nick narrowed his eyes. "What I did," he said coldly, "was save us from being turned into roadkill."

"I am not talking about that. I am talking about that—that disgusting display of macho!" Eyes flashing, she jerked her hand free of his. "Who do you think you are?"

It was the most weary, clichéd line imaginable but it stung because he knew damned well what she meant by it. Nick moved closer, gratified to see her take a couple of quick steps back until she was pressed against the car.

"You know who I am, baby. I'm the man who's gonna save your daddy's royal ass, assuming you treat me right."

She recoiled. Hell, who could blame her? What kind of drivel was he spewing? And had a woman ever made him this angry before? He wanted to grab her and shake her.

Or grab her and kiss her again and again and again until she forgot who she was and who she was convinced he was, until she dragged his face down to hers and kissed him and kissed him...

Nick thought twice, stepped back, cleared his throat.

"Get in the car."

He could see her considering things. What in hell was there to consider? She couldn't drive worth a damn.

"Did you hear me, princess? Get in the car."

She stared up at him. What now? Her eyes were blurry with angry tears. As he'd already noted, her obviously expensive outfit was a mess. And somewhere along the way, maybe when he'd thrown her over his shoulder, she'd lost a shoe.

Still, she was beautiful.

Beautiful and vulnerable, and why he should notice or care was beyond him to comprehend.

He jerked his head toward the open passenger door. She lifted her chin in defiant acquiescence, in a way that made him want to laugh. He didn't; he wasn't that much of a fool. Instead, he slammed the door after her, went around the car—and yeah, there was her shoe, lying in the grass. He picked it up, tossed it in the backseat where it joined his carry-on bag and got behind the wheel.

Seconds later, they were on the highway, this time as part of the traffic flow.

They said nothing for the next hour. Then Alessia spoke.

"The sign for the vineyard is just ahead. You will turn to the right."

The headlights picked out a small wooden plaque. It said Antoninni in gilt letters; below it was a coat of arms. A griffin or maybe a lion, a shield and a sword. Nick's mouth twisted. What would the Orsini coat of arms be? A pistol, a dagger and a stack of money?

The turn opened onto a long, straight driveway, if you could call a half-mile-long road lined by poplars a driveway. Nick could see a shape on a rise ahead. It was a villa, big, imposing and graceful.

"You may park in front."

"How nice of you to say so."

Hell, he thought, what was that all about? She'd simply told him what he needed to know. Whose fault was it if the words sounded like a command?

He pulled in front of a set of wide marble steps. By the time he stepped from the car, Alessia was halfway up those steps, limping because she was wearing only the one shoe. Nick reached in back, collected his carry-on bag and the other shoe, then trotted up the stairs. Massive double doors opened, revealing bright light and a guy dressed like something out of a period movie.

"This is Joseph," Alessia said coolly. "He will show you to your rooms."

She tossed the words over her shoulder, the royal once again addressing the peasant. Nick smiled thinly.

"Princess?"

She turned and looked down her nose at him. Still smiling, he tossed her the shoe.

"You wouldn't want to go around half-naked," he said. "I mean, that was okay while you and I were alone, but—"

Her face filled with color. She opened her mouth, then snapped it shut, spun away from him and vanished down a long hallway. Joseph, to his credit, showed no change in expression.

"This way, please, *signore*," he said, reaching for Nick's bag.

"I'll carry my own bag, thanks."

A stupid, petty victory but a victory, nonetheless.

They climbed a long marble staircase to the second floor. The place was like a museum. High ceilings. Gilded cherubs. Paintings of shifty-eyed, long-faced ancestors peering from the walls.

Not a museum, Nick thought grimly. Museums had more warmth than this.

Joseph led him to a suite. Sitting room, bedroom, bathroom. Did the *signore* wish to have his bag unpacked? Nick said he didn't. Did he want something to eat? Nick almost said he didn't, strictly out of perversity, but then common sense took over and he said yes, a sandwich and some coffee would be fine.

Joseph bowed his way out. Nick closed the door, peeled off his suit jacket, his tie, undid a couple of buttons on his shirt, rolled up his sleeves and fell back on the bed, which was about half the size of a banquet hall. He folded his arms beneath his head and stared up at the ceiling, where it was vaguely possible a shepherd and shepherdess were about to do something they shouldn't.

The villa was obviously very, very old. And very, very expensive. Was he supposed to be impressed? His triplex in

New York was probably just as big and even if it wasn't filled with antiques, even if it had been built within the last twenty or so years, it was probably equal the cost to this, given the price of Manhattan real estate.

Nick snorted.

What was the matter with him?

He didn't give a damn about things like that.

He'd spent weekends at palatial estates in the Hamptons, others at one-room cabins in the Adirondacks, and he'd never thought of one as better than the other.

He sat up, unbuttoned his shirt, tossed it over the back of a chair and headed for the bathroom. What he needed was a long, hot shower, that sandwich and then a night's sleep.

Wrong.

The shower felt great. The butler delivered a well-laden tray, not only a sandwich and coffee, but also a small salad, some cheese, fruit and crackers. The bed was comfortable. But at 2:00 a.m., Nick was still awake, standing outside on the small Juliet balcony despite the chill in the night air, staring out at a moonlit garden.

Something had awakened him....

There. A figure. A woman, wearing something long and filmy, her hair a pale spill of gold down her back, walking slowly along one of the garden paths.

Alessia.

Nick didn't think. He pulled on a pair of jeans. Shirtless, barefoot, he let himself out of his suite, went down the stairs, through the silent house to a back door and stepped out into the garden and the night. He reached her in seconds, cupped her shoulders and turned her toward him. She looked surprised but not afraid. If anything, she looked—she looked—

"Signore."

"My name is Nick," he said, his voice low.

God, she was beautiful. Exquisite. A fairy-tale princess come to life.

She hesitated. *Say my name,* he thought, as if it were a battle to be won. After a second's hesitation, she took a deep breath.

"Nicolo. What are you doing out here?"

"I couldn't sleep. Obviously, neither could you."

"*Sì.* I—I keep thinking about what happened before. On the road."

"Yeah. So do I."

"*È colpa mia,*" she whispered. "It was my fault. I—I do not drive very well."

Another time, he would have laughed. It was the understatement of the year.

"No. You don't." He reached out, tucked a strand of gold behind her ear. "But I wasn't talking about your driving." He cupped her face in his hands, lifted it to his. "I'm talking about that kiss."

Even in the moonlight, he could see the delicate rise of color in her face.

"I do not wish to discuss it."

No. Why would she? She didn't like what he was. He didn't like what she was. It was not an auspicious start for anything, not even a business deal.

And she was right. He didn't want to discuss it, either. Instead, he drew her into his arms, kissed her more and more deeply until she was clinging to him.

Then he let go of her, turned his back and walked away.

CHAPTER FIVE

NICK was an early riser.

You had to be, in the Marine Corps, and the habit stuck even after he'd returned to civilian life, though by now it was more a preference than a habit. There was something restful about early morning silence, especially in Manhattan; a run through Central Park before it was flooded with tourists, before the surrounding streets were jammed with traffic...

Unless, of course, there was a woman in his bed.

Wake-up sex was one of life's absolute pleasures.

But there was no woman in his bed today, no Central Park just across the street. What he woke to were thoughts of a woman and, dammit, those thoughts had kept him awake half the night.

Who was Alessia Antoninni? Maybe the better question was, what was she? A princess—hell, an Ice Princess. And why should it matter? He didn't like her, he resented the class system to which she belonged and there was no doubt that she felt exactly the same way about him. Heaven knew he didn't have to love a woman to want her—if such a thing as love even existed—but he sure as hell had to like her.

The situation didn't make sense—and as dawn painted the sky with streaks of crimson and pink, Nick gave up all pretence at sleep, flung back the covers, tugged on an old corps

T-shirt, shorts and sneakers, made his way down the balcony steps and took off on a run he badly needed.

Five miles. Seven. Eight. He had no idea how far he went, only that he couldn't find a way to get all his questions about the Ice Princess out of his head even as sweat blurred his vision and his lungs began to labor.

The sun was climbing the sky by the time he returned to the villa. He ran inside, up the staircase and to his suite, went straight to the bathroom, turned on the water in the sink and scooped some into his hands.

The good news was that the water was wet. The bad was that it was warm. What he wanted was a long, cool drink. Surely there'd be bottled water in the kitchen.

It was definitely worth a try.

Nick blotted his face and shoulders with a towel, draped it around his neck, shoved his dark hair back from his forehead, then opened the door that led to the hall.

The place was still quiet.

Okay, then.

He went down the stairs and headed toward the rear of the house, where he guessed the kitchen would be.

Excellent.

There wasn't anyone in sight, not a cook or a maid or the butler. The big room was empty....

Except, it wasn't.

Alessia was there, standing in front of the open refrigerator, head tilted back as she drank from a bottle of water.

The sight startled him. He came to a fast stop and the sole of one sneaker caught on the tile floor. The resultant squeak was as shrill as the cry of a nighthawk.

She spun toward him. The bottle slipped in her hand; she caught it but not before some of the water had splashed down her chin, her throat and onto her cotton tank top. Nick watched the water darken the fabric over one breast.

His belly knotted. Stupid, he thought, to react to the sight of a wet tank top.

"What are you doing here?"

She sounded as if she'd discovered him with his hands buried in a wall safe. Obviously, she hadn't expected him to walk in on her, or to see yesterday's cool, if rumpled, business-woman replaced by a woman in shorts, tank and sneakers, blond hair pulled into a ponytail, face and body damp with sweat.

And one breast—one high, rounded breast—tantalizingly darkened by that splash of water.

Without warning, he remembered how she had looked last night in the garden, her hair loose on her shoulders, her nightgown filmy and feminine in the moon's soft glow—and thought, too, of how he had kissed her, how she had kissed him back....

Nick raised his gaze to her face. Her color was high; he could see her pulse beating fast in the hollow of her throat. Was she thinking about that kiss, too?

"*Signore*. What are you doing here?"

So much for remembering last night. Nick flashed a tight smile. "Stealing the family silver."

"I didn't mean…" Her color deepened. "You startled me, that's all."

"Yeah. Sorry." He shrugged. "I was out running. I came back and wanted something cold to drink." His eyes swept over her again. "You were running, too."

Alessia swallowed hard. It was a statement, not a ques-tion, and it made no sense that it should bother her. So what if Nicolo Orsini knew she'd been out running? She ran every morning no matter where she was; she had discovered the freedom of it years ago, even before she'd left here forever, the sense that if you ran fast enough, hard enough, you could leave your old self behind.

You couldn't, of course. She knew that now. Still, she ran. She loved the burn of muscle, the rise of sweat. Her father thought it was unladylike and perhaps that was part of what made it so appealing....

Why was Nicolo Orsini looking at her that way? His dark eyes moved over her like a slow caress, lingering on her mouth, her throat.

Her body.

He made her feel as if too much of her was exposed. Not physically; she wore less than this at the beach. It was something more complicated, a realization that he was seeing a side of her that was not his business to see.

It made her recall last night. How he had kissed her, how she had kissed him back.

To her horror, she felt her nipple pebble under her water-stained tank top, her flesh lift as if in anticipation of his touch. Instinct told her to turn and run. Logic told her running would be the most dangerous thing she could do.

Instead, she lifted her chin.

"This is my home," she said coolly. "If I wish to run here, I am free to do so."

Dio, how stupid she sounded! Why did her words, her thoughts, get all twisted when she spoke to this man?

His eyes narrowed. He folded his arms over his chest. It was an impressive chest, tanned and muscled as were his arms.

"Sure." His voice was toneless. "I should have asked permission."

"No," she said quickly, "no, of course not. I only meant..." She had no idea what she'd meant, she thought unhappily. She was talking at the speed of a runaway train and making about as much sense. Quickly, she turned toward the fridge, took out a bottle of water and held it toward him. "You must be thirsty."

That won her a small smile. "Thanks."

Their fingers brushed as he took the bottle from her. A tiny electric jolt went through her. She gave a nervous laugh.

"Static electricity," she said.

"Electricity, for sure," Nick said, his eyes on hers. Then he unscrewed the bottle top, tilted his head back and took a long, deep drink. A tiny trickle of water trailed over his bottom lip, traced a path down his long, tanned throat.

The water would taste salty there, right there, if she touched her tongue to it....

She made a little sound, turned it into a cough, but it didn't help keep her knees from feeling weak.

Nicolo lowered the bottle of water, looked at her with one dark eyebrow lifted.

Say something, Alessia told herself fiercely, something clever.

She couldn't. She was tongue-tied. She, who made her living chatting up clients, being the intermediary between often hostile groups, was at a complete loss for words.

But her brain was working overtime.

Dio, this man was beautiful! She didn't like him, would never like him, but you didn't have to like a man to admit he was, in a word, *spectacular.*

Such broad shoulders. Such well-defined muscles. His shirt was wet, stuck to his skin, delineating cut abs and a flat belly that led to narrow hips and long, muscular legs. And his face. The face of an angel. Or a devil. Strong. Masculine. A hard mouth that could take hers with dark passion or soft tenderness...

"...just you and me. Together."

Alessia blinked. He was watching her, eyes narrowed to obsidian slits under thick, sooty lashes. She felt her face heat.

"Just you and me, what?"

Those dark eyebrows rose again.

"Run, of course. What else could I have possibly meant?"

"No. I don't think so. I mean—I mean..." Dammit, what *did* she mean? She swung away from him, placed her empty water bottle on the countertop beside the sink. "We'd better get started," she said briskly. "We meet with my father's people in an hour."

She swept past him, head high, spine straight, every inch the princess though he knew damned well that she'd been something else for a little while. He'd had women look at him that way before; he knew what it meant.

What he'd never before experienced was such a swift, gut-churning reaction.

That was the reason he'd deliberately lightened the atmosphere with a pathetic quip. If he hadn't—hell, if he hadn't, he'd have done what he wanted, what he damned well knew they both wanted, right here.

Grab her wrist. Swing her toward him. Capture her in his arms, cover her mouth with his. Breathe in the sweaty, earthy, real-woman scent that rose from her skin. Lift her onto the countertop, put his mouth to her throat, her nipples, suck them deep into his mouth right through her wet shirt while he put his hand between her thighs, slipped his fingers under the edge of her shorts, felt her heat, her wetness because she would be hot and wet and eager, eager for his possession...

Nick shuddered.

He watched Alessia walk down the hall, watched her until she vanished from sight. Then he drank the last of the water in one long swallow, went back to his rooms and took the longest, coldest shower of his life.

It didn't help.

Ten minutes later, getting out of the shower, he was still thinking about her and what had happened—what had *not* happened—in the kitchen.

Thinking that way was, to put it bluntly, ridiculous.

So, okay. He wouldn't think about her. Not anymore.

He toweled off, dressed in what he thought of as his investment banker uniform. Custom-made white broadcloth shirt. Deep red Hermès tie. Gold cuff links. Black wing tips. Dark gray Armani suit. Hey, one Armani deserved another, and she would surely wear her best today.

Well, so would he. The reflection that looked back at him from the mirrored dressing room wall was businesslike. Professional. The Ice Princess would still see him as a grown-up punk, but—

But, he was back to square one, wasting time thinking about her.

Thinking about the effect she had on him.

Even if he could get past the I-Am-To-The-Manor-Born and You-Are-A-Peasant crap, the lady wasn't his type. Attractive? Sure. But he couldn't imagine her trying to please a man, ever. Not just him but any man. And yes, he liked an accommodating woman, and if it was sexist, who cared?

Nick frowned, stared in the mirror, shot his cuffs, smoothed down his tie.

The only way to explain his attraction to her, if you could call it that, would be if he were horny. He wasn't. He had a healthy appetite for sex but he'd just been with a woman, what, the day before yesterday? And even if he hadn't, he'd never been the kind of man who'd jump the bones of any female just because she was there.

Besides, Alessia wasn't there, not in the real sense of the word. She'd made it clear he wasn't her type any more than she was his.

His frown became a scowl.

Then, how come she'd responded when he'd kissed her? And, yes, she had responded. A woman didn't moan into a man's mouth, didn't wind her arms around his neck, didn't press her body against his unless she was feeling something.

Hell.

A hard-on was not the right accessory for an Armani suit.

Okay. This was nonsense.

Nick drew a long, deep breath.

He was a logical man but even he had to admit that were times logic just didn't work, and this was one of those times. So, back to plan A. Yes, he'd invest in the vineyard, not for Cesare but for himself, if only because backing out of that decision now could be interpreted as weakness.

But two days was all he'd spend here. Forget what he'd told her yesterday, that he'd need two weeks.

Two days was, exactly as he'd originally intended, more than enough time to go over the vineyard's financial records. Meet with the prince's people. Eyeball the operation. Appoint an administrator to oversee things. Then he'd be on the first plane for New York—if it was quicker, he'd have the Orsini jet fly over to get him.

And if that seemed like the cowardly way out, it wasn't.

It was a businesslike approach, and business was what this was all about.

She was waiting for him at the foot of the stairs.

Yesterday's ice maiden was back, this time unrumpled.

Neat chignon, or whatever women called that bun they made at the back of their heads. White silk blouse. Black pumps. Gray Armani suit. He almost laughed. They were almost identical, if you omitted the lush rise of her breasts and the long, long legs beneath her slender skirt.

Her eyes swept over him, her look an appraising one. Nick offered a thin smile.

"It's the latest in gangster-wear in New York."

If he'd thought to embarrass her, he'd failed.

"And so much more attractive than tattoos that say 'Mother,'" she said sweetly.

"Why, princess. You've practically seen me naked. You know damned well I don't have any tattoos."

Color flooded her face.

"I have not seen you naked," she said, her voice gone cold.

Nick shrugged. "Close enough."

"And never any closer, I assure you."

He took a step toward her. To his gratification, she took a step back.

"A challenge, princess?" he said, very softly.

"A statement of fact, Mister Orsini."

He gave her a slow smile. There was something about her when she was like this, just the slightest bit off balance, that was very appealing.

"A challenge," he said again.

And then, because it seemed the only thing to do, he bent his head and brushed his mouth lightly over hers.

Her lips were soft. Warm. Did they tremble just a little under the light pressure of his? There was only one way to find out. Nick cupped her face in one hand and kissed her again, a longer kiss this time, his lips slightly parted as they covered hers and, yes, her mouth was trembling, her breathing was quick, she was rising on her toes, leaning toward him and now her lips parted, too...

She made a sound, put her hands against his chest and her eyes flew open and fixed on his. He saw endless questions in their deep blue depths, questions he suspected were identical to his. For a heartbeat, he thought of answering them all, for her and for him, by taking her in his arms and kissing her until she begged him to finish this insane thing between them.

Maybe it wasn't what was happening that was crazy.

Maybe it was him.

"Alessia."

His voice was rough as sandpaper. He took her hands in his, sought desperately for something clever to say, but nothing came. Her eyes were blurred, her breathing uneven, and he knew his wasn't any too steady.

"Nicolo," she said in shaky whisper.

It was the second time she'd said his name. How come he was so aware of that, and aware, too, that it sounded different, in her mouth? What she said was "Neekello," and how could a simple word sound like pure sex?

Nick let go of her while he still could and put a few inches of space between them. She swayed; he reached out, steadied her with a hand on her elbow. She drew a deep breath, sank her very white teeth into the rich curve of her bottom lip.

The simple action damned near undid him.

"This—this must stop," she whispered. "This—this thing between us…"

Her words drifted to silence. A muscle jumped in his jaw.

He knew that any other woman in this kind of situation would have laid the blame strictly on the guy. It made him want to kiss her again but he wouldn't. Dammit, he wouldn't. He wouldn't so much as touch her again, and absolutely, positively he was saying, *arrivederci,* ASAP tomorrow.

"You're right," he said briskly. "It has to stop. In fact, it just did. Let's go to that meeting you've set up, come back here and check out the vineyards, the winery, all of it, so I can be out of here tomorrow."

"But you said—"

"I know what I said." God, he wanted to touch her. Just one quick brush of his hands over her body… "I've changed my mind. In fact, I'll put a call in, arrange for the Orsini plane to fly over and get me. It'll be quicker that way."

"The Orsini plane."

"Yes. We have our own—"

"Of course you do," Alessia said, and all at once, her eyes were clear and cool. "For a moment, I almost forgot who you were, *signore*. *Molte grazie* for reminding me."

The temperature dropped ten degrees. If she'd slapped him across the face, she couldn't have made things any clearer.

The time was right to tell her who he was. What he was. That he and his old man had nothing but blood in common... And then he thought, to hell with that. To hell with explaining himself to Alessia Antoninni or anyone else.

"I understand, *principessa*." His tone was as frigid as hers. "Lust can get in the way of sanity."

Her cheeks flamed. She called him something he couldn't quite understand and he thought of returning the compliment but, dammit, no way was he going to let her turn him into the kind of man she believed him to be.

"Undoubtedly," he said, his smile feral. Then he gestured toward the front door. "After you, baby."

Back straight as an arrow, she spun on her heel and marched to the door. She didn't wait for him to play the gentleman; she flung it open herself and marched down the marble steps, straight toward a black Bentley the size of a not-so-small boat. A liveried chauffeur shot from the driver's seat, opened the rear door and bowed as she stepped past him into the car.

Nick followed after her. "Do not," he growled to the chauffeur, "do not even *think* of bowing to me!"

Aside from that, he was more than willing to let somebody else do the driving.

Somebody whose head was on straight, he thought grimly, as the car started majestically down the long driveway.

CHAPTER SIX

ALESSIA had arranged for the meeting to be held in the offices her father kept in Florence.

The building itself had once been a palace and was very old, dating back to the 1400s and the Renaissance, when the Medici family ruled the city.

The Antoninnis could trace their lineage to Cosimo de' Medici or, rather, to a supposedly illegitimate son of Cosimo's. Faced with his mistress's threats to make their affair a public scandal, Cosimo was said to have given her the vast, fertile rolling acres that even then were producing excellent wine. When the illegitimate son died, as so many Medicis, legitimate or not, were wont to do at that time, the mistress passed the estate on to her daughter, who married a prince of the house of Antoninni, which was when the vineyards became known by that name.

The Antoninni part of the tale was true; there was some doubt about the Medici connection but no Antoninni had ever tried to verify it. Someone in each generation always realized that tracing something that might turn out to be a centuries-old falsehood—or, worse still, a tale of murder—would serve no purpose except to disgrace the Antoninni–Medici connection.

Alessia thought the whole thing was foolish. Who had the time for titles and lineage and fifteenth-century intrigue?

Besides, the Antoninni problem right now was not one of DNA but of dollars. Orsini dollars, ones that would become Antoninni euros. That was the reason she had arranged to hold the meeting here, in these magnificent surroundings.

"An excellent plan," her father had said, assuming that she meant to impress their foreign guest.

Alessia's motives had been far less admirable.

In terms of power and wealth, Nicolo Orsini was the modern version of Cosimo de' Medici, but with one enormous difference.

Cosimo had been a man of refinement and honor.

Nicolo was not.

And if her motives for bringing him here took her down to his level, so be it.

She had no choice but to deal with him. She did have a choice as to the way in which she did it, and impressing him was not on her agenda.

What she wanted was to remind him of where he existed on the social scale, that he no more belonged in this beautiful city, this jewel of a palace, than a junkyard dog belonged in a roomful of poodles.

In other words, she wanted him to be ill at ease.

Yes, she admitted, glancing at him as the big car glided to a stop before the palazzo, it was petty. She'd permitted herself a moment of guilt but only a moment because of the satisfaction it promised. Nicolo Orsini might have a polished look to him, he might speak passable Italian, even if it was tainted by the rough dialect of Sicily. He might have all the manners, all the money in the world, but he was not a gentleman.

He wasn't even an honest businessman.

He was a bandit all gussied up in fancy clothes, and she'd known that before she ever set eyes on him. Now that she had, now that she'd seen, firsthand, how he took what he wanted, how he...he thought nothing of forcing himself on a woman who clearly wanted nothing to do with him...

He had kissed her.

Her cheeks flushed.

And...and if she had seemed to let it happen, even to participate, it was only because she was—she was—

Dio, what was she?

Why had she permitted a man like this to put his mouth on hers? Why had she spent part of the night imagining how that mouth, that hot, firm mouth would feel on her breasts?

"Principessa?"

Alessia blinked. The chauffeur stood at rigid attention beside the open passenger door of the Bentley.

She took a deep breath. "Oh. *Sì,* Guillermo. *Grazie.*"

The man dipped his head, a gesture she despised but this was no time to remind him of it, not when Nicolo had moved across the seat, not when she could feel the heated pressure of his thigh against hers.

She stepped quickly from the car; he followed after her.

"We will be ready to return to the villa in two hours," she told the chauffeur, who did that damned lowering-of-the-head thing again. "And do not do that," she said irritably. She heard Nicolo snort and she swung toward him. "Do you see something amusing?"

"Not amusing," he said lazily. "Perplexing. The man is treating you as you wish to be treated. And you fault him for it?"

"I have not asked him to bow to me!"

"You don't have to. Every breath you take makes it clear that you are part of the aristocracy."

She felt her face turn pink. "You know nothing about me, *signore,* and yet you feel free to judge me?"

The faint smile on his lips faded. "There's an American

expression, Alessia. 'Right back at you.' If you don't know what it means, I'll be happy to explain."

Dio, the impertinence of the man. Alessia swallowed her irritation and marched through the tall golden gates that guarded the palace.

"Wow."

Wow. She almost laughed. Her unwelcome guest, her father's onerous hope of salvation, sounded as she'd expected him to sound, as if he were entering a Disney World building.

"This is quite a structure. Which Medici built it?"

She stopped and looked at him. He stood with his face turned up to the spectacular gold cherubs on the building's facade.

"I beg your pardon?"

"I know it's Medici. It has to be. But was this Giovanni's work? Cosimo's? Lorenzo's? Lorenzo, I'd bet. The others were benefactors of the city, too, but he was the one with the soul of an artist. Am I right?"

"You know of the Medicis?"

Nick looked at her. He could read the astonishment on her face.

"Yes," he said coolly. "I do. Surprised?"

"No. Not at all."

She was a beautiful liar. He was damned certain she'd expected him to assume this perfect little structure had been put up by Disney.

"And you are correct," she added briskly. "Lorenzo was its benefactor."

He nodded. "That figures."

"But Cosimo is one of our ancestors."

Had she really said that? Judging by the lift of his eyebrows, she had. It was not an appreciative lift, either; he saw the boast just as much a foolish one as she did. Still, boasting, if more subtly than that, was the reason she'd brought her father's crime-boss investor to this place.

She would have to keep one thought ahead of him at all times.

A golden cage of an elevator, installed in the mid-1800s, whisked them to the third floor. The meeting room, the one she had carefully chosen, was directly opposite. It was the most glorious chamber of all the glorious chambers in the small, elegant palace.

"After you," the man she was trying to intimidate said politely, and she led him inside.

There was no "wow" this time but she could hear the intake of his breath as he took in the surroundings: the marble-topped table, the gilded vases filled with flowers, the thick silk carpet that was almost as old as the building itself, the Michelangelos and Raphaels and Donatellos hanging on the walls.

Orsini was impressed. And, she was certain, most assuredly aware that he was out of place. The thought gave her another guilty twinge but she dismissed it.

She might have to eat her pride by ferrying this man around as if he were not who he was, but it would surely be worth it.

The five men seated at the marble-topped table rose to greet him. Oh, yes, he was in over his head today. Her father's attorney. Her father's accountant. The vineyard manager. The viniculturist and the vintner.

Alessia watched Nicolo shake hands with each of them.

Then she sat back, ready to watch him eat crow. An American expression, and an excellent one.

What could a gangster possibly know of the law, of finance or of *vino?*

Five minutes later, she knew she had made a terrible error in judgment.

"Ah," he told the attorney, "what a pleasure to meet the man who won Palmieri versus Shott in Venice last year." Alessia watched the lawyer sit up straighter.

"You know of that case, *signore?*" he said, and Orsini replied that yes, of course he did, it had made headlines everywhere.

The accountant turned brick-red with delight when Nicolo said he was delighted to meet the man responsible for such an outstanding article in a prior month's international finance journal.

He made no pretence at knowing anything at all about wine.

"Except how to enjoy a good vintage," he said, which made everyone laugh, even the vintner and viniculturist, who were the worst wine snobs imaginable.

Finally, he looked around the room and took long looks at the paintings her father had not sold only because he had understood there was more to gain from being known as a man who owned such things than from giving them up.

"Magnificent," he said, and added, casually, that he'd been fortunate enough to have acquired a Donatello at Sotheby's a few months ago and had his agent keeping an eye out for a Raphael rumored to be coming on the market soon.

By the time they got down to business, her father's people were eating out of his hand.

But that changed. Once the niceties were out of the way, Orsini the gentleman gave way to Orsini the thug....

Alessia gave an imperceptible shake of her head.

No. Not fair. He wasn't a thug. Not today, anyway. Seated across from her was a sophisticated, powerful, blunt man who was as smart as anyone in the room. Smarter, she suspected. He understood finances.

And that he was being lied to.

He'd listened without expression as the accountant and the attorney danced around the questions he had asked. Why did a successful vineyard suddenly stop earning a profit? Why was it failing? More to the point, what would it take to make the place a success again?

The answers were interesting. He seemed to think so, too....

Until, after twenty or thirty minutes, he held up his hand and said, "Enough."

This was, he said, pure fiction. Nicely done fiction, but fiction nevertheless. Then he pushed aside the documents spread over the table. His obsidian eyes were as merciless as those of a marauding shark.

"Assuming I decide to put money into this operation, it will be because I see a good reason to do so."

"But we understood..." The attorney looked beseechingly at the accountant. "We understood it was your father who would make the loan to the prince."

"I will be the one making it," Nick said brusquely. "And none of what I've seen or heard makes me eager to turn over ten million euros."

"Ten mill—"

"Ten million, that's right." He looked from one man to the other, then at Alessia. "The terms of the loan have also changed. I will expect to own a fifty-one percent interest in Antoninni Vineyards."

"No," Alessia said quickly. "We are not selling our vineyard to you."

"It's your father's vineyard, and he will do whatever I ask or there will be no loan." Nick turned to the attorney and accountant. "My own people will want to see these documents. As for the condition of the vines and land..." He looked at the other men. "Can they be saved if money is diverted to them, or have they been allowed to deteriorate for too long?"

"They most assuredly can be saved," the viniculturist

said eagerly, as the vintner and property manager nodded in agreement.

"Excellent." Nick rose to his feet, motioned those three to remain seated and nodded at the attorney and accountant. "In that case, gentlemen, I'll expect the legal and financial data to be faxed to my New York office by the end of the week."

The attorney opened his mouth to protest, then thought better of it. So did the accountant. It was clear they had been dismissed as if they were errant schoolboys.

Alessia snorted. She tried to turn the sound into a cough but Nicolo's raised eyebrows said he knew the difference between the two.

"Is there something you wanted to say, princess?"

"Only what I have already said. My father will not agree to giving you controlling interest in what has been a family-owned property for many centuries."

She saw his mouth thin. Then he drew back her chair and smiled pleasantly to the three remaining men.

"The princess and I will be just a moment. Alessia? Let's step into the hall."

She didn't want to go with him. Foolish, she knew; there was no reason to avoid being alone with him and so she stood up and preceded him out the door. The attorney and accountant were gone; she could hear the faint buzz of conversation start up in the room behind her.

"You'd better accept this, princess, and so had your father," Nicolo Orsini said calmly. "I won't invest in the vineyard without an assurance that it can be made profitable, nor will I invest in it without owning a majority share."

"That's not going to happen. You knew about my father's financial woes before you came here. I know you did. And you never even suggested you'd demand ownership."

"I came here as my father's emissary. He didn't care how badly your father had screwed up, but I do."

"Because you changed the rules," Alessia said with in-dignation. "You decided to invest your own money, not your father's. Why did you do that?"

It was, Nick thought, a good question. He'd tried finding an answer before but he kept coming up empty. All he knew was that instinct told him there was more going on here than met the eye and that it somehow involved the woman glaring at him.

His life had been ruled by logic, but he had to admit, there were times a man could do better by relying on instinct. It was instinct that had kept him alive more than once in the hellholes in which he'd served his country, and while this surely wasn't a life-or-death situation, he had the sense that instinct was still the way to go.

"I changed my plans and decided to invest my own money because investing is what I do."

She laughed, and Nick narrowed his eyes. "I know you find that hard to believe, but that is exactly what I do."

"Right," she said sarcastically. "You invest in vineyards."

"In all kinds of properties, but not in ones that aren't worth my time or resources."

"Antoninni is very much worth your time and money!"

Her voice trembled; she'd been so caught up in watching him, watching how he dealt with her father's impressionable lackeys, that she'd almost forgotten what the stakes were.

Her mother's welfare.

That was what mattered, not her anger at having to deal with this man or the future of the vineyard. Mama was what counted, and what would happen to her if Nicolo didn't put millions into her father's hands. His unfettered hands, because the last thing her father would want would be Nicolo Orsini looking over his shoulder, telling him he could or could not spend ten million euros.

"Nicolo." She drew a deep breath, smiled in what she hoped

was a reassuring way. "Isn't it enough to invest in Tuscan property? There's no reason to own any. I mean, you are not Tuscan—"

She gasped as his fingers dug into her shoulders.

"No," he growled, "I'm American. Sicilian-American, and that puts me on a different plane, or so you think."

"No! I didn't mean—"

"I am an Orsini, Alessia, but that doesn't mean I am a fool."

"I did not suggest—"

"Never lie to me, princess. It's the one thing I won't ever forgive."

Her color rose; she could feel it in her face. "I am not a liar! I'm simply trying to figure out why you are so determined to take control of the vineyard from my father."

"Because that's the way I want it."

"But if he won't let you and if you walk away and don't give him the money—"

"What?" His eyes searched hers. "What is the real reason this is so important to you?"

Alessia stared at him. He was so powerful. So capable of holding the world in his hands, and never mind how he had earned that power. He was a man who could do anything; she had known that from the moment she first saw him.

What if she told him everything? About why she had agreed to deal with him. About her father's vicious threat. About her mother and how only he, Nicolo Orsini, a stranger from another world, one she detested, could save her.

"Tell me the truth, Alessia. I know there's more to this than you're letting me see."

His voice was low. His hands no longer bit into her shoulders, they cupped them instead. She looked up into his face, into his dark, deep eyes. She could tell him the truth....

And then what?

He was a ruthless thug. Forget his beautiful face and body. His manners. His ability to tell Donatello from Donald Duck. He was what he was, and she could never trust him.

"There's nothing more to this than you see, *signore,*" she said coolly. "I'm just a good Tuscan daughter, determined to do all I can for my *papa.*"

Nicolo's mouth twisted. He let go of her, walked back into the conference room with Alessia behind him.

"Gentlemen," he said, "tell me what I need to know."

The manager spoke in glowing terms of the land. The viniculturist talked excitedly of what he would do to improve the vines, given the money and the time. The vintner talked of past vintages, of future ones, of how he could return Antoninni Wines to their past glories.

Then there was silence. Even Alessia held her breath.

Nick smiled. "I'm impressed. Not just impressed, I'm pleased." He pushed back his chair and rose to his feet. So did the others, including Alessia. "If I go through with this deal, *signori,* I'll want you all to stay on."

Beaming smiles. Handshakes. The men trooped out of the room and Nick turned, folded his arms and leaned back against the table, the look in his eyes indecipherable.

"Okay," he said. "I'm waiting."

"For what?"

"For the rest of the sell."

"The rest of the…the presentation? That was all of it. Well, you will meet the mayor tonight and some others who live nearby, but—"

"Aren't you going to make a pitch, too?"

Her chin rose. His tone was insulting; they both knew it.

"The pitch, as you call it, was just made, *signore.*"

"Really?" He unwound from where he stood. There was no other word to describe the lazy straightening of that long, muscular male body, or the slow way he came toward her.

"Because it occurs to me, princess, that you might be part of the sell."

"That I…?" Her head jerked up. "I have no idea what you mean."

But she did. He could see it in her eyes as he reached out and drew a slow finger down her face, down her throat, pausing just at the demure V-neck of her silk blouse.

"Those kisses. The little moans—"

"There have been no moans, little or otherwise," she snapped, slapping his hand away.

Nick said nothing. How come he hadn't thought of it sooner? The idea had come to him while the accountant and the attorney were doing their little dance, trying to convince him the prince wasn't as desperate for money as Nick already knew he was, thanks to what his father had told him and thanks, too, to some quiet checking he'd done on his own.

"But there have been kisses, princess. You won't deny that."

"Kisses you instigated."

"Kisses you responded to."

"Only because I did not expect them!"

He raised one dark eyebrow. "You always kiss a man back when he unexpectedly kisses you?"

"I did not mean that at all!"

No, he thought, he was pretty sure she hadn't meant that, pretty sure that the Ice Princess wouldn't return a man's kiss unless her hormones had taken over for her head.

She'd set this meeting here so she could remind him of who he was as compared to who she was. He was onto all that and it certainly didn't improve his attitude toward her.

So why, despite those things, did she melt when he kissed her? Hell, why did he react the same way, losing sight of everything except the urgent need to get her into bed?

None of it made sense…unless the touch me, don't touch

me routine was part of the scheme, part of making him crazy enough to go along with whatever she and her old man wanted.

He could kiss her again, right now, and try to unravel the mystery....

Instead, he took a quick step back.

"Okay," he said briskly. "Okay, if you don't have a second part to this presentation, I do."

She looked up at him. "I told you, there is a second part. Tonight's dinner."

"Is your closet only an adjunct to the local Armani shop?"

She blinked. *"Scusi?"*

"Do you own anything except those suits?"

Alessia looked down at herself, then back at him.

"Sì. Yes. But I don't under—"

"You grew up on those acres of grapes, didn't you?"

"Well, yes, of course, but—"

"I want a tour. With you as my guide, not the viniculturist or the vintner or anybody else. Put on jeans or whatever it is you wear when you're being a real person."

"I beg your pardon, *signore!* I *am* a real—"

"A real person," he said firmly, and he laughed at the indignant expression on her lovely face and then he stopped laughing and did exactly what he'd told himself he would not do—reached for her, gathered her against him, kissed her—and it took less than a second before she moaned, rose to him and parted her lips to his.

It wasn't enough.

Nick cursed, slid his hands under her skirt, bunched it at her thighs and felt her shudder. She whispered something in soft, frantic Italian and she wrapped her arms around him, dug her hands into his hair as he slid his hands down into her panties, cupped her bottom, brought her tightly against him and she moaned again at the feel of his erection—

A knock sounded at the door.

"Principessa?"

The chauffeur. Alessia shoved her hands against Nick's chest. He drew her even closer.

"Send him away."

"Principessa? You said two hours. I have told that to the *carabiniere* but he threatens me with *uno biglietto.*"

"You're a princess," Nick whispered. "How can you get a parking ticket?"

Alessia gave a soft laugh. It made him smile. That he could make her laugh seemed almost as important as that he could make her melt in his arms.

"I understand, Guillermo," she said loudly. "Go down and wait for us, please. We'll be there in a moment."

"Alessia…"

She shook her head, pressed her hands lightly against Nick's chest and he gave in to the inevitable and let her step free of his embrace. She smoothed her hair, her jacket, her skirt. Then she opened the door and Nick followed her into the elevator. Just before the doors opened, he gave in to instinct, pulled her against him and gave her a hard, deep kiss.

"This isn't over," he said against her mouth.

"Yes," she said in a tone that didn't match the race of her heart against his, "it is. I shall see you tonight. Seven o'clock, in the—"

"You're taking me on a guided tour of the vineyard."

"Listen to me, Nicolo…"

"I am listening," he said roughly, "not to your words but to what you tell me when you kiss me." And when her lips parted in protest, he used it as a chance to kiss her one last time before he let her go.

CHAPTER SEVEN

BACK in the guest suite, Nick tried to get a handle on what in hell was happening.

He was in a baffling situation, one he didn't entirely control, and it made him angry.

Angry at the prince for creating a financial disaster that had opened the door to Cesare's intervention. At Cesare for dumping the problem on him. At Alessia, who behaved as if she were as confused by her reaction to him as he was by his reaction to her.

Or was she?

Maybe that second of insight he'd had during the meeting a little while ago was right on the money. Maybe she was playing a game as old as time and as dangerous as anything he'd ever faced, even in combat.

He tore off his jacket and the rest of his Wall Street attire because a man this enraged shouldn't be wearing the trappings of civilization.

Damn them all. His father. Her father. The Ice Princess.

"Hell," Nick swore, and, naked, he stalked into the bathroom, slapped his hands on the marble vanity and glared at his reflection in the mirror.

Why lie about it?

The person he was furious with was himself.

He was letting a woman make a fool of him.

Yes, he'd let his father use a despicable trick to get him to come here. If his mother really wanted a bit of Tuscany, why would Cesare have waited all these years to buy it for her? And why this place, this vineyard owned by a family whose roots were probably entwined not just with the Medicis but with the double-dealing and conspiracy of the Borgias?

Nick didn't give a damn. Not about Cesare's real motives or the prince screwing up an enterprise his family had owned for five hundred years. What mattered was that he was being used. By his old man, whose entire life was given over to conspiracy. By a prince who didn't know the meaning of honor.

And by a woman.

A woman who was manipulating him.

And he—dammit, he had allowed it to happen. He'd let her draw him deeper and deeper into a dark whirlpool of desire more intense than any he'd ever known.

There could only be two explanations for her behavior.

Either she was willing to do anything to make sure he invested in the vineyard.

Or she was taking a walk on the wild side.

Not that it mattered.

He'd had enough of her games, one minute treating him as if he were lower than a snake and the next going crazy in his arms. If it was deliberate, if it was real…

The Ice Princess had perfected teasing to an art. And he'd been performing like a trained seal.

A trite metaphor but there it was.

Okay. Enough was enough. He was tired of being played with. It was time to put an end to it and he knew exactly how he'd do it.

Take her to his bed. Nothing soft and gentle. He'd take her with brutal force, again and again, until she sobbed his name, until she clung to him, until whatever she'd really wanted was meaningless because by then, all she would want was him and everything he could do to her.

And when she finally lay spent beneath him, he'd get up, dress, toss a note for ten million euros on the dresser as if she were the world's most expensive whore because it was what she deserved for reducing him to this…

"Merda!"

Nick punched the mirror.

The glass shattered; drops of blood bloomed like tiny flowers on his knuckles. He cursed again, grabbed a towel, wrapped his hand in it.

And laughed.

Was this what it had come to? Was he so far gone he'd punch a mirror, indulge in a sexual fantasy that was not just bizarre but unreal, all because he'd somehow let a woman work her way under his skin?

He turned on the cold water, unwrapped his hand. The bleeding was minor. He could staunch it in the shower, which was exactly what he did.

"No more," he said grimly, raising his face to the spray.

He would meet Alessia this afternoon, but touring the vineyard wasn't on the agenda. Neither was the decorous dinner party she'd planned for tonight, no doubt to show her father's cronies what a tame *Siciliano* looked like.

To hell with being tame.

By evening, he'd have put an end to this thing. He'd be headed home. And the Ice Princess would have learned the consequences of taunting a man who carried the Orsini name.

He dressed casually. Black leather windbreaker, black T-shirt, faded jeans and sneakers.

At two minutes before one, he headed down the stairs. It

occurred to him that she might not be waiting for him, that maybe she'd figure she'd pushed the game too far.

Not that that would stop him.

He knew her rooms were in the same wing as his. It would only be a matter of slapping open doors until he found her.

But there she was, standing outside the villa, dressed as he was in a jacket, jeans, T-shirt and sneakers. Her hair was pulled back in the kind of ponytail it had been after her morning run. Had that been today? It seemed impossible.

He felt as if he had been here forever.

"Signore."

She looked up at him as he descended the last few marble steps. It was as if somebody had knocked the wind out of him. She was exquisite. How could he have ever thought her no more beautiful than other women who'd passed through his life? She didn't just have a lovely face, it was a face alive with intelligence. And the rest of her. The wide eyes a man could drown in. A long, lush body he had explored all too briefly...

Stop it, Nick told himself coldly. She couldn't go on with the game if he refused to participate, and it was time she got that message.

"Princess."

She looked him over from head to foot and gave a forced smile.

"I see you understand that touring the vineyard will not be, how do you say, a white-collar enterprise."

Nick's smile never reached his eyes. "Nothing about this afternoon will be white-collar, princess. I promise you that."

"I don't understand."

"What happened to calling me Nicolo?"

He saw her throat constrict. "I—I... Nothing happened. I just think, since this is all about business, we might wish to maintain a—"

"Never mind." He looked past her, toward the Jeep-like vehicle parked by the foot of the steps, and held out his hand. "The keys."

"*Scusi?*"

"I want your car keys."

"My car... Oh." Pink tinged her cheeks. "We shall be using a Massif, not the Mercedes, and I assure you, I will not have a driving problem on the vineyard's private ro—"

"The keys, Alessia."

She blinked. Then, slowly, she dropped the keys into his outstretched hand. Nick walked to the Massif, opened the door and motioned her inside. He didn't give a damn what they were using as long as she got the message.

He was in charge.

She gave him directions.

Take the dirt road behind the villa. Make a right at the top of the hill. A left at the crossroads. She babbled, too. Nervously, as if she sensed something was wrong, stuff about rootstock and slips and scions, about how, in ancient times, viniculturists didn't realize that cutting back a grapevine rather than letting it grow unrestrained would produce the best, the biggest crop of grapes.

Another time, he'd have found it fascinating. The only thing he knew about wine was either red or white and he liked drinking it with dinner; all these details, even now, piqued his curiosity.

But not enough to deter him from what would happen next, he told himself coldly. No way.

Eventually, Alessia fell silent.

He glanced at her. She sat rigid in her seat, hands tightly clasped in her lap.

"What's the matter?" he said brusquely. "Have you run

out of information you think even I might be capable of understanding?"

That made her jerk toward him.

"All right," she said, "all right, Mr. Orsini. Why not tell me the problem?"

Nick's mouth twisted. He pulled to a stop under a tree that stood at the end of a row of grapevines and shut off the engine.

"Why would there be a problem, *principessa?* You're the perfect tour guide."

Alessia looked at the man beside her. His tone was silky, his voice soft... And she was terrified. Something about him had changed. Where was the astute businessman of this morning's meeting? The acerbic guest who seemed no happier to be here than she was to be stuck with him?

Her throat constricted.

Where was the man who could not keep his hands off her, even though she didn't want him to touch her, to kiss her, to make her feel things she didn't understand?

Was this the man she had accused him of being, all along? The cold, heartless head of a crime syndicate, the kind of export her country had sent to America that made decent Italians cringe?

All at once, she didn't want to be alone with him in this isolated place.

She reached for the door handle. His hand closed hard on hers.

"Where are you going?"

"Outside. To—to see the vines. To make sure they've been properly prepared to endure over the winter."

Nick gave a harsh laugh. "Fascinating. The princess is also a farmer."

"I grew up here," she said stiffly. "When I was a child, I helped tend these vines. I helped pick the grapes. Besides, I thought you wanted to see things close-up. To walk among the vines and ask me about them."

"Is that what you thought, princess? That a man like me would bring you all the way out here to talk about grapes?"

She stared at him. "Yes. Yes, I did."

He started to tell her just how wrong she was. Then he took a long look at her. Her face was pale, her eyes deep and dark. Her lips trembled. Her hand, still locked under his on the door handle, was like ice.

Nick's jaw tightened.

She was frightened. Hell, that was what he'd wanted, wasn't it?

Wasn't it? he thought, and then he muttered an oath, lifted his hand from hers and flung his door open.

"What are you doing?"

"Exactly what you said I should be doing," he growled as he got out of the Massif. "I'm going to take a walk and ask you a lot of dumb questions."

"Questions are never dumb," she said in a small, girlish voice, and he knew then that whatever he'd intended to happen this afternoon was not going to happen.

She knew everything about grapes and wine.

She knew as much about them as he knew about investments and stocks.

What it came down to was that she knew a lot. And the more she talked, the more animated she grew. Her face took on color, her voice gained strength, even her eyes brightened.

Would another princess get down on her knees in the dirt with such enthusiasm, to brush away leaf litter and exclaim over the presence of a bud so small he had to get down on his knees with her to see it? Would another princess get a smear of dirt on her cheek and not give a damn? Would she talk with excitement and enthusiasm about cover crops, fall plantings of clover and peas, to minimize soil erosion during the winter?

Hell, Nick thought, watching her as she gently moved a bug aside, forget about princesses, would another woman do these things?

His sister, Izzy, maybe, because Iz was into plants and flowers and organic stuff, but a woman he dated?

No way.

He thought about the Sunday he'd taken the redhead he'd been seeing last summer to Central Park, after he'd grown weary of hearing her insist she wanted to watch him play football in the same kind of pick-up game he and his brothers had been part of for years.

What a disaster that had been.

Eeww, Nick, there are ants under this tree! Eeww, Nick, something just bit me! Eeww, Nick, there's a big thing with long legs crawling through the grass....

"She doesn't shut up, that big thing's gonna be me," Falco had growled.

The next Friday night, when they got together for beer and burgers at The Bar in Soho, Dante had exchanged glances with Rafe and Falco.

"So, how's the 'eeww' lady?" he'd said with a look of complete innocence.

"Eewt of the picture," Nick had replied, and Rafe had rewarded him with an ungentlemanly snort of beer.

Nobody would laugh, watching Alessia. She poked and prodded, sifted through decaying plant litter and when she was in the middle of earnestly explaining how, come spring, the cover crops would be plowed under and would help fertilize the earth, Nick told himself, *the hell with it,* and he reached for her, pulled her into his arms and kissed her.

She never so much as hesitated. Her arms went around his neck and she pulled him down to her.

She tasted of sun and soil, of the grapes and the seasons. She tasted of herself, warm and sweet, and of an impossible innocence.

Nick rolled her beneath him, cradled her face in his hands, kissed her again and again, each kiss deeper than the last. He could hear his blood roaring in his ears, could feel his heart pounding against hers.

"Nicolo," she whispered, all a woman could ever ask of a man in that one, softly spoken word, and he groaned and gathered her closer still, his hands in her hair, his body in the V of her legs, everything forgotten but this woman, this moment, this need.

His mouth was at her throat, his lips measuring the race of her pulse in its hollow, savoring the salty sweetness of her sun-warmed skin. Every muscle in his body had hardened; he could feel his erection swelling, swelling, swelling until it was almost painful.

His lips angled over hers. Tasting. Teasing. Her lips parted, letting him in. The taste of her made him groan. She was making little sounds, moans, whispers, and now she was arching against him, fingers digging into the hard muscles of his shoulders as her legs rose and closed around his hips. She rocked against him, her pelvis grinding against his swollen flesh, and he practically tore open her jacket, pushed up her T-shirt, found her braless, her breasts waiting for his lips, his teeth, and she gave a sharp cry, flung her head back, and his heart swelled with pleasure when he realized that she had come from that, just that, his mouth on her nipples.

"Nicolo." Her voice broke. She reached for him, cupped her hand over the denim that covered his straining flesh. Nick closed his eyes, let the feel of her touch send a shock wave through him and then, with his last bit of sanity, he took her hand from him, caught her other hand and held both between them, against his chest.

"No," she said in a fierce whisper, "no, don't stop! Nicolo, *per favore, io voglio—io voglio—*"

He kissed her. Swallowed her cries when what she wanted was what he had wanted all along, to bury himself deep, deep inside her.

But not here.

He wanted to be with her in a high-ceilinged room. To undress her as slowly as he could manage and still survive. To carry her to a bed covered in ivory linen, lay her down on it, see her golden hair loose against the pillow.

He wanted to watch her face as he touched her, explored her, all of her with his lips, his tongue, his hands.

He told her those things and watched her eyes blur.

"Tonight," she said brokenly, and he smiled.

"Yes, sweetheart. Tonight, we'll be lost in each other's arms."

"But not here. Not at the villa…"

"No." He kissed her again, softly, his mouth lingering against hers. "Not the villa, princess. I'll get us a place. The right place. I promise."

He rose to his feet, held out his hand. She took it and he drew her up beside him.

"We'll drive to Florence. Right now. And…" He looked at her. She was shaking her head. "What?"

"I forgot, Nicolo. The dinner."

"To hell with…" One glance at her face and he knew that was the wrong answer. "There's no way out of it, huh?"

"I planned it." She blushed. "It is what I do, you see? I represent people, bring them together, determine who will enjoy the company of whom. I know it is not an important occupation but—"

Nick silenced her with a kiss.

"If you do it, it's important." He brought her hand to his mouth and kissed her fingertips. "We can wait, sweetheart.

Didn't some wag once say that anticipation makes the heart grow fonder?"

Alessia wrinkled her brow. "Wag? You mean, as a dog moves its tail?"

He smiled. "That, too."

"I do not understand. Besides, it is absence that makes the heart grow fonder, not anticipation."

Nick drew her closer, cupped her bottom, heard her sweet gasp as she felt his hardness against her.

"Yeah," he said, his voice roughening, "but anticipation has its uses."

Alessia rose to him, her arms around his neck. She kissed him, touched the velvet tip of her tongue to his.

"*Sì,*" she whispered, and by the time they broke apart, it struck him as a minor miracle they hadn't turned into a column of flame.

CHAPTER EIGHT

ALESSIA had been to endless dinner parties, first as the daughter of a wealthy Florentine prince and in the last several years, as an up-and-coming associate at a publicity firm.

Some parties were dull. Some were interesting. The ones that involved her sometimes egotistically-challenged clients, a polite way of thinking of ones who were unsophisticated, were the most difficult.

She had to seem to be having fun even as she kept a sharp eye on everything.

Whatever kind of party it was, she'd long ago perfected the art of wearing a polite mask. She smiled, moved from group to group, carried on conversations about anything from art to Antarctica and did it all on autopilot.

And she was never nervous.

None of that applied tonight.

She was not just nervous, she was—there was no other word for it—a wreck.

Dressed and ready an hour early, staring at the clock in her bedroom, watching the minute hand drag around the dial didn't help and finally she gave up and headed downstairs.

Surely, there were things she could find in the drawing room, the dining room, to keep her busy.

But she couldn't.

Her father's household staff was well-trained, and she had arranged for her own coordinator to supervise things.

The drawing room was filled with light from half a dozen magnificent chandeliers; gold-rimmed champagne flutes and wine goblets that had been in the family for almost two centuries glittered on the enormous sideboard alongside an array of bottles that ranged from Cristal champagne to vintage Brunello di Montalcino, the incredibly expensive red wine for which the area was known.

The dining room table, set for twelve, was a masterwork of floral centerpieces, antique silver candelabra, her great-great-grandmother's china and sterling flatware that dated to the eighteenth century.

Alessia straightened a plate here, moved a fork there but the truth was, there was nothing for her to do....

Nothing except finally admit that her nerves had nothing to do with this dinner party and everything to do with Nicolo.

She had not seen him for hours.

They'd driven back to the villa from the hillside in silence. She hadn't known what to expect. Would he try to take her in his arms again? She was not ready for that. In fact, by the time they'd returned, she was stunned at what she'd said to him about wanting to be with him tonight and convinced she was not ready for anything to happen between them, now or ever.

The drive back had given her time to think.

What am I doing? she had thought.

Nothing sensible, that was certain.

Why would a logical woman even consider getting involved with a man she didn't know or want to know? Nicolo Orsini wore the right clothes and said the right things but that didn't change what he was.

Or what she became in his arms.

She had turned into someone else on that hillside, losing

her sense of self, of decorum, of—of morality. To have kissed him with wild abandon, to have begged him, *Dio,* begged him to take her...

All those thoughts had whirled through her head as they drove to the villa, but when they reached it, Nicolo had been the perfect gentleman. He'd helped her from the Massif, brought her hand to his mouth and lightly brushed a kiss over her knuckles.

Then he'd gone to his rooms and she had gone to hers. She had not seen him since, which was not what she'd anticipated. Despite their agreement that he would not make love to her in the Antoninni villa, she'd expected him to want to take her to his rooms, or to hers.

In fact, for the next couple of hours, each time she'd heard a footstep in the hall she'd felt her heart race, her mouth go dry because that footstep might be his, because she'd thought he might have been coming to her, coming *for* her to complete what they had started under that tree.

Just the thought had been enough to start her trembling....

As she was trembling now.

Alessia went to the mahogany bar in the drawing room and poured herself a glass of wine.

The porcelain mantel clock softly ticked away the minutes. Soon, Nicolo would come through the doorway. She had learned enough about him to know that he was a man who understood the unwritten rules of business, and this was a business dinner. She had to remember that.

There was nothing of a social nature to it.

He would be on time. And she would tell him that what had almost happened today had been a mistake.

Her hand shook. Carefully, she set the glass on a small table. It would not do for the Princess Antoninni to greet her guests with wine stains on her gown.

Her gown.

Another mistake. Why had she let her friend, Gina, convince her to wear it? It was beautiful, yes, the most beautiful gown her friend, an up-and-coming young designer, had ever made.

But it was wrong for this occasion.

Last week, over a pick-up meal of cheese and salad in Gina's Roman *atelier,* she'd told her friend about the dinner party she had to preside over in honor of an American investor of her father's acquaintance.

"An American investor," Gina had said brightly. "Is he young and good-looking?"

"For all I know, he looks like an ape," Alessia had said glumly.

"But he's filthy rich?"

"Filthy, anyway."

Gina had laughed, hurried to a rack filled with clothes and yanked a gown from it.

"Ta-da," she'd said dramatically. "I have the perfect creation for you to wear. Take a look at this."

"This" was a stunning column of gold, embellished with tiny crystal paillettes.

"This man doesn't deserve anything so elegant," Alessia had said, but Gina had insisted she try it on.

"I told you," she'd said triumphantly, once Alessia had it on. "It is absolutely perfect."

Perfectly spectacular, Alessia had thought, looking at herself in the mirror. The cut of the halter-necked gown was deceptively simple—but the back of it dipped to the base of her spine and when she took a step, a slit in the skirt revealed a glimpse of leg from ankle to thigh.

Alessia had laughed.

"My job is to convince this man to give my father a lot of money, not seduce him."

"You'll dazzle him! He'll agree to anything. Between your title, that villa and this gown, you'll have him at your feet." Gina had wrinkled her nose. "Look, you don't like this guy and you haven't even met him. Think of what it'll be like to have him groveling."

It would be wonderful, Alessia had thought with sudden clarity.

She had taken the gown. And the stiletto-heeled gold sandals that went with it.

"The only thing you'll have to add is attitude," Gina had said with a wink, "but, hey, if you think like a princess, you won't have any trouble."

They'd both laughed, though Alessia could not imagine laughing now.

She picked up the glass again.

Very well.

She could, indeed, conjure up that regal attitude Gina had joked about. She would be polite but distant, pleasant but cool. And when the evening ended, she would tell this arrogant man that she had made a mistake on that hillside….

"Good evening, princess."

Alessia spun toward that slightly rough voice and her heart leaped into her throat.

"Nicolo," she said…and knew instantly that everything she'd just told herself was a lie.

She had not made a mistake this afternoon.

She wanted Nicolo Orsini to make love to her, and to hell with right and wrong.

She'd wanted him since he'd taken her in his arms as she wept so foolishly by the side of the road, she wanted him now, and nothing else mattered. He was everything she had ever let herself dream of in the darkest recesses of the night, and she was not going to walk away from what would surely never come into her life again.

"You are," he said softly, "incredibly beautiful."

She smiled. So was he. The leanly muscled body. The wide shoulders and long legs. The hard, angel-of-darkness face. The way he was looking at her.

"Thank you." She touched the tip of her tongue to her suddenly dry lips. "You look—you look very elegant in that tux."

It was an understatement of amazing proportions. He looked as if he'd just stepped out of a Ralph Lauren advertisement.

He smiled back at her. "I'm glad I packed it. A man could wear nothing else for an evening with a woman who looks the way you do tonight."

"It's the gown." Deliberately, as aware of him as if he were a lion and she were the female he was stalking, she turned in a little circle, just slowly enough to be sure he saw the low dip of the gown at her spine and the long, exposed length of her leg. "Do you like it?"

She watched his eyes narrow under his dark lashes, saw the tic of muscle in his jaw. Her entire body responded, pulse rocketing, skin flushing, bones threatening to turn to water. And when he started toward her, it was all she could do not to fly into his arms.

Kiss me, she thought, *kiss me now!*

Forget the carefully planned dinner, the guests, the cars even now pulling into the driveway, their headlights illuminating the drawing room.

But he didn't kiss her. He didn't touch her. He spoke to her, instead, and his words were more intimate than any caress.

"You're killing me," he said in a rough whisper.

Her heartbeat stuttered. "Am I?"

"You know damned well you are." He came even closer, so close she could feel the heat emanating from him, and ran a fingertip over her lips. "How am I going to keep my hands off you tonight?"

Alessia took a long breath.

"Don't keep them off me," she said, her voice trembling.

And then the butler entered the room and announced the arrival of the first guest.

The evening was never going to end.

Either that, or she was going to go up in flames before it did.

Her guests—her father's guests—were a polished, sophisticated group. Alessia knew he'd invited them to impress a potential investor. When he'd shown the guest list to her, she, who never gave a damn about impressing anyone, had coolly hoped for the same thing.

Better still, she'd hoped the American would be intimidated.

That was before she'd met Nicolo.

She knew now that no one and nothing would ever impress or intimidate him. Just as at the meeting earlier in the day, he was completely at ease, comfortable carrying on conversations about theater and travel and politics in English and in passable Italian.

Actually, it was he who directed conversations because, by the second course, her father's aristocratic and powerful cronies, and especially their ladies, were transfixed by the handsome, intelligent, interesting stranger seated to her right.

A good thing, too, because Alessia had virtually lost her ability to speak.

The reason?

Even as the guest of honor talked pleasantly with the others, even as he ate the elegant meal she had carefully organized, sipped the vintage Antoninni wines she had selected—

Even as he behaved with impeccable decorum—

Even then, he was touching her.

Nobody knew. Nobody saw. It was a hot, hidden secret shared only by the two of them—and it was the most exciting experience she could ever have imagined.

It had started back in the drawing room, after drinks were poured and hors d'oeuvres nibbled. A brush of his shoulder. A slide of his hand on her bare arm.

His hand placed on her back when dinner was announced.

It was a simple gesture, typical of most men escorting a woman to the table.

"Princess," Nicolo had said politely.

And spread his palm over her back.

Over her naked skin.

His warm, slightly calloused hand.

She'd caught her breath, looked up at him, saw his polite smile...saw the flame burning bright in his eyes.

In the dining room, he'd drawn her chair back from the table, his hand still on her. But as she took her seat, his fingers had dipped beneath the gold silk at the base of her spine in a swift, hot caress.

"Thank you," she'd said and he'd said, "You're very welcome, *principessa*," and she'd known, without question, that if he'd chosen that moment to lift her into his arms and carry her away, she'd have welcomed him doing it.

By now, he had touched her a dozen times.

His arm brushing hers when he turned his attention to another guest. His fingers, slipping against hers when she passed him the salt cellar.

But the game changed.

As the third course was served, she felt his hand on her leg.

A moan rose in her throat. She bit it back and did what she

could to smile brightly at the mayor, seated at the other end of the table, to pretend she knew what he was saying, but how could she? How could she when all she could think of was Nicolo's touch, his caress, the heat of his palm on her knee? Her thigh.

He was driving her wild.

And she loved it.

Dio, what was happening to her? She, the soul of propriety, the woman so steeped in the rules of etiquette that her employer always turned to her if questions arose.

She was hanging on to her sanity by a thread, and doing even that was becoming increasingly difficult. The room was spinning, and she knew it was not the wine. She had limited herself to the one glass before dinner and she had hardly touched the one that stood by her plate now.

Still, the room was spinning. She was breathing faster. She was hot, even though she knew the room itself was not.

Nicolo's hand moved. Caressed. His touch was… It was wicked magic. Rough. Silken. Warm.

She put her hand in her lap. Closed it over his. To stop him. Of course, to stop him… Or perhaps just so he would do this, yes, trace his thumb across her palm, fold his fingers through hers, move his hand and hers higher on her thigh…

"Is that not right, my dear?" a man two seats away said, smiling at her.

She stared at him. She could not put a name to the aristocratic face. He was—yes. He was an art dealer. She'd met him possibly a dozen times but his name had flown from her head. As for answering his question… How could she, when she had no idea what it meant?

I am, she thought with great clarity, *brain dead.*

The thought made her laugh. Apparently, it was the right thing to do because the others laughed, too.

"It's true, then," Nicolo said smoothly. "You really did bid

on a Renoir at an auction at *Signore* Russo's gallery when you
were seven years old?"

She flashed him a look filled with gratitude.

"Yes. I did. It was an accident, of course. I was there with
my art tutor and I lifted my hand to scratch my nose."

More laughter. Nicolo leaned toward her. *"Brava, cara,"* he
whispered, and she wanted to grab his head and kiss him.

The dessert course, at last.

Tiramisu. Tiny chestnut cakes. Antique gold-rimmed li-
queur glasses of *strega* and *frangelico*. Espresso, in a coffee
service as old as the villa. Laughter. Chatter.

And Nicolo, who had taken pity on her and had his hand
on her thigh, but kept it still.

She could, at least, think.

What she thought about was him.

That she'd been prepared to despise him. That she'd been
certain he would be rough and uncultured. That he would
not be able to hold his own among truly civilized, worldly
people.

Wrong. Wrong. Wrong.

He was wonderful. And sophisticated. And very much at
ease in this sophisticated setting.

The women in the room couldn't take their eyes off him,
and who could blame them? He was, without question, gorgeous. He'd have laughed at the word but it was accurate. The
men hung on his every word. The mayor, the art dealer and
another man, a wealthy eccentric, discreetly handed him their
business cards.

He was charming to them all but she knew who really held
his attention.

She did.

And when all these people finally left, when she and Nicolo
would, at last, be alone...

The coffee cup shook in Alessia's hand. Carefully, she set it on the table.

She thought of what he had done all evening. How he had touched her. How his caresses had excited her.

She thought of how it would be, when everyone was gone and there was nothing to keep him from touching her more intimately, nothing to keep her from parting her legs, giving him deeper access to her body...

Dio.

Her pulse was thundering. She was wet and hot and she thought how readily she could give him that access now. She had only to place her hand under the table linen, place her fingers over his. Ease her thighs apart, guide his hand up and up and—

A little sound burst from her throat. Conversation stopped and she realized, to her horror, that every eye in the room was on her.

She told herself to say something. Anything. Her mind was blank. In desperation, she looked at Nicolo and saw that he knew what was happening to her.

Triumph blazed in his eyes.

Then, slowly, he moved his hand from her leg, made a fist of it and brought it to his mouth, smothering a polite but audible yawn. It was a good approximation of the sound she had made and everyone looked from her to him.

"I'm sorry," he said, with a charming smile. "*Mi dispiace.* I assure you, it isn't the company. This has been a wonderful evening. It's just that I've been on the go ever since early yesterday morning."

Everyone murmured their agreement. The guests tossed their napkins onto plates. Pushed back their chairs. Said *buona sera* and *arrivederci,* good-night and goodbye, and said it had been a delightful evening.

Nicolo politely helped her to her feet, held her elbow as they both accompanied everyone to the door. Car doors slammed. Headlights came on. A procession of elegant cars crawled down the long driveway.

And Alessia stood in the open front doorway, Nicolo beside her, smiling and waving as if she were simply a polite hostess seeing her guests off when, in truth, she was facing a moment of stark reality.

She and Nicolo were alone.

It was what she had longed for.

Now, it was what she feared.

The game they'd been playing had suddenly taken on a new dimension.

And it scared the hell out of her.

She didn't fear him. Never that. What she feared was herself. If he was not quite the man she'd thought, she was most certainly not the woman he thought, either.

Her behavior this afternoon, then this evening, surely would make him assume she was experienced in the ways of sex. Sophisticated. Worldly. A woman who was accustomed to pleasuring a man and being pleasured by him in return.

Nothing could have been further from the truth.

All of this was new to her. Everything she'd done, everything she'd initiated and responded to... She had never done anything even remotely like this before.

No, she wasn't a virgin. She was a modern woman. But what she knew about sex compared to what Nicolo must think she knew...

It was laughable.

She'd slept with a boy at school. He'd been as naive as she and, after a couple of weeks, they'd drifted back to being friends instead of lovers. Then, three years ago, there'd been an older man. A graphics artist. That had lasted all of a tepid month before he'd admitted he'd finally realized he preferred men.

Not much of a recommendation for a woman who'd spent

the last hours playing games with a man who, without question, had been with many, many women.

Beautiful women. Experienced women. He would expect things from her, with her, and she would surely disappoint him....

The taillights of the last departing vehicle vanished into the dark night. Nicolo's arms closed around her. He lowered his head to hers, pressed his lips to her ear.

"Princess," he said softly. "Whatever's going on in that lovely head?"

She could feel the heat of his body, the strength of it against her. She wanted to lean back into him. She wanted to turn and bring his mouth down to hers.

She wanted to run away before he discovered what a fraud she really was. Instead, she swallowed dryly. Forced a smile, even if he couldn't see it.

"Nothing," she said with false gaiety. "I'm just—you know, it's been a long day and—"

"Alessia." His hands cupped her shoulders and he turned her toward him. "I know something's wrong. What is it?"

She looked up at him, at that hard, handsome face, and then she dipped her head and lowered her lashes. "Nicolo. I think—I think we must talk."

He put his hand under her chin. Raised it until their eyes met.

"What I think," he said, his voice rough, "is that we've talked too much."

"We have not talked at all, Nicolo. We have—we have done other things—"

He framed her face. Lowered his mouth to hers. Kissed her tenderly, his lips moving on hers with growing hunger. He tasted of wine and coffee, of passion and of himself.

Alessia could feel her heart racing.

He tasted like every dream she'd ever had, every dream

she'd been afraid to dream. She held back, but only for a few seconds. Then she sighed and gave herself up to his kiss.

After a very long time, she put her hands against his chest.

"Nicolo," she whispered, and he lifted his head and looked down into her eyes.

"What is it, sweetheart?"

"I need to tell you… You must know…" She licked her lips. "What happened today was—it was—"

"It was the last thing either of us expected."

"Yes. That is true. My father… Your father…"

"They haven't got a thing to do with this."

"No. They do not. But—but you need to know… I must make something clear, Nicolo." *Dio,* she felt so foolish! Why was it so difficult to tell him that his expectations of her had little to do with reality? "What I'm trying to say is that you— you may have certain expectations of me—"

Nicolo swept his hands into her hair. She felt the pins that had secured it in a loose knot at the crown of her head come loose; golden strands cascaded over his fingers as he lifted her face to his and kissed her. Hard. Passionately. As if there had not been hours between those kisses under the tree on the hilltop and this one, as if they had never stopped tasting each other at all.

"The only expectation I have, princess, is that you'll let me make love to you until you tell me nothing else matters."

"Nothing does," she whispered. "Nothing could. I just—I do not want to disappoint you."

Disappoint him? What had happened tonight—Alessia's whisper just before they'd gone in to dinner, the way she'd looked at him throughout the meal, her increasing loss of control because of him, only him…

It had been more exciting than anything he'd ever experienced, and he was a man who had pretty much experienced everything.

"Truly, Nicolo, you must understand... I am not—I am not..." She drew a ragged breath. "When you touched me tonight, when you put your hand on me..." Her voice broke. "I almost—I almost—"

Jesus, she was going to kill him! Nick leaned his forehead against hers and gave a soft, ragged laugh.

"I know, sweetheart. Me, too."

She looked up at him, her cheeks flaming. "Truly?"

"Yeah." Another ragged laugh. "And wouldn't your old man's fancy friends have loved that?"

"Because—because all I could think of was what would happen if—if you touched me more. If you moved your hand, only a little—"

"Enough," Nick growled, and drew her hard against his side, silencing her with a kiss as he hurried her down the wide marble steps to a gleaming red Ferrari.

"Mine," he said, in answer to her unspoken question. "Delivered here an hour ago." He opened the passenger door, one arm curved around her as he did, with such blatant masculine possessiveness that she felt her knees go weak.

"Your seat belt," he said, once he was behind the wheel, the words an imperious command.

Alessia complied, though her hands trembled. The car gave a throaty roar as he turned the key.

"Where are we going?"

"To a place where we can be alone without the ghosts of your father or mine looking on."

Then he leaned toward her, gave her one last, deep kiss before he stepped hard on the gas and the Ferrari leaped into the night.

CHAPTER NINE

NICK drove fast, his hands light and sure on the steering wheel.

He let the Ferrari take the winding roads into the dark hills like the thoroughbred it was.

They weren't going very far. Twenty miles. Fifteen minutes, the Realtor had said, twenty at the most.

The road ahead climbed higher. Nick downshifted and thought fifteen minutes would be about all he could manage.

He'd wanted women before. Why not? He was a man in the prime of life. But he'd never wanted a woman like this, with a need so strong, so powerful, that having her was all he could think about.

It had taken him most of the afternoon, making calls on his cell phone to make arrangements for tonight. He rarely thought about the fact that he had, to put it bluntly, an almost unfathomable amount of money and the connections that went with it, but there were times having money and those connections could change everything.

First, he'd phoned a Ferrari dealer in New York, who had phoned a Ferrari dealer in Florence. Then he'd called a banker pal in London who'd called a Realtor in Siena who'd called a Realtor in Florence...

It had all been time-consuming, but he'd finished with an

hour to kill before a dinner party he wanted to attend about as much as a vampire would want to have a vegetarian lunch.

Taillights winked just ahead. Nick checked his mirror, swung out and passed the vehicle as the speedometer neared ninety.

That final hour had been an eternity.

A voice inside had kept saying, *What are you waiting for? Find her. Push her against the wall. Ruck up her skirt, unzip your fly, hold her wrists high over her head and drive into her while she sobs your name and comes and comes and comes....*

Crazy, he'd told himself, even to have thought that way.

Life was all about self-control.

He'd learned that growing up, when being a son of Cesare Orsini had made him fair game for every TV newshound in New York. He'd perfected it in combat, especially in clandestine ops where self-discipline could be the difference between life and death. It was the single most important factor that had made him the kind of gambler who won far more often than he lost, at cards and then as a financial decision-maker at Orsini Investments.

And, of course, relationships with women, in bed and out, were all about a man exercising self-control.

And why he'd been thinking about relationships when a minute earlier he'd been thinking about Sex, Sex with a capital *S,* had been beyond him to comprehend.

So he'd taken an endless shower, let the cold water beat down until he could think straight. Then he'd dressed in the tux he'd thought to bring with him, looked in the mirror at the image of a civilized man about to deal with a woman in a civilized way...

Until he got downstairs and saw Alessia.

The beautiful face. The gorgeous body. The gown that was an invitation to sin, the take-me stiletto heels.

How am I going to keep my hands off you? he'd said.

Her sexy-as-hell response had sent the civilized man inside him packing.

Somehow, they'd made it through dinner, playing a game so hot he was amazed they hadn't set the place on fire. That he'd been forced to carry on intelligent conversation while he touched her had added to it.

And then that last moment, when he'd brought her to the brink…

A muscle knotted in his jaw.

He glanced at Alessia. She hadn't spoken since she'd asked him where he was taking her. She sat very straight, hands folded in her lap, gaze straight ahead. Was she imagining what would happen next? Was her body softening as she pictured him touching her?

Or was she worried that she wouldn't—how had she put it? That she wouldn't live up to his expectations?

Was she really that naive? Or simply clever?

He told himself it didn't matter.

Hell. Why lie to himself? It mattered. A lot. When they were finally alone, what if what he did to her, did with her, was new to her? What if he was the first man to teach her things that would make her moan and beg him to end the exquisite torment, as she had today on the hilltop?

Dammit!

Nick shifted his weight in the seat. If he kept this up, they might never make it to the villa he'd rented.… And, thank God, there it was, just ahead and exactly as the Realtor had described. A narrow gravel road, leading through an open iron gate. A stand of gnarled olive trees. And in the distance, the lights of a stone house.

Villa Riposante.

And not a minute too soon.

* * *

Alessia trembled as she stepped from the car.

"Here," Nicolo said, shrugging off his jacket and wrapping it around her shoulders. "This should keep you warm until we're inside."

She nodded, though he was wrong.

She was not cold, she was terrified. Not of him. That fear was long since gone. She was terrified of herself, of the awful knowledge that no matter what he'd said, she knew she was going to disappoint him.

She had no idea where they were, only that they were in the hills high above Villa Antoninni and that this place, this beautiful stone villa, could only have been found on such short notice by a man who could ask whatever he wished of the world and get it.

He put his arm around her, led her up the stone steps to the door. The key—big, brass, old—was under a thick rush doormat. Nicolo inserted it in the lock, turned it, the heavy wood and brass door swung open...

"Nicolo." She sounded breathless and she was. This was a mistake. A mistake. To have led him on, to have let him think... "Nicolo," she said again, this time with urgency. "Listen to me—"

All at once, she was being swept up in his arms.

"Stop thinking," he said in a rough voice. "Stop worrying. Just let the night happen."

He elbowed the door shut behind him as he carried her into the villa. Alessia wound her arms around his neck and buried her face against his throat. She could feel his heart thudding against hers.

The villa was softly lit. And beautiful, what she saw of it over his shoulder. A frescoed ceiling. A floor of pale gray stone. A steep wooden staircase and at the top, a stream of ivory moonlight that led into a room lit by tapers in tall silver candlesticks. A fire glowed on a slate hearth; orchids rose like graceful ballerinas from crystal vases on the dresser and the night tables....

The night tables that framed the bed.

The bed.

A canopied bed, draped in endless, drifting layers of pale pink silk.

Nicolo let her slide down the length of his body to stand on her feet. She caught her breath at the feel of his erection. He took her hand; she thought he was going to put it against his fly. Instead, he brought her fingers to his lips and kissed them.

There was something so sweet, so touching, in the simple gesture that it made her throat constrict.

He turned away. Closed the door. When he looked at her again, his expression was unreadable. She waited for him to reach for her, to touch her, but he did nothing, he only stood still, watching her through narrowed eyes.

She understood.

He had done his part.

The car. The villa. The flowers. The fire on the hearth. It was all very romantic, but now it was her turn. She wasn't ready but that wasn't his problem, she thought, and she took a deep breath, raised her arms, reached for the tiny loops and hooks that were at the back of her gown's halter neck.

"No."

Her eyes flew to his. He moved toward her, caught her wrists, brought her hands to her sides.

"I want to undress you," he said in a husky whisper.

Could a man say anything more wonderful to his lover? Alessia's heart lifted. Her lips curved in a smile.

"It is what I want, too," she said softly, and Nick drew her to him and kissed her, his mouth moving slowly against hers, very slowly. Going slowly was what he wanted for her. Still, he might be pushing too hard, too fast… And then she groaned, rose to him, opened her mouth to his…

And he stopped thinking.

How could a man think when a woman's taste was so sweet? When she felt so soft, so right? The press of her breasts against his chest. The warmth of her arms around his neck. And those sexy high heels meant that her hips were against his.

He slid one hand down her back. Felt the silken texture of her skin. Cupped her bottom, lifted her into him, and she sighed his name against his lips.

"Nicolo."

Just that, nothing more, and yet he felt as if his heart might leap from his chest.

"Yes, sweetheart," he murmured, and he turned her in his arms, swept her long fall of golden hair aside and fumbled for the loops and buttons at the gown's halter neck, knowing those tiny bits of gold and cotton were all that kept her from him.

His fingers felt big. Clumsy. Undoing the buttons seemed to take forever.…

And then, at last, they were undone.

The bodice of the gown slipped down.

She caught it and held it against her. Nick didn't try to stop her. Instead, he bent his head and put his lips to the tender skin he had uncovered just at the nape of her neck. A soft kiss. Another. The faint nip of his teeth and she moaned. Her head fell forward; her hair tumbled over her shoulders. Nick trailed the tip of his tongue along her sweet, heated flesh, then kissed his way down her spine.

Alessia's moans became soft whimpers of pleasure and when he could take no more, he cupped her shoulders and turned her toward him.

Her head lifted. Her eyes met his and he felt his heart turn over. Everything a man could possibly dream was in her eyes, desire and need and something more, something that made him murmur her name, lift her to him and take her mouth with growing hunger.

She kissed him back, her teeth closing lightly on his bottom lip.

Adrenaline flooded his blood.

He took control of the kiss. Deepened it, until she was clinging to him. His lips moved to her jaw, her throat, her shoulder. She gasped, shuddered, her hands drove into his hair and the bodice of the gown, now forgotten, fell away.

"Alessia." His voice was hoarse. "*Mia bella* Alessia…"

His hands shook as he hooked his thumbs into the gown's deep V at the base of her spine and slowly eased it down. The silk whispered over her hips. Her buttocks. Her thighs. Nick groaned and let it slip from his hands to become a soft circlet of gold around those sexy stilettos.

"Nicolo," she whispered.

"Yes, baby."

"Nicolo. Please."

The word was a sob. A plea. Nick felt his heart thud. He knew what she was asking, knew, too, that he was as close to finishing this before it really began as he had ever been in his life. He could feel everything within him tightening, coalescing, centering low in his belly as he looked at her glittering eyes, her kiss-stung lips, the black lace thong between her thighs.

A shudder went through his big body.

He wanted to tear the thong from her, bare her to his hands, his eyes, take her again and again and again.…

Instead, he took a harsh breath, wove his fingers through hers. Helped her step free of the gown. Let go of her hands, reached for the thin silk band of the lace thong, drew it down and down and down…

And looked at her. Just looked at her.

The sight almost stopped his heart.

His princess had the face of a Botticelli angel. The body of a Venus. Small, rounded, up-tilted breasts crowned with nipples the color of the palest of pink roses. A narrow waist rising from curved hips. Endless legs, topped by a cluster of honey-colored curls. She was exquisite, a man's most perfect dream....

A man's most perfect desire.

Her breathing was quick and shallow. Her eyes were feverish, the pupils deep and dark. She started to raise her arms to cover herself, but Nick caught her wrists and brought her hands gently to her sides.

"You are beautiful," he said. "More beautiful than I could ever have imagined."

Her lips curved and he leaned toward her, brought his mouth to hers, kissed her and kissed her until she murmured his name, again and again.

"Yes," he whispered, "yes, sweetheart, yes..."

Nick watched her face as he raised his hands and cupped her breasts. Her breath hissed at his touch. God, oh, God, the softness of her breasts against his palms. The delicate weight. His thumbs rolled over her nipples.

She cried out; she trembled, her hands dug into his shoulders.

"Do you like that?" he said hoarsely, his eyes locked on her face. "Tell me what you like, sweetheart," he whispered, and he dipped his head, licked one lovely furled tip, then sucked it into his mouth.

Alessia's knees buckled and Nick swept her into his arms and took her to the bed. A bed that might have been designed with his princess in mind.

The silky coverings were as soft as her skin, the blues

as vivid as her eyes. She lay back and her hair fell over the pillows like spun gold.

His heartbeat skittered.

She was more than beautiful. She was exquisite.

Her arms rose, reached for him. He obliged, came down on the bed beside her, kissed her, then ran his hand lightly over her from throat to breast to belly. She caught his hand. Lifted it to her lips and kissed his fingers. Touched the tip of her pink tongue to his palm.

A groan tore from his throat.

He wanted to look at her forever. He wanted to caress her, to spend an eternity exploring her...

He wanted to tear off his clothes and bury himself inside her.

"Please, Nicolo," she said brokenly. *"Per favore, Nicolo mio..."*

Ah, dear God, he was going to explode.

He could feel it happening. The heat, gathering low in his belly. His scrotum tightening, his aroused sex now so hard, so swollen it was almost painful.

He wanted to end her torment and his but somehow he held back. He had to make this last. Last forever. Even now, his brain barely functioning, he understood that such a thing was impossible and yet, he wanted to find a way to make it be true....

And, suddenly, his mind achieved a terrible clarity. For all his careful planning, he had forgotten one thing.

Condoms.

He had no condoms! How could he been so stupid? The thought of stopping now...

"Nicolo?"

"Yes." Nick framed her face in his hands. "Sweetheart. Alessia. I forgot..." Silently, he cursed himself for being such a fool. This wouldn't be the most romantic of questions but it had to be asked. He could only pray she had the right answer. "Are you on—"

"The pill." She blushed. That she could blush as she lay naked in his arms only heightened his arousal. "*Sì*. There is no need to worry. I am—"

His kiss was deep and drugging. Her response was wild and he gave up any final attempt at rational thought, came down to her and gathered her in his arms. She clasped the back of his head, dragged his mouth to hers and kissed him, drew the tip of his tongue into her mouth. He rolled her beneath him, brought his lips to her breast, drew a budded nipple between his teeth, and her cry shattered the night.

She said something in Italian. The words were soft and hot and desperate. They needed no translation.

Nick reared back. Tore off his clothes and Alessia reached for him, wrapped her arms around his neck and pressed her body to his.

He shuddered.

There was so much he wanted to show her. To teach her. But she was sobbing his name, arching like a bow against him and he tried, God, he tried, entering her slowly, as slowly as he could, and when she screamed in ecstasy, he was lost.

He drew back, then drove deep again and again and again until she was wild beneath him, until he could feel the contractions of her womb....

Nick threw back his head and followed his princess into the starry night.

He slept.

She did, too, curled in his arms, her head on his shoulder, her hair silky against his lips.

The night grew chilly. He awoke just long enough to pull the duvet over them both.

"Mmm," she sighed, and he gathered her closer, told

himself he wouldn't wake her, that he would only hold her, like this. Stroke his hand down the length of her spine, like this. Repeat the caress until she made that soft little sound again and now he would rise over her, just a little, bring his mouth to hers, kiss her softly, lightly, gently...

She sighed again, and he rolled her gently on her back. Absolutely, he would let her sleep. She had to be exhausted after the last couple of days. All he would do was kiss her a little more.

Her closed eyes. Her temples.

Her mouth. Her delectable mouth.

"Nicolo?"

Her lashes fluttered. Her eyes opened. "Nicolo," she whispered. Her arms went around him. "Nicolo," she sighed, her mouth warm and sweet against his, clinging to his, and then, somehow, his lips were on her throat. Her shoulder.

Her breasts.

Her nipples, delicately beaded, their taste like honey against his tongue.

His kisses drifted lower. And lower. He heard her breath catch.

"Nicolo? What are you...?"

"Nothing," he said, his lips at her navel. "Nothing at all."

"Oh. Oh, Nicolo! You can't—you shouldn't..." She gave a soft cry as he parted the delicate petals of her labia. Inhaled her essence. Sought out the delicate bud that awaited him.

Her cry rose into the night.

He kissed her there again. And again. Stroked her. Caressed her. And when finally he entered her, this time he did as he had hoped to do the first time, entered her slowly, slowly enough to bring them both to the edge of eternity, to that moment that is part death, part paradise.

And when it was over, Nicolo gathered his princess in his arms, against his heart, and knew that whatever it was he had found in the last forty-eight hours was more than he had ever anticipated....

And more than some men found in a lifetime.

CHAPTER TEN

ALESSIA woke to sunlight, the smell of coffee…

And a heart-stopping view of her lover.

Nicolo had just walked out of the en suite bathroom, drops of water crystallizing on his tanned skin. He was toweling his hair. Which left the rest of him naked. Gloriously, unashamedly naked.

Heat swept through her veins. Such a magnificent sight!

Her lover was beautiful. So beautiful. Until now, she had not had the chance to look at him, really look at him, and appreciate the sight. He'd made love to her again and again through the long, wondrous night. The stroke of his hand on her, of his mouth, the feel of him against her…and under her, she remembered with a soft catch of her breath—all of those incredible things were now hers, forever, imprinted in her mind and on her flesh.

But she had not had the chance to see how perfect he was.

Now, she could look her fill. Without embarrassment, because he had no idea she was awake. And, oh, he was a sight to behold. The muscled shoulders and arms. The dark whorl of hair on his chest. The way it arrowed down his flat, hard belly, tapered to his navel, then flared out again as it surrounded that part of him that was flagrantly, unashamedly male.

Alessia was a child of the city of Florence. She had grown

up virtually surrounded by magnificent works of art, including Michelangelo's *David*. She'd been stunned by the artistry of the great marble sculpture...and, the same as generations of other adolescent girls, amazed by the depiction of all that intimate masculine beauty. Of course, she had stared. What teenager wouldn't?

Now, for the first time in years, she thought of the statue again.

David had nothing on her Nicolo.

Nothing at all.

The thought was totally unlike her. It made her giggle....

A mistake.

Nicolo took the towel from his head and looked at her. "Just what every man wants," he said. "Laughter from his woman, first thing in the morning."

His woman. The words filled her with joy but the expression on his face filled her with laughter and she couldn't help it, she snorted back another giggle.

He raised his eyebrows, draped the towel around his neck—his neck, she noticed, not his hips—and came slowly toward her. "The sight of me without a stitch on is amusing?"

He looked deadly serious. Had she actually offended him?

"No, of course not. It is only that—that I was imagining the statue."

"What statue?"

"*David*. You know the one. And I was thinking that you—that you and *David*—"

"Go on."

She couldn't. Oh, she couldn't. This was embarrassing. It was humiliating. It was—

She gasped as Nicolo flung himself down beside her, grabbed her wrists, hauled them high over her head...and kissed her. She could feel his lips curving against hers.

"Ah-ha," he said in a mock-growl, "the lady is a student of art."

"You are laughing at me," she said, trying to sound stern.

"Not if you tell me who won."

Dio, now she knew she was blushing! "Who won what?" she said, trying for innocent indignation and knowing she wasn't succeeding.

"You know exactly what. *David* and me. Hey, you're talking to a guy who has two sisters. Anna and Izzy spent a summer touring Europe when they were, I don't know, maybe fourteen and fifteen. The trip was supposedly all about art."

"Art is an important part of a young woman's education," Alessia said primly.

"Uh-huh." Nick grinned at the look on his princess's face. She was doing her best to sound proper. Not an easy thing when laughter glinted in her eyes. "From what they said, or maybe from the way they said it, it took my brothers and me ten seconds to figure out that the highlight of their visit to Florence was that statue."

"*David* is a revered work of art," Alessia said, trying not to laugh.

"At least tell me Dave and I came out even. Hey, you've got to keep in mind, Dave is, what, twenty feet tall?"

"Seventeen," she said, and another giggle burst from her lips.

"Yeah, well, I've seen some pretty interesting sculptures, too." He nuzzled her throat, loving the delicious mingled scents of woman and sleep and sex. It had taken all his determination not to wake her with kisses this morning but he'd made love to her so many times during the night that he'd felt a twinge of guilt at the thought of depriving her of a little more sleep. "The *Venus de Milo.* The *Winged Victory.*"

Alessia pulled one hand free and swatted his shoulder. "The *Winged Victory* has no arms and no head."

"Trust a woman to notice something like that." Nick nipped lightly at her shoulder, heard her soft intake of breath as he shifted against her. "The point is, you win, hands down."

"What is this hands-down thing?"

He pulled back. Not far, just enough so he could see all of her face.

"It means," he said, "that you're a hundred times more beautiful."

She smiled. Stroked a dark strand of hair back from his forehead.

"Liar," she whispered.

"A million times more beautiful," he said softly.

He kissed her. Moved over her. Kissed her again and again, until laughter had been replaced by passion.

"Nicolo," Alessia whispered, "Nicolo, *mio amante*."

She had called him her lover. And that was what he was, he thought fiercely, what he wanted to be, what he would be....

And then he stopped thinking and let the world slip away.

The day was overcast.

It didn't matter.

They ran a mile together, returned, showered and made love. Then they ate a huge meal—the villa came complete with staff—and talked and laughed and talked some more.

Hands linked, they strolled the grounds. The place was all Nick had hoped for. Quiet. Isolated. Nothing but a soft breeze that swept through the ancient olive trees, a small vineyard and, over a rise, a stable and half a dozen horses grazing in a paddock.

He watched Alessia as she petted the animals, watched their reactions to her touch. One big stallion snorted, tossed his head, then leaned into her hand.

I know how you feel, pal, he thought, and when his princess turned and smiled up at him, he cupped her face and kissed her.

"Happy?" he asked, after they'd climbed a hill, reached the top and found a view that stretched for miles.

"Very happy. To be here, in such a beautiful place with you… How did you find it?"

"Pay the price and maybe I'll tell you."

"It all depends on the price."

"A kiss," he said, swinging her toward him.

Alessia fluttered her lashes. "You drive a hard bargain, *signore*." She stood on her toes and planted a quick kiss on his cheek.

"You call that a kiss?" Nick grabbed her, dipped her back over his arm and she offered an appropriate shriek. "This," he said, "is a kiss!"

She laughed. So did he. But the kiss went from melodramatic to passionate to sweetly, achingly tender, and Nick sank down on the grass and drew her down beside him.

She sighed and laid her head against his shoulder, and he tried to figure out how he could ever have thought her cold and imperious.

The truth was that she was warm and giving.

She was amazing.

He had never enjoyed being with a woman as much as he enjoyed being with his princess. "Enjoy" was the wrong way to describe it. A man could enjoy a fast car. A deal he'd successfully concluded. But what he felt about Alessia was more intense. More vital. What he felt was more like—more like—

Nick blinked.

Easy, he told himself. Just slow down. Relax.

Alessia was bright. She was funny. She was beautiful. He liked talking with her, sparring with her, having sex with her, but sex was what it was. Incredible sex, especially considering that she'd had been concerned about meeting his expectations. She'd made it sound as if she was inexperienced.

Maybe. But she was the most responsive lover imaginable.

And she was on the pill. A good thing, considering that he'd managed to think of everything but protection.

But…

But, why was she on birth control? Better still, why did it bother him? Because it did. That she was using something was, as he'd just told himself, a damned good thing. Otherwise, what would they have done last night besides drive each other half-crazy?

Besides, he wasn't a male chauvinist. He was all in favor of women having the same rights as men, in sex and in everything else.

Except, suppose she was on the pill because she already had a lover. Then what? Was he sharing her with a man who had the right to touch her as intimately as he had, to explore her body's dark, sweet secrets?

Last night, she'd cried out his name.

Was there some other name she had cried out last week—and would cry out again, once he was gone?

He couldn't imagine that. She was not a woman who would go from one man to another. And despite her responsiveness, despite her being sophisticated enough to keep herself protected against an unplanned pregnancy, her reactions to what happened between them in bed were, for lack of a better word, innocent.

Her sighs. Her moans. They spoke not of knowledge but of wonder.

The first time he'd put his mouth between her thighs, she'd been shocked. *No,* she'd said, *no!* Not in fear. In stunned amazement that he would do such a thing. But he'd gone on kissing her, tasting her, and her shock had given way to ecstasy and she'd sobbed his name, come apart as he licked her....

Hell.

If he kept this up, he was going to turn her toward him, strip off her clothes, make love to her right here, on this hilltop....

"Nicolo?"

Nick cleared his throat. "Yes, sweetheart?"

"Would it be terrible of me to ask you...to ask you to take me back to the villa?"

His heart leaped. "If that's what you want—"

"What I want," she said in a low voice, "what I want, Nicolo, is you."

Her honesty made her blush. That, coupled with what he saw in her eyes, was almost his undoing. He rose, brought her up beside him, took her in his arms and kissed her. Then he took her back to the villa, to the bed, *their* bed, and as she sighed his name and welcomed him into her warmth, all his doubts vanished.

She belonged to him.

Only to him.

She fell asleep in his arms.

Nick lay holding her, his eyes fixed on the ceiling. The sun was sinking behind the hills, casting long shadows over the room. The day was ending and, damn, he hated to see it happen. Soon, it would be time to leave here and return to the Antoninni villa.

To reality.

Alessia stirred, sighed in her sleep and cuddled closer. His arms tightened around her. When she awoke, he'd tell her he'd made some decisions.

He would lend her father the money to restore the winery and the vineyard to their glory days, free of restrictions. He would not demand control of it. He'd said that in anger that was long gone.

And he wouldn't remain here for two weeks. It was an impossibility. He'd really known it when he'd said it but, again, anger had overrun common sense. He had commitments in New York. Meetings. Clients. There was no way to ignore any of it.

So, no, he wouldn't stay....

But he'd come back.

He'd make that very clear to her. Not next weekend—now that he thought about it, he had a trip to Chicago scheduled. And not the weekend after. There was something in his calendar about an appointment in Beijing. But he'd come back....

The muscle in his jaw knotted.

Planning ahead put a different spin on things. It made things complicated. Made them more serious.

And as much as he—as he liked Alessia, this wasn't serious. Intense, sure. But serious...?

Nick frowned. Why think about that now? He was here and so was she, lying warm and soft against him. Her hair smelled of sunshine, her skin of a perfume all her own.

His body hardened.

He wanted her again.

He drew her nearer, brushed his mouth lightly over hers, and she stirred.

"Mmm," she sighed.

"Mmm, indeed," he whispered and when she opened her eyes and smiled, he gave up thinking altogether and lost himself in her arms again.

Hours went by.

They slept. Showered. Had espresso on a broad terrace overlooking the olive groves and by then, it was too late to go back to the Antoninni winery.

And, really, what was the rush?

Nick had figured on flying back to New York tomorrow morning, but he could just as easily leave in the afternoon. No way was he going to risk spending hours stuck at an airport this time and since the Orsini plane was in use by one of his brothers—he'd phoned and checked—he'd be using a chartered flight. One of the advantages of renting a private plane was that it flew at your convenience, not that of others.

He made a quick call to the Realtor and arranged to keep the villa for another night.

The cook produced a meal as good as any in a five-star restaurant. Soup. Salad. Pasta. Fish. A chocolate gelato that made Alessia lick her lips in a way that meant Nick just had to taste the rich ice cream, but on her tongue, not his. The butler produced a bottle of red wine; apparently, the guy recognized *la principessa* as a representative of the famous Antoninni Vineyards and solemnly handed her the cork. Equally solemnly, she sniffed it, then sniffed the scant inch of wine he poured, tasted it, savored it, thought about it…

And burst out laughing at the look on Nick's face, which changed her from wine snob into gorgeous woman in a heartbeat, and made him lean across the candlelit table to steal a wine-flavored kiss and to hell with the butler watching.

"Tell me about New York," she said, over espresso.

"Haven't you ever been there?"

"Oh, yes. Many times." She looked at him and smiled. "I want you to tell me about *your* New York. The places that are special to you."

Nick obliged.

He told her about a museum called the Cloisters, in upper Manhattan. The narrow streets of Soho, at the other end of the island. The saloon he and his brothers had bought there, years back, to keep it from being turned into a cocktail lounge.

That had made her laugh. "You said 'cocktail lounge' as if it were a curse."

"Turning an honest-to-God bar into a place where people order drinks you have to make with a blender *is* a curse," he said, and this time it was Alessia who leaned across the table and stole a kiss.

"I would love to see the New York you have described."

Nick didn't have to think about it. He reached for her hand, ran his thumb lightly over her fingers. "I want you to see it."

She smiled. "I would like that, Nicolo."

He would like it, too—and here they were, back at the same logistics problem he'd been thinking about a couple of hours ago. Okay. He'd have to work something out. Make plans, fairly long-range plans, to keep the relationship going...

Hell. Was that what it was? A relationship?

Well, no.

It was an affair. And yeah, there was a difference...

"...a big family."

He blinked. "What?"

"This morning, you said two sisters. And now you talk of your brothers. A big family. That is nice."

Amazing. He'd told her more personal stuff in a handful of hours than he'd ever told another woman no matter how long they'd been involved.

Nick swallowed hard. *Involved?*

"How many brothers do you have?"

"Three." Her look of astonishment lightened the mood. He laughed, touched his index finger to the tip of her nose. "Hey, we're *Siciliano*. What can I say?"

Her smile wavered. "Of course."

Nick cocked his head. "Meaning?"

"Nothing." She looked down at her glass, as if her interest

had suddenly been captured by the wine. "It is only that—that I had almost forgotten who—who—"

"Who I am," he said with cool belligerence. So much for personal stuff. "Right. Not just a Sicilian. A Sicilian named Orsini."

Alessia shook her head. She raised her eyes to his and he saw that she was blinking back tears. So, what? All that had happened between them meant nothing when you got down to basics. It was the princess and the peasant again, right where they'd started.

"No," she said in an unsteady whisper. "Nicolo, you cannot be—you cannot possibly be—"

A crook. A thug. A member of *la famiglia*. Right. He was none of those things. Now was the time to tell her what a less pigheaded man would have told her from the beginning. That he was an investor. A financial analyst. That he was as legitimate as Mother Teresa—okay, maybe not quite as legitimate as that, but he could surely tell her he was an honest guy who'd worked hard for what he had, that he'd turned his back on his father and everything he represented before he'd been old enough to vote...

Instead, some terrible streak of Sicilian perversity drove him on.

"What if I can be?" he said tonelessly. "What if told you that I am exactly the man you think I am? What would you do then?"

Alessia stared at him for an endless moment. He waited and wondered why he should be waiting, and then the tears she'd tried to stem spilled down her cheeks.

"I would say, it does not matter," she said brokenly. "I might go straight to hell for it, Nicolo, but I would say, 'It does not matter what you are.' You are *mio amante,* you are my lover, and I want you, I want you, I want—"

A heartbeat later, she was in Nick's arms. And as he kissed her, he realized there was no way in the world he would fly back to New York tomorrow.

CHAPTER ELEVEN

WHEN she was a little girl, Alessia had been taught by a seemingly endless procession of tutors and nannies.

At first, with a small child's belief in the infallibility of adults, she'd believed that each of them knew everything there was to know about the world.

A stern-faced woman named *Signorina* Felini taught her otherwise.

Signorina Felini had been hired specifically for her supposed expertise in science. Almost from the start, things went badly.

When she could not explain why the moon was sometimes full and sometimes barely a sliver, Alessia went to the villa's huge library, found a book on astronomy and, with a little diligent research, found the answer. The *signorina* was not pleased, nor was she pleased when Alessia corrected her version of why there were different seasons in the year.

The end came when Alessia asked what would it would be like if an astronaut fell into the sun.

"Such a thing is impossible," said *Signorina* Felini brusquely.

"You mean, he'd burn up before he reached it?" Alessia asked.

Her teacher frowned. "The sun is up there. All else is down here. That is why no one could possibly fall into it."

Alessia's mother happened to overhear the conversation. Nella Antoninni knew little about the sun and the sky but she knew enough to put an end to the *signorina's* employment. A new tutor with a provable degree in earth sciences took her place.

One night, after Alessia and Nicolo had been together for almost two weeks, she awoke to his kisses on the nape of her neck, the sexy stroke of his fingers on her nipples. And just before she lost herself in passion she suddenly thought, *This is how it would be to fall into the sun.*

Flame. Heat. Knowing that you were burning up and not caring, never caring because soon you would be reborn...

Except, she thought the next day, as she put her foot into the palm of her lover's hand and let him help her into the saddle of the mare she'd taken to riding, except she had already been reborn.

She was Nicolo's lover. And he was hers.

Her lover. And—and her love.

The realization swept through her, left her breathless. She clung to the mare's reins, watching as Nicolo swung onto the back of a black stallion, her eyes, her very soul, taking in his beauty, his grace, his power, his air of command. He was sexy and gorgeous, a man any woman would want....

But love wasn't possible. That couldn't be what she felt. Love didn't come this quickly, not unless it happened in fairy tales and this was the real world, not a fairy tale. She couldn't love him. She was confusing love with passion. With desire. And yes, she desired him all the time. His arms around her. His mouth on her. His hands exploring her. His body, possessing hers...

"Alessia." Nicolo's voice was low. Rough. His eyes were hot as he watched her. "What are you thinking?"

Her heart was a swollen balloon, about to burst. She was

sure he knew precisely what she was thinking. All she had to do was whisper her answer.

You, she would say, as she had so many times the past days, and he would get down from his horse, hold up his arms and she would go into them and he would take her to the villa and even before their bedroom door closed, they'd be undressing each other, touching each other and perhaps this time, this time as he entered her he would say, *Alessia, my Alessia...*

"Principessa? Signore? Scusi, per favore...il principe— vostro padre—lui è qui!"

The maid who'd come after them was breathless with excitement. It was, evidently, one thing to deal with a princess— but a prince, *the* Prince Antoninni...

Alessia all but groaned. Her father was here. He would spoil her happiness. He would demand something, anything, and despite the fact that she was an adult, that she was here with her lover, she felt her heart start to plummet.

"Sweetheart?" She blinked. Nicolo stood beside the mare, arms raised, not to carry her to bed but to a confrontation with her father.

"Baby," he said softly, "come to me." And she all but tumbled into his outstretched arms.

Her safe haven, she thought in wonder. Her safe, warm haven against the world.

The visit didn't last long.

Nick wasn't very surprised. Though he had never before met the prince, he'd formed an opinion of him and it wasn't complimentary.

Antoninni's daughter was virtually living with a stranger. Yes, she was old enough to make her own choices. Still, if a man's daughter became involved with a stranger, wouldn't he want to have a conversation with that stranger, face-to-face?

Wouldn't he be interested in getting a feel for his daughter's lover?

Logically, the answer was "no." Nick couldn't recall ever meeting any of his mistress's fathers. Still, this was Italy. This was Tuscany. It was a place still caught in the cultural trappings of an earlier time.

And then there was the fact that Antoninni had gone to an acknowledged crime boss for a loan. That, the same as Alessia, he probably assumed that Nicolo, by virtue of being Cesare's son, was a thug, too.

Add it all up and that changed things, didn't it?

The simple answer was that it didn't.

Nick had expected…what? At the very worst, a demand as to what his intentions were. He had no answer to that but the question would have been valid. A father had the right to ask such a thing. At the very least, he'd figured on a thinly veiled warning that he was to treat Alessia as she deserved or there would be consequences.

Wrong on both counts, Nick thought as the prince's chauffeured limousine drove off.

The prince had greeted him with a handshake, Alessia with a cursory nod. He'd thanked Nick for the ten million euros that had been credited to his bank account, referring to it only obliquely, calling it "your investment."

Then he'd commented on a variety of things.

The weather. "I hope it will remain dry and pleasant throughout your visit, *Signore* Orsini."

The red Ferrari parked outside. "An excellent choice in automobiles, I must say. Though you must someday try a Lamborghini."

The villa. "A magnificent place, *Signore* Orsini!"

Done with small talk, he'd glanced at his watch, said he had another engagement and that he hoped to see Nick again before he left for New York. Another handshake, and Antoninni had turned to the door.

Nick, who'd stood all through the visit with his arm possessively curved around Alessia's waist, felt her stiffen.

"Father," she said. "How is Mother?"

The prince didn't bother looking back. "Your mother is fine," he said coolly.

Then he was gone.

Nick had grown up in a home in which conversations often didn't mean what they seemed to mean. Once they were alone, he turned Alessia toward him. The expression on her face damned near stopped his heart.

"Sweetheart? What is it?"

She shook her head.

"Tell me." Nick put his hand under her chin, gently raised her face so her eyes met his. "What did you mean when you asked him about your mother? Is she ill?"

Alessia hesitated. Could she tell him the truth? That her mother had lived most of the last two decades in an institution? She never talked of it to anyone, not out of shame or embarrassment but because of the way people reacted.

"Sweetheart?"

But this was not "anyone." This was Nicolo, and she took a deep, deep breath.

"My mother is in a hospital. A—a place for those who are—who are mentally ill."

Yes, this was Nicolo. Still, she prepared herself for what she thought of as the "oh, how awful" reaction, the elevated eyebrows of shock, the tsk-tsk of pity. It always made her feel not just helpless but angry.

It was the pity she could not stand.

"I'm sorry, baby," he said softly. "That must be rough."

Alessia looked at her lover. There was compassion in his

face and in his words. Not pity. Not disgust. She felt her heart lift.

"You must miss her terribly."

She nodded. "*Sì*. I do."

Nicolo drew her close in his arms. "What can I do to make things better, sweetheart? Would you like to visit her? I'll take you to wherever she is. If you let me, if she's up to it, I'd like to meet her."

That was the moment Alessia knew, without any doubt at all, that she had fallen in love, deeply in love, with the man whose arms enclosed her.

It was a two-hour drive to the sanitarium.

She couldn't believe Nicolo had offered to do it or that she'd accepted, she knew only that for the first time since her mother had been placed in the institution, walking through the doors and into the brightly lit, overly cheerful reception area didn't send tremors of anxiety through her. She never knew what to expect. Mama might be cheerful today; she might be despairing. She might not even acknowledge Alessia's presence, but no matter.

Alessia could face anything; Nicolo was with her.

As it turned out, her mother was at her best. She knew Alessia, smiled and offered Nicolo her hand when Alessia introduced him.

Nick raised her hand to his lips. "Now I know where your daughter gets her beauty, *principessa*," he said with a smile.

They didn't stay long. Her mother's private duty nurse appeared and said it was time for her nap.

"Alessia," the princess said, "you must bring your handsome fiancé to see me again."

"Oh, no, Mama. Nicolo isn't—"

"I'll see to it that she does," Nick said, squeezing Alessia's hand.

So what if Alessia's mother believed he was engaged to her daughter? Nick thought as they drove back to the villa on the hilltop. From what Alessia had said, she probably wouldn't remember meeting him. Why not let her be happy, if only for today?

Besides, the real happiness would be that of the lucky guy who could someday truly make that claim.

Nick felt a strange constriction in his throat. He looked at his lover. Then he reached for her hand and wove his fingers through hers.

Time passed with startling speed.

Nick had previously phoned his PA, arranged for her to shift meetings and appointments. He'd lucked out with the Chicago deal—the banker he was to meet with had to cancel. The same with the Beijing appointment; the Chinese associate had called to ask if they could postpone their meeting for a few weeks.

On a sunny morning, he and Alessia drove to Florence. It turned out that what he'd packed in his carry-on was only enough to take him just so far.

"Man cannot live by one suit, jeans, running shorts and a tux alone," he'd intoned solemnly that morning, to the sweet sound of her laughter, and she, female to the marrow of her bones, had happily dragged him from shop to shop while he acquired new clothes.

It was her turn, he said after lunch. Over her protests, he stepped inside a shop that bore an elegant name and instructed the beaming sales clerk to outfit his lady from head to toe.

Alone while Alessia tried on dresses and trousers and anything and everything the clerk brought out for his approval, Nick took out his cell phone and did what he'd been putting off doing. He phoned his brothers, a three-way call,

Dante and Rafe and him, because Falco was still off on his honeymoon.

"Hey," Rafe said, "where the heck are you, man?"

"In Florence. I'm, ah, I'm on business for the old man."

He could almost see his brothers roll their eyes.

"Yeah," Dante said, "we figured he finally trapped you. How's it going?"

Alessia stepped onto the round platform in front of him and twirled in a circle. The blues, greens and violets of a very short, very strapless dress swirled around her thighs.

"Nick? How's it going?"

Nick cleared his throat. "Fine. Just fine."

"What's he got you doing, anyway?"

Alessia raised her eyebrows. Nick grinned, gave the dress a thumbs-up.

"Oh, this and that," he said casually. "You know."

In New York, sitting across from each other at a desk, Dante and Rafe looked meaningfully at each other.

Uh-oh, Dante mouthed, and Rafe nodded in agreement.

"Listen, man," Rafe said, "if we can help…"

Alessia was back again, this time in a short red dress that clung to every curve.

"Nick? I said, if we can help—"

"No," Nick said quickly. "No. Thanks, but I don't need any help. Really, things are going great. I just—I might not be home for a while."

Silence. Then Dante said, "Okay, let me be blunt. This thing the old man sent you to do… Does it involve some woman?"

"No," Nick said blithely.

"Because, the thing is, if it does—"

"Whoa. Sorry, guys. The call's breaking up," Nick said, and snapped shut the phone.

He hadn't lied, he told himself as the clerk showed him a

handful of silk thongs, not at all. Because this thing, for lack of a better phrase, this thing didn't involve "some" woman.

It involved one woman. Only one. And when that one woman came out of the dressing room, cheeks rosy with indignation, and told him that the clerk said that the gentleman was paying for everything, for each and every item she'd tried on, and that if he thought she would ever permit him to do that he was crazy—

"I *am* crazy," Nick said softly, gathering her into his arms. "Crazy for you."

Alessia held Nicolo's hand as they strolled across the *Ponte Vecchio,* the beautiful antique gold heart he'd just bought at a goldsmith's shop warm in the hollow of her throat.

She was happy. No. That was too small a word for what she felt. Her heart was full of joy. Of love.

Of what she had discovered about her lover.

That he was good and kind. Generous and compassionate. That he was perfect.

Of course she'd fallen in love with him. What woman wouldn't? What woman wouldn't want to be his forever—and yes, she knew she was thinking much, much too far ahead but how could she not imagine that he might love her, too? That he might ask her to be his wife, to bear his—to bear his—

Dio mio!

She could almost feel the blood drain from her head. Her footsteps faltered; she came to a dead stop, heart thumping so loudly she thought it might leap from her breast.

No, she told herself, no! It was impossible!

She should have had her period five days ago.

And she hadn't. She hadn't! And she was always, always regular....

"Princess?"

Alessia looked up at her lover. "I—I just realized..." Stop

it, she told herself furiously. Stay calm. Somehow, she managed to smile. "I have to stop at a pharmacy."

He said he would help her find one. She said she knew of a shop nearby. When he started to walk into the place with her, she stopped him.

"I must purchase something—something personal."

He flashed that devastating grin. Teased her. Said he was old enough not to be shocked at seeing a woman buy personal things. She knew he thought she meant she had to buy tampons. *Dio, if only that were so!*

Somehow, she made herself smile in return.

"This is Italy," she said in a teasing tone. "You might not be shocked, *signore,* but others would be."

It was a lie, but he could not know it. He rolled his eyes, said okay, he'd wait outside, and then he hauled her to her toes and kissed her on her mouth and she wanted to clutch his shoulders and tell him that she was terrified.

Instead, she went into the pharmacy and bought half a dozen early pregnancy test kits.

At the villa, she told him she needed privacy to try on the things he'd bought her and choose one outfit for dinner on the terrace. He kissed her again, said she could make him a supremely happy man if she let him watch and she clucked her tongue, told him to go away and he rolled his eyes again, kissed her…

Finally, Alessia was alone.

Her hands shook as she opened the kits.

She took the tests, one after another, drinking as much water as she could between them, but the results were all the same.

She was pregnant. Pregnant! How could it have happened?

She was on the pill. She'd been on it for almost a year, ever since her gynecologist had told her it might help ease the crippling pain she suffered every month. Nicolo had asked her if she used birth control, and even though it wasn't birth control, not for her, she'd assured him that she was....

Alessia stared at herself in the mirror, hands braced for support on the bathroom sink as the world began to turn gray.

But she had not been. Not that night. She always took her pill at bedtime but she had not taken it that night; she had left the little packet in her room at her father's villa and in the excitement of making love, such incredible love with Nicolo, she had forgotten everything but him.

When had she finally taken another pill?

She sank to the cool marble floor. A sob rose in her throat. She put her hand to her lips, bit down on her thumb to muffle the sound.

Not until two days—and two nights—later, when they'd returned to Villa Antoninni so they could retrieve their things.

She had missed three of the pills. Three! How could she have been so stupid? She had messed up and now she was pregnant. Nicolo's baby was in her womb, tiny and helpless.

And unplanned. Unplanned and surely unwanted by its father...

"Alessia? Sweetheart, I've been waiting downstairs for you. Are you okay?"

Her heart pounded. She shot to her feet and swept all the EPT boxes and sticks into the wastebasket.

"Alessia. Answer me. Are you ill?"

"No," she said in a high voice that bore no resemblance to her own. "I mean, yes, *sì,* I am. I—I have my period and—and—"

"Baby. Open the door."

"No! Nicolo, *per favore,* I told you, this is a female thing."

Nick narrowed his eyes. He knew about "female things."

When you grew up in a house with two sisters, the mystery wasn't all that mysterious. His sister Isabella waltzed through her monthly cycle. Anna, on the other hand, crept around clutching a heating pad to her belly.

But he'd never heard Anna or any other woman sobbing and, dammit, Alessia had been sobbing.

Female thing or not, no way was his princess going to endure any kind of pain without him doing whatever he could to help.

"I'm coming in," he said in a tone that said he wasn't going to tolerate any nonsense.

"No, Nicolo—"

Nick swung the door open. Alessia was sitting on the edge of the marble tub, eyes red and swollen, face shiny with tears.

His heart melted.

"Ah, sweetheart…"

"Nicolo," she said brokenly, and went straight into his arms.

Nick swept her off her feet and carried her into the bedroom. He sat down in a velvet armchair, drew her head against his chest and crooned to her, rocked her gently as he held her close. Long moments went by. Her sobs eased; her tears stopped. He waited a few seconds. Then he drew back and looked at her tearstained face. This was more than pain from her period. Every instinct told him so.

"Princess." Gently, he smoothed her hair back from her damp cheeks. "What is it?"

Alessia looked at Nicolo. His eyes were filled with concern. His arms were a bulwark against the woes of the world. He was a good, kind man. He had not signed on for this.

She could lie to him. Tell him she wept because her period was agony. Tell him almost anything. He would believe her, if she told the lie well enough.

"Alessia. Talk to me." He took her hands, brought them to his lips. "Tell me why you're crying."

It was just as the poets said. Time did stand still. She took a steadying breath.

"Nicolo," she whispered, "Nicolo—I am pregnant."

CHAPTER TWELVE

PREGNANT.

The word echoed in Nick's head. Alessia was pregnant.

He felt a sheen of cold sweat break out on his forehead. If there was one word a man never wanted to hear from a woman with whom he was having an affair, that was it.

Over the years, he'd grown accustomed to hearing women say things that were upsetting. Like *I love you*. Like *I know you said you weren't interested in a serious relationship but...* And on one memorable occasion, *But what will my friends say if we break up?*

Women said those things in different ways, never mind that he always made it clear, right up front, he wasn't looking for forever. For all he knew, "forever" didn't really exist.

So, yes, he'd heard women say a lot of things but he'd never had one claim she was...

"Pregnant?" The word came out sounding rusty. Nick cleared his throat. "Are you certain?"

"*Sì*."

"How do you know?"

"I took a test. Many tests." Her hands, still enclosed by his, were trembling. "That was what I was doing in the bathroom."

"Have you missed your period?"

She blushed. And wasn't that ridiculous? he thought, as

coldness seeped into his blood. Her body had no secrets from him, not anymore, and she was telling him she was knocked up…but asking her about her menstrual cycle made her blush.

"I should have had it last week. I—I did not realize that it had not—"

Carefully, he let go of her hands. "You said you were on the pill."

"I was. I am." Her eyes met his. "But I did not have my pills with me that first night, Nicolo, and we made—we made love so many times before we went back to my father's villa and I collected my things…"

"So, you weren't on the pill. Not really, even though you said you were."

She winced. Okay. He knew the question was coldly phrased, maybe even unfairly phrased but, dammit, she had said—

Nick eased Alessia off his lap, got to his feet and paced across the room before swinging around to face her.

"How could this have happened?"

She felt everything within her collapse. She knew his real question was, how could she have let this happen? It didn't surprise her. In a world that talked about the equality of women, nothing was equal when it came to sex. She had always known that. At university, men who had a lot of lovers were sexy; women who took equal numbers of men were sluts.

As for getting pregnant outside of wedlock… Perhaps it was fine for Hollywood movie stars but it was far from fine in her world. Getting pregnant when you shouldn't was invariably the woman's fault, just as it was the woman's responsibility to deal with.

Nicolo had not said any of those things. He didn't have to. The way he felt was in his tone, his face, the very tension radiating from him.

"I told you," she said, trying to stay calm. "I forgot—"

"Are you sure," he said, his tone as brutal as it was flat, "are you absolutely sure I'm the man who made you pregnant?"

She had expected the question. Still, she hated him for asking it. She wanted to scream. To hurl herself at him and beat her fists against his chest.

How could he even think he was not the man whose seed had joined with her egg?

And yet—and yet, she thought on a dizzying rush of despair, she knew how he could think it.

She had gone into his arms after knowing him for a couple of hours, slept with him a day later. She had given herself to him fully, nothing held back. She had done things with him she had never imagined she would ever do.

But he could know nothing of that.

She knew he'd had many women; a man like him would. He moved in a world where people tumbled into bed casually, without regrets. She didn't—or maybe it was more truthful to say such things *did* happen in her world.

But not to her.

He couldn't possibly know that her friends teased her about her pathetic sex life. He couldn't know she hadn't been with a man in almost four years. So, no, she couldn't blame him for asking if the life growing within her womb was his.

She could blame only herself for being foolish enough to have thought, even fleetingly, that what they'd found was not just sex but love.

"I asked you a question. Are you sure I'm the man who—"

Alessia's despair gave way to anger. It was a safer emotion. How dare he accuse her of lying about such a thing or, at the very least, of having gone from someone else's arms to his?

"No," she said coldly, "no, I'm not. It might have been the butcher. Or the man from the cleaning service. And then there's the concierge at my apartment building in Rome and the headwaiter at a restaurant where I had dinner last week, and if not him, the drummer from a punk rock band whose publicity I have handled or—"

Nicolo covered the distance between them in four strides and grasped her by the shoulders.

"You think this is funny?"

"I think I was stupid even to tell you about this." Her eyes flashed fire. "Forget that I said anything, *signore*. This is not your problem, it is mine."

"Hey. I never said—"

"I am accustomed to taking care of myself. I do not require your help or anyone else's." Angrily, she shrugged free of his hands. "I would not have told you anything if you had not intruded on my privacy."

His dark eyebrows rose. "Excuse me?"

"The bathroom door was closed. I asked you not to open it but you did. And you found me at the worst possible moment. I was—I was surprised by what I had just learned." It was the understatement of the century, but he didn't have to know that. Alessia lifted her chin. "So, if you had not intruded—"

Nick cursed. His hands bit into her flesh as he hoisted her to her toes.

"That's rubbish and you damned well know it!" he said, his voice rough with anger. "You're pregnant. I got you that way. That makes this my problem as much as yours."

His words should have warmed her. They didn't. The pregnancy was, indeed, a problem—but she didn't like hearing him call it that. Stupid, she knew, but that was how she felt. Her mother had been her father's "problem" all his life, or so he claimed. There wasn't a way in the world she was going to be seen as a "problem" by Nicolo Orsini or any other man.

"Let go of me," she said with icy calm.

"Don't talk to me about intruding on your privacy, not when

that so-called 'privacy' involves something that's bound to change both our lives forever."

"I do not take orders from you, Mr. Orsini!"

Sweet Mary, Nick thought, what kind of nonsense was this?

First, she dropped a bomb of nuclear proportions in his lap. Then she all but told him what he could do with his help. Okay, maybe he'd left something out, the part where he'd demanded to know how in hell this could have happened and was she sure the kid was his—if you could call a two-week-old clump of cells a kid—but, dammit, what man wouldn't ask?

The lady had more attitude than any woman he'd ever known. It made him want to shake some sense into her...or maybe kiss some sense into her. One or the other and it didn't much matter which because sense was what she needed.

Did she think he'd walk away from what was as much his responsibility as hers? Yes, she'd said she was on the pill. So what? He was always a responsible lover. He should have used a condom. He always did.

Except with her.

Hell.

Nick let go of Alessia, swung around and took a long breath. Who was he kidding? Not taking her that night would have been impossible. He would have died unless he could have undressed her, kissed her, buried himself deep inside her...

Merda!

Sex was the last thing he should be thinking about right now. He'd got himself into a mess. Now, he had to find a way out and yeah, he had to find a way out of it for her, too. What was that old saying? It took two to tango.

And it sure took two to make a baby.

Well, then. It took two to deal with whatever came next. She might not like it, might consider his input another intrusion, for God's sake, but she'd have to accept it. He wasn't going to let her do otherwise.

"Okay," he said, doing his best to sound calm. "Okay, what we need to do is discuss this calmly. Very calmly, because—"

He turned toward her and his heart damned near stopped.

For all that imperious air, that "do not touch me" coldness he'd seen in her when they'd first met, what he saw now was the woman he'd come to—to care about. Care about? Even now, his muscles taut, his mind racing like a hamster on a wheel...even now, he wanted her, wanted her as he had never in his life imagined wanting a woman.

Her expression was defiant but her eyes were filled with fear. She was trembling even though the room was warm and he thought of how easily he could stop those tremors, stay her tears by taking her in his arms and kissing her, kissing her until she clung to him.

A groan of despair caught in his throat as he walked past her, out the door and out of the villa.

Hands in his pockets, head down, Nick climbed the hill behind the house. The sun was setting; shadows had accumulated in the olive grove, turning the trees into otherworldly creatures with long, lean bodies and spindly arms. The hoot of an owl added to the seeming strangeness of the landscape and to the confusion in his soul.

No way could he go on blaming this on Alessia. He was as responsible as she, maybe even more. He'd seen to it that she'd forgotten everything the night he'd brought her here, not just the birth control pills but the world outside.

He was the one who'd planned everything.

Planned? Nick barked out a laugh.

Some planner he'd turned out to be. A house. A bed. His

stupid brain hadn't gone beyond the necessities. And a supply of condoms should have been part of those necessities. He'd known that since he was, what, thirteen, sitting through the embarrassment of a sex-ed class, then snickering over what it all meant a couple of hours later with his brothers.

He kicked at a small stone, watched it tumble downhill.

The simple truth was that sex had been the only thing on his mind. Having Alessia. Making love with her. Making her his, as if sleeping with a woman marked her as a man's property.

A man didn't make a woman "his" unless he married her. And marriage was a million light-years away.

You could double those light-years when it came to having kids. Kids were not part of the plan. The best he'd concede was that maybe someday he'd want them, but for now...

No kids.

They weren't in Alessia's plans, either. Not from what he'd seen when he'd opened that bathroom door. Her tears. Her disbelief. No, clearly she wasn't in the market for motherhood.

She was young. Beautiful. So damned beautiful, with the world waiting for her to explore it.

Calmer now, he knew that whatever she decided to do— terminate the pregnancy, go through with it and keep the baby, go through with it and give the baby up for adoption—her world would never be the same again.

And it was his fault.

Nick stopped walking, tucked his hands in his pockets and gazed up at the sky. Night was coming on quickly. A handful of stars flamed against the dark blue canopy; a fat yellow moon was rising on the horizon.

Amazing.

The world changed but life went on. And, yes, his world had changed. No matter what choice Alessia made, he'd always know he'd been the reason she'd had to make that choice. He'd always know that he'd created a life that had ended before it began. Or that strangers were raising a kid with his genes, his DNA. And even if Alessia decided to keep the child, it would not have a father.

Yes, of course, he'd acknowledge the kid and support it. Maybe he'd even visit. Or maybe not. Maybe she wouldn't want his daughter to have only sporadic contact with the man who was her father in only the most scientific terms. His son or his daughter, yes, but somehow it was easier to picture a little girl with Alessia's features, her golden hair, her blue eyes...

What was that?

A car was coming up the long drive that led to the villa. A car, at this time of evening? Why should a car...

It was a taxi. It had to be. Who but a cabby would stop outside the house and blast his horn like that? It was the loud, impolite, "I'm here—where are you?" language of cab drivers everywhere.

A taxi.

Nick cursed and raced for the villa. "Dammit," he said as he ran, "dammit to hell, Alessia..."

The front door opened just as he reached it. And yeah, there she was, overnight bag in hand.

She was leaving him. *Leaving him!* How dare she? Did she really think she could take a step like that without first asking him if he'd let her go?

He stood at the foot of the steps, fists planted on his hips, eyes hot with anger.

"Where in hell do you think you're going?"

Alessia narrowed her eyes, gave him the same sort of princess-to-peasant look she had at the airport a million years ago.

"Get out of my way, please."

Please? He snorted. The "please" might as well have been a four-letter word.

"*Signore* Orsini. I asked you to—"

The taxi horn blasted. Nick shot the cabby a furious look, then turned back to Alessia.

"You are not to move," he growled.

She laughed. Laughed, damn her, and came down the steps. He caught her arm, leaned down, his face an inch from hers.

"I'm warning you, princess. Do not take another step."

"Who are you to give me orders?"

"I'll tell you exactly who I am. I am Nicolo Orsini. And unless you want to find out what that means, you will not, under any circumstances, move from this spot. *Capisce?*"

"How dare you give me orders? I am a princess. I am descended from kings. And you—you—"

Nick kissed her. Hard. Deep. He forced her head back and she gasped and struck him with her free hand and he caught that hand, brought it behind her back and went on kissing her until she moaned into his mouth and her lips parted to the possessive thrust of his tongue.

Then he let her go.

She stood motionless as he trotted down the steps, dug out his wallet and stuffed a handful of bills into the cabby's extended hand. The taxi roared away. Nick stood still for a couple of seconds before he returned to confront Alessia.

"Where," he said grimly, "did you think you were going?"

"It's none of your—"

"You tell me you're having my baby. Then you turn tail and run."

She drew herself up. "What is this 'turning tail' thing?"

"It means you were afraid to stay and face me."

"I am not afraid of you. I was—I was simply going away."

Nick folded his arms. "I'll ask you again. Where were you going?"

Where, indeed? Alessia swallowed hard.

"Away."

"You're going to have to do better than that."

"You do not have the right to—"

Nick clasped her shoulders again, his touch harsh.

"I have every right! Where were you going? What are your plans?" His mouth twisted. "Dammit, that's my child you're carrying."

Her eyes flashed with bitterness. "Are you sure?"

Okay. He deserved that. Nick took a deep breath.

"Just give me a straight answer. What are you going to do about the baby?" His eyes met hers; he could feel his anger draining away. "Listen. This isn't easy for me, either. Talk to me. Tell me what you're thinking, what you want to do."

She went on glaring at him. Then, suddenly, the fight seemed to go out of her and she slumped in his hands.

"I don't—I don't know." She looked up at him, eyes pleading for understanding. "Do you think I can decide something like this in an hour? In a day? My life has changed, Nicolo. Whatever I do, nothing will ever be the same again."

It was exactly what he'd been thinking in the olive grove. Everything had changed for him, for her. Forever. And, just that quickly, his anger was gone.

"Come here," he said softly, gathering her to him. She fought him, but only for a second. Then she gave a little hiccup of a sob. His arms closed tightly around her; she laid her head against his chest.

"You're right," he said, one big hand gently stroking her hair. "Nothing will ever be the same again for either of us. We have a decision to make, princess, maybe the most important decision of our lives."

Alessia shut her eyes. Nicolo's touch was so soothing. She longed to wind her arms around his neck, let herself lean into him, let his strength seep into her.

She didn't. She couldn't. This was a time for rational thought, not for dreams. And letting herself fall in love with this man had been a dream.

He was not hers. He never would be. But it was a comfort to know she had not been wrong about him. He was a good man. A kind man. That he had refused to let her leave, that he spoke of the decision that came next as having to be made by them both, even that he was holding her now with such tenderness, proved it.

But it didn't change the fact that their relationship was over. What else could it be?

"Alessia. Come inside. We'll sit down, have some coffee, talk about this." He tipped her face to his. "We can work this through, sweetheart. You'll see."

She let him hold her hand and lead her into the villa, take her straight through it to the terrace at the back and out into the warm night. How fitting that they should come outside to discuss what would happen next. She'd sat outdoors on a warm Tuscan evening a few short weeks ago with her father. It was where she had first heard the name Orsini.

Who could have imagined that Nicolo Orsini would become her lover? Who could have imagined his child would lie sleeping in her womb?

Nicolo led her to a love seat, drew her down next to him, held her hands so that they faced each other.

"So," he said softly.

She couldn't help offering a little smile.

"So," she said.

Nicolo freed one of his hands, used it to tuck a strand of hair behind her ear.

"Tell me what you're thinking. About what you want to do next."

She took a deep breath. "There are public clinics. Private doctors. Abortion is legal in my country."

"But?"

"But, it is not a good choice for me."

"You want to have the baby."

She nodded.

"And then what?"

Alessia caught her bottom lip between her teeth. This part wasn't as clear yet. She was a career woman. Was it right to bring a child into a life like hers? To raise it without a father? Or was it better to give it up for adoption?

There were plenty of couples who were eager for a child—but could she do that without wondering about her baby for the rest of her life? Was he happy? Was he well? And yes, already, she thought of the baby inside her as "he," a little boy with Nicolo's features. His dark hair. His beautiful eyes.

"And then what?" Nicolo said again, his voice a low rumble. "After the baby's born…what do you want to do with her?"

"With him," she said, without thinking.

Nicolo smiled. "With him. What next, princess?"

Alessia took a deep breath. The answer had been there all along. She just hadn't seen it clearly until now.

"I'll keep my baby."

"Good," Nicolo said, gathering her against him. "That's what I hoped you'd say."

Ah. Now his questions made sense. He was going to offer to support the child. She didn't want that. A clean break was best. She would work hard, earn enough money to give her baby everything he needed.…

"It's good," he said, "because that's what I want, too." He

cupped her shoulders, held her at arm's length and looked into her eyes. "Alessia. Will you marry me?"

Her mouth dropped open. It made Nick want to laugh. Or kiss her and that, he decided, was the far better choice. Slowly, he bent to her, brought his lips to hers.

"Marry me, princess," he whispered. "And we'll raise our baby together."

Alessia stared at him. "Marry you? No. It's a wonderful gesture, Nicolo, but—"

"We owe this child more than a gesture."

"I know. I mean, I understand that. But marriage…"

"Is it such a horrible thought? Marrying me? Becoming Mrs. Nicolo Orsini?"

Horrible? She fought to keep from saying the words singing in her blood, that she loved him, adored him, that spending her life with him would be the dream she'd been afraid to dream.

"Princess?"

He was waiting for her answer. She wanted to say "yes," but could she marry a man who didn't love her, no matter how noble the reason?

"What?" he said. "What are you thinking?"

Alessia touched the tip of her tongue to her dry lips.

"I'm thinking…I'm thinking, what about love?"

Nick captured Alessia's lips with his. He kissed her again and again and when he raised his head, her eyes were glazed, her lips rosy and swollen.

"What about it?" he said gruffly.

What, indeed? she thought.

And then he began undressing her and she stopped thinking about anything but him.

CHAPTER THIRTEEN

THEY would have a civil ceremony.

It was the fastest way to marry. Even so, Alessia said, they would have to wait two weeks.

"Tomorrow," Nick said the next morning, as they lay in their rumpled bed.

Alessia laughed. "Impossible."

"Because?"

"Because, this is *Italia*. There are laws to obey. Are there not laws in America?"

"We're not in America," he said, brushing his lips over hers. "We're in *Italia,* just as you said. And I am an impatient man."

"Well, *signore impaziente,* there is nothing you can do about it. The law is the law."

"And you know the law, princess?"

"I do," she said archly.

She was in public relations. She had made marriage arrangements for others. Nicolo, as an American citizen, could marry simply by filing the necessary papers. But it was different for an Italian national. For her. Banns would have to be posted for two Sundays prior to the day of the ceremony.

Nick rolled her beneath him.

"We'll see about that," he said.

"Nicolo. There is nothing to see. The law is the law."

She sounded like a schoolteacher correcting a recalcitrant pupil. It made him smile. He loved her all-knowing tone, loved the slightly exasperated look on her face. He loved—he loved…

"What are you thinking?" Alessia said softly.

"Let me show you," he said huskily, and he ended all further discussion the best possible way, with kisses, with his mouth on her breasts, with his body hard and demanding inside hers.

As he had done to find their villa, Nick made a couple of phone calls.

In midafternoon, a messenger came to the door with a manila envelope. Nick opened it, checked the contents and grinned.

"What?" Alessia said.

His grin widened. "Time to shop for a wedding dress, princess."

Her breath caught. "You mean…" She nodded at the open envelope and the papers spilling out of it. "Is that about the banns?"

"What banns?" Nicolo said and kissed her.

He took her into the heart of Florence, to a boutique he'd noticed one evening as they'd strolled the street after dinner at a small café.

"We want a dress," he told the clerk.

The woman looked from Nick to Alessia, then at him again. "Is it for a special occasion?"

"Very special," Nick said solemnly. His arm tightened around Alessia's waist. "We're getting married tomorrow."

Nick smiled. Alessia blushed. The clerk grinned. An hour later, they left the shop with a pale pink silk dress and matching jacket, a tiny gold purse and gold stilettos.

It was dusk, and the temperature had dropped. Perhaps that was why Alessia shuddered.

"Cold, sweetheart?"

She nodded and Nicolo drew her closer as they made their way to the Ferrari but the truth was, Alessia wasn't really cold. She'd shuddered because a thought had crept into her mind. Things were moving so fast. Was Nicolo hurrying the arrangements because he didn't want to give her time her to change her mind? Or was it because he didn't want to give *himself* time to change *his* mind?

She shuddered again, because she didn't want to think about it.

Nick knew he was rushing things, but he had a good reason.

Any delay and his family might somehow learn what was happening. The Orsinis, especially his brothers, were good at uncovering secrets. And if they uncovered this one, the wedding would become a circus.

His mother and his sisters would shriek with female delight and go straight into action. He'd seen it happen with Rafe, Dante and Falco. The church. The music. The reception. The cake. The menu. The flowers. The gowns. The tuxes.

And his brothers. They'd go straight for the jugular. *You know her two weeks? What, did you knock her up?* Well, yeah, he had. But as well-meaning as the question would be, he'd have to answer with his fists because this was Alessia and whether she was pregnant or not wasn't their concern. She was going to be his wife, and his decision wasn't up for a vote.

Besides, the more he thought about it, the more certain he felt that he was doing the right thing. His baby—the baby he and Alessia had created—deserved a father.

And the woman he was marrying was a joy. She was beautiful. Bright. She could make him laugh. She could make him feel a tenderness he'd never known he possessed. The marriage was sudden, yes. But it would work out. It would be successful.

In fact, after the initial shock of trying to visualize himself as a married man, the idea had become, well, it had become kind of pleasant. He liked the idea of greeting the day with Alessia in his arms and ending it the same way.

Marriages had been built on less.

Still, this one needed a little time, a little space. Bottom line? The wedding first, followed by a honeymoon. After that, he'd contact his brothers, break the news, ask them to tell his mother and sisters. When all that was done, he'd take Alessia to New York to meet his family.

Right now, the only person he had to inform was her father. The prince probably knew everyone in Florence; he'd surely hear the news and Nick wanted it to come from him, not secondhand.

He disliked Antoninni. He'd run a centuries-old vineyard to the point of ruin. Far worse, he'd left his daughter alone to deal with Cesare Orsini, and he seemed to have little affection for her.

But he was Alessia's father.

That night, while she prepared for bed, Nick phoned him, reached his voice mail and left a brief message.

"This is Nicolo Orsini. Your daughter has done me the honor of agreeing to become my wife. The wedding is to-morrow, ten in the morning, in the *Sala Rossa* of the *Palazzo Vecchio*. You are, of course, welcome to attend."

It was not a warm message but it was the right one.

And Nick, in fact all the Orsini brothers, had always been big on doing that which was right.

The next day dawned bright and sunny.

A few minutes before ten, Alessia clung tightly to Nicolo's hand as they walked into the palazzo.

Nicolo had reassured her as she lay in his arms. "This will be a good marriage," he'd said softly.

She wanted to believe him, but she was marrying him for love—and he was marrying her only because he was a responsible, decent man.

He was the opposite of her father.... And suddenly, she realized she had no idea if her father had kept the promise he'd made about her mother's care. Had he? Was Mama still safely in the sanitarium she had come to think of as home?

The mayor, who would perform the ceremony, was strolling toward them with her father a few steps behind. Alessia turned to Nicolo, put her hand lightly on his arm.

"The mayor will surely want to speak with you," she said quickly. "While he does that, I must talk to my father."

Nicolo put his hand over hers. "Can it wait until after the ceremony, sweetheart?"

Her heart felt as if it were going to overflow at the tenderness in his voice.

"This is important, Nicolo. I only need a moment, *sì?*"

Her bridegroom tipped her face to his and brushed his lips over hers.

"You don't need my permission, princess. A last private word between father and daughter? Sure. Go ahead." He smiled. "Just remember to get back here in time to become my wife."

She smiled, rose on her toes to kiss his cheek. Then she hurried to the prince and motioned toward an alcove.

The prince's smile was sly.

"Congratulations, daughter. What a coup! The wife of an Orsini. *Eccellente!*"

Alessia ignored the comment. "Tell me about my mother," she said in a low voice.

"Tell you what? She is fine."

"Have you kept her at the sanitarium, as you promised? We

had an agreement. I would be your hostess, take your place entertaining Cesare Orsini, and you—"

"And I would repay you for your actions." Antoninni smiled. "And what a hostess you were, Alessia!" He chuckled. "I knew you would do far better with the man than I ever could!"

"You mean, you always intended to have me step in?"

"Of course. Once Orsini told me he would send his son instead of coming to Florence himself…" The prince laughed softly. "Do not look so shocked, Alessia. You did a fine job. You not only secured my loan, you doubled it."

"It was Nicolo, not me. He is the one who decided to give you ten million euros."

"Ten million euros, and now I am to have one of New York's wealthiest, most powerful men as my son-in-law." Antoninni arched one eyebrow. "Are you carrying his child? Is that the reason for this swift marriage?"

"None of that concerns you," Alessia said sharply. "Our understanding was about my mother. Have you kept your word?"

A dramatic sigh. "I will."

Would he? Alessia doubted it. He'd pay for her mother's care for a while. Then he'd stop. She did a quick mental calculation of what it cost to care for her mother, what it might cost over the next years, and then she looked her father in the eye.

"You will deposit three million euros to my account immediately."

"Three mill— You joke, daughter. That is too much, even for your role in securing ten million euros, marriage to an Orsini and becoming pregnant with his—"

"Go on," Nicolo said coldly. "Let's hear the rest."

Alessia and her father spun around. Her father paled.

"*Signore* Orsini! I did not see you standing—"

"No. Obviously, you did not."

Alessia blanched. Nicolo had overheard…and, all at once, she was glad that he had. Why hadn't she shared her concerns with her lover sooner? There was nothing she couldn't tell him, not even when it was humiliating. Her father was a cold, unfeeling man; Nicolo was just the opposite. She could trust him to see to it that her father did as he had promised.

She could trust him with everything, for the rest of her life.

"Nicolo." She smiled tremulously. "I am glad you overheard our conversation. I should have told you that my father and I had an agreement—"

"I heard."

His voice was frigid, his eyes black as coal. He looked cruel and hard and dangerous, and she couldn't understand the reason…. Until, with terrible suddenness, she realized how easily he might have misconstrued her father's words, and hers.

"No! Oh, no, you don't understand—"

She gasped as his hand closed painfully around her wrist.

"I understand everything, *principessa*." His gaze dropped to her belly, then rose to her face. "Especially your touching story about being on the pill."

Her face went white. "You're wrong! I swear it, you are—"

"Say goodbye to Daddy, sweetheart. You won't be seeing him for a long time."

"Nicolo, Nicolo, *per favore*—"

"Don't look so stricken, baby." Nick's mouth twisted. "You still won the prize. I'm going to marry you. Hell, you're carrying my child. If you think I'd leave him to the tender mercies of you and Papa, you can think again."

"Nicolo." Alessia's voice trembled. "I know what you think you heard, but—"

"Get out of my sight," Nick told Antoninni. The prince, eyes wide with shock, took a step back. "If I ever see you again, so help me, I'll do what your kind has feared for the past six hundred years and use you to wipe the floor."

Antoninni scurried away like a rat. Alessia reached out her hand to Nicolo. She had never seen him like this, so furious, so vengeful, so cold. It terrified her.

"Nicolo, please, listen to—"

"I'm done listening, princess. We're here so you can finalize the deal you made with Daddy by becoming my wife."

"No! I never made such a deal!"

"Sorry. I should have said, we're here so you can improve the deal by becoming my wife."

"Oh, *Dio,* oh, God, please—"

"I'll pull the loan money," Nick said softly. "And then I'll use every ounce of that Orsini power you find so disgusting and I promise, I'll take my child away from you. What happens to you then, *principessa?*"

Alessia stared at him in horror. A muscle ticked in his jaw. He waited. Then, he held out his hand. Slowly, she put hers into it and he led her across the room, to where the mayor was waiting.

"No," Alessia said in a desperate whisper, "no, not like this!"

"Exactly like this," Nick said.

Five minutes later, they were man and wife.

He had planned to surprise his bride.

A honeymoon in Venice, at the Gritti Palace. Five days in a suite the concierge had assured him was as romantic as a newly married couple could wish, then a two-day stop in Milan so he could buy his bride a new wardrobe, and, finally a flight to New York in a chartered plane, a bottle of rare Krug Brut Multi-Vintage Rosé waiting in a silver bucket in the craft's private bedroom, the room itself filled with orchids and roses.

There would be none of that now.

Nick made quick adjustments to his plans. A stop at the villa outside Florence to pick up his things. A phone call to the charter service so he could change the arrangements he'd made, a drive to the airport where a plane awaited them without champagne or flowers.

But it had a private bedroom, he thought coldly as he kept a hard hand on his wife's elbow and climbed the steps into the cabin, because no way was he giving up the one thing Alessia Antoninni Orsini could provide him…until, of course, she delivered his child.

After that, after his son or daughter was born, he'd decide if he wanted his wife in his bed anymore or if her usefulness to him was at an end.

"Nicolo," Alessia said now, as the door to the plane slid shut behind them, "Nicolo, if you would only listen—"

It was what she'd been saying ever since he'd stumbled into what he'd stupidly assumed was a last conversation between a father before he gave his daughter into the care of the man who was now her husband. And, as he had done each time she'd asked him to listen, Nick ignored her.

Listen to what? More lies? He'd heard enough from that soft, sweet-tasting mouth to last a lifetime.

That she was sexually inexperienced.

That she had "forgotten" to take her birth control pills.

That he was her lover. Of it all, those two whispered words, *mio amante,* infuriated him the most. He'd known she hadn't meant it, that she'd said it in a haze of sexual heat. Hell, who cared what she'd called him? Still, honesty demanded he admit the truth to himself. All he was to her, all he'd ever been, was a ticket to a fat bank account.

He'd let her make a fool of him, he thought grimly as he drew her down next to him in a leather seat. He hated himself for having let even a part of his heart feel the impact of her sighs, her whispers, her caresses.

Sex, Nicolo thought coldly. That was all it had been. For him. For her. And he had every intention of making the most of it.

The plane's jet engines came to life. The aircraft moved slowly forward. And his lying, deceitful wife leaned toward him. "Nicolo," she said in a frantic whisper, "please…"

Nick shot to his feet, grasped her wrist and brought her up beside him. He walked purposefully toward the rear of the cabin, slid open the bedroom door and pushed her inside.

Then he shut the door and locked it.

"Take off your clothes," he growled.

She stared at him. Her eyes glittered, pools of darkest blue in her pale face.

"No. Nicolo—"

"Take them off. Or I'll do it for you."

Tears spilled down her cheeks. "You are not this kind of man," she whispered. "You are good. You are kind. You are—"

"I am Nick Orsini." His hands went to his jacket. Undid the buttons. He shrugged it off, unbuttoned his shirt, shrugged that off, too. "As far as you're concerned, I am exactly the man you expected me to be. I see what I want and I take it." A cruel smile twisted across his lips. "We suit each other, *principessa*. A man who takes what he wants. A woman who does the same."

He closed the distance between them, put his hand in the V of the pale pink silk dress that, only hours before, he had thought the most perfect thing a bride could wear. One hard tug, one gasp from her, and the dress tore and fell to her feet.

"Oh, God," she said, weeping, "Nicolo, don't—"

"I told you," he said grimly. "The name is Nick."

And he swept his wife into his arms and took her to bed.

He'd meant to take her coldly.

Pin her arms above her head if she fought him. Thrust his knee between her thighs. Take her hard, ride her hard, get himself off without giving a damn if she was ready or not.

Except, she didn't fight him.

She lay still, her face turned away from him. And she wept. Silently. Agonizingly. Her tears soaked the linen pillowcase; her teeth caught and held her bottom lip.

All his rage drained away. In its place was despair so terrible, so deep, that Nick felt his throat constrict.

He got to his feet. Put on his shirt. Tossed his jacket on a chair. She could use it to hide what he had done to her dress.

Then he walked out of the cabin, went to the front of the plane and sank into a seat.

And knew that he had touched his wife, his achingly beautiful, heartbreakingly dishonest wife, for the very last time.

CHAPTER FOURTEEN

THE marriage had been a mistake.

Nick sat in his leather swivel chair, his back to a massive oak desk, staring out his office windows at the narrow streets of Soho four stories below. He'd endured another day of meetings and phone calls just as he'd done for the past couple of weeks by deliberately blanking his mind to anything but business.

Now, in the waning hours of the long day, he had the one thing he didn't want.

Time to think.

It was the same every day. Work kept him busy. Busier than ever. He'd taken on meetings and calls that should have been his brothers' responsibilities. They were happy to let him do it. Things were happening in their lives. Rafe and Chiara were eagerly preparing for the arrival of their first child. Dante and Gabriella had their hands full with their cute toddler. Falco and Elle were looking for a weekend home in Connecticut.

"You sure you don't mind?" they'd say, when he offered to take a meeting in their place.

"Hey," he'd say lightly, "what are brothers for?" Or he'd flash a smile and say he'd get even some day and payback would be hell.

What he didn't say, had not said, had no intention of saying, was that he was as married as they were. His marriage, his wife, the child she carried...

Secrets, known only to him.

There was no way he could keep secrets like those from his family forever.

"Dammit," he said wearily.

Nick turned toward his desk, propped his elbows on its paper-strewn surface and put his face in his hands.

He wasn't as married as his brothers. He knew damned well that neither Rafe or Dante or Falco went home to silence at the end of the day, or to a meal eaten alone, or that any of them slept alone as he did, while his wife slept in a bedroom at the end of the hall. And he'd have bet everything that he was the only one who cursed himself a dozen times a day for having been used and trapped into marriage because he'd let himself be played for a fool.

Nick sat back and dragged air deep into his lungs.

Most of all, he was damned sure that none of his brothers lay awake at night, staring into the darkness and fighting the almost overpowering need to say to hell with all this, go to his wife's room, fling open the door or break the freaking thing down if he had to, strip away the duvet that covered her and take her again and again even if she begged him not to do it, take her mercilessly until he'd worked her out of his system forever.

Or until she sobbed his name, wound her arms around his neck and told him that he was her lover, that he was more than that, that he was her love....

"*Merda!*"

Nick shot to his feet, jammed his hands into his pockets and paced the big room.

What he needed was sex. Not with his wife. Sex with a woman who would respond to him with honesty rather than calculated pretense.

As for his unborn child... He loved that small life already, from the second he'd seen the sonogram of it, lying safely cocooned within his wife's womb.

A week after they'd reached New York, he'd broken the silence between them to announce that he'd made an appointment for her with an ob-gyn recommended to him by his personal physician. Normally, he'd have asked one of his sisters-in-law to suggest a doctor but considering that none of them knew he even had a wife, much less a pregnant one, that had been out of the question.

He'd expected Alessia to argue but she hadn't. Despite everything he knew her to be, he had to admit she seemed to have maternal instincts. She'd given up wine, ate carefully and, a couple of times, he'd seen her with one hand lying lightly over her belly.

Like the day he'd taken her for her ob-gyn appointment.

He'd stood by dutifully while she was examined, his eyes straight ahead, but his air of removal had vanished when the ultrasound technician appeared.

"Let's see what we can see," the woman had said cheerfully, and Nick's gaze had been inexorably drawn to his wife, lying on the examining table, eyes wide, her left hand forming what could only have been a protective cover over her belly.

"Move your hand, please," the tech had said and, without thinking, Nick had reached for Alessia's hand and clutched it in his.

And there it was. A black speck that was their baby.

"Excellent picture," the tech had said happily, pointing out features only she could see, and Nick had squeezed his wife's hand and she had squeezed his, and then their eyes had met and he had remembered everything, how she had lied to him with her hands, her mouth, her body...

"Hell," he growled.

Enough was enough. It was time to get his life back. See

a lawyer. Discuss his choices. Legal separation. Divorce. The ways in which they would affect his demand for custody when his child was born because, without question, he would demand it.

He would not permit his son or daughter to be raised five thousand miles away by a woman with the same duplicitous morals of her fifteenth-century ancestors. She was not fit to be a mother. What he saw now…what he *thought* he saw now— her changed diet, the hand over the belly, even the tears he'd thought had glittered in her eyes during that sonogram—

Lies, all of it. But then, lies were her specialty.

Okay. He needed to make an appointment with an attorney. Not the ones Orsini Brothers retained, not until he told his brothers about Alessia, and then he'd have to let the entire clan in on his secret and he could imagine what a mess that was bound to—

His intercom light blinked. His PA was calling. Never mind. Whatever she wanted could wait. But the light kept blinking and finally Nick cursed and reached for the phone. Even as he did, the door burst open and his sisters, Anna and Isabella, marched into the room.

Nick forced a smile.

"Hey, girls. I'm glad to see you, but it's polite to wait until—"

"We are not 'girls,'" Izzy said, in a tone that dropped the temperature fifty degrees. "We are women."

"Yeah. Right. I only meant—"

"But then, what do you know about women?" Anna said, eyes cold as ice.

"Listen," Nick said, "whatever this is, I'm not—"

"What in the bloody, holy hell do you mean by getting married and then hiding the marriage and your wife from the rest of us?"

Nick blanched. He looked past his sisters, saw his PA just behind them, saw her mouth fall open.

Say something, he thought furiously. But his mind was blank.

Instead, he strode past both Anna and Izzy. "No calls," he barked, ushering his PA out the door and slamming it after her.

"Nick," Izzy said, "we want an answer."

Izzy, normally as sweet and gentle as the flowers she loved to nurture, looked as if she wanted to slug him. Anna was breathing fire as only she could. He had a quick flash to what she'd been like as a teenager, how she'd dyed her pale blond hair black, painted her nails black, dressed in black, wore black lipstick, how she'd stood up to her brothers' teasing, their mother's hand-wringing and, most impressively, their father's fury...

"Are you deaf?" she snapped. "We were just at your place. We saw her. And we want to know—"

"What were you doing," Nick demanded, narrowing his eyes, "snooping around in my place?"

"Oh, that's perfect!" Izzy laughed with disdain. "He's going to try and lay the blame on us—but what else can you expect from a man?"

"Listen here, you two—"

"No," Anna said, tossing her blond hair out of her eyes and pointing an accusatory finger at his chest, "*you* listen! You are married. You have a wife. And you're expecting a baby."

Nick glared back. Then he let out a groan, went behind his desk and sank into his swivel chair.

"Yes."

His sisters looked at each other. Anna snorted. Izzy shook her head.

"And when," she said, "when, exactly, were you going to let the rest of the world know?"

Nick gave a strangled laugh. "I don't know. After the baby's born. After my divorce." He looked up, laughter gone, jaw flexing with tension. "Now, what were you doing at my condo?"

"We met for lunch," Isabella said. "And Anna remembered you had something for her at your place."

Nick looked blank. Anna rolled her eyes.

"I'm taking tort law this semester, remember? The day of Falco's wedding, you promised you'd give me the legal analysis from that French deal you did last year—you said you had it in your home office and if you didn't remember to courier it to me, I could just stop by if I was in the neighbor-hood and get it myself, but I got busy and forgot about it until now and—"

"And," Isabella said impatiently, "we were having lunch a couple of blocks from your condo, and Anna thought of that file. So, she phoned to make sure your housekeeper was in, a woman answered—"

"A woman answers," Anna said, picking up the story, "and I say, 'Hi, this is Anna Orsini,' and she says, 'Who?' and I say, 'Anna, Nick's sister, who's this?' and she says, 'This is his wife,' and then she bursts into tears!"

"*Merda,*" Nick said, and instead of yelling at him again, his sisters saw the misery in their brother's face, looked at each other and went around the desk. They squatted beside him and each clasped one of his hands.

"Nicky," Izzy said softly, "tell us what happened."

So he told them. Everything.

Almost everything.

He left out the part about the pain lodged deep within his heart because he'd barely begun to admit that to himself. Why should a man's heart ache over a woman who was a cheat and a liar?

But he told them all the rest. How he'd thought Alessia was

an honest, good woman. How he'd discovered, by accident, that she wasn't. That she had lured him into doing what her father had wanted, lured him into more than that, into having to marry her...

They listened.

That had always been the thing about his sisters. They both knew how to listen. They never sat in judgment. Anna, maybe because she'd been judged too many times in her black hair/black nails/black clothes/black lipstick days; Isabella, maybe because from childhood on, she'd given herself over to nurturing things that nobody else thought could be saved. They listened, and when he finally stopped talking, they sighed.

"You want my third-year, almost-ready-to-graduate-from-NYU-law-school-and-pass-the-bar, legal-eagle opinion?" Anna asked. Nick nodded, and she sighed again.

"You're screwed."

Nick looked at her. For the first time in weeks, in what felt like centuries, he laughed. Really, really laughed.

"That's your legal-eagle opinion? I hate to tell you this, kid, but if it is, you're not ready for that bar exam."

"You're screwed," his sister said softly, "because you're in love with your wife."

Nick snatched his hand from hers. "No way!"

"You're in love with her, Nicky," Isabella said, "and she's in love with you, and unless one of you comes to your senses, you're going to toss away a really good thing."

Nick jerked his hand from hers, too. A muscle knotted in his jaw.

"You don't get it," he said coldly. "Alessia Antoninni—the Princess Antoninni—is one hell of an actress. Just because she saw her chance to play another scene in this farce, just because she told you she loves me—"

Anna stood up. "What she told us was that she despises

you. That you're the most pigheaded, most stubborn, most impossible idiot she's ever met."

Nick smiled grimly. "Sure sounds like a declaration of love to me."

Isabella got to her feet, too. "Did you ever ask her to explain that conversation you overheard?"

"And hear another lie?" Nick hesitated. "Why? Did she explain it to you?"

"She didn't explain anything. She didn't tell us anything. She only said she hated you. And, Nicky, trust us. When a woman says she hates a guy the way Alessia said she hates you, what she's really saying is that she's crazy in love with him."

"That's ridiculous," Nick said, but something inside him seemed to stretch its wings. "She doesn't love me. And I don't love her. Once she's had my baby—"

"Nick," Anna said gently, "go home. Talk to your wife. Ask her to tell you what she feels about you."

"It's pointless."

Isabella smiled. So did Anna. It crossed Nick's mind that they were right, they weren't girls anymore.

"If it is," Anna said, "I know a really terrific almost-attorney who'll handle the divorce, cheap."

They blew him kisses, and then they were gone.

Nick's PA left.

His brothers hadn't been in at all that day. It was a Friday and all three had been out of town on business. They were back; Rafe and Dante had called a couple of hours ago, Falco had phoned minutes after that. All had left the same message. They'd be at The Bar at seven this evening, an old Friday-night habit, one they'd kept though they no longer stayed there longer than a couple of hours.

Nick considered stopping by for a beer. Anything to clear his head of the nonsense Anna had put into it.

No. Bad idea.

He'd tried that last week, figuring maybe it would keep him from thinking about Alessia. His brothers had spent the first hour talking about their wives and the second asking him how come he was so quiet lately and wasn't there anything new in his life?

Not a hell of a lot, he'd been tempted to say, *just a wife I don't trust, a kid I didn't plan on...*

No. He was not going to drop into The Bar.

He wasn't going to try and have a conversation with his wife, either—and he had to stop thinking of her that way. Alessia was no more his wife than she was the sweet, innocent, loving woman he'd believed her to be, he thought as he stepped from a cab outside his Central Park West condominium building.

She was exactly the cold, scheming daughter of the aristocracy he'd initially assumed her to be, and it was time to deal with reality.

Tomorrow, he'd ask a friend to recommend an attorney, meet with the guy and get his advice on how to safeguard himself and his unborn child when he divorced Alessia, which he would do as soon as the baby arrived. She could go home to Daddy or stay in the States. He'd support her; he knew his responsibilities. But his kid would be his. Entirely his. And if he had to fight for custody—

"Good evening, Mr. Orsini."

Cheerful chitchat with the doorman. It was the last thing he was in the mood for.

"George," Nick said, and started past the man.

"I hope you don't mind my asking..."

"Asking what?"

"If everything's okay, sir. With Mrs. Orsini."

Okay. George was the only other person, aside from the ob-gyn and his sisters, who knew there was a Mrs. Orsini.…

Wait a minute.

Nick stood absolutely still. Then he turned toward the doorman.

"Why wouldn't it be?"

George hesitated. "Well, I just thought—I mean, I'm not prying, sir, it's just she asked me about the nearest hospital when I hailed the cab for her and—"

"Where?" Nick's voice was rough with urgency. "Where did you tell her to go?"

"I suggested she go to Mount Sinai. I know it's not the closest but—"

Nick was already on his way.

Friday nights were not the best time to be in an emergency room. The place was full of drunks and dopers and people clutching jaws and elbows and looking as if they were on their last breath.

Alessia wasn't among them.

It took Nick ten minutes to find a nurse who might know something, but only two to convince her that he would take the place apart unless she told him where he could find his wife.

Alessia had come in half an hour before, bleeding vaginally. She'd given her ob-gyn's name. The admitting nurse knew the man, knew he had staff privileges. She'd called him and he was with Alessia now, in a private room, and if Mr. Orsini would just take a seat in the waiting room…

Nick ran for the elevator, knew he'd never have the patience to wait and took the fire stairs. By the time he reached the right floor, found the right room, he was breathing hard.

Breathing hard and scared as he had never been in his life,

not in combat, not in clandestine ops, not in anything. His wife, his *wife,* was behind the door ahead of him. His wife, whom he loved with all his heart, all his soul, with everything he was or ever would be...

He dragged in a deep breath. Knocked. Turned the doorknob...

And saw his princess, pale and forlorn-looking, in an ugly hospital gown that only made her more beautiful, in a hospital bed that seemed to dwarf her.

"Alessia," he whispered.

She turned her face toward him. Her eyes lit—and then the light in them dimmed.

"Nicolo," she said. "How did you—"

He hurried to her side, grasped her cold hand in his, brought it to his lips. "What happened? Are you all right? Where's the doctor? Why didn't you call me?"

Despite the heaviness in her heart, Nicolo's rushed questions made Alessia smile.

"I am fine, Nicolo. The doctor stepped out for a moment. As for why I didn't call you..." Her smile faded. "I met your sisters today." Her voice dropped to a choked whisper. "And—and I found out that you have not told anyone about me. About us. About the baby. And I knew then that any hope I had that you would someday want me, love me—"

Nick silenced her the only way that mattered. He kissed her. Softly. Tenderly. The sweetness of her taste filled him.

"Alessia, sweetheart...I love you with all my heart. I'll always love you."

Tears filled her eyes. "You don't. You are only saying it because—"

"I'm saying it because it's true."

Alessia shook her head. "You say it because of this. The emergency. It has made you think you love me but—"

"I love you, princess. I adore you. I was just too damned

stupid to see it, or maybe too scared to put my heart in your hands."

Her eyes searched his. Some of the sadness in their blue depths seemed to fade. Nick felt his heart lift.

"Oh, Nicolo," she whispered, "I love you so much! If you knew how I have longed to hear you say that you love me, too…"

"I'm going to say it every day for the rest of our lives, baby, if you'll forgive me for having been such a fool all these weeks."

"I was the fool. I should have explained everything, but—"

"We need to talk. I know that." Nick lifted his wife's hands to his lips and kissed them. "But first tell me what happened today. What did the doctor say?"

"The baby is fine."

"Good. That's great. But you. Are you all right? Because—because I can't—I can't lose you, sweetheart. Do you understand? You're my world, my heart, my life."

His wife's smile was the most beautiful sight imaginable. "As you are mine, Nicolo. And I am fine. The doctor says I only need a few days rest."

Nick let out a pent-up breath, tilted Alessia's face to his and kissed her.

"Can you ever forgive me? When I think of how I treated you, of what I so stupidly believed—"

"No, no, it is my fault, too. I should have told you about…" Alessia took a deep breath. "My father had threatened to remove my mother from the *sanatorio* unless I met with you. But the rest—what I came to feel for you, it was all true. I fell in love with you, Nicolo, so deeply in love that I forgot to ask what he had done about my mother. The conversation you overheard was about her future. I was trying to find a way to be sure he could never hurt her again—"

"He won't," Nick said, with such stern determination that Alessia knew his words were a promise. "I'll see to it your mother is always happy and well-cared for."

"You are a good man, Nicolo Orsini," she said softly. "I know you cannot be what—what I believed you to be."

"A thug?" Nick smiled as he gathered his wife in his arms. "It's worse than that, sweetheart. I'm an investment banker."

She laughed, looped her arms around his neck and kissed him. After a long, long time, Nick drew back and framed her face with his hands.

"*Principessa.* Will you do me the honor of marrying me?"

Alessia touched the tip of her index finger to her husband's beautiful mouth. Her eyes were as bright as stars.

"But we are already married."

"I want to marry you the right way." He grinned. "A Sicilian wedding. The works. You know. The church. The reception. My brothers and their wives welcoming you to our family, my sisters driving you nuts, my mother sobbing because I've finally found the perfect *sposa*. You in a white wedding gown… and me in a tux that makes me look like something out of Madame Tussaud's."

Alessia laughed again. It was, Nick thought, the most beautiful sound he'd ever heard. Smiling, he bent his head and laid his forehead against hers.

"Is that a yes?"

She kissed him.

"It is, with all my heart, a 'yes.' Now, *mio amante, per favore,* take me home."

And, with joy filling his heart, Nick did.

EPILOGUE

SOFIA Orsini wept with joy at the news that her fourth son was taking a wife.

The civil ceremony in Italy? It did not count. They would have a real wedding in the old-fashioned Greenwich Village church Sofia loved—the church she still thought of as being part of her beloved Little Italy. The reception would be in the conservatory of the Orsini mansion. Isabella would arrange for the flowers, Anna would deal with the menu, Chiara and Gabriella and Elle would take Alessia shopping for the perfect gown. Her veil would be the one her new mother-in-law had worn so many years before.

It would be, Sofia announced, a perfect day.

And it was.

Nick couldn't seem to stop smiling. His brothers teased him about it, but then they herded him into a corner, hugged him, got teary-eyed—although, to a man, they'd have denied it—and told him how great it was to see him so happy.

"Yeah," Nick said, his smile becoming a grin, "well, you know, I couldn't let you guys leave me in the dust."

Rafe, Dante, Falco and Nicolo all laughed. Alessia heard them, looked at her husband...

The smile she gave him made him glow.

She glowed, too. And everyone agreed that the small bump

beneath the silk of her white bridal gown only added to her beauty.

"I love your family, even your father, because he brought you into my life," she told Nicolo later that afternoon, as they swayed together on the dance floor. "Your brothers are wonderful. So are their wives. And your sisters… Why are they not married?"

Anna and Isabella, on their way to the dessert table, overheard her. They flashed their new sister-in-law bright smiles but when they'd moved past her, they rolled their eyes.

"Married," Izzy said, with a snort. "I came within an inch of telling her the reason."

"Me, too." Anna looked at a silver platter of cannoli, sighed and slid first one of the rich pastries, then another, on a plate. "Why would a woman be foolish enough to tie herself down to a man?"

"Too many cannoli aren't good for you," Izzy said primly, and snatched one from Anna's plate with her fingers. "As for marriage… It's fine for Chiara and Gaby and Elle. And now for Alessia."

"But not for us," Anna said, with self-righteous conviction. "Never, ever."

Izzy licked a bit of ricotta from the tip of her pinkie. "I'll drink to that," she said, reaching for a flute of champagne.

Anna reached for one, too. *"Salute,"* she said, and the Orsini sisters touched glasses, grinned, and each drank down the fizzy stuff in one unladylike gulp.

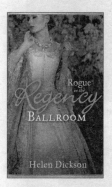

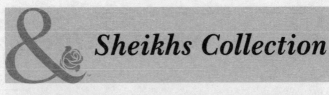

The World of Mills & Boon®

There's a Mills & Boon® series that's perfect for you. We publish ten series and, with new titles every month, you never have to wait long for your favourite to come along.

Blaze
Scorching hot, sexy reads
4 new stories every month

By Request
Relive the romance with the best of the best
9 new stories every month

Cherish
Romance to melt the heart every time
12 new stories every month

Desire
Passionate and dramatic love stories
8 new stories every month

Where will *you* read
this summer?

#TeamShade

Join your team this summer.

www.millsandboon.co.uk/sunvshade

SUNSHADEb